From Plantation to Easy Street, They Were a Family of Indomitable, Brave-Hearted Women . . .

LUCY: A plantation owner's bastard daughter, born to slavery, destined to break free and give her own daughter the chance she'd been denied . . .

SARAH: In a new century, college was hers for the asking. But she only wanted to sing—until love forced her to choose her man above all. Years of hard work flourished into success, but she couldn't save her daughter from passions of the heart . . .

BOBBIE: A shooting star in the velvety Jazz Age night, a beauty born to sing the blues—and to love the wrong man in a world where gangsters ruled supreme . . .

TESS: Child of tragedy, she loved the one man she could never have. But she would find salvation in another man's arms—and a challenging future in the fight for Civil Rights . . .

CARMEN: She was Bobbie all over again, driven to stardom, haunted by a mobster determined to see her dead. But this time the song was new—and she would walk on, proud and free at last, to raise her voice in the undying refrain begun by her people so very long ago . . .

SATIN DOLLS

SATIN DOLLS

ELSA E. COOK

Elsa E. Cook

PUBLISHED BY POCKET BOOKS NEW YORK

Lyrics from "Bye and Bye" (page 13) reprinted from *American Negro Songs and Spirituals* by John W. Work, copyright 1940, 1986 by Crown Publishers, Inc. Used by permission of Crown Publishers, Inc.

Lyrics from "Go Down, Moses" (page 84), "Custard Pie Blues" (page 98) and "Careless Love" (page 141) reprinted from *Negro Folk Music, U.S.A.* by Harold Courlander, copyright © 1963. Reprinted by permission of Columbia University Press.

Lyrics from "Sissy Blues" (pages 105–6) and "Leavin' Gal Blues" (pages 121–22) reprinted from *The Meaning of the Blues* by Paul Oliver, originally published by Cassell & Co., copyright © 1960 by Paul Oliver. Reprinted by permission of Macmillan Publishing Company.

Another *Original* publication of POCKET BOOKS

POCKET BOOKS, a division of Simon & Schuster, Inc.
1230 Avenue of the Americas, New York, N.Y. 10020

ISBN: 0-671-62327-3

First Pocket Books printing August 1987

10 9 8 7 6 5 4 3 2 1

POCKET and colophon are registered trademarks of Simon & Schuster, Inc.

Printed in the U.S.A.

Many thanks to my husband, Frank;
my daughters, Barbara Larson and Patty Grant;
my agent, Joyce Flaherty;
and my dear friends,
Jim Burnside and George Daily.

CHAPTER I

"Child! Hold still till I finish." Maybelle straightened the last corn row on her daughter's head. Pulling the braid tightly with one hand, she brushed away the tears with the other. Maybelle looked at the skinny runt of a ten-year-old, her face furrowed with sorrow. Sitting on a tree stump in the middle of the yard, finally she grabbed Lucy and held her close, rocking back and forth as she moaned softly to herself. No one else was around; the intense midday heat had driven men and animals to cool, shady spots where they would stay until the sun dropped low in the sky and a light breeze rippled across fields of stubble where there had only recently been golden-red wheat.

Lucy's forehead was beaded with perspiration, and the brightness of the sun's rays blanched her creamy tan skin. The harsh sunlight made her look washed-out, causing her dark brown eyes to dominate her delicate features. Small, even white teeth, framed by well-defined lips, peeped through a tiny smile meant for her mother. But today, Maybelle's eyes didn't sparkle as they usually did. The ominous threat of separation was too overpowering to be eased by a smile.

Images of slave auctions—slave traders, devils with white faces—were the children's bogeymen, and now the bogeyman was going to get her. No, she cried, no, no, no. Fear was replaced by anger, and she kicked the wooden bucket at her feet. It spun across the yard, spewing water and lye soap into the dirt. The strong odor of the homemade soap stung her nose. Lucy looked at it in disgust. She hated when her

1

mother washed her hair with the foul-smelling stuff, but now, as she stared at it floating in the dirty water, she wondered if she would ever have her hair washed again.

Nothin' make sense no more. Papa hate me. Miss Susan hate me. Why? I practice my letters and my music. Papa like to hear me sing and play the piano. Nobody can carry a tune 'cept me and Mama. Maybe Papa, too. Most what we sing be church music. Ain't never gonna see the church no more . . . or the pastor. Maybe I ain't never gonna talk to Jesus no more neither. Oh, Mama, I gonna miss you so. You and JimJim and Rebecca. Who they gonna play kickball with? Who be playing house with Rebecca? I be missing everybody 'cept Papa and Miss Susan. They be the ones making me get sold.

A slight breeze stirred the giant oak behind the slave cabins, and a rustic set of chimes tinkled softly across the barren expanse of yard. Lucy raised her head and listened. They were so beautiful. Why hadn't she heard them before? They were always there—the chimes, the laughter. Yesterday they were there. Tomorrow they would still be there, but she would be gone. Lucy turned and looked at the house, at the mansion, where her papa lived with his wife, Miss Susan, and JimJim and Rebecca. It was big and dark and quiet. No one laughed; the wind didn't catch the chimes there. She had been born in that house ten years ago, and she and her mama had lived there till they moved back to the slave quarters. That was when Papa married Miss Susan. There weren't no place in his heart for us after that, she thought. But it don't bother me none to live in a cabin. Just don't see why he got to sell me. Lucy dropped her chin on her chest, and her body sagged like a marionette under the blazing afternoon sun.

"It be hot, Mama." Lucy wrinkled up her nose. "We might melt into a pool of butter like the tiger be doing in the story." She forced a smile. "Course, if I melt, then I won't be sold, will I Mama?"

Tears rolled down Maybelle's face. Her body shook convulsively. "Don't make light of my sufferin', child.

I . . . I . . . oh, Lucy. What's gonna happen to you? T'ain't right him sending you off—you, his own flesh and blood."

Lucy grabbed her mother's hand, stifling her tears. "Come on, Mama. Let's go down to the creek. It's cooler there. We can drop our feet in the water."

Maybelle nodded and stood up. Stepping over the mud puddle, she grabbed Lucy's hand. Chickens strutted out of their way as they opened the back gate and passed the hen house. Covering their mouths with their skirts, they held their breaths past the pungent odor of chicken droppings, rotting plums, and horse manure that hung heavily in the stagnant August air. They hopscotched through the watermelon patch, jumping over the green humps attached to the rock-hard earth by long umbilical cords. Then, as they had done as far back as Lucy could remember, they ran the last two hundred feet, hesitated, grabbed hold of a low-hanging branch and slid down the mossy incline, barely stopping before they reached the water's edge. Lying on the bank, they gazed upward at the sunlight filtering through the black and green limbs of a huge willow. Its branches were heavy with foliage, creating a cool canopy overhead. Lucy fought to preserve the moment as she sat on the soft blanket of leaves, holding Maybelle's hand and dangling her feet in the cold, rushing water.

Until today, Lucy had been happy, wiling away the years under the adoring eyes of her mother and the distant but concerned interest of her father. She had imagined that everyone was well fed, educated, secure, never realizing those conditions were unbelievable luxuries for a slave. Now, for the first time in her life Lucy was aware of her status. Not only was she a slave, but she was a threat, an affront to the prim sensibilities of Miss Susan, Jim's wife and mistress of the estate.

Lucy looked at her mother, at her creased face, haggard and drawn but not from age—she was only thirty-one—and not from hard work if you believed Mr. McGregor, the overseer, who always complained to Massa Jim that he had too many slaves for the size of the farm. "Just training 'em to be lazy bastards," he grumbled, then headed for the barn where he kept a bottle of whiskey, a sturdy wool blanket, and routinely Missy Lou, coal black and "tight as a pig in a poke."

No, Maybelle suffered the helpless agony of losing her only child, knowing that there was nothing she could do to prevent it. Maybelle put her arm around Lucy and hugged her, crying softly as though releasing the pain buried deep inside.

Her mother's tears upset Lucy almost as much as the thought of being taken by the slaver the next morning. Maybelle so seldom cried. There had been nights when she awakened in the dark cabin with only the moonlight splashing against the whitewashed walls and seen Maybelle, hovering over an oblong wicker basket that she hid under her bed and sobbing as she pressed a velvet ball gown, dusty now but still elegant, close to her. One after another she fingered the dresses, satins and brocades, silks and lawns, all the while humming tunes out of the past: "Shenandoah," "America." She never sang them when she worked or when she took Lucy to the big house for her music lesson . . . only at night when she clutched the precious gowns to her bosom.

Just six months ago Lucy had learned that her mother had worn the dresses at the recitals that Massa Jim and his first wife, Henrietta, held in the parlor, where people from all over the county congregated and listened while Maybelle sang, and Henrietta played the piano and Massa Jim his violin. He still had the instrument, a Stradivarius, but despite his pride of ownership—he showed it to anyone who expressed an interest in music—Lucy had never heard him play it. When she asked Hattie, the Negro cook, why they didn't have recitals anymore, Hattie turned up her nose and spit out her scorn. "Dat man give up living after Henrietta passed, least ways till he took up with your mama. Seemed content enough then, and downright happy when you was born, but since dat Miss Susan come, I ain't heard him laugh more'n half dozen times . . . much less have a hoedown." Hattie turned on her heel, grabbed a blue and white bowl and dumped a half pound of flour in it. "Git on with you now," she said, her voice terse. "I got to whip up a batch of biscuits for dinner."

It was in bits and pieces of gossip and reminiscences that Lucy learned about her past and the events that led inexorably to that awful day when she learned she was to be sold.

Lucy snuggled close to her mother. The thought of Miss Susan was like a cold wind blowing through a hot room. She wondered how Jim could have married her after loving Henrietta and, even more, Maybelle. He be lonely maybe, but how could he be lonely when my mama be living with him? She shook her head. My mama still love him. He must've been good to her, otherwise she wouldn't be caring nothin' 'bout him. It ain't like he just take her, not the way Hattie tells 'bout some white massas. Will that be happenin' to me? Once I's sold, won't be nobody to care. Us slaves ain't got no rights, she thought, and somehow, I got less than none. Hattie say nigger slaves ain't worth nothing 'less the massa care about 'em. Lucy wiped the tears from her eyes and started humming along with her mother. Their hushed duet didn't disturb the crickets, blackbirds, and bees who created their own symphony, unmoved by the singers' misery or even their existence.

The words to the song they hummed jumped to Lucy's mind: "Oh, bye and bye, bye and bye; I'm going to lay down my heavy load . . ." Don't seem right one's got to die to lay down a heavy load, Lucy thought, but then, maybe for slaves that was the only way. Looking back, she remembered only two events that seemed to have changed her life. Oh, she recalled fleetingly running up and down the polished mahogany staircase, tripping over Persian rugs, and even breaking a crystal vase that stood by the front door holding red silk roses and pink carnations. But the day her mama ran out the back door of the big house clutching Lucy in one arm and a pile of clothing in the other would haunt Lucy the rest of her life. She still recalled the panic she felt when Maybelle collapsed on the dirty wooden floor of the slave cabin and bleated like an animal at the slaughter. When she was older, when Maybelle's pain eased, they adjusted, but they never forgot how drastically their lives could change in a day, an hour, or even a minute. Lucy lost her home and her special status as Jim's only child because of an unexpected visit by Susan Banks, and tomorrow, when the slaver took Lucy to St. Louis to sell her, it would be because of a chance observation Miss Susan made over a year ago.

Lucy was roused from her reverie by the chanting of the slaves as they moved from one field to another, two abreast, carrying hoes, rakes, scythes, and shovels. The sun had crept low in the sky; the day was waning—Lucy's last day at home, the last day she would spend with her mother. Lucy dropped her head on her knees and sobbed.

It had only been seven years since Lucy's life had changed; seven years since Miss Susan arrived in a big coach drawn by four horses. It was September, 1843. It had been hot, like today, Lucy thought. No one was surprised by Susan Bank's unexpected appearance. Being Jim's second cousin, it seemed natural that she would stop by to offer her condolences on Mrs. Sloan's death, until someone reminded them that Henrietta had been dead for four years. Jim explained the discrepancy to Maybelle when he summoned her to his study to tell her she had to take her clothes from his wardrobe and disappear discreetly. Stammering almost incoherently, Jim ran through a slate of excuses, apologies, and regrets.

"Susan's been living in England the past four years. Just now returning to Kansas City. Stopped by on her way home. Miss Banks is a Christian woman. Baptist, I believe. Wouldn't do for her to know we were living together as man and wife."

Maybelle nodded and, by biting her lip, managed to back out of the room and shut the door before she wailed in pain. Then, without stopping, she ran to their bedroom, grabbed her clothes and, barely slowing down to swoop Lucy off the kitchen floor, darted out the back door and across the yard. Blindly, she pushed open the door to the cabin she had occupied years ago. Clutching her child in her arms, Maybelle peered around the room. The chair, the cot, the rough-hewn table were covered with dust, and a black spider clung steadfastly to a delicately spun web. Maybelle would sweep it away when she cleaned the cabin, but for now, she was stricken. Jim's rejection stunned her, a brutal reminder that she was a slave, a powerless woman. No matter what affections he might have felt for her and for their daughter, those ties could be severed without an ounce of remorse.

Lucy tugged at her mother's sleeve. "Mama, we gotta go back. Hattie be madder'n a hungry dog if I don't set the table. Her back's actin' up again."

"Child, this be our last day together. I ain't wanting to share you with nobody." Maybelle cupped Lucy's face in her hand and gently kissed her cheek. "The table'll wait."

"But Miss Susan might get mad."

"Dat white woman can't scare me no more. And she can't hurt me no more, neither. 'Cause of her I be losing the only person I love in the whole world. A whippin' won't be nothing compared to the sufferin' I be feeling now."

"Oh, Mama. Massa Jim ain't never had nobody whipped."

"Don't have to as long as he got the right to sell a person."

Lucy nodded. "I be the only one he ever sold, and I's his daughter. Why he doing this to me?"

"Miss Susan, she the real devil. Massa Jim just go along."

Lucy never considered jealousy. Could the woman just be mean? Miss Susan was as beautiful as a china doll with honey-blond hair and deep blue eyes. Small lips occasionally parted in a smile, but Lucy had never seen her really laugh, not even on her wedding day in April, 1844.

The slaves had nominated Hattie to present their gift to the couple, and when Jim brought Susan round back to share lemonade and chocolate cake, the old woman proudly handed the mistress their gift, a brown-and-gold wedding ring quilt. "We's all sewed on it. After the work was done, we took turns till we got it finished."

Miss Susan held up a corner of the quilt and frowned. "The colors won't fit in our bedroom, but I'm sure you

7

meant well." She dropped the coverlet on the table and took her husband's arm. As they headed back to the house, Susan snickered, and Hattie heard her say, "Oh, my dear, whatever possessed them to make such a horrible quilt. Brown is such a dismal color." The gift, never claimed, was passed from cabin to cabin as the need for a handsome coverlet arose—a death, a wedding night, a convalescence.

When Jim's and Susan's first child, Rebecca, was born, the slaves didn't give her a gift, a slight that Miss Susan complained about for years. By the time their second child, James Sloan, Jr. was born, a spirit of rectitude prevailed in the slave quarters, but no gift was forthcoming. After that, the occupants of the big house and the inhabitants of the slave quarters divided their lives, touching only at work and at evensong, a richly melodic ceremony at the end of the day. Miss Susan had a series of bells installed in a gazebo, and every evening, usually at sunset, everyone on the farm congregated there. Young boys sang the English liturgy; Jim read scripture. It was traditional, formal, religious. Maybelle noticed that, unlike Henrietta's recitals, no spirituals were sung, and the adult slaves took no active part in the ritual. Miss Susan didn't like to share the spotlight on her activities. She clearly hated the slaves and she threatened to have all of them sold and replaced by Irish immigrants. "They're not much better than that horde of black devils living fifty feet from our front door," Miss Susan had said to her husband, "but at least they're white."

Massa Jim didn't argue, but the Irish girls never materialized. Lucy was chosen to be Rebecca's companion and playmate, and when he was eight, JimJim would be a singer in the farm's all-Negro boys' choir. Normally Massa Jim didn't pay attention to his wife's harangues. He had spent his life with the people on the farm. Neither he nor his father had ever sold a slave. It would take considerable persuasion for him to change his attitude on that issue, but the unexpected happened at the most unexpected moment.

Maybelle noticed it first. Except for Lucy's light brown skin and black hair, she and Rebecca were almost identical.

The older she grew, the more Lucy favored her father—the oval face, broad forehead, sharp nose, and well-defined mouth. Rebecca, five years younger, had inherited the same characteristics, the same serious mettle.

Miss Susan noticed the similarity between the two girls one Sunday morning as they returned from church. Lucy and Rebecca rode together in the family carriage, sitting on the jump seat opposite Miss Susan. They were dressed alike in yellow calico and straw hats tied under their chins with matching bows. Miss Susan studied their faces in the noonday sun, and suddenly the reality of Lucy's parentage struck her. She threw her hand over her mouth to stifle a scream and turned to her husband, her eyes asking the question her mouth could not utter. Jim followed her eyes and immediately understood.

"Susan, please. Let me explain. It isn't what you think." Jim reached out to touch his wife.

Susan's hysteria mounted. Enraged, she pounded on Jim's chest. "You're nothing but a— Oh, my God. You lived with that slave woman. She had your child."

"It was before you came. I was so lonely. Henrietta's death devastated me. Please forgive me."

"Sell her. I want her put on the block and sold. I won't have a minute's peace till she's gone." Susan pulled away and stared at Jim in contempt.

Jim glanced at Lucy; he saw the distress registered on her face. He turned back to Susan and clasped her hands in his.

"If I have to, I'll send both of them away. We'll make plans as soon as—as soon as you're able to talk about it."

Susan's features grew hard. Her lips stretched tightly over her small, white teeth. She shook her head. "No, not both of them. Only Lucy."

John flinched under the harshness of her stare. "I can't. I can't take Lucy away from her mother."

"You can, and you will. That woman must be punished for what she did." Susan freed her hands from Jim's grasp, squared her shoulders, then stared blankly into space.

* * *

"Lucy, you sleepin', child?" Maybelle nudged her daughter, who was lying quietly beside her. Lucy's eyes were closed, her breathing shallow. Her stillness frightened Maybelle.

"No, Mama. Just thinking 'bout how it be tomorrow." Lucy said pleadingly, "You got to help me, Mama. I don't know if I be strong enough. I's so scared . . . I feel like I be dying . . . all alone with nobody to hold my hand. Leastways if I was dying, I be going to Jesus, but I's afraid who I be going to tomorrow. If we pray all night, do you think the Lord'll help?"

"Don't know about the Lord, but maybe the massa be changing his mind. He got to know how bad it be, him selling his own child."

The clanging of the gazebo bells startled Maybelle and brought Lucy to her feet. "It be evensong, Mama. We better get back. Don't want to make the massa or missus mad. Just in case."

Slowly they returned to the big house, remembering happier times when they had scrambled back, bent over in the tall wheat to escape detection after stealing an extra hour of rest along the edge of the creek on hot summer days.

Was it Lucy's imagination, or did everyone shy away from her during the services? Sympathetic smiles veiled dark, submerged fears of being sold, and Lucy's situation made all the slaves suspicious. If Jim could sell his daughter, he could sell any of them.

Even worse, JimJim and Rebecca were conspicuously absent. They usually stood beside their mother, and Lucy couldn't remember when they hadn't actively participated in the service. But not this evening. Was Miss Susan afraid I'd cry and scream? Lucy thought. Or maybe even hurt them? Lucy shuddered and dropped her eyes onto her prayer book. "Don't let him sell me. Don't let him sell me. Don't let him sell me." She repeated the litany during the whole ceremony, but when it ended, Jim and Miss Susan disappeared into the dark mansion without redeeming her. Later, after everyone returned to their cabins for supper, the farm grew quiet. Even the animals were mute, as though they were in mourning. Only Hattie came by later to help Maybelle lay out Lucy's belongings.

"I can only take what'll fit in a big hanky." Tears ran down Lucy's face.

"There be room for dis ole Bible," Maybelle said with determination. "I wrote in it. See! It got your mama's name, and papa's, grandma and grandpa. Says when you was born and where. You keep it, child. It make it easy to remember your family."

"Oh, Mama. I ain't never gonna forget you."

"Didn't mean you forget. Just that sometimes names and dates and places get all mixed up." Maybelle peered at the pages, holding the book close to the candle flame. "Hopes you can read it. I put it down soon's I heard what Massa Jim gonna do. Never believed he sell you, 'specially since Miss Susan had her fit over a year past. But seems dat white woman just waiting for somethin' like this to happen so she can cause misery."

Hattie shook her head. The folds of fat around her neck rolled with each movement. "Dat woman work on Massa Jim to get rid of Lucy day 'n night. I never heard such squabblin'. I can hear her screamin' now. 'If you don't get rid of that nigger, I'll take the children and go back home. I won't let Rebecca be humiliated by her friends. Imagine, having a nigger slave looking enough like our daughter to be her twin. Why, the whole county must be laughing.' Dem's her words exactly." Hattie strutted around the small room, imitating her mistress.

"Maybe Miss Susan aggravate the massa, but he make the decision in the long run," Maybelle said. "He be a weak man, letting dat woman talk him into selling his own child."

"He don't want to lose her," Hattie said. "And dem two children—Rebecca and JimJim—mean the world to dat man."

"I's his, too," Lucy said. "Don't I count for nothing?"

"Course you do, but the man got to make a choice. He done chose dem. Dat the way it be. You and us is slaves.

Massa Jim ain't gonna pick a slave over his legitimate family."

Maybelle dropped her eyes, confused and embarrassed by Hattie's words. Is God punishing me for my sins? Ain't no god gonna punish a person for lovin'. Is Massa Jim punishing me? If that be so, why he selling Lucy and not me? Don't make no sense, and the massa won't talk about it. I beg him, but he just walk away.

At three o'clock, long before the rooster's crow announced the start of a new day, Maybelle and Lucy were up. Lucy ladled cold water into a bowl and splashed it on her face. Her eyes stung as she tried to hold back the tears, but when she looked at her mother, she collapsed, begging Maybelle to hide her before the slaver fetched her.

Before Maybelle could answer, Hattie stepped into the cabin and shook her finger at Lucy. "Dat slaver'll just come in here and drag you out. Now you get yourself together. You ain't the first child sold from your mama. You ain't gonna be the last." Her eyes were hard. "Say your good-byes 'fore that devil come tearing in here. You got your pride."

"What good's pride?"

"Hush," Hattie said, cutting Maybelle off. "You knows dey can't own you if you don't let 'em."

"What Hattie talkin' 'bout, Mama?" Lucy asked.

Maybelle sighed. "Like I told you last night. Nobody can make you a slave less you let 'em. There, in dat Bible, you got your family written down. Who your papa is, your mama, on back as far as I can remember. Your great-granddaddy was a warrior in Africa. He come from a place call Melli."

"What good's a Bible, Mama? What good it be knowing 'bout my great-granddaddy? He be a slave, too. He be bought and sold just like me."

"That what your mama tellin' you," Hattie said. "No matter what happen, you's a slave only if you let yourself be one. It's the thinking that does it, not the owning."

Lucy shrugged, unable to comprehend what the two women were talking about. But her mama had stopped crying. Maybe the Bible carried a magic spell and would comfort her, too. Picking up her belongings, all neatly tied together in the oversized handkerchief, she walked with Maybelle out into the early morning darkness. They hesitated in front of the house where Mr. Walker was lining up his pack of weary slaves.

The slave dealer was tired. For over a month Mr. Walker had traveled a prescribed circuit of farms in central Missouri collecting the slaves to be sold at the large midsummer auction in St. Louis. He had two days to get them down river. Just time enough, he thought. Normally he wouldn't have stopped to pick up a girl as young as Lucy, but, Walker reasoned, if Jim Sloan was starting to sell his slaves, he hoped Jim would remember the favor and give him his business in the future. Still, he was cutting it close, and he was tired. After the sale, he planned to take a week off.

Lucy and Maybelle clung to each other until the slaver pulled Lucy's arm, forcing her to the rear of the human chain. Without a backward glance, Lucy stumbled after the gang of manacled men and women as they marched toward the Missouri River. Walker's slaves had watched Lucy and Maybelle, and the leave-taking had stirred painful memories of departures made long ago. As they marched away, they began to sing:

> *"Nobody knows de trouble I've seen,*
> *Nobody knows but Jesus,*
> *Nobody knows de trouble I've seen,*
> *Glory, hallelujah.*
> *What makes ole Satan hate me so?*
> *Because he got me once and he let me go."*

After they disappeared around the last bend in the road, Maybelle fell to the ground and sobbed. Finally, exhausted, Maybelle pulled herself up. She stared down the deserted road. The singing voices were supplanted by the lonely cry of the whippoorwill as it greeted the dawn.

As Maybelle headed back to the slave cabins, she looked in horror at the grotesque three-story house with its gables and turrets protruding like gangly growths from the central structure. The light from the rising sun had not yet touched the gray facade. Through the dim light of a flickering candle, she glimpsed a man standing in front of a third-floor window. It was Jim. He looked haggard. Inflamed with hate, she dropped her gaze and headed back to the cabin where she sat with Hattie and waited for the world to end.

CHAPTER II

Lucy picked up her bundle and peered through the hazy mist as the coffle of slaves, six men and six women, stumbled down the gangplank onto the slick cobblestones. Searching for companionship, Lucy sidled up to a sallow-cheeked young woman whose kinky black hair was covered with a red and white bandanna. The dour-looking woman glanced at her coldly, then turned away. Cringing, Lucy stepped back several paces and was the last one to leave the boat.

The Mississippi River lapped lazily against the great steamboats moored at the St. Louis levee, the *Omega* and the *J. M. White* the most impressive. Despite her exhaustion, Lucy couldn't help but feel the excitement surging around her in the early hours of the morning. Gaslights flickered along the wharf as hulking stevedores moved bales of cotton onto waiting boats. Unwieldy kegs were lifted onto wagons. Teams of horses flicked their tails and dozed fitfully in the hot, humid night.

The sweating workers barely looked up as Mr. Walker aligned the slaves two abreast, the muscular young men in the back, women in the front, then manacled them in pairs.

Lucy, because of her size and age more than Walker's promise to Jim, was allowed to walk unfettered at the rear.

They trudged up the hill from the landing. By the time they reached the street, they were wet with perspiration.

Only Lucy raised her eyes to study the dark buildings and shadowy outlines of the city. She paused when she saw a stately-looking building at the far end of the street. Its tall pillars and huge dome shone in the moonlight, casting a white glow on the surrounding buildings.

Mr. Walker reined his horse alongside her and forcefully shoved her along. "Get a move on it. You'll be seeing all you want of the courthouse in the morning. That's where we sell our slaves—right on the front steps." Walker spoke with obvious delight. "Just like a circus only you niggers is the clowns. Oh, you should hear the hee-hawing when the bidding starts. You all sound like a bunch of hyenas."

Lucy clutched her bundle and tried to move out of his way. Everything her mama had told her about traders was true, she thought. That man's the devil himself. Tears streamed down her face, but there was nothing to do but follow the twisted figures ahead of her.

Walker laughed as he jabbed Lucy in the back with his stick. "Once a slave, always a slave," he bellowed. "Might just as well get used to it."

Oliver L. Lynch, Buyer and Seller of Prime Quality Slaves, Ages 8 to 45 read the sign hanging over a sturdy oak door. The advertisement was visible half a block away.

Lucy gasped when they stopped in front of a formidable brick building, its windows secured with heavy iron bars. But she almost fainted from fright when the door flew open and a huge black man carrying a flaming torch motioned them inside. Only the whistling bark of Walker's riding whip made her enter the prison. Lucy was stunned to see the other slaves shuffle obediently down the dark hallway.

When they reached another door, the black guard turned a heavy iron key in the lock and pushed hard against it, forcing it to move on reluctant hinges. It opened into a room twelve by twelve feet. The only ventilation came from a single window high on an outside wall. On a hot August night, the room was sweltering. The earth floor had been trampled rock-hard by thousands of bare feet. The only furniture was four wooden benches. Most of them would have to sleep on the floor. The stench from an overflowing slop jar was oppressive.

Chains were unfastened, and the men and women dropped to the floor. With stoic indifference, they segregated themselves—men on one side, women on the other.

The heat and stench were almost unbearable. Lucy leaned against a wall and gasped for air. I'm not going to live through the night, she thought. Dear God, I don't want to live. "Mama! Mama!" she cried out. "Help me."

"Hush child. Don't do no good screaming like that. Give me your hand. I'll get us a place by the window."

Still struggling to breathe, Lucy grabbed hold of the woman's hand and followed her to the far end of the room.

As they sat down, the woman put her arm around Lucy and held her close. "Don't cry so. It just makes you thirsty, and we ain't goin' get no water till mornin'." She rocked back and forth for several minutes until Lucy's sobs diminished. "There. That's better. Way you're carryin' on, I don't believe you ever been sold before."

Lucy shook her head, then nuzzled close to the woman's bosom. If I close my eyes, I can pretend I'm back home, she thought. Back home with mama and Hattie and Rebecca. A great sob gushed from Lucy's throat.

"I'm Phyllis. I been sold more times than I care to remember." Phyllis paused and stared into the darkness, as though trying to recall the first time she had been put on the block. "Been so long ago—"

"Is it always this bad?" Lucy wiped her eyes with the corner of her checkered cloth.

"Sometimes it's worse—depends. If you ain't sold the first day. Well, the slaver can get awful mean."

"What's he do?"

"Mostly he'll take the whip to you. One time I saw a

16

slaver kill a young buck. The boy just wouldn't bow his head. Ain't nobody going to buy a proud nigger. Takes too long to bust 'em." Phyllis's voice softened, and Lucy felt the woman's body relax. "But that ain't got nothing to do with you. A pretty little thing like you'll be sold right off."

Lucy hoped Phyllis was right, but she was too tired to worry anymore. The steady hum of voices had been replaced by the slaves' heavy breathing. Lucy was impressed with their knack for resting whenever they could. Pulling some bread and cheese from her bundle, Lucy nibbled at it and started to offer some to Phyllis, but the woman had fallen asleep. When she finished, she laid her head on Phyllis's lap and dozed off.

The rays of the morning sun seared the stone walls of the pen; the room became a scorching hell as a new day began. When Lucy awoke, her thirst was agonizing. She took deep breaths to control her panic. Lucy watched surreptitiously as the men and women moved about, some of them relieving themselves in the slop bucket. The stench grew in intensity. She began to cry, but this time Phyllis didn't console her.

"Ain't no time to feel sorry for yourself. Remember that nigger buck who moved us in here last night? If you make a fuss, he'll come after you with a whip that'll slice your skin like it was paper." Phyllis shook her head for emphasis. "Ain't none of us want to make him mad."

Lucy bit her bottom lip to keep it from quivering, but there was nothing she could do to stop the tears from streaming down her face. To her horror she realized she had to go to the bathroom, but as yet she couldn't force herself to walk to the bucket in the corner. Her discomfort was forgotten when the door opened and the giant guard stood in the archway.

"Line yourselves up, you worthless niggers. You're going to get scrubbed and polished so the boss gets top dollar for your miserable hides. First one steps out a line'll get ten lashes."

17

Phyllis took Lucy's hand and pulled her close. "Don't say nothing. Don't look at his face. Keep your head down. We don't want to do anything that'll make him notice us."

They pressed forward through the narrow passageway until they reached an empty room lined with two long wooden troughs. Fresh water poured from a raised conduit. Although the room was hot, a slight breeze blew in through the south windows. Everyone rushed to the trough and, sticking their heads under the dripping water, gulped greedily until they were satiated. When the guard spoke again, they stopped and listened intently.

"Strip them rags off your bodies and throw 'em in the center of the room. Scrub your skin with soap till you don't smell like mangy dogs no more. Then line up against the wall, boys on one side, womenfolk on the other. You'll get clean clothes and a pair of shoes. We want you to look real nice till we get you sold."

Lucy looked down at her dress, the one her mother had made for her. Hot tears stung her face at the thought of throwing it in a heap on the floor, but this time she didn't complain to Phyllis. She knew it wouldn't do any good.

When everyone had taken off their clothes, Lucy was appalled. Most of the men's backs were hatched with scars; the more mutilated their bodies, the more subdued their spirit. But the whip marks on Phyllis's back disturbed her the most. She wondered what the woman could have done to have been beaten. Maybe she didn't have to do anything, Lucy thought, terrified.

After their bath they were fed a spectacular meal: ham and eggs, corn bread, and coffee. It was topped off with a jigger of whiskey. For the first time since she had left her mama, Lucy relaxed. Maybe the worst's over, she thought. Even that big black nigger don't look so mean no more. I bet he was just trying to scare us so we wouldn't cause no trouble. Lucy smiled. Phyllis wiped her mouth with the back of her hand.

"That was mighty good, wasn't it?" Lucy asked as she pushed her plate away.

Before Phyllis could answer, the sharp bark of the whip

whistled overhead. Lucy crouched in fear, but didn't have time to worry. Immediately the guard lined them up against the wall. A heavy chain was drawn through manacles bolted around their wrists and ankles; not even Lucy was spared this humiliation. The whip snapped again and they shuffled into the street. Remembering Phyllis's warning not to attract attention, Lucy moved as rapidly as she could without falling over the heavy iron chain.

After they had walked a few hundred feet, Lucy realized they were going to the courthouse—the same one she had seen the night before—but now the area was crowded with people: gangs of slaves and a large mass of men milling around at the foot of the steps. Lucy's group was marched to the back of the porch where they sat and waited for the auction to begin.

Feeling light-headed and nauseated from the whiskey, Lucy followed Phyllis's example and leaned against the wall, trying to find a comfortable position. Once she was settled, Lucy stared in bewilderment at the carnival atmosphere of the slave auction. Men dressed in fancy waistcoats and large-brimmed hats milled about, pointing their gold-handled canes at brawny Negro men and long-legged women.

To the rear stood the white idlers, unshaven laboring men, who were attracted to the sale by the prospect of seeing Negro women stripped for inspection.

When the auction began, the serious buyers were allowed to move among the slaves, checking their limbs for breaks or arthritis, eyes for cataracts, and backs and buttocks for lash marks; lips were pulled back to inspect teeth and gums.

"What's botherin' you, child? You feelin' bad?" Phyllis opened her eyes and stared at Lucy with concern. "Why you whimpering?"

"Looks like they're checking horses." Lucy pointed to the two slaves standing on a raised platform. "I ain't goin' let 'em touch me."

Phyllis raised her eyebrows in dismay. "Don't you cause no trouble. All you'll get is a whippin' with a leather paddle—don't leave no marks, but it stings something fierce

19

when it hits." Her frown eased, and she patted Lucy's hand. "You let'em do what they will. It'll be over with 'fore you know it. The important thing is to get sold today so you don't have to spend another night in the pen."

"I'm scared." Lucy's eyes were frozen on the spectacle before her. "I don't want to be sold like a dumb animal."

"I know, child. None of us wants that. But mostly, we don't want to be sold down river to Mississippi. If you die on a cotton plantation, ain't nobody knowed you ever lived."

Lucy huddled close to Phyllis and tried to compose herself. She'd come this far without mishap; she didn't want to be whipped, especially in front of the leering men.

The auctioneer droned on while the sun swung wide across the southern lawn of the courthouse and moved steadily westward. By late afternoon, their gang was all that was left of the slaves, and less than a dozen buyers were bunched around the platform. The more prosperous-looking gentlemen had made their purchases, leaving poor farmers and seedy entrepreneurs to compete for the rest. Phyllis was filled with apprehension. The lateness of the day and the paucity of buyers made it all the more likely that they would have to spend the night in the pen or, even worse, would be bought cheaply by one of the crude, unshaven men dawdling away the afternoon.

Suddenly, the burly arm of the Negro guard swooped down, grabbing Lucy by the nape of her neck. Screaming in fright, Lucy was dragged down the steps to the auction block.

"How old are you?" the auctioneer asked in a booming voice. She didn't answer.

"You deaf?" Bending over, he stuck his face so close to Lucy's she could smell the chewing tobacco that driveled through a crack in his lip.

"Ten."

"What was that?" he yelled. "Speak up, nigger."

"Ten years old."

"You look healthy enough. Anything wrong with you?"

"No, sir."

"Speak up." The auctioneer grew impatient. He swatted a leather whip in the air, never taking his eyes off Lucy.

"Never been sick," Lucy said loudly. To her horror, she discovered that she couldn't hear her own voice. *Am* I deaf? she wondered. She concentrated on the man's face. If she looked at nothing else, she thought, maybe she'd live through the ordeal.

"Know how to cook and clean?"

"Yes, sir."

"Sew and bake?"

"Yes, sir."

"What else can you do, nigger gal?"

"The piano—I—I can play the piano, and, and I can sing most church songs. I—I been taught my letters."

The auctioneer frowned and stuck the whip under Lucy's nose. "Here now! It's against the law teaching a slave to read and write."

"Don't know about that," Lucy said barely above a whisper. "Just know my papa wanted me to know my letters and numbers." The man stepped back and studied her, his face twisted with suspicion. Quickly he caught himself.

"You ever been whipped?" he asked churlishly.

"No."

"Didn't hear you, nigger gal?" The auctioneer reached for Lucy's dress and started to pull it over her head. Instinctively she pulled away; then, cowering in fear, she waited, expecting the whip to slash across her face. His jaw tensed with emotion, but he didn't strike her. Instead, he squinted and stared at a carriage standing off by itself half a block away. Beside it stood a tall, middle-aged man dressed in a gray suit. He held a black hat and a dark wooden cane in his right hand. Lucy saw the man signal the auctioneer with his hat then turn to talk to someone in the carriage.

"Well, little nigger gal—looks like you got yourself a home—and a mighty fancy one at that." Without further comment, he motioned to the guard to take Lucy away.

Again the man's huge hand gripped her neck as he half-carried her off the platform. He was pushing her toward the street when Lucy broke away and ran up the courthouse steps. Her quick movement so startled the guard, it was several seconds before he caught up with her. By that time, Lucy was tearfully saying good-bye to Phyllis.

"You goin' get a whippin' yet, child," Phyllis said reproachfully.

"I had to say good-bye. I couldn't've made it without you last night and today. I'm sorry I'm bought and you're not. T'ain't fair."

The guard stood over them, his whip raised over his head. Phyllis looked up at him, her eyes filled with sorrow. He dropped his hand. "Hurry it up," he growled, then kicked Lucy for emphasis.

"Get on with you," Phyllis said. "And don't you worry about me. I'll be fine. And as far as helpin' you, well—I always hope someone gives mine a bit of love."

Lucy kissed her, then felt the strong hand reach around her neck again.

"Hold back," Phyllis said. She pulled the checkered cloth from under her skirt and handed it to Lucy. "You forgot this," she said hurriedly.

"My mama's Bible!" Lucy clutched at it as she stumbled down the steps. She tried to wave at Phyllis one more time, but the guard cuffed her cheek and held her close so she couldn't escape again.

Lucy saw nothing but the cobblestone street until they finally stopped, and she was thrust in front of her new master.

CHAPTER III

"Tell Mr. Lynch my lawyer will contact him in the morning to sign the necessary papers," the man said to the guard and then dismissed him by turning his attention to Lucy.

"I'm Mr. Priestly, Lucy," he said in a reserved tone. "And this is Mrs. Priestly." He stepped aside so the woman in the carriage could peer out at her.

Lucy mumbled a ma'am before she dropped her eyes. She was not prepared for the overwhelming presence of the man who had just bought her. With each new degrading experience Lucy felt more and more like a slave. She was an investment, not a human being. Why had the Priestlys purchased her? Nothing in their demeanor gave her the slightest clue.

Lucy looked at Mr. Priestly again as he stepped away from the carriage. I never seen nobody so tall before, she thought. He be even taller than Massa Jim, but he be dark, and my papa was fair. She stared at the brooding eyes, which were set deep in hollow sockets, and at the protruding cheekbones, long narrow nose, big white teeth, and fleshy lips. His thick black hair was streaked with gray.

In contrast, Mrs. Priestly's pale, transparent skin had a tinge of blue in it. She seemed ageless, almost ghostly; no lines or wrinkles marred her delicate complexion, yet she looked as weak as an eighty-year-old woman. As they glanced briefly at each other, Lucy thought she caught a glimpse of terror in Mrs. Priestly's eyes. The woman barely nodded to Lucy before retreating into the interior of the carriage.

"You'll ride up top." Mr. Priestly pointed to the driver's perch outside the brougham. Without changing his imperious tone, he added, "No need to be frightened anymore. We're taking you to our home."

The magnificent black gelding hitched to the carriage threw back its mane and neighed. Suddenly the smiling face of the liveryman peered down at them. He spoke with the confidence of a man secure in his position.

"We're ready when you are, sir. Seems Mr. Jefferson's tired of waiting."

"Give Lucy your hand." Mr. Priestly helped her clamber onto the seat.

Seconds later, they were off. Hair flying, Lucy clung to the railing around the padded seat. Dear God Almighty! she thought. You saved me from the lash and from the pen, now you goin' let this fool nigger shake the stuffin' out of me. Lucy squeezed her eyes shut when Mr. Jefferson charged through an intersection, barely missing a coal wagon. She didn't open them again until they had slowed down. But the relief she felt was cut short by the driver's laughter. Ain't I had enough, Lord, but I got to put up with a crazy man, too? Lucy mumbled.

"I can see you ain't used to city living," he said smoothly.

Lucy glanced at the man, trying to get a feel for him, but all she saw was a broad-shouldered Negro with a mirthful countenance who seemed to be enjoying himself at her expense.

He didn't wait for her to answer. "Name's Joshua— Joshua Taylor."

Lucy nodded, then turned her attention to the wide tree-lined street, marveling at the fine brick homes and elegant carriages.

As though reading her mind, Joshua said, "That one belongs to Clement Page, one of the officers in the Lemp Brewing Company. Jenny Belcher lives there. Related to the sugar Belchers. They own a refinery—"

Lucy leaned forward and stared at Joshua, uncomprehendingly. He stopped speaking abruptly.

"Guess you think I'm an ignorant simpleton—you been shackled and starved, bought and sold, and here I am—running off my mouth like some addlebrained fool. I'm sorry." His smile was warm now, and his eyes were filled with sympathy.

"Can't tell what I think." Lucy tried to keep the bitterness out of her voice. "Parts of what's happenin' is excitin' till I remember why I'm here. Then I get real sad."

"Must be hard, having to leave your family . . . especially being so young." Joshua shook his head, and a deep frown creased his forehead. "They'd have to beat me half to death 'fore I'd get on the block and let anybody sell me."

Lucy pulled back, startled. "You never been sold? I thought most Negroes had been by the time they were your age."

Joshua laughed. "Hey, little miss. I'm only twenty-one. Don't expect I'm ready for the pine box just yet."

"Oh, I didn't mean—" Lucy stammered.

"I know what you meant. And you're pretty much right about that. Most colored been sold long 'fore they're twenty-one. Major difference between me and most is, I'm free colored. Never been owned, and never will be."

He sounded so certain Lucy never doubted him. She was amazed to hear that there were people of her race who weren't slaves. Maybe someday Massa Jim could be persuaded to free her mother. She became so obsessed with the idea, she barely heard Joshua's monologue on the blessings of freedom. Despair had turned instantly to hope as they bumped along the avenue. Lucy jumped in surprise when Joshua nudged her arm. "We're here, little miss. Stay on the seat till I get the mister and missus inside. Then I'll come back for you."

Lucy stared at the Priestlys' stately home. Although it looked much like the other houses on the street, its elegance was accented by its shine and polish. Those folks must be spittin' all the time, Lucy thought. The white marble steps leading to two massive oak doors were smooth and spotless; two brass door knockers shone in the late afternoon light.

The severe vertical lines of the plastered facade were softened by dark green ivy that trailed over the doors and windows. The whole was topped with a gray mansard roof; a black wrought-iron fence enclosed a small front yard.

Joshua hurried her inside the house before Lucy could ask him about the Priestlys. She stared panic-stricken as Joshua tipped his hat and disappeared behind a winding staircase, leaving her standing alone in the center of the hallway. Tears, tightly suppressed, flooded her eyes as her despair returned. Doesn't do any good making a friend, she thought. He just walks off and leaves me. Guess I'll just stand here till somebody falls over me. I'd run out that door if I knew where to go. I don't want a new master. I want my mama.

Exhausted, Lucy walked toward the steps and started to sit down, just as Mr. Priestly stepped through an opening between two sliding doors.

"We're ready to talk to you now," he said, then stepped aside and motioned Lucy inside. Placing her between himself and Mrs. Priestly, who reclined on a rosewood settee, he towered over her.

"Get on your knees, child," Mr. Priestly said in a booming voice.

Dear God! He's goin' to whip me, Lucy thought. But I haven't done anythin'. Oh, why didn't Joshua warn me? She tensed her body and waited for the first blow. When it didn't come, she opened her eyes just as her new master began reading the Scriptures:

> "I will instruct you and teach you
>   the way you should go;
>   I will counsel you with my eye upon
>   you.
> Be not like a horse or a mule, without
>   understanding,
>   which must be curbed with bit and
>   bridle,
>   else it will not keep with you.
> Many are the pangs of the wicked;

but steadfast love surrounds him who
trusts in the Lord."

"Amen." Mrs. Priestly's voice could barely be heard.

Am I crazy? Lucy thought. I never saw anybody act so
peculiar. Well, better Scripture than the whip. Still, Lucy
cringed when Mr. Priestly spoke.

"Stand up," he ordered. He eyed her suspiciously. "You
have been raised a Christian, haven't you?"

"Yessir. Both my mama and papa are Christians. My
mama and me sang in the Baptist church choir."

"So I heard . . . so I heard." Mr. Priestly sat in a large
leather chair, with Lucy and his wife in his line of vision.
They both looked at him apprehensively.

"I know Mr. Sloan—Jim and I have been friends and
business associates for years. That's why you're here, child.

"When Jim realized he'd have to send you away, he asked
his friends if they would take you. I reluctantly agreed—oh,
not because of you personally. Mrs. Priestly and I don't
believe in owning people. Slavery is a pernicious blight on
the land, not to mention the debilitating effect it has on
bondsman and master."

Lucy stood rigidly at attention, seemingly compliant and
docile, but she brooded over the man's conflicting words.
Massa Jim didn't want to sell me; Mr. Priestly didn't want
to buy me; but here I be. Don't make any sense to me.

As if looking for an answer, Lucy glanced briefly at Mr.
Priestly. She was startled to see him staring at her, his
protruding eyes cold, like the eyes of a dead fish, unblinking.
Lucy quickly looked away.

"We have a daughter," Mr. Priestly said. "Amanda. She's
your age, but the Lord didn't see fit to bless her with good
health. She's been sickly all her life, never had playmates.
We've had a private tutor for her the last four years. But she
gets lonely. You'll be her companion—serve her meals,
compete with her in the classroom. Do you think you can
handle all that?

"In return, you will be treated as one of the family,
sharing Christian affection and genteel culture; you will be

27

raised as a Priestly." He nodded in approval. "Your features are pleasing, quite comely, and Mr. Sloan told me you're intelligent—quick to learn, resourceful. Of course, that's to be expected, considering your father—"

When Mr. Priestly stopped talking, the room was silent; Lucy held her breath. Only the grandfather clock was bold enough to break the stillness; its melodic rhythm comforted her.

Mrs. Priestly's taffeta skirt rustled; they watched her frail hand rise to her throat where it fluttered nervously about the lace edging of her collar. "Excuse me. I've not been feeling well lately. It's the heat. I think I'll nap before dinner." A frail smile crept across her delicate lips.

Mr. Priestly solicitously escorted his wife to the foot of the staircase, then waited as she floated up the floral-carpeted steps. She paused halfway up and looked straight at Lucy, her eyes both anxious and sad. "Welcome to our home, Lucy," she said. "I hope you'll be happy here."

Mr. Priestly pivoted on the ball of his foot and returned to the parlor. Inexplicably relieved that Mrs. Priestly had left, Lucy relaxed.

Upon entering the room, Priestly tugged at a bell pull hanging by the door. Turning, he said, "I've rung for our housekeeper, Mrs. Fitzgerald. She'll get you settled, and I expect you to do your part to ease the woman's burden, especially with regard to Amanda." Mr. Priestly waited until Lucy nodded, then he continued, "She's a little Irish woman, but her energy has diminished with age."

An Irish woman! Lucy's skin went cold at the thought of meeting anyone Irish. She stared at the door, waiting for the Irish woman to appear. Would she have wings or a tail? The last thing Lucy expected was the short, gray-haired woman who stepped into the room, eyes shifting furtively until they fell on her. The Irish woman looked as apprehensive as Lucy felt. They studied each other, their prejudices clear in their eyes.

"Shall I be taking the girl to her room?" the woman asked crisply.

"I think Lucy would like something to eat first. Some sandwiches and lemonade."

"I'll be serving dinner in less than an hour," Mrs. Fitzgerald said in an argumentative tone.

"A few sandwiches won't spoil her appetite," Priestly said sharply.

Mrs. Fitzgerald nodded. An exaggerated limp suddenly appeared in the woman's walk as she hurried out of the room.

She's blaming me for the extra work, Lucy thought. And she's the one who'll be lickin' me if I don't learn fast enough. She sighed, contemplating her bleak future, barely listening as Priestly droned on, trying heroically to justify buying another human being.

When Mrs. Fitzgerald returned, she was carrying a silver tray laden with long crustless pieces of bread filled with brown, yellow, and white spreads artfully arranged on a plum-colored plate. Lemon slices floated in a heavy crystal pitcher; chunks of ice sparkled in the pale yellow liquid. With professional disinterest, the housekeeper ignored Mr. Priestly's discourse and piled a small plate with the finger sandwiches. Then, after pouring a glass of lemonade, she handed them to Lucy, who murmured a heartfelt thank-you. It was the first time in her life she had been served by a white person.

"Will you be wantin' dinner at the regular time?" Mrs. Fitzgerald asked.

"Mrs. Priestly is resting. She's not feeling well. Serve her in her room. Lucy can help. It'll give her a chance to learn the routine."

"And will you be eatin'?"

"I have a business engagement. I'll be eating at the club." With that, Mr. Priestly picked up his cane and black hat. He looked at Lucy. "I hope you and Amanda get on. You'll be spending a lot of time together." He hesitated, straightened his shoulders, then he was gone.

He wasn't out the door before Lucy stuffed the food in her mouth, fearful that Mrs. Fitzgerald would take it away once the master was gone. Instead, the housekeeper fell onto one of the exquisite settees and fanned herself with her apron.

"Lord Almighty! That man thinks I got six hands and ten feet. 'Mrs. Fitzgerald do this; Mrs. Fitzgerald do that. Amanda cut herself; Mrs. Priestly wants her tea.'" The woman stopped and eyed Lucy with great curiosity. Her face softened, and she cracked a little smile.

"You're a mite of a thing to be sold off from your ma. Hard to imagine the mister having a slave in the house."

Lucy stopped eating. She primly pulled her skirt around her ankles. She was relieved when Mrs. Fitzgerald nodded agreeably.

"Finish the sandwiches, child. Ain't nobody else's goin' eat 'em. My Paddy and Joshua could eat the side of a cow come supper time." Mrs. Fitzgerald pointed to the silver tray. "Grab yourself some sugar cookies. They usually don't last long enough to get 'em out of the oven."

Lucy slid off the chair and did as she was told, stuffing five cookies in her checkered cloth and five more in her hands.

"Can you talk, child?" Mrs. Fitzgerald asked, suddenly alarmed at Lucy's silence.

"Yes'm, I can talk," Lucy mumbled, her mouth full of food.

A frown creased Mrs. Fitzgerald's broad face. "I work like a slave—I swear—but it ain't like being one. Know anything about cooking and cleaning?"

"Yes'm. Know both."

"Well, that'll be a help."

"Did the mister tell you about Amanda?" she asked carefully.

"Yes'm. Said she was sick, and I was to help take care of her."

"She's sick all right, but as far as you tending to her—I don't know about that." Mrs. Fitzgerald stood up and motioned for Lucy to follow. "Grab your belongin's, and I'll take you upstairs to meet Amanda and show you your room."

"I only got this." Lucy held up her checkered cloth.

Mrs. Fitzgerald drew herself up in righteous indignation. "My Paddy and me shared a suitcase when we come here in steerage. Even a young girl like you should have a change of clothes." She shook her head. "Well, never mind. Amanda has so many outfits you could wear half of 'em, and she'd never know it."

Lucy's bedroom was small and plain compared to the rest of the house, but she was delighted when Mrs. Fitzgerald showed it to her. A sturdy iron bed filled the whole left side of the room, leaving only a small aisle between it and the chest of drawers, washstand, and commode that lined the opposite wall. At the end was a marble-faced fireplace sealed shut with an ornate iron front. Lucy looked longingly at the bed, but forced herself to pay attention to Mrs. Fitzgerald, who was listing the chores she expected her to do in the morning. Lucy knew she'd never remember, so she didn't ask her to repeat them. When she finished, Mrs. Fitzgerald led Lucy into an elaborately decorated bedroom-sitting room. Despite its expensive furnishings, this room seemed heavy and oppressive.

Lucy noticed how quiet it was in the house. The evening light was dim, and Lucy peered at the canopied bed, expecting to see a wan, frail little girl lying on the puffy white pillows. But the bed was empty. Mrs. Fitzgerald looked agitated.

"Amanda! Lucy's here. Where are you?" Mrs. Fitzgerald stepped haltingly into the center of the room. Lucy was right behind her. "Amanda!"

Suddenly, from behind the draperies on the bed, a body sailed through the air, landing almost on top of Lucy and Mrs. Fitzgerald, both of whom fell to the floor protecting their heads with their hands. A screeching laugh pierced the silent room, and Lucy gasped in terror. Crouching on her hands and knees, Lucy tried to slide under the bed, but a hand clutched her wrist and held on tightly. When she opened her eyes, Lucy gaped at a little girl with long blond hair, alabaster skin, and green feline eyes that glistened malevolently.

Lucy, Lucy, black-eyed beauty
Come to play with Mandy's ghost.
Faith and love and hope and duty,
Light the fire, two toads to roast.

"Amanda! You liked to scare us to death." Mrs. Fitzgerald stood up, holding her hand to her heart. "What must Lucy think—you acting like this! I declare. You must've been planning this all day. Sometimes I just don't know what gets into you."

Amanda's eyes were glazed with mischief as she tightened her grip on Lucy's arm. "I want Lucy to play with me. I don't have anybody to play with."

"It's almost time for you to be in bed," Mrs. Fitzgerald said scoldingly, "and you haven't eaten a bite of your dinner."

"I won't eat anything that ugly old Bridget brings," Amanda said with a pout. "She put poison in it. Make Lucy eat it. If she dies, we'll hang Bridget."

"Here, now! That's no way to talk about my daughter. Nobody's poisoned your food. You're the most wasteful child . . . I bet Lucy'd eat it. She knows what it's like to be hungry."

"Lucy can feed me," Amanda said in her childish, sing-song voice. "Will you feed me, Lucy? Will you?" Amanda pulled Lucy to her feet and twirled her around in a circle, laughing hysterically as she picked up momentum.

"Here! Stop that! You'll make yourself dizzy. Sit down." Mrs. Fitzgerald grabbed Amanda and threw her on the bed. Lucy cowered behind a marble-topped table.

Dear God in heaven, the girl is mad, and I got to take care of her. Lucy's stomach knotted. I got to run away—right now—tonight.

Mrs. Fitzgerald saw the panic on Lucy's face and quietly knelt down beside her. "Don't pay Amanda no mind. She don't mean ill of you. It's just that her mind goes off sometimes, then there's nothing to do but let her be."

"Please! Don't leave me alone with her," Lucy said pleadingly.

Mrs. Fitzgerald nodded and patted Lucy's face. "You get on with you to your own room. I'll help Amanda. Don't fret yourself. She'll be all right in the morning."

Lucy shook her head doubtfully, thankful she could finally be alone. It was almost seven thirty when she staggered out of Amanda's room into her own, Amanda's shrill laugh echoing behind her. Lucy slammed the door and dropped wearily onto the bed. She closed her eyes, too tired even to cry. Falling into a troubled sleep, she dreamed of slave drivers with gold-tipped canes beating a long row of Negroes mercilessly. When a hand wrapped around her wrist, twisting it painfully, Lucy tried to pull away. Her eyes flew open when a pillow was pressed over her mouth. She found herself staring at those cold green eyes flecked with yellow. The pillow muffled Lucy's scream.

Stepping back, Amanda laughed hysterically, then threw a piece of paper on Lucy's chest. "I drew a picture of you. Don't you want to see it?"

Barely conscious, Lucy sat up. When she realized she was alone with Amanda, she curled into a ball and stared wide-eyed at the specter stalking her.

The white-robed girl, her long blond hair drifting over her face and shoulders, pointed to the paper. "Look at it," she demanded. "I drew it for you."

Terrified, Lucy picked it up and studied it. She gaped at Amanda. Amanda had sketched a young girl hanging from a gallows. The brown skin, black hair, and sack-like dress were vividly depicted.

"That's what happens to niggers who don't behave." Amanda's eyes narrowed and she studied Lucy's distraught face. "How come you're not black? Niggers are supposed to be black. You're almost as white as me. Don't matter. You're a slave, and we'll hang you anyway."

Lucy finally exploded. When, shrieking, Lucy tore the picture to shreds, Amanda turned pale.

"Stop that! I'm going to tell my daddy. You got no right—"

Lucy was on top of her. Jumping off the bed, she grabbed Amanda by the throat and shoved her across the room.

Letting go, she planted her feet firmly on the floor, hands on her hips, waiting for Amanda to strike back. But the green eyes were leery now.

"I'm going to tell my daddy you choked me. He'll have you whipped so hard your skin'll fall off."

When Lucy didn't move, Amanda said with agitation, "I'm going to call Mrs. Fitzgerald. She'll have your hide for getting me upset."

Lucy stared at Amanda, her silence threatening. The scent of honeysuckle permeated the warm, moist air, and a drowsiness crept over her when she realized she wasn't afraid anymore. After the sorrow of leaving her mother, the terror of the slave pen and the humiliation of the auction block, Amanda's threats seemed tame, indeed.

Amanda sensed Lucy's strength, and suddenly the fragile veneer cracked. Tears streaming down her face, she held out her hand to Lucy.

"Won't you be my friend? I promise—I won't draw any more bad pictures. I won't be mean. Will you help me be good, Lucy?"

Lucy pressed her lips together so she wouldn't cry out. She was so tired, so unhappy—but so was Amanda. Doesn't make sense, she thought. If we could change places—I'd have my mama, and I'd love her forever. Amanda has everything; I have nothing. Maybe we need each other. Maybe it'll work out.

"Can we be friends tomorrow? I'm too tired to think about it now."

Amanda hesitated, then nodded agreeably. "Tomorrow'll be fine." She turned and walked out of the room.

Lucy's body sagged with relief. As she fell asleep, the scent of honeysuckle filled her room with the delicate aroma of the farm, and images of her mother and Jim and Miss Susan waiting for her to come home comforted her, strengthening her resolve to survive.

CHAPTER IV

During the next four months Lucy alternated between restrained contentment and paralyzing loneliness. When Amanda was tranquil, the household ran smoothly, but when Amanda was disturbed, everyone suffered, especially Lucy, who was the first to feel the brunt of her violent harangues and unreasonable streaks of jealousy. Amanda had an insatiable need for attention. One day, lashing out in the close confines of their schoolroom after the tutors had innocently praised Lucy's diligence, Amanda yelled, "She's a nigger slave. She doesn't know anything. You're all going to be arrested. It's against the law to teach a nigger slave to read."

Later, her antagonism forgotten, Amanda demanded that Lucy help her play her mischievous pranks against their tutors. None of her tricks was original: a dead toad dropped into Miss Pratt's sack, a banister greased to inconvenience Mr. Finney. But her savage mimicry was so outlandish that even Lucy laughed at Amanda's caricature of the grammar teacher's wide hips and the Latin teacher's arthritic shuffle, all too well aware that Amanda's next victim might be herself.

Amanda's wrath, flowing like an unseen current through the household, erupted every other Friday when Miss Davis arrived for their music lessons. Lucy's playing was superior, and Mr. Priestly's smile of approval was always for her, not his own daughter.

"Play the minuet again, Lucy," Mr. Priestly said, leaning his head against the back of the chair.

"You see, Amanda," he said afterward, "Lucy's just what

we needed—someone to bring a little life into the household. And I hear your lessons have improved quite a bit."

I would have to study day and night to keep up with her, Amanda thought. Rage seethed inside her, but for her father she managed a broad smile and a coy kiss. That's one thing that little nigger can't do; she can't kiss him.

That night at dinner, Lucy paid for the compliments when Amanda threw a bowl of pudding in her face, cursing her and threatening to kill her. But by the time church services began on Sunday morning, Amanda clung fearfully to Lucy, for her father, acting as assistant pastor, preached fire and brimstone from the unadorned pulpit of the First Presbyterian Church.

Lonely, Lucy lost herself in her mother's Bible, fantasizing about the lives of her ancestors: strong African warriors, proud African maidens. She couldn't imagine their lives. Had they lived in cities? On farms? It didn't matter. They were all handsome and happy and free. Freedom. She thought about that during the long nights when she couldn't sleep. It didn't take her long to realize she and Joshua were the only people in the Priestly household who were all alone, the only Negroes. They had no loved ones, no families. So whenever she could slip away, she headed for the barn hoping to find Joshua, who was usually tending the horses or polishing the brass on the elegant carriages.

"Well, if it isn't my little miss sneaking out for a spell," he said with a sparkle in his eye.

Embarrassed, Lucy apologized for interrupting him. He assured her she was welcome in his stable.

"One of these days I'm going to put a saddle on Louise and teach you how to ride," Joshua said when Lucy, sitting on a bale of hay, shied away from the mare's nose as the horse playfully nudged her cheek.

"Mr. Priestly wouldn't ever let me go off like that," Lucy said matter-of-factly. "And anyway, I'm scared of horses."

"Aw, they're not hard to handle—just got to show 'em who's boss." Joshua brushed Mr. Jefferson's coat until it shone.

"I'm not good at doing that," Lucy said wistfully.

"Amanda takes all my handling. I barely make it through the day."

"Amanda always was a wild one. Don't know what Mr. Priestly's thinking, having you take care of her."

"What's ailing that girl? Never saw nobody act so crazy."

Joshua shrugged. "Some kinda sickness. Nobody talk about it, 'cept the time I heard Mrs. Fitzgerald say a streak of melancholia runs in the family."

"Guess I should feel sorry for her. Most of the time I hate her." Dropping her eyes, Lucy said sadly, "Being all alone, not having nobody to care, that bothers me most. Next is fear. Amanda scare the breath out of me sometimes."

Joshua looked up, a frown creasing his forehead. The muscles in his arms flexed as he squeezed the brush between his hands. "If Amanda ever tries to harm you, you just come and get me. I'm almost always here—especially at night. I sleep right upstairs." He pointed to a wooden ladder leading to a loft.

Inhaling the heavy odor of hay, horses, and manure, Lucy couldn't imagine living over a stable, but Joshua didn't seem to mind. In fact, he seemed to enjoy it.

"You always lived up there?" she asked, unable to restrain her curiosity.

"No," Joshua said, then, putting down his brush, he straddled a milking stool and leaned his arms on his protruding knees. "When my folks were alive, we lived in a shack down by the waterfront. My pa tended horses and owned a wagon. Mr. Priestly hired him to carry goods from the riverboats to his hardware store. By the time pa died, the Priestlys had their own hauling firm. Mr. Priestly owned five stores by then, and he needed more than an old darky with a broken-down freight wagon to help him. But Mr. Priestly remembered me, and when he needed a liveryman, he offered me the job."

"How long ago was that?"

"Back in the summer of 1846—four years ago, it was." Joshua shook his head. "Don't seem that long."

"Do you like working for the Priestlys?" Lucy squirmed uncomfortably on the bale of hay.

"I ain't overworked, if that's what you mean." Joshua shrugged. "They don't go out much. The missus is sickly, and, of course, they never take Amanda anywhere."

"So how come you aren't married?" she asked, innocently.

Joshua threw back his head and laughed. "Well, now, little miss—not that it's any of your business—but I'm not planning on getting married for a long time—if ever. You see, I'm a free Negro, and I ain't going to get myself tied up with a slave woman. But them's about all I meet. Ain't many free women around."

His words pricked her like a bee sting. Suddenly free and slave took on new meanings. On the Sloan farm, whites were the only ones who were free, and they were a world apart. She wondered if Joshua was ashamed to talk to her—her being a slave and all. No, she thought as she looked at his open, handsome face, she knew he would never be ashamed of his own people. But if he wasn't ashamed, why wouldn't he marry a Negro slave? She decided to ask.

"Well," he answered, "I believe a man and a woman belong to each other when they get married. Not like owning, but—well—belonging. You know what I mean?"

Lucy nodded, but wasn't at all sure she understood. Of course, the Priestlys belonged together, and so did Miss Susan and Massa Jim. But they were white. Did Negroes have the same feelings? Joshua has, and he's a Negro, she thought. And suddenly she realized she would feel the same way if she ever got married.

Joshua continued, "Ain't no way a slave woman can belong to her husband—don't matter if he's slave or free. The white man owns her, and he pulls the strings. No way a man can live with that—black or white." Joshua sighed deeply. "You understand, little miss?"

Before she could answer, Lucy heard Mrs. Fitzgerald's shrill voice calling her from the back porch. She jumped up and almost fell over her feet as she hurried to the door. "I got to go now. Mrs. Fitzgerald has me helping her fix the food for the party next Saturday. When I don't have to sit with Amanda, I shell nuts or cut out Santa Claus cookies."

"Save me one," Joshua called after her. The door slammed shut and he was alone. Always alone, he thought sadly. Would he remain a recluse forever or could he allow himself to love someone for keeps?

Lucy's eyes glistened as she stared at the sideboard laden with food, most of which she had helped prepare during the past two weeks. The Santa Claus sugar cookies, decorated with red and white icing, were hung on the branches of a small pine tree along with marzipan strawberries, bananas, and green apples. The tree would be the centerpiece for the dinner table that she was now setting with lace-edged doilies and heavy silver tableware. Later Mrs. Fitzgerald would carefully add the fine bone china plates, crystal goblets, and wine glasses.

Exhausted by the endless chores, Lucy barely had time to think about her mother and how much she missed her. For the moment, she was thankful that even Amanda was cheerful. She too had helped, shelling black walnuts and stringing popcorn to wrap around the Christmas tree.

It began to snow around noon, and by one thirty, over an inch had accumulated on the streets and walkways. By five o'clock, Lucy was almost as agitated as Mrs. Fitzgerald. Told that Mrs. Priestly wished to see her, Lucy took off her apron and slowly climbed the servants' stairwell at the back of the house. She had hoped they had forgotten. A month before, when she had heard about the party, Lucy had been asked by Mr. Priestly to sing at the musicale after dinner. She was so terrified at the prospect of singing before the Priestlys' august guests that Lucy risked a tongue-lashing by refusing. Instead of getting angry, Mr. Priestly had flattered her and promised a wonderful surprise. Reluctantly, Lucy agreed. Forcing herself to practice day after day, she reminded herself that, after all, her own mama had sung at the Sloans' recitals years before.

Well, soon it'll be over with, she thought as she rapped on

Mrs. Priestly's bedroom door. They won't be expecting much from a slave girl anyway, she told herself ruefully.

Lucy was filled with awe and excitement as she stepped into Mrs. Priestly's magnificent room. Across the expanse of an intricately designed Oriental rug sat Mrs. Priestly, looking wan and fragile amid her sumptuous surroundings.

Lucy dropped her eyes, unwilling to look into the melancholy face. Mrs. Priestly questioned Lucy gently.

"Yes'm. I've been practicing for two weeks . . . No, ma'am, I won't shake no matter how scared I am . . ."

The interrogation continued for ten minutes before Mrs. Priestly was convinced that Lucy would not embarrass her guests. Pointing a long, bony finger at her bed, Mrs. Priestly asked Lucy to fetch the box lying on top. Then, holding it on her lap, she untied the white ribbon, lifted the lid, and slowly folded back the tissue paper. Lucy watched spellbound as Mrs. Priestly pulled out a fawn-colored velvet dress, its collar and cuffs trimmed with deep brown mink.

"Oh," Lucy sighed as Mrs. Priestly shook it, allowing the skirt to tumble to the floor.

"Do you like it?" Mrs. Priestly asked, smiling.

"It's beautiful—so soft and, and—beautiful."

Mrs. Priestly chortled at Lucy's astonishment. "It's yours, Lucy," she said, handing her the dress. "We want you to look your very best tonight."

"Oh, oh, oh!" Tears welled up in her eyes. Quickly brushing them away, Lucy gingerly touched the rich velvet and ran her finger across the mink collar. "I will, Mrs. Priestly. I'll look my very best."

"I hope so. We're going to entertain some very important people. In fact, I'd like you to meet two of them now. They're waiting for you in my sitting room." She sighed. "Please—introduce yourself. I want to rest as long as I can before dinner. But do come back and help me after you dress Amanda."

Lucy nodded, then, returning the dress to its box, she headed for the sitting room. Puffed up with pride, Lucy couldn't wait to show off her new attire. Wait until Mrs. Fitzgerald and Joshua see my dress, she thought. Course

Amanda'll be a witch about it, but then—she's a witch about everything.

In her excitement, Lucy didn't even consider who Mrs. Priestly's guests might be. Lowering her head to show the proper demeanor, Lucy couldn't see the faces of the couple flanking the fireplace. When she finally looked up, she stared into the eyes of Jim and Susan Sloan.

"Dear Jesus!" she cried. She dropped her box on the floor and leaned against the arm of the sofa. Her first instinct had been to throw herself into her father's arms, but Susan's haughty stare held her in check. Jim extended his hand.

"Hello, Lucy," he said, smiling. "It's good to see you again."

Lucy curtsied, then, unable to think of anything to say, stared at them blankly.

A slight cough caught in Susan's throat as she nodded impersonally. "Rebecca sends her greetings—as does Jim, Jr." She nervously tapped her hand with an elaborately decorated fan.

Lucy caught her breath. Ignoring Susan's icy detachment, she kissed Jim, then returned to the sofa and sat down.

"How's Mama?" she asked, her lips barely moving.

"Your mama's fine." Jim stuck his hand into his vest pocket and pulled out an envelope. "She wrote you a letter."

Unceremoniously, Lucy jumped up and grabbed it out of his hand. She clutched the precious piece of paper in her fist, saving it for when she was alone. Jim nodded in understanding.

"If you have the time to reply, we'll take your letter along with us," Jim said haltingly. "Will you do that?"

"Oh, yes, sir. By tomorrow morning—if that's all right. I'll stay up all night—"

"Morning'll be fine," Jim said, then fell silent.

Did Susan still hate her? Lucy wondered. It seemed unlikely that she would have come along if she did. But if the crisis was over, why hadn't they brought her mama with them? Oh, what a joy that would have been. Susan was breathtakingly beautiful. Her long blond curls tumbled over her bare shoulders. Her throat blazed with a diamond and

41

pearl necklace, showing off the black lace-and-taffeta dress sparkling with tiny crystals. No, Lucy thought. Miss Susan will never allow Mama to come to St. Louis. She couldn't stand being around her. Well, at least she didn't make Massa Jim sell Mama, too, she thought, tightening her grip on the letter. It would have to suffice for the time being.

With less than half an hour to help Amanda and Mrs. Priestly dress, Lucy didn't have time to bemoan her fate. Amanda was docile as Lucy helped her into a pink and red taffeta dress, then brushed her long pale hair until its golden highlights shone. Lucy's mind was wandering when Amanda suddenly grabbed the brush and struck Lucy in the face. Lucy yelped. Grabbing a poker, Amanda stood in front of the hearth, her face glowing with angry passion. Lucy was panic-stricken. She ran to the door, but Amanda was quicker and blocked her exit.

"You stole my mommy and daddy from me, you nigger slave. I'm going to kill you." Amanda's green eyes glistened with excitement. "You got a prettier dress, and Daddy makes eyes over you all the time. You think you're so smart. Smarty pants! Smarty Pants! I hate you, Lucy nigger, and I'm going to kill you cause there ain't no law against killing a slave."

Amanda pushed the tip of the poker against Lucy's chest. Shrieking, Lucy grabbed the poker and threw Amanda to the floor. "How many times do I have to tell you I'm not taking your mommy or daddy away from you? If your mommy bought me a new dress it was because she wanted me to look nice tonight for her friends. If your daddy listens to me play the piano, it's because he likes music. And as for me, I don't even want to be here. I got my own mama—and only the Lord knows when I'll see her again." Tears spilled down Lucy's face. As always when Lucy lost her temper, Amanda cowered fearfully. Grinding her teeth in disgust, Lucy dropped the poker and stalked out of the room.

The next two hours were a nightmare for Lucy. She helped Mrs. Fitzgerald in the kitchen even though the temporary help crowded the pantry looking for something to do. "Takes more time to teach 'em where things is than to do it ourselves," the housekeeper reasoned. But all the same, Lucy thought, we still got to do the running.

Whenever she could, Lucy peeked into the dining room and looked sorrowfully at her father. If there were only some way I could go back with him—back to the farm, back to my mother. But there wasn't time to dwell on her misery. As soon as the guests finished eating, Lucy ran upstairs to change into her new dress, now a stinging reminder of Amanda's hateful jealousy. Still, she couldn't help but admire her reflection in the mirror as she tied a light brown ribbon in her hair. It softly accented her creamy complexion, and her thick black hair contrasted richly with the smooth mink and velvet.

At exactly nine o'clock Lucy made her way through the crowded parlor, and almost unnoticed she took her place in front of the grand piano. A slight murmur of irritation arose when people realized they were to be entertained by a ten year old Negro, but their polite attentiveness turned to real enjoyment as Lucy sang the popular tunes "Flow Gently, Sweet Afton" and "Long Long Ago." But when Lucy chose a Negro spiritual to finish her performance, the audience was outraged. They knew that slaves had used lyrics as a code to spread their escape plans, and not all of the Priestlys' friends had abolitionist leanings. When Lucy took her bows, the applause was sparse, the faces stony. As Lucy hurried out of the room, she felt the contempt in Susan's pitiless eyes.

Mr. Priestly hurried after her. "I'm surprised at you, Lucy, singing that slave song. It's not like you to be so callous toward our friends' feelings." He barely restrained his anger.

"I don't understand," Lucy stammered. "My mama taught me the spirituals. I thought you'd like it—it being about Jesus and all." Lucy turned away, unable to bear Mr. Priestly's almost possessive stare. His breath was strong with liquor.

"Don't cry, Lucy. It isn't that important." He dabbed at her eyes with his handkerchief.

"But I ruined the evening—"

"Nonsense! You sang beautifully. But next time I'll choose the music. Now, off with you. It's way past your bedtime."

"Yes, sir. Thank you, sir." Lucy was so relieved the ordeal was over, she didn't care what faux pas she had committed. Had it really been so terrible? Probably, she thought glumly, recalling Susan's icy stare.

Lucy ran up the stairs and didn't stop until she slammed the door to her room. Breathlessly, she undressed, laid her new dress carefully on her bed, and at last she opened her letter.

Her heart pounded wildly as she looked at her mother's ornate handwriting. "Dearest Lucy—" The letter rambled on for two pages. Maybelle was relieved that she was being raised like the master's own child. Though filled with love and longing, the letter offered little hope that they would see each other again.

After reading it four times, Lucy sighed and, pulling a pen and inkwell closer to her, began to write. Not knowing what was important and what wasn't, Lucy wanted to tell her mother everything about her new home, the Priestlys, Joshua, the Fitzgeralds. So little time to say it all! Then she remembered her diary. She'd been keeping it ever since she had arrived at the Priestlys. She had pretended she was writing to her mother, and now, she thought joyously, her pretending had become a reality. She opened the third drawer of her bureau and after rummaging for a minute, cried out in anguish. The diary was gone. Amanda! She grabbed the lamp and ran into Amanda's room. As she tore through Amanda's desk, she didn't hear her creep out of bed. Feeling the girl's breath on her neck she spun around, throwing up her hand just in time to deflect the poker that came crashing down.

"You're crazy," Lucy screamed. "Crazy."

Amanda's shriek numbed Lucy, filling her with terror. She grabbed the poker from Amanda's hand and shook it threateningly.

"You've gone too far this time. I want my diary. You give it to me."

Amanda laughed hysterically. Her green eyes glowed in the flickering firelight.

"I'm going to tell what you wrote in your stupid diary! I saw what you wrote about my papa."

"I didn't write nothing about your papa."

"You did. I saw it. You want him to kiss you. He won't. He loves me. He loves me. He hates you."

Lucy lunged forward ready to strike Amanda, but the look in the girl's eyes made her stop. She wants me to hit her. Lucy lowered her arm. Well, I won't. I'd be punished.

"Amanda," Lucy said, trying to control her quivering voice, "I don't know what you're talking about. I never wrote anything 'bout kissing your papa. You got to believe me."

"You're the devil. You're the devil. You want Papa to kiss you."

"And you're nasty. Making up a story like that."

Amanda pointed to Lucy's dress lying on the bed. "Papa bought that for you. You want to look pretty for him, don't you?" Her hands shook. Hatred glazed her eyes.

Lucy retreated under her stare, the sting of her wrath as cutting as a leather whip.

"Oh, Amanda, you say such terrible things. You lie. Your mama bought me that dress."

Amanda sneered. "She does what she's told. She's afraid of Papa."

Lucy shook her head. "She bought it for the party. I couldn't sing in rags."

Amanda was beyond hearing. She pressed her hands over her ears and cried, "Devil! Devil! Devil!" As though propelled by her hatred, Amanda grabbed Lucy's dress and threw it in the hearth where the dying embers smoldered.

"No!" Lucy bolted to the hearth and snatched her dress from the hot coals, but as she bent over, Amanda shoved her, headfirst, into the fireplace.

Lucy cried out in pain as she scrambled away, but too late. Soot and ashes covered the fawn-colored velvet and festering blisters spread up her arm. She sat on the floor and cried.

Amanda, her anger spent, backed away showing neither elation nor remorse.

Drawing on her last bit of strength, Lucy stood up, shook out the dress, dabbed water on the hole, and laid it on a chair. She stared at it, her heart filled with fear, sadness, and utter defeat. What if Mr. Priestly wouldn't allow her to write her mother? She would have to give them the letter before they found out about the dress. Sitting at the small table beside her bed, she wrote, not stopping till the clock struck three. The throbbing pain in her arm finally forced her to say good-bye. Folding the ten sheets carefully, she tucked them into an envelope, writing on the outside: "To Maybelle, mother of Lucy, the Sloan farm near Jefferson City, Missouri."

Knowing she wouldn't be able to sleep unless she took care of her burns, Lucy bundled herself up in a flannel gown and heavy woolen robe. Reluctant to leave the damaged clothes behind, she grabbed them up and made her way down the back staircase toward the stable. She breathed a sigh of relief as she hurriedly stepped inside.

"Lucy! What in tarnation—" Joshua looked at her in distress.

"Please! Don't yell at me. I need help. You're the only one . . ." Lucy could not stop the tears streaming down her cheeks.

As Lucy told Joshua what had happened, he was both relieved and concerned. Relieved that the burns weren't worse, concerned that Amanda was becoming more and more violent. He flinched when Lucy pushed up the sleeve of her gown and held her arm up so he could see the burns. The wounds had opened, oozing blood and fluid. Cursing under his breath, Joshua dabbed some greasy salve on Lucy's sores, then wrapped her arm with strips of torn rags.

"There, there, Little Miss. Don't cry. It'll stop hurtin' soon." Joshua looked down at Lucy, his heart filled with compassion. Such a little thing, he thought.

Lucy stared hard at Joshua. "You won't say anything to Mr. Priestly, will you? I mean, he can't know—"

"Don't you worry. I won't say a word, even though I'd like to explain a few things."

Fear spread across Lucy's face and she clenched Joshua's hand in hers. "He can't ever find out. There's nothing to be done. If the Priestlys got to choose between me and A-manda, well, you know who'll go."

"I'll do anything to protect you." Joshua gently wiped Lucy's tears with his fingertips.

"Oh, Joshua! I'd greatly appreciate it if you'd just be here if I need you. I won't come anymore at night. Don't want to get you into any trouble. If you'll just be my friend."

"I'll be more than your friend, Lucy. You think of me as family. Anytime somethin' bad happens or you're lonely, you come get me. It always helps to talk, and sometimes to get away—"

"I can't go running off. I'm a slave. Slaves don't have rights."

Joshua smiled and put his arm around Lucy, holding her close. "Listen, Little Miss. There's lots of slaves in the city. They manage to get off by themselves. They come to the church—slave and free. Young folks, too, like yourself. I'll take you there anytime you want."

Lucy relaxed. Just listening to Joshua talk made her feel good. Somehow she knew he'd make everything right. Still, there was no way Mr. Priestly would ever let her go to the Baptist church.

"We're Presbyterians" she had heard Mr. Priestly say with disdain when one of his friends had invited the family to attend an Episcopalian service.

"Mr. Priestly's very strict on that," she explained. "We only go to the Presbyterian service."

"You're a young un', but you got to learn that everything ain't up front when you're dealing with people." When Joshua spoke, it was with an air of worldly wisdom.

Lucy lifted her head and listened intently.

"What I'm saying, Little Miss, is that you can come to my church and not let anybody know."

"How'm I going to do that?"

"Don't you worry about that right now. There's plenty of time to work out a plan."

Lucy's spirits soared. She kissed Joshua on the cheek and then scurried back to the house grinning happily. Joshua had even assured her that Mrs. Fitzgerald had cleaned and patched worse disasters of Amanda's than the ruined velvet dress, and no one had ever been the wiser.

CHAPTER V

The salmon pink tulips and dusty blue hyacinths had lost the bloom of early spring, yielding to the showy beauty of purple and white peonies bordering the lush green lawn. The slanting rays of the late afternoon sun illuminated Lucy's face as she stood at the kitchen window. Today, June 1, 1857, was her seventeenth birthday. She had sprouted from a gangling, long-legged girl to a young lady with a small waist and full breasts. Her cotton dress stretched tightly across her body making her feel both ill at ease and vain. Her face had become a woman's: a shapely mouth, long, thick lashes outlining luminous brown eyes, and wisps of tiny ringlets, escaping from the mass of black hair pulled back off her forehead, framing her oval face.

A slight breeze rustled the branches of a dogwood tree on the side of the house. It had grown along with her, and Lucy tried to recall the last six birthdays she had spent at the Priestlys. But the years blended into one. Her one dream— that she would someday see her mother again—had failed to materialize, and all she could look back upon were her classes with Amanda in the mornings, followed by endless chores, despite Mrs. Fitzgerald's efforts to lighten them.

Still, there had been some pleasant moments. The

Wednesday night church services, held clandestinely in the basement of the Negro Baptist church where talk of the growing animosity between North and South over slavery was heated and vehement, had given Lucy the chance to grow into womanhood without the disabling mentality of a slave. She had forced herself to look beyond her own humdrum existence into the wider world of politics and social unrest.

Did the admission of California into the Union as a free state balance the stringent fugitive slave law that threatened all free-born blacks? Under the present fugitive slave law, no black was assumed to be free unless he could present absolute proof of his status. Harriet Beecher Stowe's abolitionist novel, *Uncle Tom's Cabin,* roused the fighting spirit of the anti-slavery forces, but the power structure in Washington seemed unaffected. Only three months before, in March, 1857, the Supreme Court had declared that a slave was not a citizen of the United States. Lucy ruefully recalled that the Dred Scott case had started in the very courthouse where she had been sold. Her memory of the day she had stood on the block still festered in her mind, the fear and humiliation indelibly marked on her soul.

In contrast, Lucy quietly relished the intensity of her love for Joshua. She couldn't remember when he had ceased being her protector and had become her confidant, then the man she dreamed about late at night. But nothing would ever come of it. He had said often enough that he wouldn't marry a slave, and there was no denying she belonged to the Priestlys. They owned her like they owned a stick of furniture or a horse.

Just as long as he doesn't up and marry somebody else and then leave me here alone, Lucy thought. I believe I can handle a wife, but I can't handle his going off. If I were free, maybe Joshua'd marry me. I know he likes me. Calls me "Pretty Miss Lucy." He's something, my Joshua. Really something.

"Lucy!" Mrs. Fitzgerald's strident voice interrupted her daydreams. "Would you mind taking Mrs. Priestly's tray to her? My legs just won't do them steps more'n once a day."

49

Lucy nodded sympathetically.

"Thank you, Lucy." Mrs. Fitzgerald moved to the pot of soup bubbling on the stove. "And watch out for the vase. It's not too sturdy. But you know Mrs. Priestly. She has to have a flower on her tray.

"I hope Mr. Priestly's guest likes home cooking. Time was I could throw a pretty fancy meal together, but that was a while back. Since the family don't entertain no more, it's enough just to get meat and potatoes on the table." Mrs. Fitzgerald paused; her frown eased into a wisp of a smile.

"Happy birthday, honey. I baked you a cake—just a wee one." Her eyes sparked mischievously. "After you tuck the womenfolk in for the night, you come back to the kitchen and we'll celebrate your birthday. You can cut the cake and I'll pour us a swallow of whiskey. I'm sure Paddy and Joshua'll join us."

Lucy grinned, then hurried up the stairs. As she rapped on Mrs. Priestly's door, she was reminded again of the progressive deterioration of the Priestly women. Mrs. Priestly never left her rooms anymore, not even to go to church. Only Lucy and Mrs. Fitzgerald were allowed to enter her sanctuary; she loathed her husband, and Amanda's constant chattering drove her mad. Until the light faded completely, Mrs. Priestly spent her days working on needlepoint or reading the Bible, resolutely rocking in her cane-backed chair. Amanda also refused to leave her room, and even the enticement of a walk in the park wasn't enough to tempt her from her self-imposed exile. There was nothing to be done about it, Lucy thought as she pushed open the door and entered Mrs. Priestly's sitting room.

"How are you feeling this evening?" Lucy asked pleasantly. She placed the tray on a small table beside Mrs. Priestly.

"Not well at all. But thank you for asking." The frail woman's dull, expressionless eyes strained to see through the murky darkness. Barely able to distinguish Lucy's shadowy form, she grabbed her hand in desperation and held onto it tightly.

"Dear Lucy," she said, almost as a sigh, "have you

forgiven us for buying you—for keeping you as a slave all these years?"

Lucy stared at the woman uncomprehendingly. "Forgiven?"

"Yes. I was just reading Jeremiah. The Lord punished the Hebrews when they enslaved their own people." The woman put on a pair of spectacles and opened her Bible to a heavily marked page. "I know it by heart almost. It says— 'and I will give them into the hand of their enemies and into the hand of those who seek their lives. Their dead bodies shall be food for the birds of the air and the beasts of the earth.'" She looked up. "Do you understand what that means?" Her voice was filled with panic.

"No, ma'am. I don't know how to interpret Scripture, and I don't think it's our pleasure to do so, either. Maybe you better talk to the minister—or Mr. Priestly. One of them—"

"They're evil. The minister has slaves, too. How can he see the warning when he's one of them?"

Lucy vacillated between fear and disgust. There was just too much hatred in this household. Hatred and horror. She wondered what had happened to all of them that they dwelt on death and evil so much. There was no laughter, no love.

"Eat your dinner, Mrs. Priestly." Lucy tried to pull away, but the woman clung to her.

"Don't go! I have something to give you. Wait! Let me think."

Lucy did as she was told, overpowered by Mrs. Priestly's command. She felt as if she was caught in a snare, unable to break the spell enveloping them.

Rummaging through a basket, Mrs. Priestly finally pulled out a crudely wrapped box. Her eyes, now bright with success, focused on Lucy as she opened the present.

As Lucy's fingers touched the fine filigree decorating the miniature gold piano, she gasped, first in dismay, then in fright. Lifting it in the air, she gazed in wonderment at the diamonds and rubies encrusting the lid. And when she opened the top, the music box played a sprightly waltz.

Tears flooded Lucy's eyes. What had possessed the woman to give her such a beautiful gift? Lucy wondered. Guilt maybe. Certainly not love. But of course I can't keep it. Amanda would have a fit if she knew it had even been offered. And the rest—Joshua, Mrs. Fitzgerald. What would they think? Looking at the exquisite music box one last time, Lucy ran her finger over the delicate design and joyfully lifted the lid, humming the lovely waltz, the only sound to break the oppressive silence in the room.

"It's yours," Mrs. Priestly said, elated that Lucy liked her present. "It's a family heirloom—and since I don't have any children—"

"What about Amanda? She's your daughter."

Mrs. Priestly leveled her eyes and stared hard at Lucy. "I have no children."

"Oh, Mrs. Priestly—" Lucy backed away, for the first time fully aware of her descent into insanity.

"Please—take the tray. I'm not hungry tonight," Mrs. Priestly said feebly, dismissing Lucy with the wave of her hand.

Afraid of creating a scene if she argued, Lucy put the music box on the tray and walked out of the room, determined to give it to Mr. Priestly as soon as she could.

Mrs. Fitzgerald agreed that that was the best thing to do and offered to talk to the mister about his wife's hallucinations. Lucy was relieved when she found Amanda asleep. She returned her tray to the kitchen and spent the next hour serving dinner to Mr. Priestly and his guest. As they retired to the drawing room for cigars and brandy, Mr. Priestly asked Lucy to join them in an hour.

Strange goings on, Lucy thought, then put the last of the blackened pots into the tepid dishwater and scrubbed them until they shone. Thankful that the kitchen chores were finished for the day, Lucy threw the dirty water out the back door, then, untying her apron, headed for the front of the house.

The whole family's daft, Lucy thought, then hesitated a moment before she knocked on the parlor door. A gnawing fear clutched at her stomach. Who was Mr. Priestly's mysterious guest? Could he be a slaver? The stubborn, almost pernicious fear of being sold never disappeared. Finally, gathering her courage, she announced her presence and stepped into the room.

Always gracious in front of guests, Mr. Priestly escorted Lucy to the center of the room where he introduced her to a dour-looking man whose fleshy pink face contrasted starkly with his black waistcoat and white silk cravat.

"Lucy, this is Mr. Jacob." Mr. Priestly's voice was warm and friendly.

Lucy nodded politely.

"Mr. Jacob is my lawyer as well as my banker. He's here—well, we'll talk about that later. Right now I'd like for you to sing for us. You don't mind if I show you off, do you?"

"No, sir," Lucy said, completely disconcerted. So! He's going to sell me. He'll get more money for me if I can sing and play the piano. That's what all those lessons were about. And I thought . . . Oh, dear Jesus! Is he going to sell me to one of those houses where the women entertain the men, where they—"

"Well, don't just stand there, Lucy. Mr. Jacob doesn't have all night," Mr. Priestly said impatiently.

Dutifully, Lucy forced herself to sing, but her voice cracked on even the simplest song. Her mind went blank and she felt herself falling. . . . Her head fell against the top of the piano.

Mr. Priestly hurried to her side. "What is it, Lucy? Are you ill?"

Mr. Jacob handed Mr. Priestly his glass of brandy and they finally forced some of it into Lucy's mouth. The unfamiliar bite of the liquor roused her. As she looked into Mr. Priestly's dark eyes she remembered his wife's admonition—that he was evil, that he'd be punished for owning a slave. What did it all mean? Lucy laid her head on her arm and cried.

"Here, here, child," Mr. Jacob said sternly. "We don't need that." He cleared his throat as he walked back to his seat.

"Mr. Jacob's right. There's nothing to cry about." Mr. Priestly cocked his head to one side, a puzzled expression on his face. "But how did you hear? I thought it was a well-guarded secret."

"Oh, please, Mr. Priestly." Lucy lifted her head, but made no effort to wipe the tears from her eyes. "Is it something I've done? Something I haven't done? I know I've been cross with Amanda when I shouldn't have, but if you'll—"

Mr. Priestly laughed when Lucy mentioned Amanda. "You're acting very strange today, Lucy. I'm sure that getting your freedom is exciting, but don't you think you're carrying things too far?"

Lucy blinked. "Freedom! What are you talking, freedom? You mean I'm—I'm—"

"That's right, Lucy. You're free." Mr. Priestly relaxed, smiling broadly. "Mr. Jacob has drawn up the papers. That's why he's here tonight. It's all legal."

"I can't tell you how I feel—I can't—" Lucy's tears splashed down her face, and it was only with the greatest amount of self-control that she didn't hug Mr. Priestly and Mr. Jacob, both of whom, she felt, would have disapproved of such fervor. "It's a dream come true—it's like being born again—it's—"

Mr. Jacob's dour expression hadn't changed, and now he stepped forward and stared hard at Lucy. "Freedom has many faces, child, one of which is earning your own living. I'm sure you'll agree, and since you have musical talent, I'll be happy to recommend you to my clients. Quite a few are looking for a music teacher for their children. You won't make a lot, but—"

"Lucy doesn't have to worry about making a living," Mr. Priestly interrupted. "I expect her to continue as she is—taking care of Amanda, running the household. Of course, she'll take on more responsibilities now that she's older—seventeen today, as a matter of fact. I always intended to free her when she turned seventeen. She's been a big help in the past, especially since Mrs. Priestly's illness prevents her from performing her duties."

Mr. Jacob fidgeted with the gold chain attached to a handsome pocket watch. His agitation increased as Mr. Priestly rambled on about Lucy's future, his round, fleshy face reddening with embarrassment at his patron's apparent obsession with his young charge. Clearing his throat, he flipped the front of the watch open, exclaimed over the lateness of the hour, and, turning on his heel, left hurriedly, barely grunting a reply to Mr. Priestly's good-bye.

"Now, back to you," Mr. Priestly said.

Lucy fidgeted with the lace edging around her cuff, unable to contain her excitement.

"I have so many plans for you, Lucy. You'll stay here—with us. But I intend to spend more time with you; teach you how to be the perfect hostess; how to run a household. With Olivia—Mrs. Priestly—almost a recluse, you can see why I need someone I can count on." Mr. Priestly pressed closer to Lucy, the smell of liquor strong on his breath.

Lucy pulled away, trying to hide the turmoil inside her. How much longer do I have to pretend? she wondered. I don't care about your household; I don't care about Mrs. Priestly or Amanda. Her smile broadened, and she spoke softly so as not to provoke Mr. Priestly.

"I can hardly wait to share the good news with Mrs. Fitzgerald and Joshua. I'm sure they'll be as overwhelmed by your generosity, your Christian charity, as I am."

Nodding agreeably, Mr. Priestly dismissed her with the promise of continuing their talk later, pointedly pleased with Lucy's response to his humanitarian deed. Under his benevolent eye Lucy slid off the piano bench and, just short of a run, hurried out of the room.

Mrs. Fitzgerald and Lucy hugged and cried and laughed. Hearing their jubilant cries, Joshua and Paddy dropped their saw and rushed inside. Overcome with joy, Lucy sputtered out her pronouncement again and again. When Joshua grasped the full import of Lucy's excited words, he spun her around the kitchen, his face gleaming with happiness.

When they finally sat down at the kitchen table, Mrs. Fitzgerald cut the birthday cake, and Paddy poured a bit of

Irish whiskey in everyone's glass while Joshua, apologizing for his modest gift, presented Lucy with a delicate brooch of three hand-painted violets on white porcelain.

Lucy pinned it to the bodice of her white muslin dress proudly. Paddy, who had been sipping his whiskey all the while, refilled his glass and self-consciously proposed a toast to liberty, to love, and to a long life.

Joshua had just pulled his chair closer to Lucy when Bridget swooped through the room. The Fitzgeralds' only daughter, still unmarried at the crucial age of eighteen, spent most of her spare time at the St. Louis cathedral saying novenas and stations of the cross in the hope that Jesus or Mary or someone in the calendar of saints would send the right man to her doorstep. Perennially jealous of Lucy, she forced an artificial smile when told of Lucy's good fortune, then tugging at the crumpled kelly green dress that barely disguised her thick hips, she thumped across the kitchen and out the back door. Mrs. Fitzgerald looked up apologetically, but Lucy was indifferent to the girl's rudeness; nothing could dampen her euphoria. "I'll be able to go see Mama!" Lucy bubbled delightedly.

"The fugitive slave law can get you into a lot of trouble," Joshua said frankly. "Any white folk who wants can claim you're a runaway slave. You can be sold, and nobody'd know what happened to you."

"But I'll have my papers. They'll say I'm free colored. Mr. Priestly said it was all done legal."

A smirk distorted Joshua's lips when Lucy mentioned papers. "Lucy! Put your thinking cap on a minute. If a man's determined to have you, a piece of paper won't make no difference."

"It's against the law to kidnap a person," Mrs. Fitzgerald said indignantly. "Certainly somebody'd take the man to court."

"Who? The man who bought her or the one who sold her?" Joshua said sarcastically. "Didn't you hear about the new ruling? A slave can't sue nobody in a government court—a slave don't have no rights. Lucy ain't a slave no more, but how would she prove it?"

"Oh, please. I didn't mean to get you upset." Lucy shrugged resignedly. "There's nothing to be done. If it's meant for me to see my mama again, then it'll happen. If not . . ." Lucy looked around at the faces of her friends. They, too, were her family. She had lived with them almost as long as she had lived with her mother. Lucy smiled wistfully. She didn't want to leave them either, but to stay with the Priestlys—Lucy's stomach knotted at the thought.

I'm free, she told herself. Free to say yes or no or maybe, free to come and go, within reason, of course, and free to marry Joshua—if he'll have me. But he will—I just know he will. There'll be no maybe on that if I play my cards right. The Lord sure works slow, she thought ruefully, but at least he's not sleeping.

Lucy looked at Joshua, her eyes filled with love. "Would you take me to church tonight? I think it'll be safe. Surely the sheriff won't arrest two church-going Christians. I have some praying to do." Lucy smiled. "And don't you think the folks'll be pleased as punch to hear about my being freed?"

"Since we been doing it illegally for years, can't imagine it'd hurt now." Joshua stood up and offered Lucy his hand. Ignoring Mrs. Fitzgerald's questioning look, they ran out the back door, down the steps, and across the yard, and still holding hands laughed exuberantly, relishing their youth, their independence, their very existence. A spring rain sprinkled their faces, and feeling feverish, joyous, impassioned, they raised their heads to allow the cool, tingling drops to splash on their eyelids, their lips, their throats. Feeling the burden of slavery lighten with each passing moment, Lucy lost her inhibitions and shouted at the top of her lungs.

With their arms entwined they circled a sapling, and as they caught their breaths, Lucy and Joshua fell in love all over again. Joshua's rock-hard muscles bulged from under his shirt sleeves, and his broad chest heaved as he leaned his head close to the tree trunk and pulled Lucy toward him. His kiss was warm at first, light and curious. Lucy responded hungrily to his touch, and his passion flared; embracing her, his massive hands gripped her shoulders while his heavy cotton trousers stretched tight across his narrow hips. When they separated, they were breathless, unable to speak, unable to move.

"I was afraid I was going to have to break my promise to myself and marry a slave," Joshua said, smiling.

"I don't understand."

Joshua brushed a lock of hair from Lucy's face and stared at her tenderly. "I been in love with you forever, Pretty Miss. From the first day, when I helped you up on the carriage, when I brought you home. Oh, I didn't love you then like I do now, but if anybody'd ever laid a hand on you, I'd've killed him. No doubt about that." Joshua cocked his head to one side. "It was maybe three years ago—when you started to fill out, when you started to pout and laugh and flirt—that I knew it was hopeless. I was in love with you—like I feel right now, all hot and weak and crazy."

"But why didn't you tell me?"

"I had to work out this slave thing. Mr. Priestly owned you, and to tell the truth, it didn't seem likely he was going to give you up. He sure seemed to take a fancy to you."

"Oh, bosh! You and Amanda been imagining things," Lucy chided. "Mr. Priestly enjoyed my musical talents, but Mr. Jacob let it slip that I was expected to earn my living giving music lessons. That was the real reason for all that practicing and performing. Mr. Priestly knew I'd have to earn my own way when I grew up. And I do love to sing."

"Don't matter—not now. We can get married and nobody can stop us." Joshua stammered, then cleared his throat. "That is, if you want to marry me—I mean—do you love me, Lucy? Will you—?"

Lucy answered him with a kiss. Glancing over Joshua's shoulder, she saw under the large oak tree the looming figure of Mr. Priestly stepping out of the shadows. He was dressed all in black, only his grave white face and the gold handle on his walking stick reflecting the light from inside the house. He raised his cane in apparent anger and seemed about to shout something, but before he did, a carriage drew up in the front of the house and he hurried to it, disappearing inside. A whip cracked overhead and the cab vanished down the empty street. Lucy started to tell Joshua what she'd seen, but he was already pulling her toward the cobblestoned alley that led to the Negro Baptist church.

Entering the small, clapboard structure they walked down the center aisle where two parishioners were dusting and scrubbing the floor around the pulpit. When they learned that the Reverend Mr. Taney had just left, Lucy, bubbling with joy, told the women her news. Flo Luckett kissed her and gave her a congratulatory hug, while her sister, Nettie, hung back, nodding pleasantly. With scrub brush in hand, Flo watched as Lucy and Joshua withdrew, bowing their heads to pray.

"Looks to me like we'll be hearing more about those young'uns," Flo said. "Did you see how Joshua looked at her? It's been more years than I care to remember since a man looked at me like that. All the same, ain't it wonderful she's free?"

Nettie shrugged. She knew it pleased Flo whenever someone was freed. It gave her hope that maybe someday the spinster who had owned her for twenty-five years, Freda Bates, would free her.

Too excited to go back to the Priestlys, Lucy and Joshua walked the block and a half to the reverend's home. As they sat at the kitchen table sipping glasses of lemonade with the rotund, moon-faced reverend and his buxom wife, Lucy realized that she had been one of the few Negroes still in bondage—most who came to the church were free blacks.

For the first time in her life Lucy could plan for the future, but she felt strange and not a little frightened promising Mrs. Taney that she would be the new choir leader now that she could come to Sunday services. She slipped a thin hymnal into her pocket, already thinking about practicing some of the harder songs at home.

Lucy was aware of Joshua's eyes on her; a feeling of pride mingled with desire welled up in her. She knew Joshua would be embarrassed if he could read her mind, but she couldn't help admiring his body, his long, thin face, his finely chiseled features and expressive brown eyes. He was a beautiful man, she thought, mentally tracing his full lips with her fingers.

"We'll see you Sunday, then," Mrs. Taney said.

Lucy stared at her uncomprehendingly.

"Sunday—at the picnic," Mrs. Taney said.

"Picnic?"

Mr. Taney laughed. "Our little nightingale hasn't been paying any attention to us. Where you at, child? Looks like you're a million miles away."

Lucy stammered an apology and nervously fingered Joshua's pin.

"Never mind," Joshua said. "I'll see she gets here." He walked to the window and peered out at the darkness. "Guess we better mosey on back. Don't want to get caught on the streets after curfew."

"I'd be more afraid of being snatched by a slave trader than being arrested by the sheriff," Mrs. Taney said with real fear in her eyes. "We'll watch till we can't see you no more. But you better run on now. The later it gets, the more danger you're in."

Lucy kissed Mrs. Taney good-bye, then followed Joshua out the door. They were silent as they hurried along the alleyway, not pausing as they crossed streets or stumbled upon stable boys rolling dice in secluded corners of rotting sheds. Fear gripped Lucy until she said good-night to Joshua on the back steps of the house. Timidly, he bent over and kissed her again, and her body yielded to his touch like a young, supple willow yielding to the wind.

"I love you, Lucy." Joshua nuzzled his face into her thick black hair.

Lucy inhaled the strong, pungent odor of hay. As long as she lived, she would love the scent of horses and stables. "And I love you, Joshua."

Turning to go into the house, she coyly glanced over her shoulder. "I'll love you forever, Mr. Taylor, so you better not be playing any games with me."

The easy smile vanished from Joshua's face as he grabbed Lucy's waist. "You and me is going to get married." His voice, bereft of romance, was filled with grim determination. "You're the one's playing games. You ain't said one way or another if you want me."

Lucy snuggled close to Joshua. "I'm sorry. I was just teasing, but I guess this isn't the time to tempt fate. Ever since Mr. Priestly told me I was free, I feel differently than I did before; I feel like I can laugh and joke, and I can say 'yes, sir' and 'no sir' out of respect and not fear. I can tease you because I know you love me." Lucy stepped back and kissed Joshua lightly on his mouth. "There! You see, I love you. I want to marry you—just as soon as I can stitch my wedding dress. And we'll have to tell the reverend so he can reserve the church for us, and we'll—"

"Stop! I don't want to know anymore than I have to," Joshua chided her. "All I wanted to hear was a simple yes."

"Then—yes."

Joshua's eyes glistened as he nodded. Kissing her hard, Joshua hugged Lucy fiercely until at last she turned and ran inside.

I'm free. I'm free and I'm in love. The words reverberated as Lucy threw herself on her bed. A breeze stirred the hem of the lace curtains, and minutes later, Lucy fell into a deep, dreamless sleep.

It was almost three o'clock in the morning when she awoke with a start. Her body felt chilled from perspiration. But it was an ominous phantom, an unseen heaviness in the room that had disturbed Lucy's sleep. Frightened she sat up. Trying desperately to pierce the darkness with sleepy eyes, she cried out, "Who's there? Is that you, Amanda? You better not jump out of the shadows at me or I'll whip you good. I'm done with all your craziness and your—"

"It's not Amanda. It's me."

Lucy stared at the massive figure approaching her. Before she saw the face with its brooding eyes and sensuous mouth, before he had spoken, Lucy knew it was Mr. Priestly. She knew he had been there a long time, watching her sleep, running his finger along the outline of her chin, mumbling words both incoherent and terrible. He reeked of liquor as he sat beside her on the bed.

61

"Don't be frightened. You must know I'd never do anything to hurt you." His speech was slurred and his head drooped as he struggled to keep his balance.

"Is something wrong, sir? Is someone sick—Amanda? Mrs. Priestly? I mean—the time. It's so early—or so late."

"I just returned from my club. I wanted to talk to you before you got carried away with plans for your future." Mr. Priestly paused, then lighting a kerosene lamp, placed it by Lucy's bed. "There. That's better. Now I can see you. I never tire of looking at you."

Lucy blushed, but a lifetime of servile obedience prevented her from ridiculing him. Spellbound, she listened as Mr. Priestly revealed his plans for her. The words companion, nurse, housekeeper, confidante all blurred in her mind when he finally summed up his intentions: she was to be his mistress, his lover, his whore. He had waited for her to grow up—waited for seven years, but she had to have her freedom before he took her; he couldn't abide her being a slave. She was too beautiful, too talented, too perfect.

Lucy felt like laughing and crying. Poor, lonely man, she thought. He's suffered as much as anyone in this household. But I haven't come this far to worry about him, she thought. There's nothing I can do to help, and I sure don't intend to live with him, mistress or not.

"It's too late, sir," Lucy said forcefully. "So many things have happened to me today. I'm seventeen years old. I'm a woman. Most girls—most women—my age are married—have their own families, their own homes. I can have those things, too, now that I'm free. And I want them. More than anything else, I want my own family."

Mr. Priestly smiled benignly, like a father smiles at an errant child. "You needn't concern yourself with thoughts like that. You have a home, right here, with me. And as far as a husband—well, of course, there can be no marriage, but arrangements will be made. You'll always be taken care of—you and any children—"

Lucy shook her head, her expression registering shock and disbelief. "Mr. Priestly, I don't mean to sound disrespectful, or ungrateful, but I'm not stupid. I know what you're asking of me, and I can't do it. I can't live here and sleep with you, not under the same roof as Mrs. Priestly and Amanda and Mrs. Fitzgerald."

Lucy cringed as Mr. Priestly grasped her hand and fondled it affectionately. I'm still his slave, she thought, filled with revulsion. Why isn't he listening to me? He can't imagine that I won't meekly submit to his wishes. He thought it would be enough to teach me to be submissive as a slave; he didn't think he'd have to teach me to be submissive as a woman too. A sadness enveloped Lucy as she studied Mr. Priestly's leering glance. Am I just an amusement, a satin doll, to be petted and then discarded without a backward glance?

"What I'm trying to tell you, sir, is that I'm going to get married. I'm in love, and just as soon as—"

"Married! When did this happen? Who gave you permission even to consider such a ridiculous thing?" The furrows deepened in his lined forehead. "Have you been running off nights without my knowing?"

"Didn't have to run off—Joshua's been right here all the time."

"Joshua—Joshua Taylor. My stable boy?" Mr. Priestly stared at Lucy in disbelief. "Were you the tart that was kissing and carrying on earlier this evening with that nigger? I thought it was Bridget. She's such a coarse, unlettered goat." Mr. Priestly's face reddened in anger. He grabbed Lucy by her shoulders and shook her violently. "Did he do anything else to you? I demand to know. Did he touch you?"

"Mr. Priestly! I don't want to hear such talk. You have no right. I'm free now. I don't belong to you anymore."

"But I can tear up the papers. I can tear them up, and then I'll own you forever."

Suddenly, Mr. Priestly lunged and was on her. Lucy froze with fear as she felt his weight bear down on her. Caught in a vise, Lucy struggled for air, biting and kicking as she tried to regain her freedom. But his passion was wild, like an animal's, and his groans deep. Lucy winced when he opened his mouth and pressed his lips on hers, rubbing her cheek raw with his wiskers. Momentarily, the pressure eased, and freeing her arms, she flailed at his chest and head, trying to beat him off. But his hard body pinned her to the bed. She felt his heart pounding furiously as he thrust his thigh roughly between hers, forcing them open. She prayed that he would kill her when it was over. I'd rather be dead than be a slave again, she thought. I can't bear to live with the humiliation.

He was tearing her gown now. His hand, damp with perspiration, squeezed her breast. Lucy cried out in pain, but she didn't fight anymore. When he finished with her, she would take her penknife and slash her wrists so she wouldn't have to see Joshua's face when he heard. Oh, my dear, sweet Joshua! Please forgive me. Tears cascaded down Lucy's cheeks when Mr. Priestly lifted himself up, pulling off his trousers. Flinging them onto the floor, he rolled back on top of her, his chest heaving under the strain of his perversion. Closing her eyes when he came down on her, Lucy sobbed hysterically. Neither of them saw the door open, and neither was prepared for the harsh shriek that filled the dimly lit room. Lucy's eyes flew open, and she stared straight into Amanda's frenzied face.

Mr. Priestly shouted at the girl to get out, to leave them alone. But Amanda, faced with the reality of her father's adultery and blaming his sins on Lucy, ran to the fireplace and grabbed the heavy black poker. Her eyes blazing, she raised the shaft over her head, then brought it down full force toward Lucy's head. But in the seething cauldron of arms and legs and bodies, Amanda missed and struck her father, who had reached out to her to ward off her assault. His eyes filling with pain, he fell heavily on top of Lucy, blood spurting from his fatal wound.

Beside herself with fear, Lucy pushed him off and jumped up, but was too late to catch Amanda, who had dropped the poker and run screaming into her room. "My God, he's dead!" Lucy shook her head, thinking frantically. Maybe he's still alive. I've got to get help. Clutching at her torn nightdress, Lucy flew out of the room for the stables. In less than a minute she was in Joshua's arms, weeping, the words tumbling out disconnectedly. He stared in disbelief when Lucy told him that Amanda had struck her father, had possibly killed him. Joshua asked no questions, not even after he noticed her torn gown. He grabbed Lucy by the hand and they raced back to the house, bumping into Mrs. Fitzgerald.

"Get Paddy!" Joshua cried, racing up the stairs with Lucy in tow. When they reached the second floor, the smell of smoke was already strong.

Joshua pounded on Amanda's locked door, but it didn't open. Undaunted, he ran into Lucy's room only to find the door between Lucy's room and Amanda's was also bolted. Only after Lucy followed him inside did he finally turn and look at Mr. Priestly's body. The expression on Lucy's face told him all he needed to know—that and Mr. Priestly's half-naked body. He threw a cover over the man, and they returned to the hall.

"I've got to get inside Amanda's room. Is there any other way—"

Lucy shook her head.

"Paddy and I'll have to break down the door. It smells like that crazy girl is trying to burn the house down."

When Paddy finally appeared Mrs. Fitzgerald was right behind him, ringing her hands and mumbling a litany of Hail Marys. Paddy and Joshua heaved their shoulders against the stalwart oak door. "We won't break this one easily," Joshua said, and after several tries their shoulders were so bruised and painful Joshua told Paddy to stop. Paddy suggested an ax. Minutes later, he returned to the smoke-filled hallway with the biggest one in the household.

Joshua's body glistened with sweat and Paddy's face was red from exertion as they alternated at chopping and splitting the heavy door.

"Amanda! Where are you?" Joshua's voice bellowed above the crackling fire when the door gave way.

Lucy gasped when she saw the flames enveloping the damask drapes, the curtains around the bed, and the exquisite furnishings that had decorated Amanda's sitting room. She pushed forward. There, in the corner of the room she saw Mrs. Priestly and Amanda clinging to each other, their faces filled with terror. Mrs. Priestly held out her hand pleadingly, but she didn't move from her spot only feet from the flaming draperies.

Joshua tore off his shirt and pressed it against his face to attempt to run into the room, but Paddy stopped him.

"It's too late. We can't save 'em." The Irishman's eyes were wet with tears.

"But we must!" Lucy lifted her dress to protect her face as she tried to run through the flames, but the heat was so intense she was forced to stumble back into the hallway, collapsing in Joshua's arms. Seconds later, after a loud, cracking sound, they watched, mesmerized, as the outside wall collapsed, burying Amanda and Mrs. Priestly in a blazing pyre.

"Get out before the roof caves in." Paddy grabbed his wife and half carried her down the stairs.

Joshua started to lift Lucy in his arms, but she angrily pushed him away. "No. I have to get my mama's Bible. It's all I have left in the whole world."

"It's not safe . . ." Joshua's warning was lost in the roar of the fire as it rolled in on itself, destroying everything it touched. Lucy was gone before he knew what had happened.

"My God, hurry up, Lucy. This whole place is a tinder box!" Joshua shouted over the din.

"I put it in the bottom drawer, but it's gone." Falling on her knees, Lucy rummaged through the piles of clothes and cried in despair. "If Amanda took my Bible again . . ."

"Lucy!" Joshua's voice choked with panic. They couldn't stay any longer. She's in shock, he thought; she doesn't understand the danger. This whole floor could crumble. Desperately, he reached down to grab her, but she pulled away. Finally, she raised her arm and triumphantly held the Bible over her head.

"Here it is. Amanda didn't take it." Lucy's eyes filled with tears as she pressed the pages to her breast. "I'll have to apologize to her. Poor Amanda! She gets blamed for everything."

Joshua shook his head. Picking Lucy up in his arms, he ran out into the street. Smoke poured from the second story and soon the whole house was engulfed in the flames. Tears coursed down Mrs. Fitzgerald's face while Paddy and Joshua stared silently at the holocaust. Lucy, collapsed on the lawn, stared uncomprehendingly at the destruction, her eyes blank. Tenderly, Joshua caressed her. The bond between the Priestlys and Lucy had been severed forever.

CHAPTER VI

"Lucy, you goin' pull that dress apart if you don't stop tuggin'. It take me three months to hand stitch that gown. It gonna take you three minutes to have it in shreds."

"Sorry, Mrs. Oates, but I never been married before. It's a scary business."

"Way you carryin' on, I hopes you don't be doin' it again." The woman frowned and thrust a bouquet of daisies and white roses, pruned just hours before from her garden, into Lucy's hand. "Here. Grab onto these, but don't pick at 'em. In this heat, we lucky if they last the afternoon."

Lucy's maid of honor, Honey Sweet, a sprightly girl of sixteen, stepped forward. "No need to get yourself in a stew, Lucy. You is beautiful. Joshua got to be the luckiest man alive."

Lucy smiled, then, burying her face in her bouquet, sniffed the sweet scent of roses. "I just wish it was over. I feel like I'm melting into my shoes."

"You pick the hottest day of the year to get married," Mrs. Oates said with little sympathy. "Think of the men in them black suits. They got to be wiltin' by now."

Lucy nodded, and the sound of piano music drifted to the

67

back of the church. Mrs. Humphrey was playing the prelude to the wedding march. Honey stepped forward, and the ceremony commenced.

For the next half hour, Lucy moved and spoke without thinking. She saw the minister. She felt Joshua move close to her. She repeated the marriage vows. Only when Joshua kissed her, when she was finally Mrs. Joshua Taylor, did she respond. The joy of their union made her want to shout her happiness. Instead, she cried. Joshua smiled. Together, they turned and marched down the aisle, Lucy's eyes shining, Joshua's pride spread across his face.

A half hour later, the men had hung their wool jackets on the backs of wooden chairs; fiddles and horns were pulled from frayed cases. A quartet settled themselves under a leafy oak tree to entertain the wedding party. Members of the Ladies' Guild filled the long, wooden tables with the best of their homemade fare—crisp salads and cooked greens, boiled ham and spicy ribs, cakes, pies, puddings—and in the center of it all sat Joshua and Lucy. Enthroned on two chairs, they laughed and chatted and occasionally leaned over and kissed. Roars of approval were followed by ribald quips. Lucy blushed. Joshua squeezed her hand.

A hot wind blew across the churchyard, whipping the white tablecloths, scattering the colorful wrappings that had decorated the wedding presents—handmade quilts, tatted doilies, glass pitchers and painted plates—like bits of confetti. The sun waned. At last, Joshua and Lucy climbed into a carriage festooned with ribbons and wilted flowers and were off. As Joshua guided the horses out of the churchyard, Lucy turned around and waved one last time. Tears flooded her eyes.

"Mrs. Taylor, what's this I'm seeing?" Joshua said. "Tears on your wedding day! You ain't sorry you got hitched up with me, are you?"

Lucy shook her head. "Sorry! This is the happiest day of my life. Why do you think I'm sorry?"

Joshua laughed. "You're blubbering like you just lost your best friend."

"I'm blubbering 'cause I'm so happy."

Joshua sighed. He slapped the reins across the horse's rump. "Guess I got a lot to learn 'bout women. Don't figure a person'd cry if she's happy."

Lucy wiped her eyes and laid her head on Joshua's shoulder. "We both got a lot to learn. Lucky we got a lifetime to try."

That night when Lucy undressed behind a screen adorned with peacocks and lacy ferns, she wondered how patient Joshua would be when he discovered how ignorant she was about the mysteries of lovemaking. Before when he had kissed her, she had felt an unfamiliar flutter somewhere deep inside. Was that enough to stir her passions? No time to worry about it, she thought, then stepped from behind the screen. Joshua was waiting. He put his arms around her, and when he kissed her deeply, she forgot her fears in the delicious passion of loving Joshua. Later, as they lay side by side, Lucy felt his breath on her cheek. It was soft and sweet, like his lovemaking.

"I love you," Joshua whispered.

Lucy laughed, pleased with herself. "I love you more than life itself. Promise me it'll always be this wonderful, that I'll always be this happy."

"I promise. As long as it's in my power, I promise."

Lucy squinted her eyes as she tried to recapture a dropped purl stitch on a sock she was knitting for Joshua. It was a cold, blustery day, much too cold for March. It unnerved her as she listened to the wind rattling the poorly fitted window sash in the bedroom that was usually a cozy sanctuary in the winter. She pulled a wool afghan around her shoulders, then, distracted by her throbbing headache, she laid aside the unfinished sock and rested her head on the back of the rocking chair.

Normally Lucy didn't reminisce; the good times were always uppermost in her thoughts and the bad times were best forgotten. But today, as she waited for Joshua to harness the horse and buggy so she and Chin Lee could go to market, she mused about that time two years ago when she had waited for their sign to hang over the door of the Taylor

Tavern and Livery Stables. She smiled as she recalled the grand opening of their business, just blocks from the busy Mississippi levee. Shots of whiskey were fifteen cents to the businessmen and traders who thronged the area during the day and the sporting gentlemen who visited the brothels at Almond and Third streets at night. They gladly paid the seventy-five cents to board their horses before cantering home after their night of pleasure.

The Taylors had prospered, and the profits were put back into the business—enlarging the stables, renting loft space to stevedores, and hiring a cook, Chin Lee.

But, Lucy sighed, there was still one problem: she had been married two and a half years and hadn't had a baby. Lucy's feelings varied from mild distress to chronic melancholy. Looking for reasons, she had anxiously considered her lack of enthusiasm when she and Joshua performed their marital duties. I love him more than life, she thought, but when we're lying together and doing all those things, I can't respond. I just can't. Is it because of Mr. Priestly? If I love Joshua, I should be able to share his bed without cringing.

"Lucy, it takes time." Joshua always had a sad look in his eyes when he comforted her.

Time, yes, but it's so hard to wait, Lucy thought. She sighed. I just wish I didn't feel so terrible. This headache's just about to do me in.

"Missy Lucy! Chin Lee ready go market." The cook's high-pitched voice startled Lucy, rousing her from her reverie.

"In a moment, Chin." Lucy slipped into her sturdy blue twill coat.

Forcing a smile, she walked through the tavern and blew a kiss to Joshua, who was moving kegs of whiskey behind the bar. Outside, the cold wind almost knocked her over, and she rushed to the enclosed cab, sinking gratefully onto the soft leather seat. She was thankful that Chin Lee was driving the carriage; she wouldn't have to listen to his singsong chatter all the way to Soulard, the great open-air market with the freshest and cheapest fruits and vegetables in the city.

Hovering behind the canvas flap enclosing one of the stalls, Lucy watched Chin Lee skip from one stand to another, squeezing potatoes, thumping cabbages. In nice weather, Lucy enjoyed marketing, but today, with the blustery winds and overcast sky, she wished she were in bed. Wearily she leaned against the wooden stall. Her body was hot with fever, and she barely felt the wind whipping around her. She forced herself to look up when she heard someone call her name.

"Lucy! Over here. Yoo-hoo!"

"Mrs. Fitzgerald!" Lucy held out her hand in greeting. "How are you? It's been such a long time."

"It has that." The woman pressed her worn coat collar close to her face. "Paddy and me talk about you all the time, wondering how you're getting along. Hope it's better'n us. Hasn't been so easy since . . . well, you know."

"Oh, I'm sorry." Lucy tried not to notice the holes in the woman's cotton gloves.

Mrs. Fitzgerald clicked her tongue against the roof of her mouth. "Tch, tch. We're paying the rent and putting food on the table. I really got nothing to complain about. But, my, look at you. All growed up and married to Joshua, I hear. Mrs. Joshua Taylor, eh! And a fine-looking missus you are, too."

"Three years come August. We've had a bit of a struggle, too, but other than this flu that I seem to be coming down with, we've had our health. And we make a living with the livery stable and tavern we own on Front Street."

The woman's face wrinkled in concern. "You do seem under the weather. This is no place for you to be if you're feeling bad. You better get to bed. Put some hot bricks under the covers. Warm your feet."

"Oh, I'll be all right. Don't believe in giving in to a cold. Makes me feel worse."

"Maybe, but we liked to lose our little one this winter. Scarlet fever. Started out with chills." Without pausing,

Mrs. Fitzgerald brought Lucy up to date on her family, describing the boarding house they bought in Kerry Patch with the money they inherited from the Priestlys. "Poor souls," the woman said as she crossed herself. "Poor, tormented souls."

"What's happened to Bridget?" Lucy asked, preferring to change the subject. "I heard she got married too."

"Marry in haste, repent in leisure." Mrs. Fitzgerald shook her head. "She got herself a good-for-nothing. Hasn't worked six months since they been married. Course, she had three boys right in a row—one, two, three. Barely had time to roll over in bed. To tell you the truth, that's where she spends most of her time. Never did like to work."

Lucy just smiled. "I envy Bridget her sons. We haven't been blessed."

"Depends on who you're asking if you think three little ones is a blessing. Especially now, times being what they is. Paddy says there's going to be a war."

"Let's hope it doesn't come to that," Lucy said quickly.

Mrs. Fitzgerald nodded, then, after hugging Lucy briefly, she turned her back to the wind and disappeared into the crowd. Poor woman, Lucy thought. Life hasn't been good to her since the Priestlys died.

Searching the crowd for Chin Lee, Lucy spotted him buying a bushel of apples. Feeling faint, she waved her handkerchief to catch his attention and motioned for him to hurry. As he reached her side, Lucy's knees buckled under her and she fell unconscious into his arms.

An hour later Lucy was buried under a pile of quilts, her teeth chattering like sleet on a tin roof. Her eyes were glazed from the fever that climbed steadily upward. Voices, soft and seemingly far away, drifted about the room, compelling Lucy to speak, but when she tried to open her mouth only a deep moan escaped her lips. Someone tried to move her, and she moaned even louder. She pulled her legs up as she tried to ease the terrible cramps gnawing at her stomach. Crying now, she moved her lips and pleaded for a sip of water. The voices grew dimmer and finally faded away.

"It be cholera, Mr. Taylor. Ain't no sense me lying to you. Your missus gonna be mighty sick for the next three days, that is, if she makes it."

"Ain't no question 'bout her making it. My Lucy won't die. You just tell me what I got to do." Joshua's voice was firm, his body rigid with determination.

"If you want to help, fetch me some rice water," said Mrs. Jenkins, the Negro nurse whose secret nostrums were famed for their curative power. "We be lucky if we keep it down your missus, but we got to try. Cholera dries 'em up so. Ain't much hope if we can't be putting the water back she be losing."

"How long will it be 'fore we know?"

"Like I say, three days . . . maybe a week."

Joshua and Mrs. Jenkins took turns sitting with Lucy, gently coaxing the rice water through her parched lips and dabbing cool compresses on her face and neck.

For three days Joshua watched as the disease progressed. He was morbidly fascinated by the changes ravishing Lucy's body. Her skin, parched and wrinkled, shriveled on her bones. Her lips, caked with blood, developed deep cracks from dehydration. Then, almost miraculously, Lucy's temperature fell. She opened her eyes and gazed in bewilderment at her husband's haggard-looking face.

Joshua's eyes filled with tears. He clutched her arm. "You made it, my love. Thank the Lord. You're going to be well."

After the fever passed, Lucy's health steadily improved, but Mrs. Jenkins refused to allow her to leave her sickbed. To brighten her spirits, Joshua presented Lucy with a spray of violets. Lucy, propped against a mountain of white pillows, pressed the damp petals against her cheek and smiled.

"They're beautiful." She threw Joshua a kiss.

"Not as beautiful as you, sitting up in bed with a pretty blue ribbon in your hair." Joshua bent over and kissed Lucy's forehead. When he stood up, he frowned. "You not be rushing things, are you?"

"Not likely with Mrs. Jenkins keeping an eye on me. She

73

won't even let me take a bath." Lucy shrugged. "She did tie the ribbon around my hair. I feel so much better. Don't you think I look better? If only I could get out of this bed."

"T'ain't likely you be getting up for quite a spell, girl," Mrs. Jenkins said as she swished into the room.

Joshua nodded a greeting. "Just brought my girl her breakfast. Her appetite's coming back. Figure she be up and about soon."

Mrs. Jenkins felt Lucy's forehead, then took her pulse, all the while observing her breathing, her bright eyes, the color in her cheeks. She nodded. "No doubt about it . . . you be getting well. How you feeling?"

"Wonderful! Except I'm bored. I want to get back to work."

"There be no hurrying to get up, girl. You been mighty sick, and now we got complications."

"Complications? What kind—"

"Just hold your tongue, Mr. Taylor. I's trying to prepare you for the news. Usually the woman know already, but with the missus being so sick and all—"

Lucy's eyes flew open. "Oh, Mrs. Jenkins! Is it possible?"

"What?" Joshua looked at one woman, then the other.

"You going to be a papa, Mr. Taylor."

Joshua hesitated a moment, then let out a yell. "That's the best news I heard since you said you'd marry me. I'm going to be a papa. Ain't that something!"

Mrs. Jenkins rapped her finger on the brass footrail. "'Fore you go getting all excited, remember your missus just had a bout with cholera. No telling what damage been done."

Lucy brushed her hand across her stomach. She started to speak, but Mrs. Jenkins held up her hand to silence her.

"Ain't no sense asking questions. I not be knowing the answers. Right now you gots to build up your strength. Eat hardy, keep off your feet, and don't be worrying. Fretting just makes things worse." Mrs. Jenkins picked up her bag. "I be back in a week 'less you take a turn." She didn't wait for Joshua to walk her through the tavern.

Lucy looked at Joshua. Tears streamed down her cheeks.

"The good Lord wouldn't take our baby, would he?" she asked.

Joshua shook his head, then fluffed Lucy's pillows before he returned to work.

As Lucy began her long recuperation, war fever swept across the country. By August, 1860, businessmen felt the strain on commerce when the movement of manufactured goods to Southern ports slowed to a trickle. Money was scarce. There was a dearth of credit. Everyone wanted cash. Secessionist talk by Southerners frightened Northern manufacturers, and Joshua felt the pinch. Stevedores, who had filled the tavern only months before, vanished. They either stayed on board ship or unloaded their cargo and moved upriver.

By October, Joshua told Lucy he believed everyone in the city had gone mad. Presidential elections were a month away, and tempers flared whenever the name of Abe Lincoln was mentioned.

"No doubt I'd vote for the man if I was allowed. Stupid city ordinance won't let free colored vote," Joshua grumbled. "Guess them slavery people scared of us, knowing where we'd put our X. They feels so strong about it, there's talk of more states leaving the country if Lincoln gets elected. They call him 'that black Republican.'" Joshua stared fretfully at Lucy. "Wonder if the Southern states'll really pull out."

"Can't see why they would," Lucy retorted. "Lincoln never promised to help us. Fact is, I heard he'd like to send all the colored back to Africa. His only worry is keeping more states from rebelling."

"Whether he says it or not, slavery be the main issue." Joshua dropped the subject, wearying of his people's attempts to predict an uncertain future.

St. Louis was a microcosm of the country at large. Newly arrived immigrants found slavery offensive and resented having to compete with chattel in the labor market. The city was like a citadel under siege.

75

Joshua paced the floor of the tavern awaiting the birth of his firstborn, who finally arrived at eleven o'clock at night after a particularly cruel confinement. Mumbling a prayer of thanksgiving that it was finally over, Joshua hurried into the bedroom. Mrs. Jenkins was washing the baby, who was squalling angrily. After giving the boy a cursory glance, Joshua sat on the edge of the bed and pecked at Lucy's cheek.

"You look a little peaked." He gripped her hand.

"Fancy you would too if you'd been through what I been through."

Joshua smiled. "The boy seem healthy enough. Is he all right?"

"Seems so. Course something could develop . . ." Lucy bit her lip, and tears rimmed her eyes. "Oh, Joshua! Pray that he'll be well."

"There, there. Listen to the boy holler."

Mrs. Jenkins wrapped the baby in a thick cotton blanket and brusquely wedged her way between Joshua and Lucy. "You snuggle him for a bit while I give your husband instructions." Mrs. Jenkins motioned for Joshua to follow her out of the room.

Once outside, her stern expression eased. "Don't look good. His coloring's off. Might be nothing. Might be something wrong with his lungs. Just thought to warn you to watch him close."

"He seem all right to me. And he got healthy kin. Lucy and me ain't been sick a day in our lives, least ways not till the cholera hit."

Mrs. Jenkins offered no words of comfort. "Keep a pan of hot water by his crib. Steam help sometimes."

"What if it don't?"

"Take him to Dr. Anderson on Grand Avenue. The man don't usually tend coloreds, but he be seeing the baby if you tell him I send you. And get yourself a woman to come in. Don't look like Lucy'll be up and about for quite a spell."

"Can't you stay?"

"Nothing I can do. Keep the room moist and get yourself a praying woman." Mrs. Jenkins nodded good-day and in her crisp, efficient way turned and disappeared down the hallway.

Joshua forced a smile when he returned to Lucy and their son.

"Shuu . . . he's sleeping." She eyed her son wistfully.

"I'll put him in his crib so you can rest."

Reluctantly Lucy handed him the baby. She waited a moment before she voiced her suspicions, hoping they were just that—suspicions. "What did Mrs. Jenkins say?"

"Say! Nothing. I mean . . . she say I should hire help for you. She expects you'll be in bed for a while."

"What did she say about Baby Joshua?"

Joshua stared at Lucy. "Baby Joshua . . . since when?"

"Since I knew I was expecting."

"You never said nothing to me 'bout naming a boy Joshua."

"Didn't want to get into an argument about it. I love your name, and I want our son to be like you in every way."

"Two Joshuas be confusing, but if you got your mind set—"

"Kiss me and let me get some rest," Lucy said, love in her voice.

Joshua stirred the fire before he walked to the door. Turning, he said, "If you need anything, call out. I'll hear."

Despite their optimism and Mrs. Jenkins's care, Baby Joshua's breathing problem grew progressively worse through the winter. Hoping to relieve the infant's hacking cough, they built a small tent over his crib to trap the steam rising from a pot of boiling water. It didn't help. Lucy was terrified. A dozen times she wanted to tell Joshua to hitch up a wagon and take the baby to Dr. Anderson's, but fear of the rising violence in the city kept her at home. She had heard rumors of Negroes being cornered outside the colored neighborhood and whipped or hanged by drunken whites.

Much of the unrest was due to Lincoln's election. South Carolina seceded from the Union, and pro-Southern sympathizers in St. Louis immediately roused themselves, demanding that Missouri do the same. By February, 1861, six other states had seceded, but Lucy was relieved when St. Louis remained staunchly in the Union camp even though the state was pro-Southern and pro-slavery.

By April, 1861, after the formation of the Confederate States of America and the firing on Fort Sumter, tensions in the city mounted again. Federal troops were being mustered across the river in Illinois, while Southern troops moved up from Arkansas to spearhead a drive to St. Louis.

Fear for his family forced Joshua to close the tavern early. He secured the shutters, then joined Lucy and Baby Joshua in the back room. Even though it was May, Lucy had closed the windows.

"What is it?" Joshua asked, when he entered the sweltering room.

"He's giving up." Tears flooded Lucy's eyes. "He just can't fight anymore."

"No! We're not going to let him die. I'll hitch the wagon. Meet me out front in five minutes. We got to get him to the doctor."

Fifteen minutes later Lucy sat on the jump seat next to Joshua. He tried to steer the horses through the crowds of youths, riled by liquor, who threw rocks at them and yelled a string of curses. As Joshua tried to break through the mob, one of the ruffians jumped onto the wagon and, slamming a club at Joshua's head, knocked him to the floor. The youth grabbed the reins and headed west, ignoring Lucy's cries until they had traveled several blocks.

"Shut up or I'll throw you all on the street." He spit the juice from his chewing tobacco into the wind. "Gotta get to Lindell Grove. Heard there was some fighting goin' on. Sure would like to get me a Union man. How 'bout you, nigger gal? You like them Union boys, don't ya?"

"Please! My baby. He's sick. Let us go. If you take us to the doctor's, you can have the wagon."

"I already got your wagon, nigger gal." The man's laughter mingled with the roar of the crowd.

Lucy tried to reach Joshua, but whenever she grabbed hold of him the wagon lurched and she lost her grip. Little Joshua was wailing now, his breathing becoming more labored. She screamed hysterically when she saw Lindell Grove filled with a violent, armed mob and both Union and Confederate soldiers. A gun went off, a man fell. There were more shots. Confrontation turned into a rout as the people ran to safety, stampeding across the hilly terrain. Frightened by the noise, the horses bolted, dragging the wagon across the open countryside. As the wagon careened down a hill, Lucy, Joshua, and the baby were thrown into weeds.

It was dawn when Joshua awoke, the gash on his head crusted, the throbbing pain almost unbearable. Squinting through a blurry mist, he saw Lucy sitting upright in a stand of high grass rocking back and forth. He hurried to her side only to stop several feet away, paralyzed by the expression on her face. He saw the same calm, the same distracted blankness that had glazed her eyes when the Priestlys were killed. She stared at him, pressing the lifeless infant close to her bosom.

CHAPTER VII

Lucy yelled in surprise when she spied the unexpected visitor. Hugging the top of the ladder to keep from falling, she smiled down at the puzzled face of Mrs. Taney, the minister's wife.

"Gave you quite a fright, eh," the large, fleshy woman said matter-of-factly. "Was in the neighborhood, and thought I'd drop by and say hello. Everyone at church misses you. Feeling any better lately?"

If Joshua put her up to this, I'll kill him, Lucy thought. But she kept the smile on her face as she scurried down from the ladder, grabbed a rag from a chair, and pointed to it. "Excuse the mess, but I've been housecleaning. Hard to keep the place clean. The dirt from the stables seeps through the walls."

"Didn't come here to admire your place." Mrs. Taney dusted off the seat with her gloved hand and sat down. "Truth is, we need you at the church. Got refugees pouring in from Arkansas, Tennessee, Kentucky. Thousands of runaway slaves are sleeping in the streets because we can't find a place for them to stay. Children are hungry—"

"I'm sorry, Mrs. Taney." Lucy nervously wrung the rag into a knot. Anger made her callous. "I know the fine work the churches are doing to help, but I also heard you're giving food and clothing to white soldiers. Southerners. I can't abide that."

"Lucy, we give what we can to the Sanitary Commission. They dole it out to the needy. Our own colored soldiers get most of the things we donate, but, of course, some of it goes to the white boys. Southern or not, many of 'em are children—fifteen, sixteen years old. One lad I saw at the hospital lost his leg at Shiloh, and another—"

"I'm sorry there's so much suffering, but I can't forgive. It doesn't matter if they're six or sixty." Lucy waved her hand as if to erase the memories of slavery like cobwebs in her mind, then she walked to the door and shouted, "Jennie. Come here, child."

Seconds later a young girl appeared. Her dark brown skin seemed to hang on her frail, bony frame, and twenty small braids secured with colorful red ribbons covered her large head. Big brown eyes encompassed the room in one glance.

"Jennie, you remember Mrs. Taney. She's come to visit. Please heat some water for tea. You remember how I taught you. The water and then the tea leaves. Be careful when you pour."

Jennie curtsied and then disappeared. Lucy sat down on the settee, ignoring the stains on her dress.

"Jennie's been with us two months now. She won't talk. Won't or can't. She and ten fugitive slaves came north last winter. Walked all the way from Arkansas without shoes. She lost two toes to frostbite, but they would have walked to Canada if they'd've had to to get their freedom. That was the second or third time they tried to escape. The first time, Jennie's mother was chained to a pillory and whipped to death right in front of the child. The master thought it'd teach 'em a lesson. All it taught 'em was to try again and again." A slight tick grabbed at Lucy's face and her right cheek jerked spasmodically. Staring straight ahead as though in a trance she continued, "Jennie hasn't spoken since that day."

"Oh, my dear! Surely you must know how I detest everything you're talking about—slavery, violence, the hatred heaped upon our race. But hating back won't solve nothing. I can show you a hundred—a thousand Jennies. They all need our help. They need your help."

"I'm afraid." Lucy broke down sobbing. "I'm afraid of all the memories. I want to forget."

"Well, girl, you forget the bad, but remember the good," Mrs. Taney said softly. "You remember your mama and remember what she thought was important. You was to be God-fearing, and use your beautiful voice to praise Him. When she taught you the spirituals, she meant for you to pass 'em on."

More to get rid of Mrs. Taney than anything else, Lucy reluctantly agreed to help the church handle the refugees, and on the following Monday morning, Lucy stood in the center of the church basement studying the silent, questioning eyes that gazed from fifty expressionless faces. She was afraid. She had no idea how to reach the children who had herded themselves into a compact group. All she was aware of was the oppressive silence. What do I do now? she wondered.

Taking a deep breath, Lucy stepped forward and forced herself to smile. Then, folding her arms across her chest, she spoke, softly at first, introducing herself, and assuring them that they wouldn't be harmed. She asked for volunteers, anyone who could read or write, even a little. Lucy paused, but no hands shot up.

She tried again. Walking among them to inspire confidence, she told them they wouldn't be punished for knowing how to read.

No one moved.

Lucy paused, studied their stalwart faces, and sighed. It was obviously going to take more than an impromptu speech to gain their cooperation. She smiled broadly and clapped her hands.

"At least we can get to know each other's names," she said. "How about starting with this young lady?" Lucy pointed to a dark girl with purplish black skin and huge, expressive eyes and a pixie face. The girl gingerly took Lucy's outstretched hand and whispered her name.

"I's called May, ma'am."

"How old are you, May?"

"Ten years 'bout, ma'am."

"Ten years!" Tears sprang to Lucy's eyes. That's how old I was when—no time to think about that now.

Lucy put her arm around May and hugged her. The tension broke. One by one they recited their names. At first Lucy was amused, then surprised, and finally shocked when she realized they were calling out names of pets, not human beings: Sweetums, Sugar, Ham, Wednesday, Grunt, Hambone. How could a child become a self-respecting adult with the name of Grunt?

"Have any of you been baptized?"

No response.

Lucy's smile softened. The inner turmoil bubbling inside her had subsided, replaced by a feeling that she had a mission to save souls and bodies and minds. "Just as soon as you learn about Jesus, the minister'll baptize you, then we'll give you Christian names."

The children eyed her skeptically. No one spoke.

Well, at least they're not screaming, Lucy thought. She kept the smile pasted on her face and continued.

"We have fifteen minutes before lunch. Would you like to sing some songs?"

Only May nodded.

Lucy walked to the piano with May in tow. As her fingers flew across the keys and the ageless tunes—spirituals and slave songs—burst forth, not a body swayed nor a foot tapped. Lucy's depression returned. Her lighthearted veneer was beginning to crack.

Perched like magpies on a fence, they listened, attentive and polite, as Lucy played "Patty-Roller Get You," "Black-Eyed Susie," and "Shock Along, John," all of them as familiar and as meaningful to slaves as "The Star-Spangled Banner" was to whites. Only May nodded her head from side to side in time with the music.

After they had gone upstairs for lunch, Lucy dropped her head in her hands and cried. Mrs. Taney found her a half hour later, red-eyed and perplexed.

Mrs. Taney cleared her throat and straightened the white apron covering her cotton dress. "Certainly ain't your fault," she said curtly. "Should've warned you. I've been so busy. This batch of ragamuffins came in just a few weeks ago. Never knew their fathers and hardly knew their mothers. Can't tell you where they been or where they going. They're children from breeding farms; their parents were put there just to have 'em, then they were raised by anybody who'd find the time. When they got to be anywhere between ten and sixteen, off they'd go to the block to be sold like a bale of cotton. They were bred to work like animals. Never had love. They're barely human."

"Oh, my God. How cruel. I heard about those farms, but I never saw anyone raised on them. Oh, those poor children."

"Don't go worrying about their past. What we got to worry about is their future. You can turn 'em around. They're still young, and they're God's children. Nothing happens in a day." Mrs. Taney pulled a handkerchief from her pocket and handed it to Lucy. "Dry your eyes and get upstairs before all the food's gone. And, if you don't mind my saying so, don't dress up so fancy tomorrow. The children'll take to you better if you don't look like some mistress on a plantation."

The frigid wind and ice-covered streets didn't deter the Negro Baptist congregation from attending an emergency meeting called by the Reverend Taney to discuss President

Lincoln's Emancipation Proclamation. Swathed in heavy woolen blankets and shawls, many wearing mourning, they trooped into the dim church hall, their shoulders drooping, arms wrapped around themselves for warmth.

Joshua was standing rigid and austere at the foot of the pulpit, acknowledging the parishioners as they took their seats and waited for the meeting to begin. "Evenin', Miss Hattie. Mr. Biddle. Mighty cold out there."

"Yes'ir, Mr. Taylor. Sure 'nough is."

"Miss Connie! Howdy."

"Evenin', Mr. Taylor. Wouldn't be surprised if we got three more inches of snow by mornin'. Some of the old timers 're sayin' the Mississippi might freeze over. Sure do hope they's wrong."

"Maggie! Didn't expect to see you tonight. Hear Henry's ailing."

The bent old woman shook her head in despair. "Seems the Lord sees fit to make life burdensome for us, Mr. Taylor."

Lucy sat at the piano with May at her side. From her first class of students two years before, only three were still with the church. The others had moved to Chicago, Cleveland, New York—wherever there were families willing to take them. May, a tall, overweight girl, quick to learn and hungry for affection despite her slow, plodding movements, was Lucy's protege. May found solace in music, as Lucy did, and the church had become her home. Tonight May would play a piano solo to commemorate the momentous occasion. She chose "Let My People Go," and everyone joined in:

> *"Go down, Moses*
> *Way down in Egypt land;*
> *Tell old Pharaoh,*
> *Let my people go."*

After the blessing, the men congregated around the potbellied stove.

"Don't make a lick of sense," Louis Oliver said, straightforward and determined. "That Abe Lincoln goin' and freein' slaves he can't get to, while us, here in St. Louis, we're helping with the war, sending our boys to the battlefields, and we got to stay put. Ain't right, and I ain't gonna sit around and be herded into no slave pen when this here war's over."

"What you think, Joshua?" a stooped, white-haired man said. "I been around a long time, and I don't think the colored gonna stand for slavery no more. We been waiting too long. What do the white folks say? Are we gonna be rounded up and sent to a camp in the middle of the state? By God, they'll have to hog-tie me 'fore I'll let 'em do that."

"No truth to it at all," Joshua said, straightening his six-foot-two frame, accentuating his natural bent for leadership. "There's all kind of talk in the tavern. Everything from mass lynchings to slave camps, but it's all talk. I don't like it that President Lincoln didn't see fit to free all the slaves, but the North is bound to win, and once it's over, we'll be seeing the end of slavery."

"My own mother's a slave, not fifty miles from here," Louis said angrily. "How much longer we got to wait?"

"Not much longer, son. Not much longer." Taney put his arm around the young man to console him. "You just be sure she's got a son waiting for her when she gets her freedom."

Louis pulled away. "I won't be looking for trouble, but I'm not going to hide from it either."

The next morning, Lucy was back at the church, welcoming a new group of youngsters. With two years experience behind her, and the utterly devoted May at her side, Lucy had the children responding warmly by the end of the first day.

May's company was sufficient for the school, but Lucy wished she and Joshua could talk as well. Their love had lapsed into a silent, shimmering ghost of affection. Gone were the days when he would grab her up in his strong arms and carry her off to bed.

Was it her fault? she wondered. Had Baby Joshua's death killed something inside her? She wished they could talk about it, but whenever she tried she burst into tears, and Joshua, normally so patient, would shake his head and walk away. His hurt seemed deeper than her sorrow; his inability to ease her pain seemed a greater burden than the pain he carried silently in his own heart. They isolated themselves, keeping their emotions tightly in check. Lucy waited, biding her time, hoping for some miracle to restore their love.

In the meantime, Joshua became a leading church elder, and lost himself in his work. "This dang war's gonna be the death of us," Joshua always said as he rushed into the tavern to talk to Chin Lee or to the stables to talk to Walt, the new livery boy. Joshua's latest adventure was a small, rundown hotel, which he had bought using the tavern as collateral.

"But we could lose everything," Lucy had argued. "The tavern. Even the clothes on our back. Those bankers won't give a hoot about us if we get behind on our payments."

"Woman, you got no business sense," Joshua replied. "Look at the location. We're just a few blocks from the levee. River traffic's been peaking ever since the battle of Vicksburg opened up the Mississippi down to New Orleans."

Lucy shrugged. "Maybe so. Just don't seem right us making money on the refugees coming into the city, but if we don't make 'em pay, we lose everything. Cat'n mouse, that's what it is."

Joshua kissed Lucy and nudged her playfully. "You tend to your church business, and let me worry about the tavern business."

The two were combined on January 14, 1865, when Lucy and Joshua celebrated the signing of Missouri's emancipation bill, freeing the state's slaves. They spent the week preceding the ceremony decorating their establishments with red, white, and blue bunting. The Stars and Stripes hung on every wall. Joshua ordered extra kegs of beer, and Lucy herded her students into the tavern early Saturday morning to prepare them for the festivities.

"May"—Lucy pointed to a stack of plates in the kitchen—"set those out front on the long table by the bar.

We'll put the ham and cheese out later. Don't forget, fifteen cents a plate. Take the money before you serve the food."

"Yes, Miss Lucy."

"Where's Walt? Has he brought up the kegs of beer from the cellar? And the glasses? Are they out?"

"Yes, Miss Lucy."

"Oh, stop saying 'yes, Miss Lucy.' It's enough to drive a person crazy."

"Yes, Miss— Sorry ma'am. I'll get the children to help."

"No. Let them stay in the parlor till it's time to go. No need to add to the confusion."

"Gonna be quite a day." May stacked the plates on the linen tablecloth.

"There's never been anything like it," Lucy said, beaming. "Governor Fletcher's going to make a speech, then there'll be a sixty-gun salute. Can you imagine?"

"Mighty exciting," May said laconically.

Lucy paused and smiled. "One nice thing about having you around"—she patted May's head—"is that you don't add to the confusion." No sooner had the words slipped out of her mouth than she was twirling again. "Where's Joshua? I swear! He disappears at the worst times."

"He's at the hotel, ma'am. He flew by while you were talking to the children. Said he'd be back by opening time."

Promptly at one o'clock, Lucy and May lined the ten children into two rows and pulled caps over ears, slipped mittens onto little hands, and buttoned the top buttons of their coats. Then Lucy grabbed Joshua's arm and they stepped out into the cold, snappy winter wind. The day was brilliant, sunny and sparkling. A band played a medley of popular tunes, including Lucy's favorite, the "Battle Hymn of the Republic." When they struck up "My Country 'Tis of Thee," the people started to sing along. Abruptly, the conductor stopped the music and, raising his hand to denote quiet, asked that the Negroes in the audience sing it alone. For the first time they'd be singing it as citizens and as a free people.

When Lucy and Joshua tumbled into bed after two the

next morning, Lucy snuggled close to her husband, happy and content that her greatest wish had come true. They were free, every last one of them. It grieved her that it had come too late for her mother.

Jim Sloan had sent her a note, in 1861, soon after the war started. It was brief and unemotional, telling her that Maybelle had died. There was no mention of the cause of her death nor the place where she was buried. Her father retained his cold, austere facade up to the end. Lucy wondered if Miss Susan stood beside him as he wrote the letter. Didn't matter, she thought. Just knowing that her mother was at peace gave her a sense of relief. Maybe now the hatred she felt toward Jim and Susan could also be laid to rest.

Before she dozed off, Lucy's thoughts drifted to the future. What would freedom bring?

The end of the war was almost anticlimatic after the explosive joy of emancipation. There were parades and speeches and prayers of thanksgiving, but soon the euphoria of peace and freedom withered and died as a new age dawned. The Union was saved, but the scars of battle festered under the onslaught of reconstruction. Northern radicals, the righteousness of their cause vindicated by victory, rode into the South with the fury of an avenging god. Scalawags and carpetbaggers pressed the purity of their beliefs onto a defeated people, and hatred bubbled out of the fertile loam.

"The last year certainly hasn't been a time for the timid." Mrs. Taney set her cup of tea in a saucer nestled on her lap. "No sooner did the Lord lift the curse of slavery from us but the president was shot. Now I hear from my cousin, Ollie, in Nashville, that he can't get a job unless he signs a contract. If he don't like the work, he can't quit. Colored can't vote; they can't carry a gun. All our rights are being chipped away. Pretty soon we'll be slaves again. It scares me, Lucy. It really does."

"You don't have to go to Nashville to see what's happening. Business is bad. Colored can't get anything but the worst jobs." Lucy shook her head despondently. "But it's not like you to quit. During the war, you were like a one-woman army."

"I never been a quitter, but it gets harder and harder every day. Here it is 1870. The war's been over for five years, and what do we have to show for it?"

"We have our freedom. We'll never give that up. As for the rest, it takes time. We can reopen the school. Instead of children, we'll teach the grown-ups. Negroes need to learn how to become citizens just like the white folks."

"No." Mrs. Taney's voice fluttered between fear and indignation. "It's more serious than that. Ollie writes that there's a bunch of hooded men who ride through the colored section of town carrying burning torches, hollering and shouting. And there better never be a darky ten miles around if a white woman gets raped. Them KKK people, that's what they call themselves, the Ku Klux Klan, are always looking for trouble. And they usually find it."

"What can we do? We can't let them get by with breaking the law. We have rights."

"None anybody cares about." Mrs. Taney rubbed her hands together as though trying to wash her troubles away. "I think we should make ourselves as inconspicuous as possible. Oh, no matter." She shook her head as if she wanted to dispel the awful truth of what she had just said. She forced a smile. "You didn't invite me here to ramble on about the KKK. Show me your new house. I noticed how elegant it is. You're a mighty lucky woman, Mrs. Joshua Taylor."

"Lucky!" Lucy shrugged. "It took a lot of hard work."

"Oh, I didn't mean—" Mrs. Taney stuttered. "Nobody deserves it more'n you and Joshua. Now give me the grand tour 'fore I leave."

Proudly, Lucy showed Mrs. Taney through her home, pointing out the elaborately carved dining room set of warm cherry wood and the settee with its needlepoint upholstery. Lace curtains and polished silver added to the elegance of the room. The pink marble fireplaces were beautiful in their simplicity, and fine Persian rugs covered the polished wood floors.

"Goodness!" Mrs. Taney exclaimed. "I never saw so many pretty things outside an antique store. I do declare, the white folks would approve heartily." She beamed with pride.

"White folks? What are you talking about?"

Mrs. Taney was taken aback at Lucy's sharp command. "I thought I already explained. If we copy the whites, then we'll be more accepted. We should do everything they do."

"We can't change the color of our skin."

"Of course not, but we can dress like them, talk like them, act like them."

"That's ridiculous." A frown creased Lucy's forehead and she pointed her finger at Mrs. Taney. "So that's what you meant when you said we should order new hymn books."

"I don't know what you're talking about," Mrs. Taney said defensively.

"Oh, yes, you do. You want me to stop teaching spirituals to the church choir. You want us to forget our own music."

Mrs. Taney cleared her throat and tugged hard on her shirtwaist. "Well, since you brought it up, I do want to talk to you about the spirituals. They're just too Negro. Reminds a person about slave days, days best forgotten."

"Do you think God will like us better if we sing white folks' songs?"

Mrs. Taney tittered nervously. "I didn't say that. Anyway, I think you're making too much out of this whole thing. It was just a suggestion."

"Well, ma'am, just because a few people want to turn themselves inside out and make black white don't mean we got to do it too."

"You're a fool, Lucy. I'm black 'nd I'm proud of my heritage. Just don't make sense shoving people's faces in it."

"If we don't hang onto our pride, white folks'll stamp it right out of us. Germans have their own newspapers. Jews got their synagogues. Catholics still pray in Latin. Why do blacks have to give up everything?"

"They're not lynching Germans."

Lucy's face flushed with anger. "I'll resign as choir director tomorrow," she said coldly. "You can get someone who believes the way you do to replace me."

Mrs. Taney coughed nervously and nodded. "That's probably the best thing for now." She headed for the door. "Later, if you have a change of heart—"

"Until tomorrow then." Lucy opened the door.

CHAPTER VIII

In 1877 America was still suffering from a severe economic depression. Graft and corruption ran rampant among politicians, who bought and sold favors at every level of government. Faith in the Republic was dismally low, and mediocre, uninspiring leaders did nothing to revive the nation's vitality. Big business was at the helm of state, and lynchings, burnings, and racial hatred rose to dangerous levels. Responding to the growing financial unrest, Joshua sputtered and fumed and doubled his efforts to save his flagging businesses. Because of the crash of '73, they had already lost their beautiful house, and home was the apartment in back of the tavern. One night after they had closed the tavern, Joshua asked Lucy to sit with him. Over a cup of coffee, he confided in her for the first time in years.

"Bound to lose the hotel." Joshua's face was etched with worry.

Lucy smiled. "Been expecting that for a long time. Can't say I'll be sorry to see it go."

Joshua looked up, startled. "You don't care?"

"No, sir," she said emphatically. "Working at the hotel and here at the tavern is killing you. I say it'll be a blessing."

Joshua leaned back in his chair and shook his head in dismay. "Woman! You don't know what a relief it is to hear you say that. I didn't want you worrying about money, especially now." Joshua laid his hand on top of Lucy's and squeezed it. His eyes were filled with love. "Might've known you'd take it this way."

"The bright side is that you'll be home more."

"Yes, yes. You shouldn't be home alone so much. A woman in your condition—"

"Oh, Joshua," Lucy squealed, "isn't it wonderful? My condition! I love to hear you say that."

Joshua grinned. The loss of the hotel suddenly seemed unimportant as he studied Lucy's radiant face. "Whoever would've thought. After all these years."

Lucy nodded. "The Lord knows what's best. We're losing something, but we're gaining something much more important." Lucy patted her swollen stomach. "Everybody at church says I'm too old to have a baby. Can you imagine? I'm only thirty-seven."

"You ain't young, woman. I want you to take care of yourself. No worrying, you hear?"

Lucy shook her head. "I only worry about you. Everything else'll take care of itself."

Joshua took a sip of coffee and looked around the tavern. Despite constant scrubbing, it always looked dirty. Not much of a place to raise a child, he thought, but he didn't dare share his misgivings with Lucy. She never seemed to care much where they lived as long as they were together.

He smiled at her tenderly. "What names you got picked out for that youngun?" His voice was filled with wonder and a little embarrassment when he realized they hadn't even talked about a name for their unborn child.

"Don't know about a boy, but if it's a girl we'll name her Sarah. With everybody carryin' on about how old I am, I feel like Sarah in the Bible. Abraham's wife. She was ninety when she had her first child." Lucy laughed. "Seems only fitting."

"Sarah's a beautiful name. If it's a boy, how about Abraham. After all, he was the father."

"Abraham's a noble name. And Abraham freed the slaves. Our boy'd be in fine company with a name like that."

"I pray every night that it'll be healthy," Joshua said solemnly.

"It will be." Lucy paused, thinking of Baby Joshua. "I haven't been sick one day this time. We'll have a healthy baby. I know we will."

Turning down the gas lights, Joshua said, "Time for bed," as though fearful of tempting the gods. "Got to talk to the bankers tomorrow. Want to be wide awake for my funeral."

Lucy wrapped her arm around Joshua's waist, and they retreated to their bedroom at the back of the tavern. They usually fell asleep immediately, but tonight they lay together, Joshua cuddling Lucy in his arms. He put his hands on her stomach and waited for the baby's kick.

"I'm the luckiest person alive," he said dreamily. He kissed the nape of Lucy's neck.

"That tickles. And what do you mean, stealing my line?"

"Your line?"

"Yes," she said, laughing. "I'm the luckiest. How can we both be the luckiest?"

"Go to sleep, woman. Sometimes I don't know if I'm coming or going with you."

Lucy's confinement was over almost before it started. When the midwife presented her with a baby girl, Lucy sobbed. Joshua knelt beside her and wiped the perspiration from her face, barely conscious that he too was crying.

"The Lord blessed us," Lucy said. "He knew we needed perking up."

"She's beautiful. Looks just like you," Joshua said after the baby was washed and dressed and laid in a satin-lined bassinet.

"I think she looks like you."

"The bald head, but not my potbelly. Shouldn't baby girls have hair? And she's so light. Shouldn't she be darker?"

"She'll darken."

Joshua shrugged. "Well, her granddaddy was white. Guess she comes by her color naturally."

"Oh, Joshua, you worry about the silliest things. She'll darken. Really she will."

But she didn't. Not very much, anyway. The neighbors came and stared at her, and Lucy wondered what they said when they left. She knew that some of them would be tempted to pass as white if their skin was as fair as Sarah's. But Lucy also knew there would be no "passing" in her family. Racial pride had nothing to do with skin color.

May was the first one to visit. She brought a bouquet of flowers, kissed Lucy and Sarah, then sat by the bed and stared at the mother, then at the daughter. At twenty-four she had already borne five children. The reverend seemed to be making up for all the years he and his first wife had been childless. Lucy still found it hard to call her Mrs. Taney even though the first one had been dead for six years.

"Sure is a beauty," May said, "and her name's fittin'."

Lucy looked at May in surprise. "'Fittin'! What's that supposed to mean?"

"Ain't no truth in it, but some of the congregation say this baby somethin' special. Like it's touched from beyond." May dropped her eyes as though too embarrassed to continue.

"May! What a thing to say. You think my Sarah's the devil's baby?"

"Ain't what I think at all, Miss Lucy. It's just that, you being up in years, some say the baby was born under a sign."

"The devil's, I suppose," Lucy said angrily. "Those superstitious goats—how dare they?"

"No need to get riled. Nobody means harm. But best get Sarah baptized soon as you can."

Only May's insistence caused Lucy to relent and allow Reverend Taney to officiate at the ceremony on July 29, 1877. Lucy, drained by the ordeal, spurred Joshua to push the horses to their limit. Giving them free rein, they were home in fifteen minutes.

The day after Sarah was born the bank called in their note, and they lost the Empire Hotel. Lucy stalwartly insisted that the hotel wasn't any more of a loss than their home had been.

"I'll be happy just as long as we have a roof over our heads," she said, repeating the refrain she had uttered the day the movers had arrived four years before to transfer the remnants of their furnishings to the back of the tavern. She had shed her tears the day of the auction when strangers tramped from room to room, sitting on the cherry wood settees, fingering the damask drapes, flicking the edges of the crystal goblets. Joshua had spent the day at the tavern, leaving her to face the horde of potential buyers and curiosity seekers. Those are my things they're buying, she thought. It pained her to have to give up her treasured possessions.

"Coloreds can rise as high as whites," Joshua had said, then proceeded to prove it.

But her personal dream of middle-class prosperity had ended when the auctioneer sold all of their belongings. Still, Lucy had thought philosophically, life went on. Tragedies were only tragedies for a little while; good news balanced the bad.

When Chin Lee told them he was leaving to join his brother in Chicago, Walt took his place. Bad news, good news. There's a rhythm to all this, Lucy thought.

But Joshua lacked her stoicism. "Don't seem right we got to work so hard in our old age," Joshua said one morning before dawn as he finally undressed for bed. "People claim we doing everything backward—starting a family, moving to the tavern. We should be taking it easy. Instead, we got to work harder than ever."

Lucy scolded him for complaining, repeating her standard quips. "We have our health and Baby Sarah. Food on the table and a roof over our heads. Can't ask the Lord for much else."

But she noticed Joshua's slower gait, the increasing pain in his injured knee, a constant reminder of the horse that had kicked him ten years before.

Because she chose to be cheerful, Lucy didn't comment on her weariness after fourteen-hour days of cooking lunches for the workmen who came into the tavern at noon, then washing the dishes, scrubbing the floors, and somehow finding time for Sarah. Her daughter's playground was the tavern floor, and her friends were the stevedores and entertainers who were patrons.

When Sarah was five, Lucy and Joshua began planning their daughter's future. By scrimping on their clothing budget, they scraped together enough money to send Sarah to a private school. Joshua loved her quick mind, her inquisitiveness, her startling beauty. "She could even become a doctor or a lawyer," he said proudly.

"She's a girl and a colored one at that," Lucy reminded him, "but maybe she could be a teacher."

"By the time she's grown up, it'll be the twentieth century," Joshua argued. "Things got to change for the better by then."

Enthroned on a dictionary next to the tavern's battered piano, Sarah watched, mesmerized, as Lucy's hands flew across the keyboard. Soon Sarah recognized her mother's favorite spirituals and ballads, and could sing along in perfect key. Never able to finish a lesson without interruptions, Lucy would leave Sarah at the piano while she paid a delivery boy or stirred soup in the kitchen. It was then that Sarah, stretching her hands on the keys, pounded away until she was close to the tune her mother had been playing. Sarah taught herself to play by ear, and only later, at Lucy's insistence, did she learn to read music.

Joshua thought the tavern was too tough for his little girl and made it off limits for Sarah at night when the lonely drinkers, the prostitutes, and the itinerant musicians wandered in off the street. But these people attracted the lonely little girl. Sarah would crawl out of bed, scoot behind an empty beer keg, and watch the parade of outcasts traipse through her life.

Mama Nellie was her favorite. Big and black, with hennaed hair, Nellie swooshed her huge hips onto the piano bench, then, poising theatrically, fluttered her jeweled hands in the air. Once she had everyone's attention, she slammed her hands onto the piano keys and played the syncopated sounds of ragtime. Before long everyone was clapping and stomping—including Sarah.

Only later when Sarah put on her mother's jewelry and pranced around the apartment singing, as she said, like Mama Nellie, did Joshua put a stop to Sarah's late night visits to the tavern. He couldn't, however, stop Sarah's incessant pleas for singing lessons. Joshua gave in, but he warned, "No lessons from Mama Nellie. You'll learn church music, not those ragtime numbers."

As much as Sarah loved the church and its music, she couldn't forget the blues and ragtime performed every night in her father's tavern. Forbidden to set foot in the place after seven o'clock at night, she could still hear the loud, raucous music pulsating through the apartment. Unable to sleep, Sarah would lie in bed and dream of becoming the world's greatest singer.

Everyone agreed that she had a beautiful voice, even her parents. But Sarah had cringed when she heard Lucy suggest she study opera. Ugh! Staring at herself in the mirror she stuck out her tongue and crossed her eyes. Opera singers were ugly. They had big breasts and huge chests. How else could they hold those high notes? Embarrassed, Sarah turned away. All through her adolescence she had thought she was misshapen. What right did she have to criticize how others looked? She cried for hours, lamenting her awkwardness. Finally, when she turned sixteen, lumps became curves, giggles softened into laughter, and somehow her body grew in proportion to her head.

"Goin' over to Ginny's," Sarah shouted to her mother.

Ginny, her best friend, had a piano and both her parents worked. The girls loved to practice the forbidden music that was all the rage: blues and ragtime.

On afternoons when Sarah escaped from her chores at the tavern, the girls adorned themselves with beads and laces, then smeared their cheeks and lips with almond paste mixed with beet juice. Hair piled high on their heads, they strutted onto an imaginary stage and wailed the familiar blues:

> *"I'm going to tell you something, baby,*
> *Ain't going to tell you no lies,*
> *I want some of that custard pie.*
> *You got to give me some of it,*
> *Before you give it all away."*

Their show might have continued indefinitely if Ginny's mother hadn't come home early one day.

Over Sarah's protest that she had heard Mama Nellie sing "Custard Pie Blues" and be rewarded with a rousing ovation, Joshua threatened Sarah with the prospect of spending a month alone in her room. A new set of rules was laid down. Blues and rag music were forbidden—as were visits with Ginny unless the girls were properly chaperoned.

Sarah sulked for a week, taunted by the unfairness of it all. Ginny had gotten off scot-free. Later Sarah discovered that being the daughter of a tavern owner tainted her in the eyes of the respectable citizens of the community. Ginny's mother was the worst, but Mrs. Patterson's views paled in consequence when Sarah realized her own parents believed it too.

CHAPTER IX

"But Mama, I don't want to go to Morehouse College. I don't want to go to Atlanta, and I don't want to study classical music."

Lucy glared at her daughter, unable to comprehend such rebelliousness, such ingratitude. "Well, then, you can just stay here with us and mop up spilled beer and polish spittoons because your papa'll never let you join a road show."

"But Mama—"

"Coon songs! Is that what you want to sing? I heard'em in the minstrel show that came through last year, a Negro minstrel show at that. It was embarrassing and insulting. Songs like 'He's Just a Little Nigger, but He's Mine' and 'Every Race Has a Flag but the Coon.' No! I won't have a daughter of mine living in rundown hotels and ridiculing her race just for the empty glamour of being in show business."

"But Mama, those songs were written by Negroes. And what about the blues? You said yourself they're our music."

"Sarah! I'm dog tired and I don't want to talk about this anymore. Get a bucket and wipe off the tables while I finish washing the beer mugs. I want to get to bed sometime before dawn."

Sarah slapped the wet rag over the splintered wooden tables. "How can you stand this? If I thought this was all there was to living, just scrubbing this dumb old tavern every night and serving beer to those smelly men every day, I'd—I'd—well, I'd just up and quit."

"Oh, Miss High and Mighty, I think you better remember hard work puts food in your mouth and clothes on your back."

Lucy dismissed Sarah with the flip of her rag, then wearily grabbed up the bucket and, stepping into the deserted street, threw the dirty water into the gutter. Pausing for a moment, she relished the stillness and solitude of the early morning hours. Thirty-eight years, she thought. I've been cleaning this place all that time. Lucy sighed. Where had the years gone? And what had happened to her youthful dreams? She was fifty-five; Joshuah was sixty-six. They were still poor and most of their race was even poorer. Negroes and whites were separated in schools, businesses, and neighborhoods, and now Sarah wanted to join a road show. Lucy's spirits sagged when she realized she couldn't hang onto her strong-willed daughter anymore than she could recapture the dreams of her youth.

Mulling over her problems, Lucy didn't see Joshua as he turned the corner and headed toward her. "Woman! Move on inside," he shouted. "You want to get yourself killed?"

"Joshua! You liked to scared me to death. Where you coming from? I thought you were out back."

Joshuah grabbed Lucy's arm and, after pulling her inside, shut the door and bolted it. "I was helping Moon move scenery in his theater. Earned a few bucks—"

"Moon Moran," Sarah said excitedly. "You know Moon Moran? Oh, Papa! Please, can I see one of his shows? If I could just talk to him, maybe he'd hire me. You wouldn't mind if I worked for Mr. Moran, would you? You know him."

"Sarah, you still talking that nonsense? Your mother wouldn't sleep if you was traveling all over the country, God knows who with."

"Oh, but what if we found a minstrel show that was respectable? Like Mr. Moran's. You'd trust him."

Joshua shook his head. It hurt him to see Sarah so unhappy, but he knew her unhappiness was nothing compared to what Lucy's would be if Sarah ever left. "Never knew you to be so determined," he said in distress.

"It's our fault," Lucy said, "for letting her watch the singers and dancers. Looks mighty exciting when you're scrubbing tables."

Lucy caught the hurt in Joshua's eyes. She patted his arm. "Now don't go getting your feelings hurt. We work hard, but we got it better'n most. I see the colored men on the levee begging for a job, a meal, anything. I see 'em sleeping on the cold stones when the sun goes down, and they don't have a dime in their pockets. We look mighty rich compared to them."

Joshua nodded. "When you put it that way . . . but I haven't forgotten my promise to buy you a pretty house and fancy clothes."

"Papa!" Sarah's eyes flickered with shock. "You can't be apologizing for us living here. Why, I love the tavern. Where else could I have seen dancers like Williams and Walker and musicians like Mr. Handy. They're all special, Papa."

"I don't want to hear about Mr. Handy or Mr. Williams or Mr. Anybody," Lucy said. "All your sentimental talk about Negro minstrel shows and colored dancers isn't going to change my mind. Any singing and piano playing you do'll be done at the neighborhood Baptist church."

"Oh, Mama!" Sarah threw down her rag and stomped out of the room, positive that her parents were the most stubborn, the most old-fashioned people who ever lived.

The summer of 1895 seemed to be flying, along with Sarah's dream of joining a minstrel show. The arguments with her parents abated, and Sarah surprised herself when she realized she might enjoy going to college in the fall. After all, look at the Fisk Jubilee Singers. Singing Negro spirituals, they had become the most popular group in America.

Sarah and Ginny were friends again. Since Ginny had decided to become a teacher, her mother trusted her daughter with Sarah, and the two girls were careful never to mention show business in her presence. But one day while they were sitting on the floor in Ginny's room, Ginny shyly pulled out a ticket tucked in the pocket of her bloomers. She handed it to Sarah. "It's a free pass to see the new minstrel show, the Happy Coons, at Moon Moran's."

Lucy stared at the ticket as though it were a million dollars. "Where did you get it?" Her voice quivered with excitement.

"The manager, a Mr. Monroe, gave Papa ten tickets if he would put a sign in his window advertising his minstrel show."

"But how did you get it? You didn't steal it, did you?"

"Course not," Ginny said indignantly. "I found it on the floor. Here. You take it. I'd love to go myself, but decided I'd never have enough nerve."

"Oh, well, I guess if you found it . . ."

The girls studied the ticket apprehensively. The trouble over their singing escapade seemed minor compared to what might happen if their parents discovered the ticket.

Sarah hesitated, then quickly grabbed the ticket from Ginny's hand.

"Swear you'll never tell." Sarah wondered if they shouldn't prick their fingers in some kind of blood ritual to insure eternal silence.

"I'll die first."

"Thank you, Ginny. You'll be my friend forever."

Once home, Sarah told her mother she had been invited to Ginny's for dinner the following evening. Finding it difficult to control the quiver in her voice, she kept her eyes downcast, but Lucy didn't even glance up from the table she was scrubbing. When Sarah repeated herself, Lucy finally stopped and stared hard at her.

"What's the matter with you, girl? You act like you're asking to leave home. Course you can go to Ginny's, but right now I'd appreciate some help with these tables."

For the next twenty-four hours Sarah was in torment. As her lie ate at her conscience, she found it difficult to look at her parents without crying. Time and again she assured herself she was committing no crime. It's just a stupid old show, she thought. There's no harm in it. All the same, the ticket seemed to burn a hole in her pocket. When the time finally arrived for her to leave, she waved good-bye as nonchalantly as she could; then, once on the street, she ran till she reached the end of the block. Halting, she glanced furtively over her shoulder to be sure Joshua wasn't watching from the window, then headed toward the theater.

Minutes after Sarah left, Joshua returned from the stables. Standing at the doorway of the tavern, he watched as Lucy stacked clean glasses behind the bar. Wisps of gray hair fell across her face, and her eyes reflected years of toil and a lifetime of worry. Got to be more to life than this, he thought. In a spontaneous show of affection he grabbed her waist and spun her around, kissing her hard on her mouth.

"What in heaven's name . . ." Lucy pulled away and stared at Joshua, her face beaming.

"Seems like I still got what it takes to make you smile."

"Never said you lost your charm, but this is hardly the time or the place." Self-conscious, Lucy glanced down at her faded cotton dress.

Joshua stepped back, his eyes following her. "Well now,

seeing as how it's a slow night, I'm going to close the tavern, and you'n me'll have a party. You spruce up a bit while I lock the door."

Lucy looked at him in wonder. "Think we should?"

"Yes. I think we should."

"Then I accept your invitation, Mr. Taylor." Lucy curtsied, then ran out of the room.

When she returned her hair was brushed back from her face and coiled in a knot at the nape of her neck. She wore her Sunday best, a light blue batiste decorated with her old pin of violets. When Joshua saw her, he hurried to her side and escorted her to a table, its beer stains hidden under a white tablecloth. The musty odor of the tavern was camouflaged by the scent of pine rising from a flickering candle. A bottle of wine rested in a bucket of ice, and the strains of a waltz floated from a gramophone on top of the bar. Bending low, Joshua held out his hand. "May I have this dance?"

Lucy laughed as she put her arm on her husband's shoulder. "I haven't danced in years."

"Neither have I, but we won't tell."

Joshua spun Lucy around the tables, their laughter filling the room. When the gramophone shuddered to a stop, Joshua escorted Lucy to the table and filled their glasses with a sparkling white wine.

"To you. To the most beautiful woman in the world."

"Now you're pulling my leg."

"No. I mean it. I always thought you were beautiful. From the first time I saw you. Remember?"

"I'll never forget it." Lucy turned her face toward Joshua's and caressed him with her eyes. "You saved my life."

"How's that?"

"If it hadn't been for you, I might have killed myself. I was so scared and so miserable."

"Lucky for me you didn't."

"Lucky for me, too."

"We've had some bad spells," Joshua said, pulling himself back to the present.

"None we couldn't cope with."

"You never been sorry?"

Lucy's eyes narrowed. She stared hard at Joshua. "Sorry?"

"Sorry you married me."

A smile spread across Lucy's face. "I'm only sorry we don't have more'n one lifetime to share. You and Sarah have made me the happiest woman alive."

Joshua courted Lucy with all the ardor of a young suitor. They drank wine and danced, kissed and reminisced. Having reached the twilight of their lives, in the shadowy darkness of the tavern, they reaffirmed their love. The world was outside, waiting, but for the moment they had each other.

Keeping her eyes downcast, Sarah handed her ticket to the young man at the door, then scuttled inside the theater. When she was safely seated in the back row, she looked around, taking a professional interest in her surroundings.

It's so elegant, she thought, and beautiful. Everything looked new: the purple stage curtain edged in gold braid, the gilded chandeliers. Oh, I knew it'd look like this, she thought. Sarah gazed starry-eyed at the audience, the orchestra pit and, even though she could barely see him, the piano player, who entertained them with foot-stomping rag music before the show began.

By the time the minstrel show came on stage, the men and women in the audience were ready for their raucous humor. Whistles and shouts greeted sixteen black men as they strutted up front—their faces painted with burnt cork, their lips grotesquely enlarged with white grease paint. Wearing baggy pants, mismatched patchwork jackets, and huge, flapping shoes, they sang an upbeat song as they entered. Taking their places in a semicircle, they waited for the command shouted by the interlocutor—"Gentlemen, be seated."

Rolling his eyes and stretching his grease-painted lips in an exaggerated grin, the interlocutor introduced the Happy Coons.

"Folks, I want youse to know dat dis is the authentic,

original, bone-fide black minstrel show featurin' true, honest-to-goodness American Negroes with unbleachable complexions and the laziest bodies their side of the Congo River."

"Here we go, everybody," Brudder Bones shouted. "Da authentic minstrels is here, 'nd we's offerin' you a show dat's a copy of da Negro shows put on durin' plantation days. Now if dat don't make no sense to nobody, youse just sit back and enjoy da fun 'cause we's got rhythm, 'nd we knows how to laugh. Ain't dat right, Brudder Tambo?"

"Dat's right, Brudder Bones." The laughing, cork-faced Negro slapped his thighs and pulled at his suspenders. "Do ya know why de firemen wear red suspenders?"

"No, I don't rightly know," Brudder Bones said, screwing up his face trying to remember.

"To keep his pants up," Brudder Tambo said, accompanied by a chorus from the audience.

Sarah laughed with the rest of the audience at the antics of the showmen, but her humor was tinged with embarrassment. She recognized the pathos in the acts: the buffoon run over by a trolley, a farmer tricked out of his money, a losing player in a never-ending crap game. Sarah recognized the characters from the down-and-outers who came to her father's tavern.

Suddenly, a low, growling roar filled the theater as Sadie LaTour sauntered on stage. Billed as the sultry bombshell from Pittsburg, the chocolate-skinned singer bumped her hips to the steady beat of the drums as she smiled and waved at the crowd. For ten minutes Sadie taunted them. Whenever the applause subsided, she kicked her leg from a slit in her wine-colored velvet gown, ground her hips, and raised her arms over her head. At the pitch of excitement, Sadie nodded to the orchestra leader. Standing in the middle of the stage, her legs spread slightly apart, Sadie put her hands on her hips and launched into her song.

"I dreamed last night I was far from harm,
Woke up and found my man in a sissy's arms.

> *Some are young, some are old,*
> *My man says sissy's got good jelly roll."*

Sadie shimmied when she sang "jelly roll." A dozen men bolted to the edge of the stage and tried to grab her dress. She shook her finger at them and stepped out of reach. Without missing a beat, she continued.

> *"My man got a sissy, his name is 'Miss Kate,'*
> *He shook that thing like jelly on a plate."*

Sadie lifted her arms and pirouetted around the stage. Winking at the leering men, she finished her song.

> *"Now all the people ask me why I'm all alone,*
> *A sissy shook that thing and took my man from home."*

Sadie blew kisses as she sauntered off stage. Only a rousing cakewalk subdued the hysterical crowd. The show ended with the fabulously successful song "All Coons Look Alike to Me."

The audience responded by throwing everything from plucked chickens to gold coins on stage.

As the theater emptied, Sarah stood up, straightened her hat, and walked purposefully to the piano at the foot of the stage. Plunking at the keys, she played "Oh Dem Golden Slippers."

"Ma'am, sorry to disturb you, but—"

Sarah raised her arm and started to swing her handbag at the man who had touched her shoulder.

"I'm Benny Monroe. The manager. Please, don't scream. I won't hurt you."

Sarah dropped her arm and blushed in embarrassment. "I'm so sorry." She threw her hand over her mouth and stared wide-eyed at the young man.

"I'm Benny Monroe."

"I recognize you—from the poster outside."

"Whew! I'll never walk up to someone ever again without giving 'em a warning."

"It was my fault. I shouldn't even be here."

"Oh, you're not breaking any rules. You're more than welcome."

"I meant I shouldn't be here—at the theater." Sarah noticed the questioning look on his face, then shook her head. "Oh, never mind. It doesn't matter. I'm leaving."

"No. Wait." Benny ran after her. "You didn't introduce yourself."

"I beg your pardon." Sarah turned and looked at him in surprise.

"I watched you before I came down. You were so lovely . . . playing the piano. You looked like a vision. The phantom of the theater!"

Sarah laughed and offered her hand. "I've been called lots of things, but never a phantom. My name's Sarah, and I can't tell you any more because I don't exist."

"Since you don't exist, should I lock you inside for the night?" Benny fell in step with her as they walked to the lobby.

"You could lock me in here forever, but . . ." She sighed and smiled wistfully.

Her frivolity faded when she stepped outside and saw the deserted street, dark now except for the gas lamp at the corner. "Looks like everyone's gone."

"No one's meeting you?"

"Well, no . . . you see. Oh, my. I'm really in a pickle." Sarah explained why she wasn't meeting anyone.

"You must let me escort you home. A young lady on the streets alone at night—it's too dangerous."

Sarah weighed the danger of walking home alone against the danger of meeting her father while with Benny Monroe. Both were risky, but she finally chose Benny. Still, she insisted that they say good-bye half a block from the tavern. At the front door, glancing over her shoulder, Sarah saw that Benny had waited until she was safe. She risked a quick wave and then hurried inside. Trying to look nonchalant, Sarah smiled at Joshua as she headed toward the apartment. Busy as usual, he barely looked up. Lucy was nowhere around. Thank the stars, Sarah thought. I don't think I could hide my happiness. Mama'd see it and ask why I'm grinning like a fool. Then I'd have to tell her I've fallen in love, and I'm going to run away and join Benny Monroe's minstrel show.

She couldn't fall asleep until four o'clock. She plotted and schemed; not only did she have to convince her parents to let her go, but she had to get Mr. Monroe to hire her. When finally she fell asleep, Benny Monroe's broad, handsome face lingered in her dreams.

When Sarah stumbled into the kitchen at six thirty in the morning, barely awake but smiling from ear to ear, Lucy eyed her suspiciously.

"Must've been quite an evening at Ginny's."

"I met the most interesting man. Mr. Monroe. The Pattersons rent him a room over their store." Sarah bit her lip until it pained her. Lies, lies, lies. God's going to punish me for lying to my mama. Sarah filled the blue enameled coffeepot with water and grounds and set it on the stove. Taking three dozen eggs from the cooler, she broke them into a large earthenware mixing bowl. I got to work and not talk, she thought. But the stories come so easily. Please forgive me, Mama, if you ever find out.

"And who is Mr. Monroe?"

"He's the manager of the Happy Coons minstrel show."

"Oh!"

"No, not 'oh,' Mama. Mr. Monroe is a businessman—just like papa. He works hard, and his show makes people laugh, and—"

"How do you know so much about the minstrel show?"

"I hear people talk. Even Papa said it was good."

Lucy sliced three loaves of homemade bread, spread them with butter, and arranged them on a baking sheet ready for the oven. "Guess I can't complain if an evening with your friends makes you this happy."

"You know how much I enjoy talking about show business."

"Just as long as that's all you did—talk."

"Yes, Mama. That's all we did."

It was ten o'clock before the last of the breakfast crowd

left. Lucy poured two cups of coffee and handed one to Sarah.

"Sit a spell." Lucy pointed to the chair next to her. "You been working hard this morning—and no complaints." Lucy took a sip of coffee, then stared blankly into space. "I hate to ruin your good humor, but your Papa's not been feeling well lately."

"Why didn't you tell me before? I should have noticed. I've been so wrapped up in myself—"

"He would never admit to being under the weather. Says his blood's just slowing down." Worry lines creased Lucy's forehead. "Wanted to warn you not to upset him—and the two of us got to pick up some of his chores. Already talked to Walt. He'll tend bar in the evenings. You and I can divide—"

"Don't worry, Mama." Sarah grasped Lucy's hand. "I'll do whatever needs to be done. You just tell me."

"Papa didn't want me to say anything, but when you started talking about minstrel shows again, I thought—"

"You did the right thing, Mama. I should know when you and Papa got problems." Sarah crinkled her eyes in sympathy. "No more talk about show business or Morehouse College either."

"Papa still wants you to go to college. Best not mention anything. Course, if he should ask—"

"I'll say whatever he wants me to say. Now don't you worry."

Instead, Sarah worried. She saw her future slipping away, and there was nothing she could do about it. Benny ate lunch and dinner at the tavern every day for a week. She introduced him to Lucy and Joshua and was happy to see they enjoyed talking to him, but that was as far as it went. No invitation to Sunday dinner, no stern discussion on the rules and responsibilities of courting.

By the second week Sarah was desperate. Joshua had bounced back from his sickbed, reclaiming his original work schedule over Lucy's stern opposition. Sarah heard him seriously discussing enrolling her in Morehouse for the fall. Tears rolled down her cheeks when she talked to Benny, whom she was surreptitiously meeting at Ginny's.

"You passed the audition with flying colors," Benny assured her. "Everyone agreed that you would be a good change after Sadie blasts 'em out of their seats. We could bill you as the demure innocent—the essence of youth, the—"

"Phantom from St. Louis." Sarah smiled through her tears. She shook her head in disgust. "That's just what I'll be—a phantom. Sarah Taylor! The Girl Who Almost Made It."

Benny scratched his jaw. "I worked with Joshua at the theater. He congratulated me for being practical. 'Hard worker. Down to earth.' Those were his exact words. Maybe if I talked to him . . ."

"Do you think he'd listen? It's our only hope."

"I'll come by tonight—after the show."

Lucy and Joshua sat on one side of the table, Benny and Sarah on the other. Joshua had closed the tavern early. "Family business," he exclaimed, then ushered the last drunk out.

"We got nothing against you or your show." Joshua tried to keep his voice under control. "But it's a rough life. You got to admit that."

Benny nodded.

"Entertainers come into the tavern all the time begging a meal and a drink. Usually a drink. They tell me how it is on the road. Rough. Especially for colored. You know that as well as me."

Benny nodded again. He's going to let me hang myself, Benny thought. He knows it's not an easy life, but then, running a tavern isn't either.

Joshua leaned on his elbows, his eyes hard and piercing. "Is it true what they say about the signs?"

"Signs?"

"In the South . . . the signs they got on the edge of town. 'Nigger! Read and Run. If you can't read, run anyway.' Ever seen one of them?"

"Yes, sir. One or two. They got Jim Crow laws all over the

South. Colored got to be out of town 'fore sundown." Benny paused, embarrassed by the ugliness of it. "But we're only going to cities—Memphis, Cincinnati, Indianapolis. We'll end up in Chicago."

This time Joshua nodded. He brushed the tears from his eyes with his shirt sleeve. "Sure would hate to see my little girl exposed to something like that. Mr. Handy . . . you remember him, don't you girl? Writes songs . . . blues. He came by couple months ago. Told me all that hatred was getting to him. Said it was a real mean life traveling the circuit, moving from town to town, running out of money, having whites biting at your heels. If somebody attacked my baby, who'd care?"

Lucy stared at the table, unable to speak.

"I've never had any trouble like that," Benny said. "It's hard work, it's uncomfortable, and it pays poorly, but I never had no real race problems. Course, I don't go looking for trouble."

"There's always a first time," Lucy interjected.

"Ma'am . . . Sarah has a beautiful voice. One of the best I ever heard. She's got the drive to be an entertainer, too. Just seems a shame not to give her a chance." Benny shrugged. "Might be the only way to get it out of her blood."

They talked for another hour, arguing, threatening, and finally agreeing that Sarah could join the Happy Coons minstrel show on certain conditions: She was to keep her parents informed of her whereabouts at all times; she was not to expose her body in a revealing costume; her songs must not be ribald or off-color. Then, as an aside, Joshua gave Sarah train fare home that she was to use in case of an emergency.

A week later Sarah kissed Lucy and Joshua goody-bye, waited as Walt secured her trunk on the wagon, then, climbing up beside him, grabbed her hat with one hand and waved with the other as they headed for the train station where Sarah would meet the rest of the troupe.

Early the next morning as Lucy and Joshua were getting ready for bed, Lucy casually glanced at herself in the long mirror by her dresser.

"Joshua! When did this happen?"

"What?" Joshua's eyes filled with fear. "What is it?"

"My hips—look at my hips. They're huge. When did I get fat?"

Walking over to her, Joshua put his arm around her. "What are you talking about, woman?"

Lucy dropped her head and tears ran down her cheeks. Sobs racked her body. "We're getting old, Joshua. Life's done passed us by. I'm fat. My hair's turned gray. I got arthritis in both my knees and . . . and nobody needs us anymore. Our Sarah's gone. . . ."

Joshua patted Lucy and soothingly rocked her back and forth in his arms. "Honey, you ain't put on a pound of fat in ten years. The gray hair softens you, woman. Makes you look real sweet and gentle. As far as needing . . . I need you. Always have. Couldn't've hung onto the tavern without you. You make the hardest work seem easy and ain't never complained. Don't you go starting now."

Lucy wiped her eyes, but the tears wouldn't stop. "First Mama"—her voice choked with emotion—"then Baby Josh, and now Sarah. They're all gone. . . ."

"That's what life's about, Pretty Miss. Comings and goings. Ain't nothing ever stays the same—'cept you and me. That's how we started, and it's how we'll end up. Think you can bear up under that?"

Lucy turned around and kissed Joshua on his lips. "As long as I got you. Just as long as I got you."

CHAPTER X

Dirt and soot blew in the open window of the Illinois Central's Cannonball Express, headed south from Chicago to New Orleans. The troupe would get off at Memphis.

Sarah leaned her head against the back seat, but the jarring motion of the train made it impossible for her to rest.

I'm the only one who can't sleep, she thought as she looked around the car. Benny was curled up on a hard chair across from her, his coat collar turned up toward his face. They had barely had time to say "hi" at the station in St. Louis; he was busy moving boxes and suitcases, and everyone was asking him questions. "When will we get to Memphis?" "Will we have decent rooms?" "Can I have my ticket now?" "Where's our car?" Wanting to ask him her dozen questions, Sarah had refrained, for she could see by his face that he was about to explode.

After the train stopped at Carbondale, Illinois, the tooting of the whistle as they pulled away woke Benny, who stood up and stretched. He pulled a bottle of whiskey from his coat pocket and sat next to Sarah. "Thirsty?"

Sarah turned up her nose in disgust. "It'd make me sick. I don't suppose you have any water?"

Benny took a gulp of whiskey, then replaced the cap. "Should've asked at the station. Water's hard to come by when you're traveling. Especially heading south. Never can tell if there'll be either water or toilets. There are white and colored for both, but I've seen toilets fouled so bad they couldn't be used and buckets for water that were either empty or full of mud."

Sarah gagged. "You warned me."

"When you're talking, it isn't ever as terrible as when you're experiencing it." Benny smiled. "There are always ways to get by. You go in the bushes, you carry a jug of water. Didn't bother this trip because it was so short."

Sarah fell silent and looked out at the pretty night. Stars were shining and the air was cool. She smiled to herself. A million times she had imagined herself traveling with a show, but she had always sat in a first-class coach. Doesn't matter, she told herself. I'd rather be sitting beside Benny Monroe in this uncomfortble car than riding in luxury with some ugly old man. Still, it would be nice to have a cushion.

Benny squirmed on his seat trying to get comfortable. "Pure torture, isn't it?" he said, almost reading her mind.

"I've sat on softer." Sarah turned away self-consciously. Oh, dear! He's going to think I'm an idiot. He must have seen everything, done everything. I've never known a man put together so well. Even better than Papa. Sarah's spirits sagged. It's not fair. We had so much to talk about in St. Louis. I got to try, she decided. As she turned to say something Benny opened his mouth. They laughed. When they tried again, the same thing happened. The third time Sarah pointed to him with her hand and waited.

"Want to talk or would you rather rest?"

"Oh, talk. I want to know all there is to know about show business." But how will I ever find out? Guess I'll ask him about himself. That way he can talk and I won't seem so inexperienced.

Benny laughed when Sarah questioned him about his past. "There aren't any deep dark secrets."

"I don't mean to pry."

"It's okay. You got a right to know who you're traveling with." Benny leaned back. His eyes seemed to be looking at something deep inside himself.

"Mama was a quadroon in New Orleans, a hostess in one of the houses there. Very fancy, very expensive. Catered to white men, old-line French Creoles. Jesse, that was my mama's name, did all right for herself as long as she obeyed the rules. The ladies couldn't get old, or sick, and they couldn't sleep around. Had to save themselves for that high-class Creole blood." Benny hesitated.

"Jesse broke all the rules. She got older, twenty-five or so; she messed around with a Negro cornet player; and she got pregnant."

"What happened to her?"

"Got kicked out of the fancy house. Her cornet player left town. She picked up men on street corners and in bars. Jesse supported both of us for five years doing that, then one day she had a fight with another woman over a customer. Mama killed the woman and was sent to prison, and I was sent to a Catholic orphans' home."

"Oh, I'm so sorry. Your poor mother."

"Missed my mama, but the home wasn't so bad." Benny tried to sound nonchalant. "Learned how to read and write. Never would've if I'd stayed with Jesse. And I learned how to play a cornet—just like my pappy."

"I wouldn't have liked being raised in an orphanage."

"I left when I was sixteen. Me and four other guys organized the Original Basin Street Funeral Band." Benny laughed. "We really had a nerve. Thought we were the best jazz band in all of Louisiana. We made enough money to eat. That's about all. Played at weddings and funerals. Managed the band for four years, then I organized the minstrel show. Been doing that for four years . . . which brings me up to today."

Sarah stared at Benny in wonder. "You must've traveled all over the country."

"The South mostly. Course I've been to Chicago and New York."

"That sounds exciting!" Then, feeling a tinge of sadness as she looked into Benny's eyes, Sarah asked what had happened to Jesse.

"She died in prison. Stabbed to death."

"How awful for you."

Benny shrugged. "It happened a long, long time ago."

By the time the train pulled into the Memphis station, the troupe was awake and moaning about their sore muscles and the cricks in their necks. Benny organized his helpers: Charlie Floyd, who was Brudder Bones on stage; Bert Jenning, the comedian; Skeeter, the human rubber band; Jake Abernathy, the juggler; Moses Hughes, the man who dressed like a woman. Together they transferred the luggage and crates to a caravan of carriages that took them to Beale Street.

Sarah was startled and then curious when Sadie elbowed her way into Benny's carriage and sat beside him, giggling and batting her eyelids at him all the way to the hotel. "Gonna come up for a nighcap?" she asked as they all tumbled out of the cab.

"Got no time to socialize," Benny said curtly. "I intend to get into bed as soon as I can, and I suggest you do likewise."

"Depends who I go to bed with," Sadie said in a sultry drawl. "Who you gonna snuggle with, honey, your little St. Louie woman?"

"That's enough, Sadie." Benny said angrily, noting Sarah's startled look. "Now get on into the hotel and get the key to your room."

Sarah groaned when she walked into the dirty little cubbyhole that was to be her room. "Are they all like this?" she asked Benny in surprise.

"Some are worse."

"I argued with Mama when she put a bar of her lye soap in my suitcase, but I guess she knew more than I gave her credit for. Looks like I got some cleaning to do."

"I'll help." Benny laid her satchel on the narrow, iron-framed bed.

"No you won't. I know how to scrub. I've had plenty of experience. Anyway, it's so late I'll probably wait till morning."

"If you're sure you'll be okay . . ." Benny hovered near the door.

"Benny Monroe! Something's bothering you, and it isn't my suitcase or my room." Sarah eyed him suspiciously.

Benny stammered like a schoolboy. "I'd like to explain about Sadie. We've had a few drinks together. We were friendly, but it didn't mean anything. We weren't engaged or—"

"Please. You don't have to explain." Sarah was embarrassed by his nervousness.

"Don't get the wrong impression. I don't take up with every singer I hire. It's just that Sadie—"

Sarah smiled. "I think I know what you're trying to say, but your relationships with the members of the troupe are none of my business."

"Hold on a minute. I'm only explaining because you're special—I mean your friendship is something special to me. I wouldn't want you to think—"

"Can't we talk about this some other time? I feel uncomfortable discussing your relationship with Sadie." Sarah managed to slip the slightest hint of hurt and indignation into her voice, but not enough to make her appear jealous. But she was jealous, and she felt vulnerable and inexperienced when she compared herself with the worldly bombshell from Pittsburg.

"Yes. Of course. You must be exhausted." He paused at the door and smiled broadly. "I'm glad you're here, Sarah. Really glad."

Sarah's self-assurance faded and died the next day at rehearsals. When she had casually dismissed Benny the previous night, she didn't realize he might not have time to talk to her again.

Benny conducted the rehearsals with the razor-sharp tongue of a tyrant. By noon, Sarah realized glumly that Benny didn't even know she was in the theater.

Almost in tears, Sarah approached him during the lunch hour. He, Brudder Bones, and Brudder Tambo huddled together in a corner with their ham sandwiches and beer, arguing about lighting. Benny barely looked up when Sarah cleared her throat and, forcing a smile, stepped forward.

"May I have a word with you?"

"Sarah! Sorry if I've been ignoring you, but we've got a million problems to settle if we're going to open tonight." He took her arm and led her to the piano on the opposite side of the stage. "As soon as we finish eating, Mel will go over this song with you."

Mel smiled and tipped his hat.

Sarah gripped the edge of the piano, trying to control her anger.

"One song! I'm only going to have one song!" Suddenly Sarah didn't think she was in love with Benny anymore.

"We have room for only one song until I can revamp the whole show and work you in." Benny patted her knee and smiled. "It's not much, but you'll get some exposure. I'm cutting one of Sadie's songs, so if she starts yelling, just send for me. I'll cool her down."

Sarah nodded, afraid to speak for fear of crying.

"You okay?"

Sarah nodded again.

"I'm going back to work. If you need anything, let me know." Sarah didn't know if she should be angry at him or herself. Why hadn't he warned her that she wouldn't be the star of the show? Why hadn't she realized she was a dolt not to be thankful for one song? After all, her only audience had been the congregation at the Baptist church.

Squeals and giggles emanating from behind the curtain distracted Sarah, and, curious, she stood up and peeped through an opening. Susie and Betsy, two of the chorus line dancers were bending over a large trunk filled with gowns, scarves, and shoes. Sarah stepped closer.

"What be the matter, honey?" Susie asked "You don't look so good."

"I'm all right." Sarah peered into the trunk. "What's in there?"

"All kinds of wonderful things," Betsy said, grabbing a handful of gems and holding them in front of Sarah's startled face.

"My God! What are you doing?" Sarah stepped back, her mouth falling open. Her eyes were frozen on the diamond and ruby pendants, the gold and emerald bracelets, and the glittering diamond tiaras. "Does Mr. Monroe know there's a fortune sitting here—unguarded? Anybody could steal it."

118

Susie and Betsy looked at Sarah in disbelief, then they doubled over laughing. "Honey, them are just paste," Susie said. "They ain't real jewels. They be junk—make-believe. Everything about the Happy Coons be make-believe."

Sarah flushed in embarrassment. In the harsh gaslight, she saw the emeralds and rubies were only dull pieces of glass; the edges of the gold-painted bracelets were tarnished, exposing the tin underneath.

Feeling foolish and exposed, Sarah threw the jewels back into the trunk and burst into tears as she ran out into the alley.

Benny found her fifteen minutes later. "No sense crying, Sarah. Ain't been one of us that hasn't made a mistake or two in our life."

Sarah turned her face to the wall. "I'm stupid, stupid, stupid. I should've known the show wouldn't have a fortune like that, just like I should've known I wouldn't be the star singer my first night on the road." Sarah wiped her eyes, but the downcast expression remained. "Susie's right. There's nothing real here. Everything's make-believe—you, Sadie, everybody in the show."

"We're real." Benny took her hand. "But all Negro minstrel shows are make-believe. Look at Sadie—she isn't a big star from Pittsburg. She's just a singer from a small town in Georgia. It takes awhile to separate the real from the fake, but you'll get the hang of it." His voice grew softer, and he turned Sarah around to face him. "Ready to go back? It's okay, you know."

Sarah shook her head. "I can't. Everybody'll be laughing at me."

"You can't stay out here."

"I can go home."

"You still have to face 'em."

Sarah took a deep breath and pulled away from Benny. "All right. I'll go in, but how am I going to learn my song with 'em giggling behind my back?"

"Best way I know is to laugh right along with 'em. That'll take some of the sting out of it."

119

No one seemed to notice when Sarah crept back inside. Betsy and Susie were still bent over the trunk. Taking a deep breath, Sarah approached them.

"Found any more jewels?" She forced a smile.

"Where you run off to?" Glancing at Sarah, Susie giggled. "That sure be funny—you thinking that junk was real."

"Yeah, sure was." Sarah said.

"Hey! Look here. I found you a gown for your openin'," Betsy said seriously. "It be too big, but Susie 'n me can pin it on you. Go 'head—try it on."

In the shadowy darkness, Sarah saw a lovely wine-colored ball gown. Taking it from Betsy, Sarah saw that it was covered with dust, the hem was ragged, and the back seam was torn from the waist to the floor. Well, at least I wasn't fooled this time, she thought. How would it ever be presentable by tonight? Draping it over her arm, she shrugged. I'll worry about that later. Right now I have to practice my song with Mel. If I don't learn that, it won't matter what I wear. As she started to walk away, Susie yelled at her.

"Honey! Leave the dress. We be fixing it for you. We take care of it."

Sarah watched her first minstrel show as a performer from the wings, pacing back and forth as the troupe performed its acts: the comedy team of Bert and Violet; the Amazing Skeeter who stretched his body like a human rubber band; Jake Abernathy who juggled plates, oranges, and iron balls, keeping them in constant motion. But the hit of the show was Moses Hughes, a small-boned, delicate man with a beardless face and tiny hands whose soprano voice and fluttering eyelashes made him the loveliest "prima donna" on the circuit. The audience exploded when he finally stripped, revealing a slim, muscular body and a bald head. As Moses took his bows, wearing baggy red underwear and sporting two oversized breasts that hung slightly askew, he got a rousing ovation.

A tiny smile creased Sarah's lips. My, I look elegant, she thought. Susie had pinned and tucked the ball gown until it hugged her body. The décolletage, embroidered with seed pearls and garnet-colored beads, highlighted her long neck. Betsy had decorated her long, black hair with a rope of pearls, then entwined them in a thick braid and coiled it on top of her head. Betsy said she wanted her to look like Sarah Bernhardt. But, Sarah wondered nervously, did Miss Bernhardt's audience sip whiskey from tin cups and chew on chicken legs during a performance?

Loud laughter rose from a makeshift dressing room backstage as Sadie flirted with Charlie Floyd between acts. She's just trying to make Benny jealous, Sarah thought, wondering where Benny was. I know I told him I didn't want any special attention, but he didn't have to believe me!

As if in a dream, Sarah heard the overture to her song.

Woodenly she walked to the yellow mark on stage. She looked at the audience; the audience looked at her. No sound came from her mouth when she opened it to sing. Mel played the introduction twice before Sarah forced herself to raise her arms, take a deep breath, and begin. Her voice was too soft to be heard beyond the front row. Mel motioned wildly at her. Her throat constricted even more. Aware the crowd was growing testy, Sarah dropped her head, trying to hide her fear. But instead of seeming scared, Sarah was transformed into an aloof, sultry apparition.

> "I've been dogged and mistreated till I done
>   made up my mind,
>   Gonna leave this old country, and all my
>   troubles behind."

Sarah moved a few feet downstage and leaned forward as though trying to get closer to the crowd. Some of the women in the front were humming along.

> "Get my ticket at the junction and flag
>   the four-day train
>   I'm going to leave this country
>   before I go insane.
>   When I leave this morning, papa,
>   pin crepe on your sleeve,

121

> *Ain't coming here no more,*
> *you can love just who you please."*

"Know what you talking 'bout, girl," someone shouted.
Sarah warmed up.

> *"If the blues kill me,*
> *tell everybody the news,*
> *Here lays a woman died*
> *with the leavin' gal blues."*

The audience erupted into loud applause, crying for an
encore. Sarah's eyes misted. Only minutes before she had
wished she would never have to go on stage; now, intoxicated by the audience's response, she never wanted to leave.

When she ran off stage, she almost tripped over Benny.

"Oh, Benny, isn't it wonderful? It's the most exciting,
goose-bumpy feeling hearing all those people clap. They
liked me, didn't they?" Sarah's enthusiasm dampened as
she studied Benny's face. He was smiling, but he wasn't
radiant. "You didn't like my song. What did I do wrong?"
She turned and pointed toward the crowded theater. "They
liked me. I heard them—"

"Of course they did. You have a great voice, but we'll have
to work on your delivery. You're still a little shy."

"Was I awful?"

"No . . . like you say, they're clapping." Benny put his
arm around Sarah's shoulders. "I'm sorry. I don't mean to
be critical. You were good—if you weren't, that crowd out
there would throw rotten fruit at you!"

Sarah looked up and forced a smile. "Thanks for not
telling me that before I went on."

"You have talent. All you need is experience." He smiled
benignly. "Once you get that, you could be one of the best
colored singers on the minstrel circuit."

Sarah's spirits rose. "For sure?"

"For sure."

Sarah resolved to practice until singing was as natural as

breathing, and her presentation as spontaneous as walking. When she pushed on the dressing room door, Sadie swished past, sneering derisively.

"Hope you ain't thinkin' to add that sweet little number to the show. It be makin' us the laughin' stock of the whole circuit."

Benny spun around, enraged. "I'll say what songs get sung and what ones don't. I don't need any trouble from you, Sadie. Watch where you stick your nose."

Sadie shrugged and sashayed on stage. The men responded as had those in St. Louis and all the other cities where she had sung about a sissy taking her man from home. Half of the male audience offered to befriend her while the other half whistled and yelled. Sarah, sitting at her dressing table, knew what Sadie was doing everytime the crowd roared. The volumn rose when Sadie winked, when she pulled her skirt above her ankle, when she pushed out her breasts. Licking her lips, she allowed the tip of her tongue to glide over her mouth while she seductively ran her fingers through her henna-tinted hair. Even from the dressing room, Sarah could hear the audience's excited response to Sadie's seductive bumps and grinds. Sarah threw her hairbrush across the room and buried her head in her hands.

I'll never get them to cheer like that for me, she thought. Sadie's right. I got to be livelier—and louder. But I'll never be able to move my hips like that. Maybe Betsy'll help me. I'll ask her tomorrow.

The *Memphis Dramatic Mirror* ran a rave review of the Happy Coons minstrel show, with a special mention of their new singer, Miss Sarah Taylor. "She sings the blues like a professional," the reviewer wrote. He was less than enthusiastic about Sadie's bawdy act.

By the end of the first week, Sadie lost another song to Sarah. Just as they were breaking for lunch, Sadie cornered Benny.

"Calm down, girl," Benny said. "You got yourself all riled

123

up because of Sarah, and there's no need. You sing different styles. You aren't competing."

"Then how come I got to give up another song?"

"I think her style's good for the show. Gives us some variety."

"It ain't her singin's got you strung out like a bull in heat. You think you gonna get some of that? I tell you 'bout your prissy little honey. She ain't waitin' round for you. Her and Charlie be goin' at it behind your back. You just too love blind 'n too stupid to see it."

"Sadie—this time you've gone too far."

"I ain't lyin', honey. I seen 'em." Sadie moved closer to Benny and grabbed his arm. "Come on. Let's you and me be like we was. Send that little prissy home to her mama."

Harshly, Benny pushed Sadie away. "If I ever hear you repeat that story about Sarah and Charlie, so help me, I'll see to it you never sing in a minstrel show again."

Sadie stared at him, her body shaking in indignation. "You be seein' I ain't lying. Your fine lady ain't nothin' but a cheap carnival hussy."

Benny raised his arm threateningly, then quickly dropped it. "I swear, you make me want to smash you against that wall." He turned away. "Go on back to the hotel. You're through for the day."

CHAPTER XI

In Louisville, Kentucky, the troupe was relegated to the worst part of town. My God, they must think we're animals, Sarah thought.

Doesn't seem like these folks are in the mood for a

colored minstrel show, Sarah thought as she studied the faces from her perch on top of the luggage wagon. The hotel entrance faced a garbage-strewn alley, and when they entered the lobby, the smell of stale tobacco and sour beer assaulted them. Dirt caked the floors, and the wallpaper was torn and grimy. Some of the players threatened to leave rather than stay there.

In desperation, Benny told Skeeter to round up some neighborhood boys, some cleaning pails and strong soap, and have them scrub the rooms.

Having mollified the angriest of the troupe, Benny collapsed on a rickety chair in the lobby and waited for the cleanup crew. Something was wrong—he could feel it. Sadie! Where was she?

The next morning Benny walked into the hotel's small dining room and shoved a piece of paper under Skeeter's nose.

With raised eyebrows, Skeeter handed the note back. "So Sadie's left the show. Don't worry, boss. We find somebody to take her place. How 'bout Sarah?"

"Be serious. If Sarah tried to sing like Sadie, they'd boo her off stage. Anyway—Sarah's a real lady. I'd never allow it."

"Just a thought, boss." Skeeter scratched his head, then nodded reassuringly. "Just leave everything to me. Something'll come to mind."

"That damn Sadie. I swear. I'm never going to get mixed up with a woman again. She's ruined everything!" Benny smashed his fist into his hand and cursed under his breath.

"Weren't your fault. Gal was crazy. Anyway, Sadie weren't the whole show. We can work around her act."

Benny shook his head. "I don't think so. She was popular. There'll be a lot of mean men in the audience if we don't find a replacement."

"I be hitting the streets, boss, looking, while you at rehearsal. Don't worry. I find us a dancer and a singer."

When Benny announced Sadie's disappearance to the rest

125

of the cast at the theater, a disgruntled moan filled the room. Susie and Betsy turned to each other in shock, and Susie began to cry.

"Sadie's my best friend—next to Betsy. How we gonna have a show without her? I miss her. It won't be fun without Sadie."

Sarah was panic-stricken. "I can't hold the show together!"

"I'd take her place, but the men might get mad if they find out I'm a phony twice in one night," Moses said, smirking.

"I'm not changing anything," Benny said firmly, looking straight at Sarah. "We'll go on as usual. You're good performers. If the show can't hold up without Sadie, there wasn't much there to begin with, and I don't believe that. Besides, we're already looking for a replacement."

Benny's lively speech buoyed everyone's spirits, at least long enough to get them through opening night, he thought. He headed for Sarah.

"Sorry I didn't tell you about Sadie," he said, leading her to the back of the hall. "I hope you weren't too scared. I never expected you to take her place."

Sarah's temper flared. "Why? Don't you think I'm good enough?"

"Of course you are. Where did you get the idea you weren't as good as Sadie?"

"From you. I've had good reviews ever since we left Memphis, but you're never satisfied." Sarah's voice was shaky. I want him to notice me. I want to be someone special, she thought.

Benny stared at her in surprise. "I don't have time to rave about everyone in the show. If you're bad, I'll tell you. I expect the best from everyone." Benny tried to be stern, but as he looked at Sarah it was hard to keep his emotions in check. She's so beautiful, and so talented. Passion shot through him every time Sarah brushed against him, every time she smiled. He heard her talking and tried to concentrate on what she was saying.

"I want to be able to sing anything, anytime. Not just blues and ballads. I know I have a good voice. All I need is experience." Not that I'll get it from the likes of you, she thought. You think I'm such a goody-goody girl. Well, I can swing my hips as wide as Sadie did.

Benny finally found his voice. "There should be two singers: one that brays and one that coos. You're very good at cooing."

I guess that's the best he can do, Sarah thought. "Thanks." She smiled. The flushed feeling that overwhelmed her at times when she was near Benny subsided.

"I really mean it, Sarah." Benny leaned closer to her.

"I wasn't begging for compliments."

"Can't I tell you how wonderfully you sing without an argument?"

"Yes—as my boss and as manager of the show, but not as a man who happens to like my voice. I want professional critiques. That's the only way I can improve." A touch of haughtiness crept into her voice. She turned as though to leave, but Benny grabbed her arm.

"Tonight—after the show—will you have dinner with me? There must be a restaurant around here. I'd like to talk."

The unexpectedness of the invitation caught Sarah off guard. She knew her mouth must has dropped open as she gaped at him.

"Unless you'll be too tired . . ."

"No. I'll be fine. I'd love it." Sarah grinned in spite of herself. "I'll meet you after the show."

Benny watched as Sarah walked away. Well, now I've done it. We'll have dinner, some wine, she'll tell me about her dreams to become a great singer, and I'll be plotting to keep her all to myself. Oh, hell, maybe it won't be like that at all. Maybe we can just be friends.

At nine o'clock, Benny stepped to the center of the stage and the show began.

When at last Sarah stepped forward, the crowd accompanied her as she sang a medley of popular tunes—"The Band Played On," "After the Ball," and a rousing rendition of "Ta-Ra-Ra-Boom-Der-É."

127

The crowd roared its approval, but when Sarah walked offstage, they stirred uneasily. The men especially glanced at the wings, expecting Sadie to strut out, blowing kisses. Benny waited until the last minute to tell them Sadie wouldn't be performing; she had been called home to attend to her sick mother. Benny thought the crowd took the news very well, but he didn't waste any time getting the troupe back onstage for the grand finale.

As he watched from the wings, Benny realized that without Sadie's brashness the show was flat. Silently contemplating the imminent death of the Happy Coons, he didn't see Charlie till the wisecracking Brudder Bones stepped beside him.

"What do you want?" Benny asked, eyeing him uneasily.

"I want to know how long you gonna keep the show going without Sadie. Without her, you got nothing 'cept a bunch of colored folks shufflin' and clappin'."

"If you think you can manage better'n me, you're welcome to try." Benny's eyes flashed angrily.

"Don't have to be a genius to know what the trouble is. Seems to me you could figure it out."

"Okay, Floyd. Let's get it out in the open so we can handle it. What's eatin' you?"

"This two-bit show. It stinks. We need a gal like Sadie. Without her, you ain't got a show. How many times I got to tell you?"

"Maybe you can tell me where to find another Sadie."

"Hey, you're the manager. That's your job."

"Then I'll handle it, thank you."

Arrogant bastard, Benny muttered as he watched Charlie strut away. Benny's hands shook as he bit off the end of a cigar. His anger, he realized, was because he knew that Charlie was right. He had to find another singer, but where? As he lit his cigar, he heard footsteps behind him. He spun around, expecting to see Charlie again, but Sarah stepped out of the shadows.

"You look angry. I didn't keep you waiting, did I?" She adjusted her hat.

"No." Benny smiled. "You didn't keep me waiting." He paused for a moment. "Is our date still on?"

"I wouldn't miss it for the world." Sarah slipped her hand into Benny's and together they walked out of the club. The streets were deserted, and the stillness along the waterfront surprised Sarah. She was used to a hustling and bustling riverfront, but the only sounds were the whistles of the boats plying the swift-flowing Ohio. For a brief moment, Sarah felt the sting of nostalgia. She was back home, helping her mother finish the night's work. Even the tavern they entered resembled her father's, except it looked like it hadn't been scrubbed in years.

Benny waited until Sarah slid into a booth, then he went to the bar and ordered two ham sandwiches, a beer, and a cream soda.

"About to close up," the bartender said gruffly.

Benny apologized and laid a quarter on the bar, hoping to entice the man to stay another half hour. The man nodded. As Benny waited for his order, he noticed a woman sitting at a corner table, her head lying on her folded arms. Drunk, Benny thought. Before he turned away, the woman looked up and stared at him through bleary eyes.

Returning with their food, Benny sat across from Sarah. He loved watching her talk. When she laughed, her eyes sparkled; her smile radiated pleasure. More and more he wanted to spend all of his spare time with her, sharing his hopes and ambitions as well as his problems. Just being with her helped somehow.

After supper, Benny leaned back and lit a cigar. "You know," he said expansively, "we been worrying too much about Sadie's numbers. The audience liked your songs. Maybe we don't need her after all."

Sarah was thoughtful for a moment, then shrugged. "The show didn't fold when she walked out . . . still, something's missing. She was loud and sometimes downright obscene, but she was funny too. I think everyone wishes she hadn't left."

"Skeeter promised he'd find a replacement before Chicago, but I don't know—"

"Speaking of Chicago"—Sarah was determined not to spend their time together talking about Sadie—"what are you going to do when the show's finished? Retire? Organize another one?" She laughed. "The cast is actually taking bets."

"And what did you bet?"

"That you'd put another show together. You don't seem the type to work for someone else . . . and I think this life's in your blood."

"Not so. I'd love to own a tavern like your papa's. That, or have my own theater. But you need money, and I can't seem to hold on to any long enough to make it worthwhile."

Sarah's face brightened. "Then you're thinking of settling down?"

"So far that's about it—just thinking."

"You wouldn't miss the life?"

Benny laughed. "Miss what? The boredom, the loneliness, the swelled heads? No, I wouldn't miss it, not anymore. How about you? You still find this exciting or has the tinsel turned a little green around the edges?"

"Both. I like singing, but I don't think I'd like to be on the road forever. I'd really like to be with a show that stays put for a while, but there's not much chance of that, is there?"

"Not for Negro entertainers. One thing's for certain—if I do put a show together, you're going to be my star singer."

Impulsively Sarah grabbed Benny's hand and squeezed it. "I'd have to go home and visit Mama and Papa, but then I'd love to join your new minstrel show."

Benny pointed to their empty glasses. Sarah agreed to stay for a glass of wine. "Helps me relax," she said.

As Benny waited at the bar for the drinks, he saw that the drunken woman sitting at the corner table was awake. She stared boldly at him, then stood up and walked toward him, weaving.

"Buy me a beer," she slurred.

The bartender swung around and told her to get out, threatening her with his fist. She ignored him and grabbed Benny's arm.

"I told ya to leave the customers alone!" Bolting from

behind the bar, the bartender grabbed her arm and dragged her to the door. "I ain't puttin' up with your shit no more, you two-bit tramp. Get your ass out of here and don't you never let me see you no more." The burly Negro raised his hand and slapped her across her face. Then, opening the door, he threw her out into the street.

Sarah and Benny stared in shock as the bartender dusted off his pants and walked toward them.

"Sorry if I was rough, but that tart been hanging 'round here three days begging for drinks and something to eat. She won't be bothering you no more." Then, peevishly, he added, "Finish your drinks so's I can close up. It's getting late."

"I'm finished right now," Sarah said indignantly. Brushing past the bartender, she hurried to the door.

Benny caught up with her outside. "No need to get riled. The man was a little rough, but—"

"But! She wasn't hurting anyone, and it seems to me he could've given her something to eat. Papa fed people like her all the time."

"Your papa's special."

"No, he isn't. He's a Christian, and he believes charity begins at home. There's nothing special about that."

They fell silent, each sorry about the way the evening had ended. Benny saw all his romantic overtures sabotaged, while Sarah seethed with resentment at the two men's cavalier behavior. Sarah stormed ahead. Then her foot caught on something, almost throwing her to the ground.

"What in heaven's name . . . !" Sarah pointed to the body of a woman lying amid broken bottles, refuse, and dirt in a dimly lit entryway.

It was the woman from the tavern. Despite Benny's objections, Sarah knelt down and tried to wake her. After several moments, the woman opened a swollen, bloodshot eye, screamed in terror, and shoved Sarah against the wall. "Coppers! Coppers!"

"Let's get out of here," Benny said terrified. "If the cops come, we'll be in for it. They'll think we're trying to roll her."

Sarah ignored him. Once Sarah promised her a shot of whiskey, the woman agreed to follow them to their hotel. Benny was so furious he refused to talk the rest of the way back.

In the safety of her room, Sarah lit a kerosene lamp and took a good look at her guest. The woman's face shocked her. This was no woman; this was a girl, a young girl whose chocolate brown skin looked coarse despite her youth. There was a hardness around her eyes, but under all the dirt, Sarah thought, she was quite beautiful.

"Where's the whiskey?" The girl glanced suspiciously around the room.

Sarah looked pleadingly at Benny. "I don't have any—do you have a bottle?"

"Hey, if you ain't got no whiskey, I'm leavin'." The girl started toward the door.

Benny glared at Sarah, but she stared him down. "Hang on—I've got some in my room."

When Benny returned, he poured two drinks. One for the girl, one for himself. The girl began to relax.

"I'm Sarah, and this is Benny. What's your name?"

"Dory. No last name . . . least not a real one. I make it up as I go."

"I guess a name's not important," Sarah conceded. "What is important is that you were sleeping in the street—and that bartender hit you. He could've knocked your teeth loose."

"He don't give a damn 'bout nobody—the bastard." Dory gulped down the liquor and eyed Benny, gesturing for more. Benny ignored her.

"Why did you hang around his place? Seems like you could've found another tavern—one where the bartender wasn't so mean."

Dory looked up and studied Sarah as though trying to figure her out. "What's your interest, lady? You want me to do some funny stuff with you and your man here?"

Sarah blushed. "Of course not. What ever made you think—"

"You want somethin'. Haven't figured out what."

"Nonsense. I just want to help you. My papa owns a tavern in St. Louis. He helped so many people—it seemed natural—"

"Better watch who you pick up. I can tell your man's got the right idea. Don't trust nobody."

"It's not a matter of trust—it's a matter of helping. We have nothing to steal."

"Suit yourself, lady. Ain't much you can ask that'd shock me."

"I assure you—"

Benny stood up and walked across the room. Stopping in front of Dory he pointed his finger in her face. "Cut the crap. Sarah says she wants to help, and that's the way it is. Personally I'd give you a buck and send you on your way, but I have a feeling it won't be that easy. Now do you want to tell us why you're down on your luck—if you are—or do you want to get the hell out of here?"

"Benny! Do you have to be so—"

"He's right, lady." Dory sat down on a straight-backed wooden chair. Her arrogance was fading; she looked tired and shopworn. "I got no call talking to you like you're a bugger. Fact is, I'm more scared than I let on."

"Scared! I would think you'd be terrified. Why, you could have been raped."

Dory laughed. "Lady, you don't know the half of it. Getting raped ain't so bad as long as there ain't no knife at your neck."

Sarah gasped. "Then why do you hang out in bars and sleep outside where anyone can get his hands on you? Surely there's someplace you can go for help."

"Not me. I'm a roamer—no friends, no ties. The only reason I was hanging around that tavern was to keep an eye on the theater across the street." Dory stood up, brushed past Benny, and poured her own drink. "I was a singer with the Marvela minstrels till last Saturday when that smooth-talking nigger, Marvin Marvela, ran off with the show's money. Left everybody stranded in this dump of a town. A rat trap boarding house is holding my suitcase till I can scrape together two bucks."

Sarah nodded. She'd heard about disappearing road managers. There weren't many professionals who hadn't been stranded once or twice in their career.

"I'm sorry," Sarah said. "I'd be terrified if that happened to me. Of course, Benny would never run off."

"Benny?" Dory turned and studied Benny's face. A spark of recognition fluttered in her eyes. "Benny Monroe! Hey, I know you. You the manager of the Happy Coons, ain't you?"

When Benny nodded, Dory slapped her leg and snorted. "Well, I be damned."

"You heard about us?" Sarah looked at Dory's unkempt appearance, her dirty hair, and streaked makeup.

"Sure have. Circuit ain't that big that I ain't heard of the Happy Coons. Had a few run-ins with your singer. What's her name? Sadie something."

"Sadie's not with us anymore," Benny said. "Maybe she ran off with Marvin."

"And maybe this is our lucky night," Sarah said.

Benny eyed her suspiciously.

Stepping close to him, Sarah whispered in Benny's ear, "Dory could take Sadie's place. She says she can sing."

Benny rolled his eyes, then, taking Sarah by the arm, excused himself as he led her out in the hallway. Once outside, he pinned Sarah to the wall with his hand and shouted in her face.

"Are you daft? What're you suggestin'? That I hire that—that streetwalker? Woman, you're crazy. How do we even know if she can sing?"

Sarah bit her lip. Benny had never spoken so harshly to her before.

"All you have to do is listen," she said as calmly as she could. "Just listen. If she can't hold a tune, you don't have to hire her."

Benny rolled his eyes in exasperation. "Oh, great! Even if she can sing, I wouldn't want her in the show. She smells."

"You'd smell too if you slept in a pile of rubbish."

Benny shook his head. "But why?"

"Because she's all alone."

"So are a lot of people."

"I know, but there's something about her. She's hurting real bad. I feel sorry for her."

Benny looked at Sarah suspiciously. "Somehow I get the feeling I'm being set up. It's too much of a coincidence—us finding Dory just when I need a singer."

"Who'd set this up?"

"I don't know. Maybe you. Maybe Charlie."

"Oh, Benny. I would never do anything like that, 'nd I don't think Charlie's smart enough."

"Okay. Okay. So it's a coincidence."

"Maybe not such a coincidence. There must be a lot of singers floating around this area. There are a lot of clubs, most of 'em closed."

Benny leaned against the wall, thinking. When he finally shrugged his shoulders and stepped forward, Sarah knew Benny would give Dory a chance.

Sarah paused. A limp smile spread across her lips. "Before you ask her to audition, I think I better confess—"

"Confess what?"

"When you asked me why I wanted you to hire Dory, and I said I felt sorry for her—"

"Yeah—"

"Well, that's only partly true. I do feel sorry for her, but the real reason is that you do need a singer, and Dory may be your last chance to replace Sadie. It'll take a while to break in a new singer. We want her to be ready when we get to Chicago."

"Why didn't you say that before?"

"Because you're the manager. I didn't want you to think I was running the show."

Benny laughed. "Why not? Everybody else has been puttin' in his two cents worth."

"Everybody?"

"Well, Charlie Floyd . . ."

135

"If Dory can sing, you can tell Charlie that the manager has hired a new singer."

After Dory's audition, Benny agreed to hire her. Her renditions of Sadie's show-stopping songs were equally natural, equally exciting. Like her predecessor, Dory caught the attention of the men in the show. Charlie and Skeeter argued over which of them would help her reclaim her trunk. By show time, Dory had made friends with the dancers, asked for and received approval on her costumes from Benny, and promised Charlie she would have a drink with him after the show. The audience was enthralled, and even Benny was pleased.

Sarah and Dory were the major attractions in Cincinnati, and the crowds and the receipts grew. Benny helped Dory perfect her act, to be more subtle, more sophisticated.

"Don't wiggle your hips so much," Benny said as he watched Dory gyrate to the sensuous beat of her song.

Dory smiled. "Just can't seem to slow down." Pulling Benny to her, she placed his hands on her hips and said, "Now you just show me how much you want me to move."

Benny dropped his hands and stepped back. "All you need is a little more practice." He cleared his throat. "It'll come."

When he sat down, he felt Sarah's cold stare. After fifteen minutes he couldn't stand it any longer and called a lunch break. Dory sauntered to his side.

"I ain't real hungry." She smiled sweetly. "Sure appreciate it if you'd help me with my songs."

Benny coughed and tugged at the stiff, white collar that seemed to have tightened around his throat. "Sorry, Dory. Got business to attend to. Maybe Betsy'll help."

Dory's bottom lip drooped in a pout. "Well, if my act ain't as good as Sadie's, don't come complaining to me." She stomped off the stage. Minutes later she reappeared, holding onto Charlie's arm, and sauntered out of the hall.

Tart, Sarah thought meanly as she watched Dory disappear. She's nothing but a tart, carrying on with all the men in the show. I wish I'd've let her stay on the street. Sarah sat on a rickety wooden chair at the back of the stage and nibbled on a sandwich. She felt betrayed. The least Dory could have done was be grateful to her for getting her the job. I'll never do that again, she thought. She sniffed at the air and mumbled "ungrateful tart" under her breath. The more she said it, the better she felt.

By the time they opened in Indianapolis on September 4, 1895, Sarah barely spoke to anyone. The city sizzled under a heat wave, and the usual trek from the railroad station to the hotel taxed everyone's nerves.

Determined to do her share, Dory jumped on top of a wagon and pulled and tugged until she had the larger pieces secured. A round of applause and a traveling bottle of whiskey eased the tension, but Sarah fumed all the way to the hotel.

"You'd think she'd learn to act like a lady," Sarah said as she paced back and forth before a bewildered Benny.

"Sarah! I don't know what's the matter with you. Dory's doing everything she can to make you like her." Benny looked at Sarah with a puzzled frown. "What happened? Dory's here because of you. Doesn't make sense you being mad at her all the time."

Sarah's voice rose in pitch. "I certainly don't think she should be sleeping on the street, but I don't know why everyone treats her like she's the star of the show."

Benny nervously jiggled the coins in his pocket. "You know, Sadie said the same thing about you when you first joined the show."

Sarah's eyes flashed in anger. "What's that supposed to mean?"

"It means that you're jealous of Dory."

"Nonsense. I'm not jealous."

"Oh, you don't think so?"

Sarah's voice grew louder. "No. I am not jealous."

"Damn! I just don't understand you." Benny grabbed his straw hat and walked to the door. "I don't have time to argue. If there's trouble between you two, handle it. I don't like being the middleman."

"You handle everyone else's troubles." Sarah picked up a fan and nervously flipped it open.

"Only if they listen. It's a waste of time talking to a bullheaded—"

A light rapping on the door spun Benny around. "Wonderful! I guess the management's going to complain about our yelling."

"You're the one who's yelling." Sarah stomped to the door. Dory stood in front of her. "What do you want?" she asked rudely.

Dory pushed past her. "Got something to say. Hope you don't take it wrong, but I—"

"What is it, Dory? Benny and I are busy."

"Yeah, I can see that." She glanced at one, then the other. "You're mad at me, ain't you? Something I've done."

"Nonsense. We're just discussing the show," Sarah said.

"And me, too. I ain't no dumbbell, Sarah. I know what you think about me. It ain't true."

"What ain't true?"

"That I'm trying to—oh, never mind. I just came in to say I'm leaving. There's nothing but arguing around here, 'nd it's my fault."

She's blackmailing us, Sarah thought as she stared at Dory, her eyes sparking angrily. She glanced at Benny, wondering what he would do.

"Nobody's leaving the show till we finish the circuit," Benny said, scowling at Sarah. He waited for her to speak. When she didn't, he continued, "If we're going to make it to Chicago, we got to work together, bury the hatchet, shake hands."

"Kiss and make up," Sarah said indignantly.

"Oh, hell. I give up," Benny said angrily.

Dory pressed her hands on her hips. "To hell with you, Benny Monroe. I don't want to quit, but you and Sarah treat me like I got the clap. I'm sick 'n tired of all this squabbling. I'd just as soon be back on the streets than listen to you two go at it all the time. I've had it." Dory spun on her heel and stomped to the door. "It's your show. If this is the way you want to run it, then good luck." She walked out of the room, slamming the door behind her.

Benny started for her, but Sarah grabbed his arm.

"Let her be for now. She's not going anyplace. That was all a grand performance for your benefit."

Dory's in love with you, Sarah thought, but she said, "I'll apologize. I admit I've been a real lemon."

Benny looked at Sarah questioningly. "Woman, you change faster'n the weather. Never thought I'd hear you say that."

"It isn't all my fault. Dory does demand a lot of attention, but I said I'd apologize, and I will."

She turned away. You oaf, she thought. Of course you don't know Dory's in love with you. You don't know I'm in love with you. Suddenly she felt a kinship with Dory, and Sadie too.

Benny picked up his hat to leave. Damn women! Never had so much trouble before, except with Sadie. But that was different. He didn't care about Sadie. But he was worried about Sarah. Suddenly he wanted to grab her in his arms and kiss her; he wanted her to be happy the way she had been when they first met.

"What do we do now?"

Sarah's anger faded. "We can talk. Start all over again."

Benny's spirits rose.

"Let's get something to eat. Maybe if we get away from this damn theater . . ."

Sarah grabbed her hat and purse. With a smile on her face, she followed Benny out of the room.

After they finished the catfish and a carafe of wine, Benny leaned back in his chair and studied Sarah's face. Her eyes were large and luminous, the sparkle radiating from deep within.

"Look, if Dory upsets you so much, I'll let her go. I can put Betsy in her spot. We'll muddle through till we get to Chicago."

Sarah looked up in surprise. "You'd do that for me?"

"Yeah. Sure. If it'd make you happy."

Sarah dropped her eyes in embarrassment. "Now you're making me feel like a fool."

"What do you want?"

I want you, she thought but didn't say. No sense making a fool of myself twice in one day. "I want us to be friends."

Benny arched his eyebrows in surprise. "We're more than friends. We're . . ."

"We're what?"

Benny clasped her hands in his. He felt like a schoolboy sitting next to the prettiest girl in the class.

"I'm in love with you, Sarah Taylor."

"In love!" Sarah's stomach churned. It was such a simple thing to say, but what did it mean? she wondered. Would he marry her? She told herself it didn't matter, but it did. She wanted to be Mrs. Benny Monroe.

"Are you sure it's not just infatuation?" Sarah felt like a schoolgirl sitting next to the handsomest boy in class.

"As sure as I can be."

Sarah smiled. "Then I guess I can say it too. I love you."

"Why didn't you tell me?"

"I thought I did. Every time I looked at you. You were always so distant. I thought you and Dory—"

"My god! Is that why you were so upset? You thought I loved Dory?"

"She is pretty, and she likes you a lot."

"Oh, Sarah, it's always been you."

"Then why did you carry on so with her?"

"I didn't carry on. Anyway, as I recall, you were the one who wanted her to join the show."

Sarah laughed. "We both fell under Dory's spell, I guess."

"I guess we did. I admit I felt sorry for her too."

Sarah squeezed Benny's hand. Her eyes danced with happiness. "You think we can forget Dory for a while?"

Benny nodded. "We may have her to thank for bringing us together, but for now, I'd rather talk about us."

They left the restaurant and walked along the levee, watching the fishing boats bob up and down as the river churned past them. The sky was bright with stars, and the moon crept over their shoulders, bathing them in a silvery glow.

Sarah nestled in the circle of Benny's arm. She felt the slow thudding of his heart. He looked down at her. His eyes were smiling. She turned to him. His kiss was warm and tender like the night. He held her close in his arms, exuding strength and virility.

"I love you, Sarah. I love you."

Passion mounted inside her. She pressed her lips to his, feeling the wetness of his mouth. Her excitement grew.

How long will it last? she wondered. She thought of Dory and Sadie and all the women who wanted Benny, but he loved her. For how long? a voice whispered inside her head. For how long?

Sarah pulled away. They walked on. She would give herself to him, but for how long? In her head, a song echoed:

> Love, oh love, oh careless love
> Can't you see what careless love do to me?
> You made me roam, made me lose my happy home.
> It was love, oh love, oh careless love.

CHAPTER XII

Benny ran alongside the train as it pulled away from the station. "I'll write," he yelled, but his voice was drowned by the shrill wail of the train whistle and the clackety-clack of the metal wheels on the iron rails. The last he saw of Sarah was her handkerchief whipping forlornly in the scorching midday heat.

Sarah dabbed the stinging tears in her eyes and collapsed into the wooden coach chair. Opening her handbag, she pulled out a smudged piece of paper. She unfolded it along the worn creases and read her mother's message for the hundredth time. Her father was dying; she must come home at once. Sarah waited three days for the train to come through the small farming town where the show had played a one-night stand. Benny and Dory had waited with her, their depression mingled with hope that Lucy might have exaggerated.

Oh, Papa! I'm so selfish. I don't want you to be sick. I love you and Mama, but I love Benny too. She felt as though she was being forced to choose between her father and her lover.

Sarah had clung to Benny when they said good-bye while Dory hovered in the shade of the station house. "Promise you'll write," Sarah begged Benny. "And if . . . if it's as bad as Mama says, please . . . come to St. Louis. Will you do that?"

Benny promised, murmuring how much he loved her. Then he and Dory returned to the rooming house where they packed their belongings and caught the next train heading north.

It was dusk and eight hours later when they pulled into Union Station in St. Louis. She'd telegraphed ahead. Sarah adjusted her hat on her tangled hair and wiped the dirt from her face. Walt was beside her the minute she stepped onto the platform.

"How is Papa?"

"Badly, ma'am." Walt's laconic manner was tinged with grief. " 'Twas a stroke. Doc come right away, but it hit so fast. He carry a keg from the cellar. I tell him to let me do it, but you know your pa. Weren't one to put off."

Sarah nodded. "Stubborn old man. Never would listen . . ." She followed Walt to a waiting carriage. They sped down Market Street toward the river.

No reason why it should've changed, Sarah thought as she stepped out of the carriage and looked hard at the tavern and the neighborhood. But there were changes. The front window was covered with a layer of grime. Litter had accumulated around the entryway. Sarah hurried through the tavern to her parents' room in the back. The door was open and she halted, stunned, when she saw her father's frail body lying on the large four-poster bed. The hollow cheeks, the sunken eyes and heavy breathing were all signs of a dying man.

"Mama," Sarah whispered.

Lucy sprang from her bedside vigil and let out a cry. "Oh, Sarah. Dear, dear Sarah. Thank God, you've come."

"Did you doubt I would, Mama?" Sarah said tearfully, overcome with guilt.

Lucy clung to Sarah and rocked back and forth. "Wait and see. That's all the doctor says," Lucy exclaimed bitterly. "Can't do nothing for him 'cept watch him die."

"Papa isn't going to die." Sarah led her mother to a chair and gently pushed back the wisps of hair falling into her eyes. "He's going to get well and then you two are going to close the tavern and take it easy. You're too old to work so hard."

"Got to eat, child." Lucy frowned.

"I'll see that you eat, Mama." Sarah patted Lucy's knee. "Right now, all I want you to do is tend to Papa. Walt and I can handle the tavern."

Despite Lucy's almost constant care, Joshua's condition only worsened. He died on Christmas Eve, 1895. Lucy insisted that the wake be held in the tavern. The bar, draped in white satin and adorned with sprigs of green holly, served as a backdrop for his coffin. Sprays of flowers replaced the rows of liquor bottles behind the bar. On the day of the funeral, May, playing the out-of-tune piano, accompanied the church choir as they sang Joshua's favorite spiritual. They no sooner began than the mourners joined in. "I looked over Jordan and what did I see, coming for to carry me home . . ."

Lucy had stood beside the casket for two days accepting the condolences of friends. The Reverend Taney, old now and retired, said the eulogy, praising Joshua's life as a Christian, a husband, and a father. Sarah stared in wonder at the more than fifty carriages that made up the funeral cortege going to the cemetery.

The weeks seemed to pass quicker now as Sarah tried to establish a routine for her mother, Walt, and herself. Work had always been a panacea for Lucy, but it wasn't long before Sarah realized that her mother's obstinate will to survive had finally broken. Lucy talked endlessly about Joshua's life and death.

Innumerable times during the course of a day, Lucy walked by Joshua's photograph and paused, grief-stricken.

"He never suffered," Lucy said as her fingers gently touched the picture. "Just went to sleep and never woke up."

"I know, Mama. That's something to be thankful for. I miss Papa, too, but you got to get on with living, Mama." Sarah rubbed the back of Lucy's neck. Her slight widow's hump had grown more pronounced. The laughter had disappeared from her eyes.

"Yes, yes, I know. Papa wouldn't want us to grieve." Lucy became pensive, then she smiled at Sarah. "Be a good girl and slice the potatoes for the salad. I want to read my diary for a little while." Lucy drifted into her memories. "The day your papa and I were married. I forget what color dress I wore. Must've been white 'cause I was . . . oh, never mind. I'm rattling on like an old fool. When the luncheon crowd comes in, call me."

Sarah went into the kitchen and cried. There were no potatoes to peel, no luncheon crowd to feed. For six months the regulars, the stevedores and day laborers who had eaten at the tavern for years, for decades, had deserted them. But Sarah hadn't told her mother. She's got enough to worry about, she thought, then allowed Walt to serve the tramps who came in at night and bought their drinks on the cuff.

As she studied the books, Sarah realized the number of customers had been dwindling for years. The neighborhood had changed. The population was moving west. Is that what killed Papa? she wondered. He blamed himself for the decline in business so he worked himself to death. Sarah dropped her head in her hands and allowed the tears to roll down her face unchecked. They dropped onto Joshua's neat columns of figures, blurring the ink on the ledger sheets.

Sarah shook her head and wiped the tears from her eyes. I can't be thinking about the past. She forced herself to go over the figures again. Very little money, but at least there weren't any outstanding debts. We can live for six months if we scrimp. We have to plan, but I can't do anything without Mama. Just as soon as she gets over the shock of Papa's passing, we'll talk.

For two months Sarah scanned the *Post-Dispatch* for news of the Happy Coons, but if they were in the city, the state, or the Midwest, the paper made no mention of it. It was as if they'd never existed, as if Benny had never existed.

What's happening to me? I don't care about anything anymore. A singing star! It seems a dozen years since I sang for the show. And Benny! He promised he would write. He promised.

Slowly, Sarah and Lucy began packing a lifetime of possessions. Lucy wanted to save everything.

"Mama, we'll be moving into an apartment or flat. We won't have sheds and basements to keep all your stuff. If you haven't used something in the past year, throw it away."

Sarah developed insomnia that spring. Up before dawn, she sipped her morning coffee in the deserted tavern and watched as the night faded into a misty blue haze. There was no way to hurry her mother. Sarah's agitation grew with each passing day. How many times had she told Lucy she couldn't spend a week going through every box? Her mother wouldn't listen. "Oh, look Sarah," she would exclaim. "My wedding dress. You see? It was white, with blue forget-me-nots around the neck. They matched the brooch your father gave me for my seventeenth birthday." Lucy knelt over trunk after trunk, scattering clothes, pictures, and newspaper clippings on the floor. Sarah doubted if they'd be moved by Christmas.

A man was coming to bid on the horses, the wagons, and all the other stable gear that day, and she asked May to take

Lucy shopping so there wouldn't be any tears. "I just want to be done with it," she told Walt. "Tell the man we'll take any reasonable offer."

By ten o'clock the man had come and gone, and Walt stood passively as Sarah angrily paced back and forth in front of the bar shouting. "He offered half what it's worth. He knows we're desperate, but I won't sell. Do you hear me, Walt? We just won't sell."

"I knows about another man, Miss Sarah. If you like, we's can get another bid," Walt said hesitantly.

Sarah threw herself onto a chair, her chest heaving. "I guess so," she said in disgust. "We've got to sell. What in the world would I do with a stable full of horses?"

"Yes ma'am." Walt tipped his hat and headed for the door.

"I'll be in the back packing." Sarah grabbed a rag from a bar stool. "Call me when he comes."

It was close to noon when Sarah finally stopped and looked at the clock. Lunchtime, she thought. She went into the lavatory to wash her hands, then, heading toward the kitchen, she heard voices, loud and argumentative. Sarah hurried into the bar. Another low bid, she thought. Well, I'll tell that crook what I think of him and his kind.

"I'm sorry, ma'am, but this man say he want to see you. I tries to tell him you busy."

When he turned around, Sarah felt her legs weaken. She threw her hand over her mouth to stifle a scream. "Benny. Oh, my God! You've come! You've come!"

Benny grabbed Sarah's hands and held them tightly, never taking his eyes off her face. "You're still so beautiful," he said softly. "When I dreamt about you, I couldn't believe you had really been that lovely."

Stuttering, Sarah asked Benny a dozen questions without waiting for an answer. She pointed to a chair, then told him to wait until she dusted it. She dismissed Walt, then asked him to serve sandwiches and coffee. An hour passed before Sarah relaxed and listened to Benny bring her up to date on the Happy Coons.

"Lost my magic," he said casually. "When you left, I didn't care about the act anymore. Still, a man's got to eat. Put another show together in Chicago, but nobody got along. The dancers could barely kick their feet an inch off the floor. Well, maybe they weren't that bad."

Sarah smiled. "It's not like you to exaggerate."

"I booked us through the Theatre Owners Bookers' Association." He grinned wryly. "They don't call that bunch 'Tough on Black Asses' for nothing. We played in the worst fleabags in Dixie. We finished the show in January, and I was broke. In fact, I was broke the whole time. That's why I didn't write."

Benny held Sarah's hand as she told him about her father's death and Lucy's slow adjustment. When she admitted she couldn't keep the tavern open and planned to sell it, Benny became thoughtful. He stood up and slowly walked behind the bar checking the stock, the ornate beveled mirror, and the brass cash register, tarnished now but its beauty still plainly visible.

How can I get him to stay? Sarah wondered. He's so kind, so energetic. As always, he looked natty in his trim black jacket and tight-fitting green and black plaid trousers. She imagined him tending bar as Joshua had done, smiling and greeting customers. Some people were made to serve the public.

Benny ran his finger across the top of the dusty bar. Solid oak, he thought. Wouldn't take much to get the place in shape. We could make enough to support all of us until something better came along. He lifted his eyes and stared at Sarah, feeling like the prodigal son.

They both spoke at once. Laughing, Benny let Sarah go first.

"Will you stay and help us? We can't pay much, but we'll share whatever we have. I know something about running a tavern. I'll help. So will Walt and Mama."

"You read my mind, woman. You sure you got enough faith in me to go through with this?" Sarah fell silent.

"I'm sorry." Sarah looked at Benny wistfully. "I was

147

thinking about Papa. He'd be happy that we're going to stay."

When Lucy heard the news she tried to hide her distress. Nobody can take Joshua's place, she thought, but I can't say no. Sarah might up and leave, and I need her so. Lucy eased her sorrow by reminding herself that she could stop packing. And if Benny changed things around a bit, Joshua would understand.

"Funny in a way," Lucy said as she swished her mop in a bucket of dirty water. "A year ago you were wanting to leave this place so bad, now here you are, scrubbing and cooking just like always."

"It's different now, Mama. I got Benny." No sooner had Sarah spoken than she wished she hadn't. "I'm sorry. Sounds like I didn't love you and Papa. That's not true. It's just that—"

"I know how nice it is to have somebody." Lucy said smiling. "I'm glad you got Benny. He works hard. I feel safe with him here."

"Papa said he was a hard worker, too." Sarah was melancholy. Her eyes misted, and she looked away.

"I don't know about you and Benny. You got all those big plans." Lucy swept past Sarah. "You better have one foot on the ground just in case your dreams fall through."

"Why should I? I'm happy, Mama. Doesn't cost anything to dream and do a little planning on the side."

Lucy wiped her hands on her coarse linen apron. "You two thinking of marrying up?"

Sarah shrugged. "I think about it all the time. Don't know about Benny."

"Benny seems to care for you, girl, but I wonder if he's the marrying kind."

"Who knows till a man asks? Anyway, Benny's tight-lipped when it comes to his personal life."

"Seems to be." Lucy then added in a whisper, "Guess he never said where he runs off to every day around noon, huh?"

"It's none of our business, Mama." Sarah tried to sound indignant despite her own growing curiosity.

Lucy ran her wet rag across the top of the bar. She caught a glimpse of sadness in Sarah's eyes.

That night after Lucy went to bed, Sarah and Benny went over the day's accounts. Benny held himself in stiff reserve. Their relationship was strained, superficial. Sarah heard her father's warning: "Men in show business don't get attached. They thrive on conquests, then they're back on the road again."

And I'm a fool, Sarah thought. Still, her hand shook when it brushed against Benny's.

"Looks like we might turn a profit by the end of the month," Benny said. His eyes scanned the neat rows of figures.

"We couldn't have done it without you."

"And I couldn't have done it without you and Lucy." Benny looked up. His eyes were brimming with joy. Sarah's heart throbbed with desire.

She forced herself to think about money. "We should talk about a salary for you. You haven't taken a dime for all your work."

"I never expected anything. I thought we had a deal. We were going to be partners."

"Oh, we are." Sarah shook her head. "I mean—oh, I don't know what I mean. It's so difficult trying to figure out what's best. I don't know what your plans are."

"I plan to stay here as long as you need me," Benny said in amazement.

"We haven't talked about it, have we? You never speak of the future. Since you've been here—it's like we're strangers. You've been so kind. You work so hard. Still, you go off on your own." Sarah hesitated, wondering if she had gone too far. "Are you putting together another show?"

"Sarah, don't you know I wouldn't do that without telling you?"

"Mama and I . . . we've come to depend on you." Sarah's face flushed and tears welled up in her eyes. "You run off

149

every day, and when you return, you're withdrawn. Once you said you loved me, but you never once mentioned it since you've been here. You've never kissed me. You're a stranger." Sarah dropped her head in her hands and sobbed.

Benny's reserve collapsed. When he spoke, his voice was filled with tenderness. "My darling Sarah. Life isn't as simple as it seems. I've wanted to take you in my arms and hold you, to kiss you till you couldn't breathe, but I didn't want to hurt you. Now I see that I've hurt you more than ever. I should have told you the truth. I thought by keeping silent I could protect you."

Sarah's eyes fluttered open. She looked at Benny, a terrible fear strangling her. "How could you hurt me?" she asked in a childish whimper.

"When I leave during the day, I visit Dory."

"Dory!" Sarah pulled back as though she had been struck.

"She followed me here—to St. Louis. I didn't know at first. She sent me a note. She was down on her luck again. I felt the same way you did when you saw her lying in the doorway that night. Oh, hell. You know how Dory sucks people in. I took her food. I gave her a little money. She promised me she wouldn't hang around, but she did."

"Oh, that woman. She's beastly."

"Don't get all jealous again. She doesn't mean a thing to me. I'd do the same for a stray dog. You would, too. I'm not apologizing for what I did. I just wish I'd told you the truth right away."

Sarah stared at Benny, not knowing whether to laugh or cry. The gaslight hissed on the wall behind her. A chunk of ice dripped noisily into a metal pan. The familiar sounds gave her a hold on reality. Ravished by Benny's confession, she still realized he had done nothing to warrant her anger. His sense of caring was, after all, one of the things that made her love him.

"Then you still love me?" she asked plaintively.

"More than ever. I want to marry you. I wanted to ask you a hundred times, but I didn't because I got nothing to offer you. No money. Nothing. If I didn't work here at the tavern, I'd be out in the street, just like Dory."

"But we do have the tavern," Sarah said, her enthusiasm returning. "And we have the future."

Benny's frown eased, and his fertile mind, always alert to possibilities, responded to Sarah's words.

"It'd be a jumping-off place. It'd support us till I could open my own club." Benny pulled Sarah to him. His chair tipped back, and they fell on the floor, laughing, kissing, both talking at once. Benny stroked Sarah, passion inflaming them both.

"Marry me." His breath was hot on her cheek.

Sarah stroked his face. "Yes. Yes." The gaslight hissed, and the melting ice dripped languorously into the metal pan.

The wedding was small. Sarah redecorated Lucy's wedding dress, replacing the faded forget-me-nots with medallions of Chantilly lace. The same lace edged her fingertip veil. She carried a bouquet of white roses and heavy-scented gardenias.

Lucy cried as she stared at her daughter standing in the back of the church, waiting for the music to start the ceremony. She remembered her own wedding and thought, if only Joshua was here. A wisp of a smile broke across Lucy's face. Men don't take naturally to weddings, she mused, but they somehow get through 'em. Sarah's got herself a nice young man. Joshua'd be proud to have him for a son-in-law, and, oh, how proud he'd be of his little girl. Lucy hugged Sarah, reluctant to let go.

"Sweet, sweet Sarah. I'm so happy for you."

"Thank you, Mama." In a rush she added, "I wish Papa was here. I miss him."

Lucy smiled. "Oh, he is. He is here. He's standing right beside us."

Sarah patted her mother's face. "Well, you take good care of him. We're going to have ourselves a wonderful time today."

When the music started, Lucy kissed Sarah one last time, then walked down the aisle on the arm of her old friend, Walt.

Sarah smiled. Her family had grown from two to five. Walt, who had been a mere shadow in their lives for so many years, working quietly and diligently in the tavern and the stables, had suddenly become part of the household. Benny had drawn the man out of his shell, urging him to take a more active role in running things. Walt had blossomed as had the meals he planned and prepared.

Dory now had a singing job that paid her enough to live on, ending her dependency on Benny's handouts. And Sarah, assured of Benny's love, was proud of the fact that she had risen above her petty jealousy. In her spare time Dory worked at the tavern, taking over most of Lucy's chores, especially the more noxious ones: scrubbing tables, washing dishes, and cleaning spittoons. She had been thrilled when Sarah asked her to be in the wedding.

Dory stepped forward, her face beaming with pleasure. "This is the happiest day of my life, Sarah. I can't never thank you 'nough for asking me to be your bridesmaid. You 'nd Benny 'nd your mama's the only family I got. It sure do me proud knowing you's my friend."

The tempo of the music changed, and the strains of the wedding march drew Sarah out of her revery. She adjusted her veil, straightened her back, and marched down the aisle, her eyes never leaving Benny.

After exchanging their vows, the bride and groom hurried out of the church, and later, in the confines of Lucy's flower-decked courtyard, the one Joshua had built years before outside the apartment so Sarah had a place to play as a child, enjoyed Walt's elaborate wedding supper with Lucy and Dory. After they finished eating, Benny raised his glass in a toast.

"To us, my darling." He stared lovingly at Sarah. "To long life, to riches, to eternal love."

Lucy beamed and Dory coughed. Idle chatter and forced laughter filled the courtyard as Dory attempted to be merry. After dinner, when Lucy excused herself, Dory too stood up to leave, saying she had to be at work in a few hours.

Sarah sighed audibly after they left and threw her legs

over the chaise longue. "It's been a long day, my darling." She smiled lazily at Benny.

Benny poured two more glasses of champagne. "We don't have to stop celebrating just because everyone's left." He sat beside Sarah, letting his hand fall across her knee. He leaned over and kissed her.

"What was that for?" she asked mischievously.

Benny laughed and blew at the ringlets of hair curling around her ear. "Can't a husband kiss his bride without being asked why?"

"I think it's very nice."

Benny kissed her again. Sarah wrapped her arms around his neck. "It's so wonderful. Just think. I'm Mrs. Benny Monroe, and I'll be Mrs. Benny Monroe tomorrow when I wake up, and the next day and the next."

"Till death us do part." Benny set his glass on the table. With his eyes burning with desire, he picked Sarah up in his arms and carried her into their bedroom.

CHAPTER XIII

"Hallelujah! I think I can get a loan." Flying through the tavern, Benny grabbed Sarah and spun her around the room. "If Lucy'll just sign the papers. I got to have collateral, babe. Do you think she'll do it?"

"What are you shouting about?" Sarah asked, pulling away.

"The bank is going to lend me the money to open a club. All I have to have is some collateral." Benny's happiness radiated throughout the room, barely dampened by Sarah's cold response. For two years they had scrubbed and cooked and filled thousands of glasses of beer, but despite their efforts, they barely made enough to pay their bills. The thought of another debt made Sarah feel sick.

"Benny, for goodness sake, slow down. What are you talking about? A loan! When did we discuss getting a loan?"

"We didn't discuss it." Benny's smile faded. "I've been working on it for the last three months. I didn't want to get your hopes up."

"My hopes up! You mean my fears. The last thing we need is someone dunning us for another bill."

"I want better. Not just for myself. I want to make Lucy's life easier. I want us to have a nice home 'n kids someday. I thought you wanted those things too."

"I do, but not now. I don't want the responsibility of a family yet. I don't want a big house. I want to try my hand at singing again—if a show would just come to town."

"If you're in a show, you got to travel, and I for one won't allow that." He shrugged. "Anyway, when would you find time to sing when we work around here eighteen hours a day?"

Sarah sat at the table and watched the long shadows of late afternoon spread across the semi-deserted street in front of the tavern. He's right, she thought. We work ourselves to death and have nothing to show for it. Mama's not getting any younger. But do I have the right to ask her to give up the tavern? What if we lose it? What if the new place doesn't make money?

Benny's enthusiasm returned. He spoke glowingly of the warehouse he wanted to renovate. "It's perfect. It's big enough for a dining room and a gambling room. We can even have a little stage built. You could be the star singer, at least for a while, until we start our family."

Sarah shook her head. "Where is this fantastic place?" she asked skeptically.

"On Twelfth Street near Market."

"That's on the fringe of the sporting district. Mama'll never allow it."

"We won't have girls," Benny said quickly. "It'll be

legitimate. A high-class dining establishment with high-class entertainment. It won't take much to renovate. Some gaudy wallpaper and splashes of gold paint."

Just like the paste jewels in the minstrel show. She had to admit that the tinsel world of show business was enticing. Could I spend another year fixing sandwiches and trying to scrub away the smell of stale beer? No, I couldn't. And neither could Benny. She slapped her hands on her thighs and stood up. "Okay, I'll ask Mama if she'll sign the papers."

Benny hugged her so tightly Sarah thought her ribs would crack. But he bowed out when it came to confronting Lucy. As it turned out, Lucy was easier to convince than Sarah had been. "I'm old. I got my memories. There's nothing sacred about living here. Joshua'd want us to move on if we can better ourselves."

Sarah saw a glint of sadness in her mother's eyes and admired her courage. It wasn't easy following a dream at her age, but maybe, Sarah concluded, that was why at fifty-eight Lucy had outlived most of her contemporaries.

The tavern and livery stable were put up as security for the loan. Then their work began in earnest. Benny's exuberance was quickly tempered by sixteen-hour days—eight or more at the tavern, seven or eight supervising the renovation of the new club. Late at night when Benny dozed fitfully or fell into an exhausted sleep, Sarah calculated their expenses. She was appalled at their rising debts. In the morning she confronted Benny with his extravagant expenditures for gold-tasseled velvet drapes and hand-decorated washbowls for the lavatories.

"You said you'd skimp." She could barely control her temper.

"If we're going to have the fanciest club in the city, we can't skimp. Remember, we're going to cater to whites and colored. And rich ones at that. The place's got to be showy if we expect 'em to spend their money."

"How much money can they spend eating dinner?" Sarah shouted back.

"You forget the gambling, the floor shows, rag contests. We'll even have light opera." Benny smiled and put his arm around Sarah, lightly kissing her hair, her nose, and her ears until she laughed despite her annoyance. When she finally pulled away, she sighed in disbelief. "I either married a dreamer, a fool, or both. But I'm stuck with you, for richer or poorer . . ."

The Creole Club opened in April, 1899. Sarah and Lucy, seated in the center of the ornately decorated dining room, stared in wonder as black-suited men and elaborately costumed women swept along the carpeted corridor and into the room. They recognized the Negro businessmen, Jewish bankers, Irish lawyers, and German doctors. The assistant street commissioner arrived full of curiosity that quickly turned to awe. Mayor Zeigenhein was equally impressed.

They came to see the new Negro cabaret and to be seen by the affluent members of the community. They also came to listen to the most ballyhooed rag cutting contest to be held in St. Louis. Four Negro piano players, Tom Turpin and Scott Joplin being the most famous, would try to outdo each other.

After Turpin's and Joplin's unforgettable piano playing, an orchestra stepped into the main salon and played while the diners feasted on a seven-course meal. The gamblers moved to the gaming tables where they played roulette, twenty-one, and other games of chance on hand-carved mahogany tables covered with bright green felt.

Sarah floated from table to table, greeting friends, introducing herself to strangers. "You're an absolute dream," Benny whispered as he passed her on his way to the bar. Sarah smiled and straightened her shoulders. She felt elegant in her beige silk gown with its swirls of gold lamé around the décolletage and hemline. A pair of gold earrings, the finespun scrolls encrusted with diamond chips—a gift from Benny—glittered when she moved her head.

At two o'clock in the morning, Benny helped the two exhausted women into a carriage and sent them home. He promised to follow shortly, although he knew it would be dawn before he left the Creole Club.

"I knew that man would make good," Lucy said ecstatically. "Joshua said he was a hard worker."

"Mama! We all knew that," Sarah chided her, forgetting her own criticisms and complaints during the months before the Creole Club opened.

"Does this mean we're rich?"

"Not yet, Mama. But if I know Benny, we will be."

"Oh, how lovely. I think I'll enjoy being rich."

"Me, too, Mama. Me, too."

Sarah tapped her foot, the band members picked up their instruments, and the old minstrel number "Oh, Dem Golden Slippers" bubbled from her lips. Standing in the middle of the stage at the Creole Club, she felt on top of the world. It was wonderful to be singing in a club; it was heaven to be singing in her own. Her voice and singing style attracted large crowds who loved her sparkling raggy tunes.

Lucy sat at a corner table and greeted old friends, but all conversation stopped when Sarah sang. Watching her, Lucy's face filled with pride, thankful that Sarah hadn't listened to her when she had tried to dissuade her from singing. The girl would be miserable without her music, Lucy thought. She's a born entertainer.

Lucy was astonished by the number of celebrities who came to the Creole Club. "Lordy! Your programs look like gilt-edged lists of ragtimers and blues singers. Some of 'em been around since I was a youngster—I swear, the Creole must be somethin' if all those folks come here to be seen."

"We offer the best show in town," Sarah said proudly. "As much as I love singing, if we didn't have variety, we'd fold in a month." Sarah patted Lucy's hand and stared lovingly into her eyes. "You're not upset about me singing anymore?"

"Why should I be? Still, nice as it is, guess you'll quit singin' one a these days and start on a family, eh?"

"Mama, you're as subtle as a pound a garlic in a pot a greens."

"T'ain't none of my business, but—"

"You're right. It ain't. I know you're achin' for a grandbaby, but not yet. I want to sing. Benny'd make me quit in a minute if I was expectin'."

"Sometimes our plans get all messed up when we're not lookin'. Got to be prepared for anything."

Sarah agreed, but during the next six months, no one enjoyed the excitement of the Creole Club more than her. Benny added a chorus line, and the girls danced a version of the cancan, adding an international flavor to the show.

In June Benny opened an outdoor beer garden, and the clientele moved outside where brightly colored umbrellas dotted the brick courtyard. By the end of August Sarah was ready for cooler weather. She blamed her headaches, upset stomach, and her malaise on the steamy temperatures. When September arrived, she couldn't ignore the absence of her monthly period. Sarah couldn't bring herself to confide in Lucy or Benny. Benny found out by accident when Dr. Payne congratulated him on his impending fatherhood. That night as they prepared for bed, Benny, with a look of pained rejection, asked Sarah the truth.

"It's not that I don't want our baby," she said softly, clinging to Benny's hand as they sat across from each other on the bed, "but not right now. I wanted to wait."

"How long? You're twenty-three. It gets harder when you're older."

"I'm as healthy as an eighteen-year-old," Sarah retorted. "And I'm very happy about the baby, just as long as I can sing afterwards."

Benny had his back to her. "Never."

"We could find a good nurse."

Benny looked around the small bedroom that had been Sarah's as a child. They still lived in the back of the tavern. "We're so cramped together now, where will we put the baby, much less a nurse?"

"We could find someplace . . ." Sarah followed his glances around the room with a scowl on her face.

Benny laughed. "Ain't no sense worryin' about it now. Problems got a way a workin' out, not that I think us having a baby is a problem. You're makin' it into one."

"You would, too, if you had to give up the club 'cause of the baby."

"That's different."

"Only thing's different is it's me giving up, not you."

Benny set his jaw, trying to hide the bitterness he felt. Sarah's words struck an angry chord inside him. Women were supposed to want babies, he thought. Was she afraid he couldn't support a family? Hell, I'm working my tail off. We got the tavern and the Creole Club. Benny was sure it was just a matter of time before the money would be rolling in. He knew the tavern business. He knew show business, and he was willing to work day and night to make his business a success. He vowed to himself that he'd be a rich man before he was forty.

He watched in pained silence as Sarah unwound her hair in front of her dressing table. It cascaded down to the small of her back. Benny shivered. He ached to touch it, to bury his face in the silky black strands. Cautiously, he stepped forward and, taking the brush from Sarah, continued brushing with soft, gentle strokes.

"I love you, Sarah," he whispered. "I want our child."

Tears quivered in Sarah's eyes. "Oh, Benny, I know you do. How I feel has nothing to do with wanting or loving. I guess I'm afraid."

"Afraid of what?"

"Of change. Of being a mother. There are so many things I want to do."

"You can do anything you like. Even sing if you want to. No reason why you can't sing."

Sarah spun around, a smile creasing her face. "Do you mean it?"

"Sure. You just got to give me time to get used to the idea."

"Oh, darling." Sarah clung to him, laughing and crying at the same time.

Benny dropped the brush on the floor and pulled Sarah up. They kissed with a passion that had lain dormant for months, drained by exhaustion and ambition. But tonight their love-making filled the hours of the long, placid night. Only the small porcelain clock ticking away on the mantel recorded the passage of time.

Just before dawn Sarah opened her eyes. The shrill whistle of a steamboat moving downriver awakened her. Benny's hand pressed against the curve of her buttocks. She curled her body close to him and listened to his rhythmic, steady breathing and stared at him in a half-sleep. They were truly one. Soon there would be the baby, she thought, and she was afraid to share his love—as though sharing meant diluting. Disgusted, she realized she was jealous of their unborn baby. Horrified, Sarah clung to Benny. She wanted him to tell her he loved her, but knew he could never assure her enough. She would always need more.

CHAPTER XIV

Sarah pulled a wool afghan around her shoulders and shuddered as she peered out the frost-covered window. Few people were about, and those who braved the biting cold found it hard going on the ice-glazed cobblestones along the wharf. River traffic was at a standstill, and the only sound she heard was the forlorn whistle of a freight train as it crossed the Mississippi River on the Eads Bridge. It was the worst December in memory.

In her fifth month of pregnancy, Sarah was sick all the time: morning sickness, the flu, and now chills brought on by the icy drafts creeping through the floor boards of the rooms behind the tavern. Lucy, too, had taken to her bed with the grippe, and Walt did his best to tend the two women in between helping Benny at the club.

Sarah spent her afternoons staring out the window, crying. She missed Benny. Feeling more isolated with each passing month, Sarah demanded more of his time. Instead of bringing them closer, though, Sarah found that her pregnancy was pulling them apart. Benny tried to make her understand.

"With the baby coming, honey, I got to make more money. You know what the competition's like out there. If I lose my customers, Turpin picks 'em up, and we go broke."

The clock on the mantel chimed twelve. Sarah roused herself. It was time to give Lucy her medicine, then fix lunch. The thought of food made her ill, but she knew her mother would be hungry. Slowly she picked up the Bible that had been lying on her lap and laid it on the bed. Just then Benny burst into the room and exuberantly kissed the top of her head.

"Good heavens! What're you doin' home this time of day? Did the club burn down?"

Benny laughed and patted her stomach. "How ya feelin'?"

"Horrible."

"How's Mama?"

"Terrible."

Undeterred, Benny pulled Sarah out of the chair and kissed her. "Great. Get your coat. We're goin' for a ride."

"Now I know you're crazy." Sarah stared at him in wonder. "I'm not goin' out in this weather."

"Oh, come on, honey. Little cold weather never hurt nobody. You need to get away from here for a few hours. It's like a prison."

"Glad you noticed."

"Well, then, let's go."

"Who goin' fix Mama's lunch?"

"Walt's in the kitchen right now."

Out of excuses, Sarah allowed Benny to bundle her up in a heavy woolen sweater and long black coat. A carriage waited outside, and Benny tucked a lap blanket around Sarah's feet. They were off, heading west on Washington Avenue.

Sarah was sure her legs were frostbitten by the time Benny

turned onto a private street, snow-packed and barren except for a few homes humped on the frozen ground like huge whales on a frozen white sea. Benny stopped in front of a handsome brick and stone house. Sarah stared out the window of the cab, impressed by the size.

"Come on." Benny held out his hand. "It's cold out here."

Sarah lumbered up the steps mumbling as she went. "Benny! If this is one of your politician friends, I'll never forgive you. You'll get to talkin' and plop me in a corner, or worse, I'll be stuck with his dull, ole wife."

"Woman! I believe you're gettin' more disagreeable every day. Babyin' don't seem to agree with you."

"Oh, and I guess you'd like to sit in the back of that awful tavern and never get out and never see anybody and be sick all the time."

Benny kissed her and smiled sheepishly. "I'm sorry, pet. Of course it's hard on you. That's why . . ."

With a flamboyant gesture, Benny pulled a bright copper key from his pocket and turned the lock. He stepped back and, with a grand flourish, motioned for Sarah to enter.

Warily, Sarah stepped into the hallway and looked around the shadowy interior. An arched hallway opened into the sitting room, and a grand staircase led to the bedrooms upstairs. They were all beautifully appointed with gold-trimmed cornices, white marble fireplaces, and crystal chandeliers.

"What d'ya think?" Benny asked, assaying the room with the air of a connoisseur.

"I think it's beautiful." Sarah peeked around the corner into the dining room as though expecting the owners to pop out of the woodwork. "Who owns it?"

"We do, babe. How long will it take us to move in?"

"Oh, Benny!" The impact of ownership finally hit Sarah. "I don't ever want to leave. Who needs furniture and pots 'n pans? Let's keep it just the way it is."

"Wouldn't be fittin' for my lady to sit on the floor. Wouldn't be fittin' for our guests, either."

"Guests?" Sarah eyed him skeptically.

"Of course. When we entertain. I figure I can bring friends and business associates here instead of takin' em to the club."

Sarah's face brightened. "And you'll be home more?"

Benny laughed and kissed Sarah's lips. "More'n you'll want, I promise."

Sarah's smile faded. "Don't wanna sound like a hypocrite, 'cause I really want you home, but with me pregnant and Mama sick, don't know how I'll keep up."

"Nothin' to worry about. Gonna get us a housekeeper—then you can be a lady of leisure."

Sarah shook her head in dismay. "Where'd you get such highfalutin ideas? A person'd think you been rich all your life, and we barely got enough to pay our bills."

"Then one more won't matter. I figure in a few months, a year at most, we'll be rich, really rich. You married yourself a man who's movin' up."

Tallulah was dropped on Sarah's doorstep by Walt, who had found her scavenging behind cabbage crates at the Soulard market. "She ain't got no home, no money, nobody." Then, in his usual brusque manner, Walt added, "Told her you needed a hard worker. All you two got to do is figure her salary."

Sarah looked at the forbidding woman. Her six-foot, large-boned frame towered over Sarah, but her face, handsome in a manly way, was open and expressive.

"Just cause I ain't got no money, don't mean I can't work. Had me a string of bad luck, but I'm honest, loyal, and even-tempered."

"I can understand bad luck," Sarah assured her, then hired her on the spot.

By the end of the week Sarah wondered what she would have done without Tallulah. When they closed the tavern, the woman packed its glasses and china, which they donated to the church. Then she started on their personal belongings. In two weeks, Tallulah, along with Walt and Benny, had moved everything to the new house. Once there, she became housekeeper, cook, and nursemaid to the bedridden Lucy, who had never recovered from influenza.

Sarah adored Tallulah and obeyed her as a child would a strong and loving adult. It was several months before she noticed Tallulah's strange mumblings. What Sarah had presumed to be a dialect from Tallulah's West Indies home sounded more and more like an incantation. When questioned about it, Tallulah openly acknowledged that she practiced voodoo.

Sarah left the room in a quandary. Could a Christian family allow a devil worshipper to live with them? Who knew what curses she might put on the household? But firing Tallulah was out of the question. In a month Sarah's baby would be born and Lucy needed almost constant care. Plus, everyone loved Tallulah. Oh, hang it all, Sarah thought and returned to the kitchen.

Sarah reluctantly assured Tallulah she could practice her "beliefs" as long as they didn't affect anyone in the house. If she burned dolls or performed black magic, Sarah would appreciate it if she did it in the stable.

"Voodoo ain't somethin' you turn on 'n off," Tallulah said, miffed. "I won't never do nothin' to hurt you or yours, ma'am. You got my promise on that."

"How do, Mr. Monroe. 'Preciate you seein' me on such short notice." A tall, gray-haired man extended his hand.

"Mr. Claybourne." Benny motioned his guest to a soft leather chair. Mr. Claybourne was one of the most influential Negroes in the community. He owned taverns, clubs, and houses of prostitution. Visits to his competitors were not casual get-togethers.

"Fine club you have here." Mr. Claybourne's voice was modulated, his attitude businesslike. He paused and lit a cigar.

"The Creole Club has been a success since opening night," Benny said proudly. "Combination of ragtime and gambling seems to be a winner."

"Yes, yes. Good choice." Mr. Claybourne drew on his cigar. "Makes a difference when your business is legal. It's cheaper. Less risky."

Benny tapped the top of his desk with his pen. "Profits aren't as great though." He wondered where the conversation was going.

"Would you agree that men in our business should stay clear of the law?"

Benny's expression became serious. "Definitely."

Mr. Claybourne leaned forward. Lowering his voice he spoke intimately. "I expect to pay the police for their 'extra protection,' but they'll only provide such services if there aren't any excessive brawls. None of us wants to see his name on the front page of the *Post-Dispatch*."

Benny, his attention riveted, gripped the pen in his fist. "Definitely," he repeated, "but you certainly don't think I'm going to give you any trouble."

"And I don't intend to embarrass you. Still, we both have a problem. Her name is Dory. She works at the Red Lantern, one of my clubs. It's also a sporting house. I hired Dory to sing and serve drinks to the men while they waited for their women."

"And?" Benny was perturbed and not a little angry. If that damn woman's got herself in another mess, he thought, I'll let him hang her.

"Dory decided to branch out on her own. While the men were waiting, she'd take 'em out back—actually laid 'em in the alley." A smile parted Mr. Claybourne's lips. "She's quite a hustler, but, of course, when my girls found out what she was doing, they were crazier'n bitches in heat. They beat her up. The little tart didn't even charge the men."

"If you fire her, I'd say she had it coming."

"Oh, I've already done that. Had to. My girls threatened to quit. But I like Dory, so when she told me you were old friends, I agreed to talk to you. She seemed reluctant to ask you for any favors."

"My wife—"

"I understand."

"I'll get to the bottom of this."

"Woman respects you. I'm sure she'll listen to you. If you can help her out—"

"I can't give her a job at the club, but she won't bother you or your girls anymore. I promise."

"Appreciate it." Mr. Claybourne stood up. For a moment a light flickered in his otherwise somber eyes. "Dory is very different from the rest of my girls."

"She can be coarse at times."

"It's more than that—none of my girls are known for their refinement."

"I'll talk to her."

Benny escorted Mr. Claybourne to the door. "By the way," Claybourne said, "have you heard the rumors about a world's fair comin' to St. Louis?"

"Who hasn't?"

"Us colored businessmen better make sure we get in on the plannin' stage. Them white boys at city hall got a bad habit of ignoring us."

"I'm not relying on any help from city hall," Benny said. "I'm buying real estate here and in East St. Louis. Figure that's where the money's gonna be."

"Probably right. Still, it takes a lot of work keeping up flats and apartments unless you just let 'em rot."

"Rot or no, it costs money to buy buildings. I need cash up front."

"How much?"

"Three thousand'd do it."

Mr. Claybourne took two more steps then paused. He stuck his cigar in Benny's face and stared intently at him. "Contact Hiram Solomon. Tell him I sent you."

Benny smiled broadly and held out his hand. "Thank you, Mr. Claybourne. I sure will. I appreciate it."

Mr. Claybourne was a man of his word. Benny barely had time to make an appointment to see Mr. Solomon when Dory appeared, contrite and frightened.

"I can't handle your problems anymore," Benny said the minute he saw her. "Mr. Claybourne—"

A great sob gushed from Dory, and she collapsed in the leather chair, overcome with remorse. "I done it again, ain't I? Hurting you like I do. You must hate me. But it weren't my fault. Them bitches—"

"Never mind about 'them bitches.' What about you? You losing your mind? Just lucky the girls didn't beat you to death and dump your body in the Mississippi. You were cuttin' in on their territory."

"Ah, what they got to be scared about? A little competition . . ." Dory opened one eye and chanced a quick look at Benny. When she saw he wasn't as angry as before, she straightened up. "Guess I gave 'em a run for their money."

"And I'm gonna give you a run—right out of town."

"You ain't serious."

"Bet me."

Dory stiffened. "I ain't going."

"That's up to you. I'll give you a loan if you promise to leave St. Louis. If you stay, you're on your own."

"You know I ain't gonna get no work for a while. Claybourne's bitches got everybody in town thinking I'm a bad one." Dory looked at Benny craftily. "How 'bout me singing at the Creole Club? What with Sarah being pregnant and all—"

"You really are crazy. You know what Sarah'd do if she even knew you were here? She'd clobber me, and you too. Then she'd leave me."

"Bosh!"

"You want me to tell Sarah what kind of trouble you're in now?"

"No." Dory was sullen. "I respect that woman. Lord knows I envy her." Tears rolled down Dory's cheeks. "She already thinks I ain't nothing but a tart."

Benny studied her curiously.

"You thinkin' of somethin', ain't you? I can tell. I do any kind of work, scrub floors, wash dishes . . ."

Benny smiled. "It's ridiculous."

"Tell me what you thinkin'."

"I'm thinking of opening a house on the east side. If I can

167

get the money. I'll need somebody to run it." Benny shook his head. "Naw, it won't work. If Sarah found out . . ."

The thought of hurting Sarah almost made him change his mind. Dory baffled and irritated him. Her ineptness always seemed to be a ruse, but something kept him from sending her away. Each time she asked for help, he promised himself it would be the last, but ruefully he admitted it probably wouldn't be. Call it loyalty, call it fascination, he found it impossible to turn his back on Dory.

Whatever second thoughts he may have had, he waited too long to express them. Dory was out of her chair. She ran behind Benny's desk and hugged him.

"I ain't gonna tell Sarah. Poor thing got 'nough to worry about, havin' a baby. This can be a secret 'tween you and me. It be a money-maker. I promise. I knows lots of tricks." Dory winked at Benny.

"I don't expect you to work with the customers. I need someone I can trust to run the place."

"Honey, I's as honest as a newborn day. Everything out in the open. I never do you or Sarah dirty."

"Don't mean that kind of trust. Course that's important too. I mean I got to trust you to keep your mouth shut. Keep the girls in line. I don't want any trouble with the police. I got to pay 'em, but if there's trouble, the price goes up."

"Won't be no trouble. Them white boys'll be eatin' out of my hand—or someplace thereabouts."

Benny smiled, dismissing the apprehension he felt. Dory had the bent of mind to run a house of prostitution. He took two ten-dollar bills from his pocket.

"Get yourself a room and stay out of trouble. I'll know within a week if we got a deal."

Dory stuck the money in her well-defined cleavage. Her face gleamed. "I know you get the money 'n we got us a deal."

Benny's skepticism returned as he watched Dory walk to the door. Was he going to talk Mr. Solomon out of thousands of dollars to open a cathouse?

Two hours later Benny explained his real estate plans to

Mr. Solomon, tactfully omitting any mention of a house of prostitution.

Mr. Solomon questioned him. "Seems like you could get a loan from a bank to buy real estate. Interest's a lot cheaper. I charge twenty-five percent."

Benny cleared his throat. "Expensive money."

"It's not because you're colored."

"Didn't think so."

"When people come to me, they're usually desperate or they're planning something shady. Either way, I take bigger risks than the bank."

"I can handle twenty-five percent." Benny nervously adjusted his tie.

Mr. Solomon nodded and drew a packet of legal documents from his top drawer. In fifteen minutes, Benny had signed the papers and walked out with the means to buy his fancy house.

CHAPTER XV

At the end of April, 1900, one month after Benny settled Dory into a rambling house in a once-fashionable neighborhood now gone down, Sarah went into labor. Benny had decided to wait until the baby was born before he refurbished the bordello and upgraded the neighborhood, a necessity for attracting the clientele he envisioned coming to visit his girls.

He was ecstatic when Walt scampered into his office with the news of his impending fatherhood. "Better hurry, boss. Sometimes them things go fast." Walt had just heard one of the cooks discussing the matter in the kitchen. Benny stuck his ledgers into a desk drawer, ran out of the club, and hurried home. He almost collided with Tallulah as he ran up the stairs two at a time.

"Lordy, Mr. Monroe. You be all worn out 'fore this be over. Miss Sarah just starting."

"Doesn't matter. I couldn't have worked anyway." Benny stuck his hands in his pockets, unsure what to do next. "How is she? Can I see her?"

"Course you can see her. I's fixing a pot of tea." Tallulah leaned close to Benny and whispered, "Ain't told Miss Lucy yet. Poor thing's so weak, don't want to get her worrying."

"You did right." Benny then rushed past her and headed toward the bedroom.

"How you feelin'?" He bent over and kissed Sarah.

"All right, I guess. Course Tallulah says things're just starting." Apprehension showed in her eyes.

Benny held her hand. "I won't leave. You just take all the time you need."

Tallulah brought in a pot of tea. Sarah dozed fitfully between contractions for the rest of the afternoon. By evening her pains had worsened, yet she was no further along than she had been that morning. Tallulah stood at the foot of the bed and frowned as she watched Sarah struggling. She motioned for Benny to follow her out of the room.

"Nature take its course with most babies I help be born. Dis one havin' trouble. Might be you should fetch Dr. Payne."

Benny was back in half an hour hustling the winded doctor up the stairs. Dr. Payne motioned for Benny to wait outside, and Sarah watched him leave. She barely had time to ask him not to go far when another contraction gripped her, and she cried out.

A white cotton coat covered the doctor's street clothes when he approached Benny.

"Don't get all upset," the doctor said, putting his hand on Benny's shoulder, "but we got complications. Nothing serious."

"What kind of complications?"

"Mrs. Monroe is going to have twins."

Benny leaned against the wall and stared at the man in disbelief. "Twins! Why didn't you tell us?"

"Sometimes it's hard to know unless I can hear two heartbeats."

"Does Sarah know?"

The doctor nodded. "She's not too enthusiastic about it now. Maybe later, when it's all over." He turned and headed toward the bedroom. "I'll stay till it's over. If you have a blanket, I'll sleep on the couch."

The long, arduous vigil began as Benny, Tallulah, and the doctor took turns sitting with Sarah throughout the night. But no one slept. Benny hovered nearby as Tallulah wiped Sarah's forehead with a damp cloth, and mumbled eccentrically. Periodically, Tallulah disappeared into her room for an hour, sometimes less. When she reappeared, her lips were pinched, and she kept her eyes riveted on the floor. As the second night approached and Sarah still writhed in agony, time seemed to have stopped. They passed each other as though in a trance, jarred out of their stupor only by Sarah's piercing screams.

"Help me, please." She clutched Benny's hand.

Dr. Payne stood at the foot of the bed and shook his head. "There's nothin' to be done 'cept be patient."

Benny jumped up. "The hell with bein' patient. My wife's sufferin', and I'm gonna get her to a hospital."

"Too dangerous. Jostling might start her hemorrhaging."

"She'll die if we don't."

Putting her arm around Benny's shoulders, Tallulah led him out of the room. "Come with me. You needs some food in you and a shot of whiskey."

Benny pulled away. "I can't eat."

"Then you get yourself a drink."

Exhausted, Benny followed Tallulah to the kitchen. He poured a whiskey, downed it, and poured another.

"I knows you ain't gonna believe me, but in a hour dem babies'll be born. A hour. Mark my words."

"What you talkin' about, woman?" Benny looked at her skeptically.

171

"I tell you, dem babies be birthed in a hour. You just hang on."

A shrill scream pierced the quiet of the house. Benny bolted up the back staircase. "Tallulah," he yelled, "tell the boy next door to hitch a wagon. I'm takin' Sarah to the hospital."

When he reached the bedroom, Dr. Payne was standing beside the bedpost staring at his patient. Benny shoved him aside. "Get her ready. We're goin' to the hospital."

"She'll never make it."

Benny shoved him again. "She'll never make it lying here. Now do as I say." Benny turned and ran out of the room. "I'll get a cot."

"Tallulah." Benny glanced around the kitchen, then out the back window. Tallulah was gone. "Where the hell are you? We got to get Sarah—"

A loud moan came from Tallulah's room. Benny pounded on the door. "Tallulah. Come out. You got to help." Without waiting for an answer, Benny stormed into the maid's room. He reeled in disbelief when he saw Tallulah kneeling in front of a large metal tray filled with hot coals. The foul odor of burning plants and singed flesh filled the room.

"What the hell's goin' on?"

Tallulah didn't respond. Instead, she swayed back and forth, mumbling incoherently and staring into the fire.

Benny grabbed her arm. "Get up!"

The woman's powerful body resisted. She continued swaying, her voice rose, and finally, throwing her hands over her head, she let out an ear-piercing scream. She threw a handful of dust into the fire which blazed momentarily then died. The room grew still.

"My God! What the hell!" Benny bent over Tallulah's prone body. "Woman, can you hear me? Get up. We got to help Sarah." He slapped Tallulah's cheeks. Her head rolled from side to side. Her skin was cold. Now what the hell do I do? he wondered. He was about to call Dr. Payne when Tallulah opened her eyes and a smile spread across her face.

"You sick?"

Tallulah shook her head. "Everythin' all right. Like I told ya. Sarah havin' dem babies now. Girl come first, then the boy."

Benny lit a kerosene lamp and stared at Tallulah's face, then at the smoldering remains in the metal pan. He recognized the head of a charred rat.

"Voodoo! Devil worship! Is that how you planned to help Sarah?"

"We got no time to argue." Tallulah was on her feet and heading out the door. "That fool doctor upstairs alone."

Outside Sarah's bedroom, they heard Dr. Payne yelling, "Keep pushin'. The head's crownin'. Keep pushin'."

Minutes later the doctor handed Tallulah a baby girl, and still later, a boy, both perfectly formed, both squalling loudly.

Benny slunk down the hall to the water closet and vomited. When he returned, Sarah was resting, the anguish on her face already fading. The housekeeper shuffled back and forth, cooing and aahing at her new charges.

"Ain't they somethin'? I never seen such beautiful babes. Spittin' images of their papa and mama."

Sarah sighed. "I hope they satisfy you, cause I'll never do that again."

"Two's plenty." Benny wiped Sarah's face then peeked at his children. Smiling, he said, "They look like oversized golden brown raisins."

"Fat 'n plump," Tallulah added.

Benny turned to the housekeeper. Still smelling the foul odor of dead rats, he decided he didn't want Tallulah to take care of his children. "Maybe we should hire a nurse for the babies."

"No," Sarah said. "Tallulah and I'll manage. I don't want a stranger takin' care of our children."

"We'll see how things go," Benny said. "No need to worry 'bout that now."

"Much as I like to tend these babies, Mr. Benny got the right idea," Tallulah said. "I got the house to tend, cookin', and takin' care of Miss Lucy. My time already stretched to the limit."

At the mention of Lucy, Sarah raised her head off the pillow. "Quick. Tell Mama we got twins. Oh, she'll be so thrilled."

"In a minute." Tallulah wrapped the infants in soft flannel blankets and laid them in their cribs. She wiped her forehead then discarded her blood-spattered apron. "Right now I got to write down their birthday and the time. Important to keep records." Grabbing paper and a pen, she looked at Benny. "Lordy, I done lost track of time. What date them babies born on?"

"April thirtieth. It took Sarah almost three days—"

"April thirtieth!" Tallulah screamed. Her hands shook. She spun around three times then threw herself on the floor, mumbling and crying loudly.

"What're you doin', you crazy fool?" Benny grabbed her arm.

"I try to help." Tallulah sobbed. "I believe Sarah gonna die. I do a spell so dem babies be born and the missus not die, but I forget to check the date. April 30 is Walpurgis Night, the witchcraft sabbat. Now dey is under the spell. Dey belongs to dem on the other side. 'Less I do somethin', they die terrible deaths. Oh, I's so sorry. Can you ever forgive me? Didn't mean no harm. Sarah would a died."

"Fool!" Benny said angrily. "Just as soon as I can find someone to take your place, I want you out of this house."

"I can't leave! I got to find a way to turn around the spell. I got to be near dem babes."

"Let her be," Sarah said, strain returning to her voice. "We're Christians. We don't believe in voodoo. It can't hurt us."

Benny stepped back. "You're right. Nothin' to worry about. I just don't want any more of that nonsense."

"I ain't never gonna bother you with spells no more," Tallulah promised, then hurried out of the room.

Benny walked to the cribs and looked pensively at his babies. Don't look like much for all the commotion they caused, he thought. Boy looks like me, though. Guess the girl looks like Sarah.

"What're you thinking?" Sarah held out her hand.

Benny sat on the edge of the bed. "I'm thinkin' we got two beautiful babies, but we got to name 'em."

"Roy for the boy. Had that one picked out long time ago. Don't know about the girl. Lucy, maybe, after Mama."

"Roy and Lucy." Benny nodded. "Sounds okay to me."

"No. Doesn't sound right. Roy and Lucy. Think of a name that matches better'n Lucy."

Benny thought for a few moments.

"Roberta."

"Roberta. Roy and Roberta. Oh, Benny! It's perfect. Where'd you get the name Roberta?"

"One of the dancers in the minstrel show was named Roberta. Always loved her name. Sweet little thing."

"Sweet, indeed," Sarah said indignantly.

Benny laughed. "Not as sweet as you." He stood up to leave. "You get some sleep. You sure earned the right to some rest."

Sarah threw him a kiss. "You did, too. We're all gonna need our energy to keep up with our new family."

For four years Sarah watched from the sidelines as Benny doubled, then tripled, their income. Occasionally, when he presented her with a diamond brooch or a gold bracelet, Sarah wondered where Benny got the money. As far as she knew, all they owned was the Creole Club and a few flats in East St. Louis. It didn't seem like they'd be worth the thousands of dollars Benny made each month. When she asked him about it, offering to keep the books just to stay busy, Benny scolded her for allowing Tallulah to run the household and raise Roy and Roberta while she frittered away her time planning to come back to the club.

"And why can't I?"

"You're my wife. I won't have my wife singing in a club or working on books. Your job is to raise our children, not stay out half the night in some smoky room entertaining a bunch of drunks."

"Oh! Is that what it's come to, a bunch of drunks? I

thought we had a higher class of people at the Creole—or has the clientele gotten a little seedy since I left?"

"You can come and see for yourself," Benny shouted in exasperation.

Sarah said she would, but she never did. Instead, she spent her time with Lucy, who was permanently bedridden now. At least Mama enjoys my singing, she thought. She had a piano installed in Lucy's bedroom and spent hours singing her mother's beloved spirituals. As Roy and Roberta grew older, they too entertained Lucy, strutting an exaggerated cakewalk around her room.

That was the most fun they had until Benny announced they were going to participate in the opening-day ceremonies of the St. Louis World's Fair.

"Guess city hall had to have some black faces there," he said dismally. But that didn't dampen anyone's excitement for long.

After a month of shopping for new outfits during the day and listening to Benny practice his speech in the evening, everyone was ready for the April 30, 1904 opening. Benny paced the front hall for half an hour waiting for his family to get ready. When they finally appeared forty-five minutes late, his temper was boiling.

"Who wants to listen to a bunch of speeches, anyway?" Sarah said as she swooshed past him, sticking a gold-plated pin in her new beige straw hat.

Tallulah, looking like a mammoth firecracker in a red and black silk dress, swept down the stairs behind Sarah, pulling her two charges with her.

"You're determined to ruin my day," Benny said, exasperated. "Not many colored were asked to be in the official activities. Just Mr. Claybourne and—"

Sarah soothed her husband's irritation by commenting on how nice he looked. Benny grabbed up the reins, and at last they were off.

"We represent all the colored families in the city," Benny said as they drove to the fairgrounds. "Some folks said Negroes wouldn't be allowed on the grounds. But the boys at city hall knew they'd have a fight on their hands if they tried to keep us out."

"I don't believe they even consider it," Tallulah said. "We's got as much right as the next."

Sarah nodded. "And I hear that Mr. Joplin is going to perform." She laughed. "I wonder if John Philip Sousa is as happy about it as we are. From what I hear, he thinks he's the only conductor good enough to entertain."

"He just plays dumb ole marches," Roy chimed in. "Mr. Joplin's gonna write a new piece for the fair."

Their eyes lit up as they entered the fairgrounds. Sarah wanted to spend the day visiting the pavilions dedicated to mankind's progress in science, industry, and education while Benny opted for the politicians' podium where mayors, governors, and even the ex-president of the United States, Grover Cleveland, would be making speeches. Roy and Roberta only saw the Pike, the magnificent fairway featuring Egyptian camels, Indian elephants, and a world of exotic thrills. All of them tasted the new foods featured at the fair: ice cream wrapped in a crisp brown waffle and called an ice cream cone, and a roasted long wiener cradled in a bun called a hot dog.

After Benny made his speech to a receptive audience, the family trudged for eight hours from one end of the fair to the other, ending their day with a ride on the 260-foot Ferris wheel that was both terrifying and awe-inspiring. The lights were still sparkling like tiny jewels when Benny laid the sleeping children beside Tallulah on the backseat of the carriage and headed home.

The next morning Sarah laid their cache of souvenirs on Lucy's bed while Roy and Roberta clambered up beside her.

"Look at my Kewpie doll," Roberta said. "Papa won it for me. He threw five balls at some milk bottles and knocked 'em all down."

Not to be outdone, Roy thrust a Bengal sword in the air, its tin handle resplendent with red, green, and blue glass chips. "I killed a tiger with my sword." His brown eyes glowed.

Sarah described the six thousand electric lights that President Theodore Roosevelt switched on from the White House.

Lucy marveled at their stories. Excitement, mingled with melancholy, brought tears to her eyes.

"If only Joshua—"

"None of that, Mama," Sarah scolded. "Papa sees us, and he knows we're happy."

"Oh, I'm just an old fool, living in the past. Lying in bed, all I got is my memories." She smiled and patted Sarah's hand. "Funny how the mind works when you get old. I can see Amanda and the Priestlys like it was yesterday. Joshua, too. Him hitchin' up them horses and cleanin' out that smelly stable. But I can't remember what I ate for lunch yesterday. I think I'm goin' daft."

"No, Mama." Sarah laughed. "I do the same. Just old age creepin' up."

"You! Old! Why you're barely twenty."

"No, Mama. More'n twenty. The years been creepin' up on us, and we barely noticed."

CHAPTER XVI

Life was placid for Sarah in the decade following the 1904 world's fair. She dutifully tended to her family, but spent most of her energy as choir director of the Third Baptist Church. Occasionally she spent an evening at the Creole Club, but she felt a gnawing loneliness as she watched the young girls perform on the stage she had always thought was hers. In 1910 she was thirty-three years old. Much too old to be dreaming about a singing career, she thought. She had felt so much more alive then.

Nickelodeons appeared a year after the fair. Sarah stated flatly that they would never replace the legitimate stage, surely never vaudeville.

Benny was more impressed with the activities of the Wright brothers, who were experimenting with human flight. "Can you imagine? Maybe someday we'll be able to fly to Chicago," he said one evening, his face hidden behind the newspaper.

Benny accused Sarah of ignoring the momentous events happening around them, things like Jack Johnson, a Negro, winning the heavyweight championship title in 1908, and W.E.B. DuBois's helping to found the prestigious Niagara Movement, a vehicle for black Americans who wanted to work for equality. Later, in 1909, Sarah and Benny were charter members of DuBois's second interracial organization, the National Association for the Advancement of Colored People.

"That husband of yours still making money?" Lucy asked one afternoon.

"Course, Mama. We got more money than we know what to do with." Sarah paused. "Why do you ask?"

"You seem out of sorts lately, like you aren't happy."

"I'm very happy. Even better, I'm contented. Taking care of you and the children fills my days."

"What about Benny? You don't have to take care of him?" Lucy's face twisted in a scowl.

"Don't you go making up problems that don't exist. I take care of Benny, leastways when he's at home."

"Which isn't often enough for you. Am I right?"

Sarah shook her head. "Takes a heap of work to make a heap of money."

Lucy sighed. "I thought rich folks didn't have to work as hard as poor folks."

"I thought so, too, but Benny lives to work. He thrives on it."

"None of my business, but I think you and the children need him as much as the Creole Club does."

"There's no talking to him." A tiny smile creased Sarah's face. "Don't you worry about it. When I get fed up enough,

179

I'll talk to the man. Till then, I'm content. Still, I thank the Lord I have you to talk to."

Lucy's body sank heavily into the feather pillows. "I won't be around forever, child, and neither will the twins. You got to make your man understand you need him in a special way. Course that don't mean you got to nag."

"Nagging never moved Benny before. Don't expect it would now."

Did she know? Sarah wondered as she sat beside Lucy's bed and stared at her mother's lifeless body and listened, terror-stricken, to the rasping sound of death rattling in her chest. I guess she wanted to make things right before she passed. Mama never did let loose strings stay untied. Lucy stirred and moaned. Sarah stood up and tried to turn Lucy onto her side. As she struggled, Tallulah came up behind her and touched her shoulder.

"Woman, you gonna be in the bed next to her if you don't rest a spell. You ain't left her side for three days."

"I don't want her to pass alone."

"Honey, she don't even know you're here."

"Yes, she does," Sarah said vehemently. "Look how calm she is . . . not fighting like she was yesterday."

Tallulah nodded. "That be true, but she don't need you round the clock. You rest a spell. I'll sit with her."

Reluctantly Sarah moved away. "You will call if . . . if . . ."

"I call." Tallulah sat in the chair vacated by Sarah.

For two hours the quiet in the room was broken only by the chiming of the clock sitting on the mantel of the white marble fireplace. The sunlight faded and the closed room, reeking of death, grew dark as Tallulah, her head sagging on her chest, nodded fitfully. Out of the shadows came a moan, then mumbling, as Lucy tried to speak. Tallulah's eyes flew open and she grabbed Lucy's hand.

"I's here. You hear me? I's here."

Lucy's lips moved, but no words formed, only a light gurgling before her body went limp.

Tallulah stepped back, frightened by the specter of death.

Throwing her hands over her face, she ran wailing, out into the hall.

By the time the rest of the household rushed into Lucy's room, Sarah was holding her mother's body in her arms, rocking to and fro.

"I knew I shouldn't have left. Mama died without me. Oh, Mama! Why'd you go when I wasn't here?"

Benny sat beside Sarah and tried to comfort her, but the more he assured her that Lucy's death had been peaceful and expected, the more hysterical Sarah became.

"We were both with Papa when he passed. I should've been here."

"She weren't alone," Tallulah said, hovering at the foot of the bed. "I loved that woman. She weren't alone."

Only the wails of Roy and Roberta distracted Sarah enough for Benny to pull her away from her mother. After the funeral, Sarah retreated to Lucy's room, transfixed.

"She was seventy-four years old," Benny said four weeks later. "You can't mourn Lucy's death forever, and crying isn't going to bring her back. She was sufferin'. You know she just finally gave up. Now she's with Joshua. You got to be happy for her. She's at peace."

"But I miss her," Sarah wailed, refusing to be comforted.

The funeral wreath remained on the front door; Sarah continued to wear her mourning clothes. Tallulah restrained the children as best she could, but had a hard time checking her own good humor.

"Shush," she cautioned fourteen-year-old Roy one day when he bounced a basketball down the hallway, the noise echoing up the spiral staircase.

"Aw, Mama isn't sick. She just wants us to feel sorry for her."

So much like his Papa, Tallulah thought. Tall and angular with the lithe body of a runner, Roy found the physical restraints of the household oppressive. Although he missed Lucy as much as anyone, he couldn't sit in his room all the time.

Roberta considered herself grown-up, and her temper flared when Sarah made promises then promptly forgot them. When Tallulah refused to sympathize with her, Roberta ran to her father.

"Mama won't even look at me. What's the matter with her? She's never been like this before."

"She can't handle Lucy's passin', honey."

"How long is Mama going to cry?"

"I don't know." Benny patted Roberta's hand.

"Can't we help? Maybe if Mama went back to church. She hasn't been for a long time. She loved the choir."

Benny's face brightened. "It's worth a try. I'll talk to the reverend tomorrow."

Reverend Amos Bailey wasn't a man to mince words. "Should've come to me right away," he said forcefully. "Mrs. Monroe's illness is a sickness of the heart. Only thing to cure it is working for the Lord. Just so happens, we needs workers. We'll be celebrating the church's twenty-fifth anniversary in the fall."

"Then you'll talk to her?" Benny said.

"Within the week."

The pinched look on Sarah's face eased as Reverend Bailey outlined his plans for the anniversary celebration.

"I'm planning a grand affair. Singin', preachin', baptizin'. We'll all be witnesses to the Lord. No need to feel burdened by your sorrow, Sister Sarah. The church is needing you. Can you find enough love in your heart to help?"

Sarah's face relaxed for the first time in weeks. "It'll be a memorial to Mama. I'll teach the choir all the old spirituals, church music, Negro music. All kinds. It'll be just for Mama—and the Lord."

"Praise be to God," Reverend Bailey bellowed when Lucy accepted. "He's calling Sister Sarah back to the fold. He works in mysterious ways, but he never lets us stray too far."

Sarah floated blithely through the mass of people crowding into the church at half past seven. She wore a new dress and her hair, coiffed in the latest style, was wound close to her head, ear-muff fashion in the front, while the back was restrained with a colorful wraparound bandeau. With the aplomb of a born leader, she handled the last-minute crises calmly. She had managed to persuade the famous W. C. Handy to play at the anniversary and nothing else mattered.

Mr. Handy introduced his blues not as his own compositions, but as a mosaic of Negro music going back to Africa.

There wasn't an idle foot or still hand when Handy played his newest compositions. The crowd stood up and moved into the center aisle when he played "Memphis Blues"; they shouted their approval when Roberta joined Handy in a duet of his famous songs, ending with "St. Louis Blues".

Afterwards, Benny led Roy and Roberta to the basement for punch and cake.

"Eat some cake," Benny said. "I'm going to congratulate your mother." He peered at the crowd milling around the tables.

"I wouldn't look too hard," Roberta said nastily. "She's probably all over Reverend Bailey cooing and aahing. Sometimes she acts so silly. Sister Janis has been talking about 'em for weeks."

Roberta's words hung heavily in the air as Benny and Roy stared at her in disbelief. Benny yanked Roberta's arm, pulled her close to him, and shook her until she cried out in pain. Only then did he release her—"not because I give a damn about your feelings," he said through clenched teeth, "but because I don't want to embarrass your mother."

"You ought to make her stay in her room a year for saying that." Roy's mouth was pinched in anger.

Benny didn't hear him. "I don't know why you said that about your mother, and I don't care, but if you ever do it again, I'll beat you to within an inch of your life."

Roberta's eyes were huge as she looked at her father. "I'm sorry, Papa. I didn't mean it." Tears rolled down her cheeks.

Benny wasn't mollified. "Get your jackets. You're going home."

"Can't I have a piece of cake?" Roy asked.

The sharp snap of his father's neck and the cold glint in his eyes was answer enough. As they marched up the stairs, Roy glared at his sister.

"This is all your fault. You're always causing trouble." Sarah waved at them from the corner of the basement. She was surrounded by a bevy of admirers. Reverend Bailey stood beside her.

"Benny! Where are you going?" She could barely be heard above the crowd.

Benny motioned that he was taking the children home.

"But I haven't—"

Benny didn't wait for Sarah to finish.

A startled Tallulah promised she'd hurry the children to bed when Benny escorted the twins into the kitchen, then spun around and was out the door as quickly as he had arrived.

By the time Benny returned to the church, most of the people had left and a coterie of diehards surrounded Sarah. Forcing a smile, he begged their forgiveness, grabbed his wife's arm, and marched her across the floor.

Stunned, Sarah followed until they reached the steps, then, like a bridled donkey, she resisted.

"We're leaving."

"You're leaving, not me."

"Shall we argue about it in front of everyone?"

"There's nothing to argue about."

"Sarah! I said we were leaving."

Their voices drowned out the hushed murmurs of the others. Sarah felt their eyes on her and she blushed in embarrassment. Biting her lower lip, she stormed past Benny and ran up the stairs. It wasn't until they were in the car that Benny asked if anything was going on between her and Reverend Bailey. The silence that followed was profound.

Sarah dabbed her forehead with her handkerchief. Finally, she asked Benny where he had heard such nonsense. "Probably from Sister Janis. She's jealous because her husband'll never be a minister."

"It wasn't Sister Janis. It was your daughter."

Sarah glared at Benny, dumbfounded at his statement. When she regained her composure, she lashed out, accusing him of listening to gossip from a child. "How can you not trust me? I have never been unfaithful. I never wanted—"

"Please, Sarah. Don't talk. I don't want to say anything I'll be sorry for later."

Teary-eyed, Sarah stared out the window but saw only the shadowy outlines of deserted streets. When they finally stopped in front of a boarded-up building ready for the wrecker's ball, she groaned.

"Why? Why did you bring me here to Papa's tavern?"

"I wanted to go back to where we started. It seems so long ago."

Sarah shook her head. "You can't go back. I don't want to go back."

"If we can find our love again, will you?"

"I've never stopped loving you." Sarah reached out and touched Benny's hand.

"Are you sure? I've been such a fool. Leaving you alone, never really sharing."

Softening, Sarah assured Benny there was nothing between her and Reverend Bailey. "He's a kind man. Maybe too friendly, but there was never . . ."

Benny dropped his head, avoiding Sarah's eyes. "I didn't really believe you were unfaithful."

"Then why?"

"Guilt. I'm the one who's been unfaithful."

Sarah gasped. "You! But—"

"Please, let me finish."

"No. I don't want to hear about it." Sarah didn't think there was any pain as terrible as the thought of Benny with another woman. All those nights he came home late. The nights he never came home at all. She felt sick to her stomach.

Benny saw the anguish on her face and took her in his arms. "No, not with a woman. There's never been anyone but you. I've never even been tempted." He hesitated, remembering the evenings he'd spent talking to Dory and her "girls." Had he been tempted? He wondered. It didn't matter. He had been faithful. "Money tempted me. I wanted to be rich—richer than anyone I knew. I wanted the money for us, but I also wanted it for myself so I wouldn't be just another 'colored boy' when I was fifty years old. It took a lot of work. But it might have cost me my marriage."

"I can't stop loving my man, no matter what." Sarah's eyes sparkled, tears of pain mixing with tears of relief. "We can work out our problems. They're not so awful."

Sarah cupped Benny's face in her hands and kissed him.

Weak with relief, Benny gushed with plans for their future. He would sell the flats in East St. Louis, train someone to manage the Creole Club. They'd take a vacation, all of them. Soon Sarah was caught up in his enthusiasm.

"I'd love to go to Atlantic City." She voiced the fantasy she had had since childhood. "Oh, it must be elegant."

"Atlantic City sounds fine to me." Benny smiled. "Course I don't know if colored are allowed in the casinos, but, if not, I'm sure we can find a crap game in town."

"Oh, silly." Sarah laughed and hugged him.

A light rain was falling when Benny finally pulled away from her grasp. He started the car. The streets were empty and so quiet—the time Mama loved most, Sarah thought. She whispered good-bye as they headed westward to another age, another world.

"I love you, woman." Then, glancing sideways, Benny smiled. "It's never too late, is it? We still have the rest of our lives to share."

CHAPTER XVII

Benny didn't sell the flats in East St. Louis. He didn't sell anything. The influx of Negroes into the city created a demand for rooms and apartments. He wished he had a dozen more, at least until Willie Jackson told him how much it would cost to refurbish them. "You don't want to own a string of derelict buildings, do you?"

Benny mulled over Willie's comment for weeks. He paid the young man good money to manage his affairs—that was one promise to Sarah he had kept. It would be senseless not to consider Willie's advice.

Benny adjusted his feet on the top of his desk and yelled, "Willie! Hey, Willie. Come in here, please. The boss wants to talk to you."

A tall young man with handsome features and short, nappy hair strode into the room with the confidence of a man whose opinion was often sought and usually accepted. Benny had never regretted hiring Willie; in fact, he considered himself extremely lucky to have found him. Three years before, when he had begun looking for an assistant, Walt had suggested his son—his illegitimate son—in Birmingham, who wanted a more challenging job than cleaning a barbershop restroom. After talking to Willie for ten minutes, Benny knew he had found his man. Bright and energetic, Willie eagerly accepted more and more responsibility. For the first time in years, Benny spent five evenings a week with his family. He still reserved Friday and Saturday nights—their biggest—for the club.

Willie's mother was a teacher, and he was well-educated

despite the poor schools provided for Negroes in his hometown. Walt was filled with pride every time he saw Willie and Benny discussing business.

"Was just talking to Pop about the food for tonight's dinner," Willie said. "Pop's a pro. Too much food, and it spoils. Not enough, and you turn people away. Good planning has allowed you to keep your dinner trade longer than most."

Benny chided Willie, telling him he didn't have to extol his father's virtues to him, and then noted how good business had been.

"It's the war," Willie said. "Lots of jobs up here. Must be millions of Negroes moving up from the South. There won't be any colored left down there if this keeps up. Colored want a piece of the pie too."

"Dory says she could hire twenty more gals."

"It's money in their pockets, but the gals really don't like that kind of work. Most of 'em came up from the South expecting to get legitimate jobs."

"Yeah . . . and starve instead," Benny said. Willie was young, intelligent, not the kind who would sit in the back of a streetcar just because he was a Negro. Of course that's where Willie would sit if he rode streetcars, Benny thought. That's where we'd all sit. But the war might change things. By the time I'm forty, I might see some real progress in this country.

"They wouldn't starve," Willie retorted. "There's plenty of work in the war factories."

"War! War! War! Everybody thinks the world's going to be perfect after the war. Even President Wilson told Congress it was a war to make the world safe for democracy."

"Changes are already happening. Us colored won't go back to the cotton fields, not after Harlem and the Southside of Chicago. But how long's the war going to last? We want to be at the right place at the right time."

The talk of war and injustice depressed Benny. Forcing himself to think of more pleasant things, Benny was tempted to get Sarah and go on a picnic in Forest Park. They had done it often in the past three years, indulging themselves with a ride in an open auto. Equally exciting, if the house was empty, was an afternoon of lovemaking. The memories of those times were often more vivid than the reality, Benny thought as he visualized Sarah sitting at her dressing table pulling the tortoiseshell combs from her hair, streaked now with the gray that softened her still beautiful face. Remembering, he watched as her hair cascaded over her shoulders and hung midway down her back. She stood up and walked toward him, her long satin gown clinging to her firm breasts, hips, and thighs. When they touched, she wrapped her arms around his neck, their lips pressed together, their bodies melted into one as he pulled her to him. It felt good, the ease of her body on top of his. She moved rhythmically; her hair fell across her face, partially hiding the ecstasy that distorted her features. Benny's forehead was wet with perspiration.

"My God!"

"Mr. Monroe. Are you all right?"

"Oh, Willie! Yes. Of course," Benny said, stammering with embarrassment, shaking himself back to the present.

The days grew longer and hotter as summer entrenched itself in weary St. Louis. Despite the war fever, which was at its peak in 1917, nothing much had changed in Benny's life. Roy and Roberta had been graduated from the academy— Roy, summa cum laude—and Roberta sang the school song at the graduation ceremonies.

Roy's transition into the business world had been simple and quick. He kept the books for his father's many enterprises. Plans were made for Roberta to study music at Howard University. Sarah blanched when she remembered her mother insisting that she attend Morehouse College, but somehow, with her own daughter, it made sense for her to go to school.

"I think she'd be better off at Lincoln University in Jefferson City," Benny said, reluctant to send his daughter as far away as Washington, D.C., especially with a war on.

Roberta thought she'd be better off not going anyplace, preferring to get a singing job in one of the new Negro clubs.

Benny didn't argue with her; Benny didn't argue with anyone, but Roberta made sure her mother knew how she felt. Considering Roberta's youth and talent, Sarah wasn't dead set against a singing career for her daughter. But she did worry what the people at church might think.

Roy loved working at the Creole Club, and his eyes lit up when Benny strode in at noon, impeccably dressed in a white wool suit accented with a light blue tie.

Roy leaned back in his chair and eyed his father enviously, commenting that no matter how hot it was, Benny always looked cool.

"Well, my good man, that's because I let you and Willie do all my work. I'm here to decorate the office and check on how I'm doing financially."

"According to the books, you're a very rich man." Roy's voice was filled with pride, and he made no attempt to hide his admiration for his father. Even though they looked alike, Roy realized he lacked Benny's steely drive and determination. Maybe when I get older, he mused.

Roy spun the ledger around and pointed to the bottom figures. "Five thousand dollars. You netted that in one week at Dory's place."

Benny knew how much he netted from all his businesses, but he enjoyed listening to Roy.

"Either she's cut expenses to the bone or they're working day and night." Roy tapped his pencil on the desk. "One thing's for sure, she's honest. Every cent's accounted for."

"Dory goes back a long way," Benny said casually.

"She was a singer with the minstrel show, wasn't she?"

"Yes, son."

"How come you and Mama never talk about her?"

Benny's face darkened. "Oh, you know how it is, friends come and go."

"Does Mama know she's running the house?"

The bluntness of Roy's question startled Benny. He hesitated, wondering how much of the past he wanted to discuss. He cleared his throat. "I've been meaning to talk to Sarah about that, but the time never seems right. Your mother's life is different now. I don't think she'd understand. She thinks of Dory as an old friend. Thought I'd just leave it at that. She's just an old friend."

And silent lover, Roy thought. He shook his head. Not fair. Dory may love Papa, but to him she's just a business partner. It happens that way. Can't be helped.

Roy changed the subject. "Only the tenements in East St. Louis are losing money. Willie thinks you should sell. I agree. They'll never be worth anything. Population's moving away from the river, and after the war everything'll change. If you want to stay in real estate, pool your money, buy some land, and build bungalows and apartment houses."

Benny was astounded. He knew Roy and Willie loved to discuss ways of quadrupling his money, but he hadn't known how smart Roy was about business. My boy's going to be a millionaire someday. He smiled. Chip off the old block.

"You're right—you and Willie. Sometimes it's hard to know when to sell property. This could be the time. There's been some trouble in East St. Louis . . . trouble between blacks and whites. Might be a good idea to get out before they burn the place down."

Benny flipped through his desk calendar. He finally stopped and pointed to a date in bold red coloring. "I'll call Gus Redding. He's been wanting to buy my flats for years. I'll let him have 'em cheap just to get rid of 'em."

"Not too cheap," Roy quipped.

Benny looked at the calendar. "Today's the twenty-eighth. I can probably get over there Monday, July second. It'll be a relief to get that settled. On the Fourth your mother and I are off on a holiday . . . a well-deserved one, I might add. She's been working like the devil—one of her causes. This time it's the Negro Servicemen's Club. She and the ladies have done a great job."

"You better not forget Roberta if you're handing out compliments. She's at that Club every night, singing and dancing." Roy was grudgingly proud of his sister's extraordinary talents. "I think she'll be the only person in the world who'll be disappointed when this war ends."

"You're not going to wear your wool suit today! It's going up in the nineties. You'll boil." Sarah poured Benny another cup of coffee and sat down beside him at the breakfast table. Sometimes he astonished her. A wool suit in July . . .

"I have a business appointment. I'm selling the flats in East St. Louis." He scowled at the steaming cup of coffee. "This stuff's worse than the suit."

"No need to get snippy." Sarah paused. "You're not selling them because of me, are you? I mean, I know I've been ranting about the time you spend on business, but . . ."

Benny smiled. "I'd like to tell you I'm selling 'em because of you, but the truth is, they're losing money. Both Roy and Willie think I should get rid of 'em." Benny straightened his tie as he stepped onto the back porch. "I'll be home for dinner."

"Take care, you hear. I hear people's nerves are on edge out there these days." Sarah watched as Benny drove away, disappearing behind the hollyhocks. I wish Willie were going along, she thought, then shook her head to dispel her fears. I'm going daft reading about all the bloodshed in the world. It's a wonder anybody's sane.

Benny turned onto Olive Street and headed east through the downtown area. Automobiles wove in and out of the heavy traffic, honking their horns at the slower carriages and horse-drawn wagons—holdovers from a more leisurely era. Women dressed in long, slim skirts and lace-trimmed blouses held onto their hats as the trolley they rode picked up speed only to screech to a halt at the next intersection.

By the time Benny reached Missouri Avenue in East St. Louis, the heat and humidity were unbearable. The traffic fumes were making him nauseated and light-headed. He wished he had listened to Sarah and not worn his wool suit. Deciding to take off his jacket and loosen his shirt collar, Benny fumbled with his tie as he scanned street signs looking for State Street. When he finally found it, the street was empty. Where are the people? he wondered. It's mid-morning. There should be shopkeepers, office workers, street traffic. Benny slowed down. He sensed trouble; he smelled it. Three blocks away on the corner of State and St. Clair Avenue a gang of men wielding clubs and shotguns stood four abreast blocking the intersection. As he watched from the safety of his car, one of the men broke ranks and swung his club at a glass window, shattering it.

Benny was shocked. Was there a strike at the stockyards? He had heard about the violence associated with striking workers, but he had never imagined they could take over a city. Whatever it was, Benny knew he didn't want to get involved. Should he go forward or try to return to St. Louis? The appearance of two foot patrolmen made him decide to go on. Inching his car forward, he leaned his head out the window and, cupping his hand around his mouth, asked what was going on. Their cold stares bewildered him until he looked down at the curb and saw three Negroes lying behind a trash can less than ten feet from the officers. Their heads were smashed; blood still pumped from their wounds.

Benny jumped out of the car and ran to them. "For Christ's sake, help me." He pulled a handkerchief from his pocket, but when he knelt beside their inert bodies, Benny realized they were beyond help. Looking up, he saw the hatred in the policemen's faces. He stood up slowly and moved toward his car.

One of the policemen raised his nightstick and thrust it menacingly in Benny's face. "You better get out of here, nigger, if you know what's good for you. White folks in this city been killing every nigger bastard they can get their hands on. If I was you, I'd move my black ass as fast as I could."

The rabble at the corner watched the confrontation for several minutes, then, roaring like a rampaging pack of dogs, they loped toward Benny and the policemen. Their guttural chant filled the street. "Get a nigger. Get a nigger. Get a nigger." Benny watched, mesmerized. He couldn't escape. They were blocking the intersection.

Suddenly, to the north, a violent explosion ripped across

the city. Flames shot upward; billows of black smoke obliterated the scorching midday sun. As rioters fell to the ground in terror, Benny ran to his car. Throwing it in gear, with the engine banging and popping, he shot past them. He turned onto St. Clair Avenue and the carnage swelled. More broken bodies, dead horses, smoldering automobiles. It looks like a city under siege, Benny thought. His tear-stained face twitched as he passed the naked body of a black boy not more than ten years old. Bastards! Dirty, lousy bastards, he thought. Why? What the hell happened to cause this? Jesus Christ! I have to get out of here.

Benny turned down an alley, shooting past two young white men who were banging their clubs on trash cans. His only hope was to reach the Negro neighborhood.

The streets were deserted there, too. Pushing the car to its limit, Benny raced toward his flats. Turning left off the main thoroughfare, he chugged down a cluttered alley to a dilapidated shed. The door was off its hinges; there were holes where windows had once been. Benny jumped out of the car and pushed the remnants of the door across the splintered opening. Crouching low, he darted toward the flat.

"Open up in there." Identifying himself, he pounded on the door, then peered through a soot-covered window.

Two deep-set eyes ringed with fear peered out at him, then quickly disappeared. A bolt slid across metal; the door opened. An old man with a wrinkled face beckoned him inside. They embraced.

"How ya doing, Charlie?" Benny said to the old-timer who did odd jobs for him in return for a basement room where he had a cot, a stove, a table, and a few chairs. "Looks like we're in a fine mess, eh? What the hell's going on?"

Charlie led Benny down the rickety stairs to the cellar. "We's havin' us a race riot, and we's right smack in the center of it." Charlie shook his head in dismay.

A single candle barely lit the gloomy basement, but Benny spotted a young woman cowering in a corner. Two little girls were lying on a soiled quilt beside her.

"That's my sister's girl, Martha, and her two, Bess and

Ruthie." They had all been in hiding since the previous night. "There be a shooting. Six whites was killed by a gang of colored. Feelin's been running hot in this town. Blacks is accused of takin' jobs from whites. Or if there be a strike, the bossman hire colored to fill in. With the coloreds moving up from the South, der's plenty competition for the jobs."

"But why didn't I hear about it? For Christ's sake, I live just across the river."

Charlie shrugged. "It be bad since last night. 'Fore that, seems like it was being handled."

Martha sat up and wiped the tears from her eyes. "I got caught last evenin'. Me and my girls was on a streetcar when this bunch of white men ran in front. We stopped and they let the conductor run away, then they rocked the car from side to side, broke the windows and climbed in. They cut their own hands and arms, but didn't bother 'em. I saw 'em grab an old woman and beat her face with a club. Poor thing was screaming . . . I grabbed my two and pushed open the front door. Two white women was yelling, 'Get the black bitch. Kill them little niggers.' I was so scared, I shoved my fist out. Hit one of 'em in the nose. We ran like we never ran before. Finally got here. Been hiding ever since."

Benny gripped Martha's hand. "The police'll round 'em up 'fore dark. It's just a few crazy people who hate Negroes. We'll wait here till things calm down a bit."

For the rest of the afternoon they burrowed themselves in the basement, feeling relatively secure and comfortable. Charlie shared a pint of whiskey. Sarah'll be madder'n hell when she sees my suit, Benny thought ruefully when he bothered to look at the blotches of oil, dirt, and blood staining the fine white fabric.

The whiskey made everyone sleepy and they dozed fitfully. Benny felt intimidated by the ominous quiet. There were no sounds of traffic from outside, no mothers calling for their children, only an apprehensive hush.

At dusk, close to eight thirty, a loud wail broke the silence. Benny's eyes flew open. The sounds of rushing feet and screams were followed by the howl of human voices. Benny grabbed a wooden box and, craning his neck, looked out the basement window. A crowd of white men had surrounded a four-family flat across the street. Standing shoulder to shoulder, they blocked the front of the building, and a half dozen wild-eyed adolescents threw flaming torches through the broken windows. The dried wood caught flame instantly. When the fire reached the second story and fanned out across the roof, the tenants scurried out the front door. Women clutched their children to their breasts while the men wielded makeshift clubs. They ran straight into the denim-clad ruffians who grabbed the black women by their hair and beat them with iron pipes. Felled, heads were split open; limbs were torn from quivering bodies. Making a game of it, the men locked arms, encircled their prey, and knocked them to the ground where they stomped on them until all that remained was a pulverized mass of flesh and blood.

Benny fell backward in revulsion and loathing. He grabbed a chair and slammed it against the wall. The crash of splintering wood frightened Bess and Ruthie, who screamed in terror. Salvaging two legs, Benny held them like mallets and headed toward the stairs. "I'll kill at least one of those bastards before I go down."

Charlie grasped Benny's arm, begging Benny not to do anything foolish. "Ain't no time to be a hero. We needs you to get us out of here. They be burning this place next. Least ways we can try to save the little ones."

Tears of anger and frustration rolled down Benny's cheeks. "Our only hope is to get to the bridge—over to St. Louis. There is no one in this city who'll help us."

"It's five miles to the river," Martha said. "We'll never make it."

"Oh, yes we will," Benny said with iron determination. "I'll stake my life on it."

Single file, they crept out of the house and crossed the moonlit yard. Hugging the weather-beaten side of the shack that housed the automobile, they waited until Benny checked the alley. There was no one in sight. Terror almost immobilized them as the roar of the mob and the cries of its victims filled the hot night air.

Martha tugged at Benny's sleeve. "Let's take the car."

Benny shook his head. "Too risky. Makes too much noise. Attracts too much attention. We're better off on foot. If one of us gets caught, the others can get away."

Martha nodded and Benny took the lead. They snaked down the alley, staying in the shadows. When a dog barked, they stood statuesque and waited. When no one appeared, they moved on.

One block, five blocks, sixteen blocks. They had covered a mile without incident.

The seventeenth block posed a threat. Garbage pails, beer casks, and whiskey bottles littered the ground in back of a tavern. Inside a dozen men lolled around rough wooden tables. Benny squeezed through piles of rubbish to get a better view. As he stepped over a rotting mass of fish heads, a trash can crashed to the ground. Benny stiffened. He held his breath when he heard a screen door open and feet pad across the dirt-packed yard.

"Who's there? Who's making that noise?"

The air rushed out of Benny's lungs when he saw a terrified boy squinting into the darkness. After a cursory glance, the boy hurried back inside.

How in the hell did I get myself in this mess? Benny wondered, dropping his head in relief. He thought of his flats, and a bitter smile crossed his face. Won't be anything to sell after tonight.

The group pushed on. They covered two more miles before they stopped to rest, collapsing under a clump of spiny bushes.

"We've been going at it pretty hard," Benny said. "How you feeling?"

"I like it better when we move." Martha gulped air into her constricted lungs. "But I can see the girls need a rest."

"We don't have much farther to go." Benny glanced to the northwest where flames and smoke rose from the area around the stockyards. The closer they got to the river, he reasoned, the more dangerous it became. Benny tied his handkerchief around his forehead to keep the perspiration from running down into his eyes. He motioned for the others to do likewise.

When they reached State Street and Collinsville Avenue, they flattened themselves against a building while Benny studied the scene. Dozens of men loitered on State Street, some around a fire, its flames flickering from a metal can, some holding kerosene-soaked torches whose light created gigantic shadows on the buildings. Corpses lay in the street.

Faceless men pressed around a keg of beer, holding tin cups under the spigot as the last of the brew trickled out. When it was empty, a man kicked the wooden cask, then stared at it as though waiting for it to refill.

An approaching streetcar attracted everyone's attention. "Maybe we can use it as a shield to get across the intersection," Benny whispered.

Before they could move, the mob, jolted out of its lethargy, attacked the streetcar. A Negro woman was dragged to the street where they beat her and, in a final act of bestiality, gouged out her eyes with bits of glass. A black man was shot in the face. All the while, half a block away, five Illinois militiamen watched impassively.

Martha was crying hysterically. "I ain't going out there. I'd rather put my girls in a garbage can than let them animals get their hands on 'em."

Benny's spirits sagged. They had gone so far. Was it all going to end just blocks from the bridge, from freedom? He told Martha to get hold of herself. Martha whimpered, but nodded her head. They retreated to an alley where they were to wait until Benny signaled that it was safe to follow. They were to come immediately. The charged atmosphere could change in half a minute. They squeezed hands for luck, then Benny, hugging the buildings, moved to the corner. The mob was toying with the blacks they had caught on the streetcar. No one noticed as Benny hurried across the street. Jumping behind a stack of packing crates, Benny signaled with his handkerchief up and down. He waited. No one appeared. He signaled again. Damn, he thought. Martha's panicked. Benny girded himself to go back and get them.

Cautiously he peered around the corner of the building. He would have to hurry. The mob was losing interest in its bloody amusement. Staring across the street, he tried to see Charlie or Martha. Nothing. No silhouettes, no movement, nothing. He had to find out what had happened.

Bending over, Benny had barely reached the curb when one of the rioters shouted, "There's one. Get 'im."

Benny froze as fifty eyes turned in his direction. Seconds later the rabble was moving toward him. Without hesitating, Benny spun around and spurted down the street. Rats scurried out of his way as he knocked over trash cans. His lithe muscles stretched like rubber bands as his long legs hurtled him forward, his heart pumping furiously as he gasped for air. After he ran a block, only two men were still trying to catch him, and they were losing ground. Benny emerged at an intersection and was about to cross when he felt his knees buckle under him. His body crashed forward, his head hitting the curb. He couldn't move. A blinding thud echoed within his skull. As he threw up his hands to protect himself, a loud, piercing scream escaped his lips. He rolled from side to side in agony. Benny knew he had his eyes open, but he couldn't see anything—a warm trickle of blood coated them. A booted foot smashed into his groin, then pushed him onto his back. Wiping the blood from one eye, Benny saw the blurred image of a policeman standing over him.

"Nigger! You shouldn't be running down no dark streets this time of night. White folks trying to keep crime down, and what do we find but a nigger boy running like the devil's after him. Seems to me niggers don't run less they's causing trouble."

"There he is. Policeman got 'im." A swarm of dirty riffraff surrounded Benny's body. "Look at that head spurtin' blood. Them darkies bleed more'n stuck pigs."

Benny couldn't defend himself. Pointed sticks jabbed at his testicles; a club smashed the side of his face. As he slipped into unconsciousness, Benny's hands dropped from his face; the pain subsided. He was lying in the grass in front of his home. Sarah was running to him, smiling and calling his name. He tried to warn her to stay away, but he couldn't speak. Closer and closer she came, her long white gown floating lazily around her beautiful slim body. As he tried to lift himself up to tell her to stop, the pain returned. In the distance he heard someone shout, "He ain't dead yet. Let's hang him . . . there . . . on the lamppost." Hands grabbed his ravaged head. Flailing his arms, Benny screamed.

"I got him." Sticking his hand into Benny's gaping wound, a man pulled the body upright. When he withdrew his fingers from Benny's skull, pieces of brain oozed from his filthy, blood-caked fist. The mob tied a rope around Benny's neck, then, throwing the other end over a lamppost, hoisted his mangled body several feet above the ground. The body swung limply in the hot summer night, and was beaten until it was a mass of blood. Finally exhausted, the mob gave the body one last kick before slowly trudging away, the light from their torches silhouetting Benny's swinging body onto the dark, deserted street.

Minutes after the mob departed, an old man stepped from an alley, tears streaming down his face. He took a broken knife from his pocket and cut the rope, gently easing Benny's body onto the street. Charlie wrapped his shirt around Benny and dragged him into an alley where he hid him behind two garbage cans. Wasting no time, he pulled Martha and the girls from a doorway and told them to hurry. Running and weeping, they cut across the railroad yards, and half an hour later, they crossed the Eads Bridge to safety.

CHAPTER XVIII

"Willie! Willie Jackson! Can you come here a minute?"

Willie strode into Roy's elaborate office, which was all brass and wood. A phonograph played a Mamie Smith record. Roy looked up from his books.

"You sound just like your dad," Willie said wistfully. "Many's a time he called me in his office just like that."

"I know . . . I was thinking about him." Roy looked at the calendar on his desk. "January, 1921. It's been three and a half years and I still can't forget."

"None of us can."

"He'd be surprised at how quickly I learned the saloon business." Roy's tone lightened. "Opening up my own tavern tonight. Whoever would've thought . . .?"

"Some tavern." Willie glanced around. "The Savoy is the fanciest black club in the city. You'll make a fortune."

"*We'll* make a fortune." Roy corrected him. "You're my partner, remember? Couldn't have done this without you."

"We work good together," Willie said matter-of-factly. "You're a chip off the old block, as they say."

Roy shook his head. "Mama will never get over his death. She and Tallulah have séances every night trying to talk to him." Roy sighed, remembering how upset Sarah used to be when Tallulah practiced her "witchcraft." Now Sarah practiced it too. At least she didn't cry all the time.

Roy pointed to the books lying on his desk. "Why didn't you tell me how much it cost to buy illegal liquor?"

Willie laughed. "Everything illegal is expensive—liquor, women, guns—"

"I'm only interested in the liquor. Who's our contact?"

"A little Italian name of Tony Gianino. But you leave him to me. I'll handle the man."

"Since when do you have to 'handle' a man just to buy liquor?"

"Since 'the people' decided they didn't want alcoholic beverages sold in this country. Since the passage of the Eighteenth Amendment. Since—"

"All right! All right! I got the point." Roy laughed. "Do we have enough for tonight? I'm expecting a big crowd—I don't want anything to go wrong."

The two men checked the club one last time, Roy making mental notes as they passed from room to room: linen tablecloths, spotless; lighting for the bandstand, in place; food, plentiful and fresh; liquor, enough to float a battleship.

"And Sid has the reservation list in order?" Roy asked.

"Sid Cox has everything in order. A bouncer like him— used to work in New Orleans's old Storyville section—he isn't likely to overlook anything. He's seen it all in that red-light district."

"Don't use the word 'bouncer' at the Savoy," Roy said lightly. "Here he's a maître-d', and he better be as good as you claim. Drunken brawls'll close a club faster'n an outbreak of syphilis."

Satisfied, they had just returned to Roy's office when JoJo, a slight, mousy boy of fifteen, knocked on the door.

Sheepishly, he handed Roy a folded piece of paper. "A lady give me this. Say to give it to you. It very important."

Roy tipped the boy a nickel and dismissed him. A frown creased his face and he crumpled the paper and threw it across the room.

"That bitch! I'll bust her ass for this. Polly can't sing tonight," Roy shouted. "We're five hours from show time and she tells us she's quitting. Who in the hell does she think she is?"

"A tart. An inexperienced, untalented tart who doesn't seem to be bothered about ruining the show."

"What the hell are we going to do?" Roy asked in despair.

Before Willie could answer, the door opened, and a young woman dressed in a short, low-cut white satin dress stepped inside. "I'll tell you what you're going to do—you're going to hire me," she said, pursing her lips seductively.

"Roberta!" Roy moaned.

"That's my name."

"What the hell you doing here?"

"I'm offering my services for the night. I heard the bad news about Polly—but then, I wouldn't worry too much about her. She was a terrible singer."

"Just get out! You can't work here."

"Take it easy, man." Willie stepped between Roy and Roberta. "Let's listen to her. If we can't get Polly back, Roberta might be our only choice."

"I'm glad someone around here knows what he's talking about." Roberta smiled sweetly at Willie. She frowned when she spoke to her brother. "Don't think Polly's coming back. She's on her way to Kansas City. She would have ruined your opening. I told her if she wasn't on the first train out of St. Louis this evening, I'd see to it that she never sang around here again."

"You did what?" Roy's eyes bulged.

Roberta sat down in Roy's leather desk chair. "You know I can sing rings around Polly. I'm the best blues singer in town."

"But I don't want you here. Papa would never have allowed it."

"Papa's dead."

"Christ! I don't believe you—"

"Well, you better believe I want this job."

Before Roy could reply, Willie pulled him aside. "You two been at each other's throat long enough. Don't you think it's time to bury the hatchet?"

"I've tried."

"Well, try harder."

Grudgingly, Roy turned and faced his smug, self-satisfied sister. "Okay. But just for tonight. Tomorrow I'll find a replacement for Polly."

"Thanks, sweets." Roberta jumped out of the chair,

grinning. "You won't be sorry. I'll give your audience the best performance of my life."

"And you'll get paid half what I was paying Polly."

"That's not fair."

"Yes, it is. Polly had experience—you don't."

Roberta shrugged. "When I get a following, you'll have to pay me double what you paid that broad."

"You work tonight, and that's all!"

"We'll see." Roberta sauntered toward the door. "By the way, my stage name is going to be Bobbie Evans. Be sure the posters spell it right—B,O,B,B,I,E. So long, sweets." The door slammed behind her.

Bobbie barely made it to the end of the hall before her veneer cracked. Her ruse had worked, but she took little joy in it. He should have asked me first, she thought—he knows I've always wanted to be a singer. When we were kids, I'd dress up in Mama's old gowns and pretend I was Ma Rainey. Roy promised that if he ever took over Papa's club, he'd hire me. I'd be the star, he used to say. Ha! Some promise. He opened his own club and wouldn't even let me audition.

Tears rolled down Bobbie's cheeks as she headed for the dressing room. She felt like a spider caught in a web, spun by her parents and her brother.

"You're only twenty," Roy had said.

"Get your education, first," Sarah had said. "Papa didn't want you to be in show business."

It wasn't her fault she wanted to sing—all her life she had been surrounded by people in show business.

Benny's death had destroyed their lives. They weren't a family anymore. Bobbie, Roy, Sarah—they were all caught in a nightmarish loneliness. With Benny's death, Roy had become the rooster; he crowed, strutted, and spread his wings, domineering, callously indifferent to Sarah's and Bobbie's pain.

Bobbie's face hardened. She picked up a powder puff and dabbed at her nose and red-rimmed eyes. Guess I showed him, she thought. He's not going to run my life. Never again.

Bobbie's whirlwind performance had left Willie bewildered. "I don't ever remember her being so obnoxious."

Roy's anger had dissipated. He sat in the chair vacated by his sister and lit a cigar. "Sometimes I hate her. Other times I ignore her. There's not a lot of love lost between us, but I admire her determination. She gets what she wants. In that sense, she's a lot like Papa."

"I know she can sing, but can she sing well enough for the Savoy? I'm only concerned about tonight. How you two feel about each other is your own business."

"She can sing better than anyone I know. She has talent. Only her personality stinks." Roy spoke softly, almost wistfully. "She'll put on a great show. When she's in front of an audience, she's a star. I'm not worried about tonight. It's tomorrow and the next day . . ."

The opening night crowd at the Savoy glittered. The women, in brilliant short silk dresses, were wrapped in fur stoles, and encrusted with diamonds. The men resembled an army of penguins. Black and white faces huddled over tiny tables each illuminated by a single candle. Everyone had come to hear blues and jazz—new music, Negro music—which was just being discovered. Everyone wanted to drink the illegal liquor and tease the scantily clad dancers whose skin tones varied from ebony to coffee-and-cream.

Roberta pranced back and forth in her small dressing room, which, she had complained, looked like a doghouse and smelled worse. Roy had left the details of her musical debut to Chuck Jones, the band leader, who had grumbled, "Polly wasn't great, but at least she knew how to perform. Roberta's never even stood in front of a band before."

"Not Roberta," Roy had corrected him, "Bobbie."

"Bobbie, Roberta. Shit! What the hell difference does it make if she folds in one night?"

Roy had thrown up his hands and walked away.

Bobbie sulked at her image in the chipped mirror. She didn't notice the band leader until he tapped her shoulder.

Bobbie jumped. "Don't you believe in knocking before you enter a girl's room?" She turned to face him.

"The door was open."

Bobbie leaned against the dressing table and stared at the man who was smiling at her. He held a lit cigarette in his right hand. Only his left hand, jiggling coins in his trouser pocket, betrayed his nervousness. She smiled back, responding to the magnetism in his brown eyes.

"I hear you're my new girl."

"Hope you don't mind." Bobbie tried to sound sophisticated.

"Not if you can sing."

"I can sing—better than Polly if that's what you're worried about."

"A good singing voice isn't all that's important." Chuck flicked his ashes on the bare wooden floor. "You got to have stage presence . . . lots of oomph."

With one step, Bobbie was inches away from Chuck. He smelled like Scotch and tobacco. Square face with strong male features—firm jaw, small, well-formed lips, bright, clear eyes above straight, square shoulders, and slim hips.

Bobbie felt woefully inadequate in the arena where men and women sparred. Her only contact with members of the opposite sex had been with schoolboys. They croaked and moved their lips as though nibbling for the bait when a girl walked by, but were blissfully ignorant of the line attached to the bait. Bobbie sensed Chuck's interest in her, but was unable to determine whether it was personal or professional.

"When I sing, I have loads of oomph."

"I'll give you the benefit of the doubt, but I'd like to hear you sing before the show."

"Anything you say." Bobbie smiled, then turned and closed her eyes. When she faced him again, she was transformed into a sultry blues singer. In a low, seductive voice, she sang "Fogyism," about a woman who lost her man. She was oblivious to her altered surroundings, so enmeshed in her performance that she could have been singing at the Met.

Chuck raised his eyebrows in surprise. "You *are* better than Polly. Why didn't Roy hire you?"

"Because he hates me."

"I think it'd be hard to hate you."

"Thanks." Bobbie dropped her seductive pose. "Maybe I ask for it sometimes. We fight a lot."

"Really?"

"It's not always my fault. Ever since Papa died, Roy's been telling me what to do. 'Stay home.' 'Take care of Mama.' I feel like I'm buried alive."

"Sorry to hear that, kid, but you know, we all got problems."

"Some more'n others." So, he was callous too. Men! "Oh, I don't know why I'm telling you all this. It's got nothing to do with you." Bobbie chewed on the tip of her thumbnail. "It was the way Papa died. That's what we can't bear to think about."

"I knew Benny. Sure was sad."

"Everybody knew him."

Chuck glanced at the gold watch prominently displayed on his left wrist. "Got to go, Miss Evans. There's a lot to do before show time."

"Yeah." Bobbie leaned against the back of the chaise longue piled high with costumes and sequined accessories. "Maybe we can talk later. After the show."

"Sure. After the show."

Bobbie's shoulders slumped after Chuck left. She felt exposed, foolish, yet talking to Chuck had made her feel lighter somehow. It was not in her nature to trust anyone, yet she had chipped a tiny hole in her shell, let a stranger peek inside. It was both intoxicating and frightening.

Spreading a layer of grease paint over her face, Bobbie circled her eyes with black eyeliner, painted her cheeks with bright red rouge. A matching red lip gloss was the finishing touch. She felt sophisticated and grown-up, but when JoJo rapped on the door and yelled, "Show time," Bobbie downed a shot of brandy to quell the butterflies in her stomach.

Hurrying to the wings, she waited the prescribed ten seconds after Chuck's introduction, then swept across the floor to the bandstand. The houselights dimmed, and she was enveloped in the glare of a spotlight that transformed her sequined, knee-length red dress into a sparkling firecracker. Bobbie's voice exploded across the room as she launched into her favorite, "St. Louis Blues."

The familiar strains caught the crowd's attention, and they listened, enraptured with her music, enchanted with her charm. Bobbie wailed, she growled, she was seductive, she was lonely—she was that "St. Louie woman," and the people loved her. The normally sedate supper-club crowd gave her a thunderous ovation. Bobbie threw kisses, bowed, then ran offstage.

Roy was in the wings. Sheepishly he congratulated her, then he excused himself, mumbling something about spoiled liver pâté.

With only twenty minutes between numbers, Bobbie hurried to her dressing room to change. She was ecstatic. I showed them, she thought as she unzipped her dress. She started as a figure emerged from the shadows.

"Mama! What in the world?"

Sarah smiled sadly. "I just had to see my baby sing. I wouldn't've missed your opening for anything."

"But how did you know?"

"I heard you talk over the phone. You children don't think I know anything, but I do."

"Mama, I would have asked you to come, but I didn't think—I mean, you haven't been out of the house since . . . since Papa died."

"But for an occasion like this . . ." Sarah sat on the chaise longue and twisted her fingers around her handbag.

Bobbie looked around. "Where's Tallulah?"

"Tallulah didn't come. Did you expect her?"

"You mean you came alone? How did you get here?"

"I took a taxi."

"Oh, Mama . . ."

"It was fun. And I'm not an invalid. Anyway, I didn't know if Tallulah'd let me come, and I didn't want to take the chance." Her smile blossomed. "You were wonderful, dear. I remember when I sang with the Happy Coons. I thought I was the best singer in the world. Not bragging, but I was good. Still, you're better."

Bobbie took Sarah's hands. "People still talk about how beautiful you sang and how beautiful you looked. I'll never be as good as you."

"I'm sure you would be, dear, but unfortunately, we'll never know. You have to come home. It was fun. You had your debut, but it's over now. We're expecting you—"

"What are you talking about, Mama? Home? I've only performed once. I have three more shows."

"No, dear." Sarah was adamant. "Papa said you could sing one song, but that's all. He doesn't want you to be in show business."

"Papa's dead. We don't know how he'd feel, Mama."

"I know. I talk to him. He tells me what he wants us to do."

"That's impossible." Bobbie panicked as she realized her mother was serious. "You can't talk to him. You just think—"

Sarah clutched Bobbie's hand and sobbed. "I can't blame you for not believing, but Tallulah reached him. We had a séance. I didn't believe it at first either, but Benny and I talk every day now. I don't even need Tallulah."

"Mama, Mama." Bobbie's eyes, too, filled with tears. She glanced at the clock on the dressing table. She had less than ten minutes before the next show. She ran to the door and asked a dancer waiting in the wings to get Roy. He rushed in expecting the worst.

"Mama wants me to go home with her. She's been talking to Papa, and she wants me to go home and just stay buried there until I die."

"Take it easy." The furrows deepened on Roy's forehead. He turned to Sarah. "I know Papa wanted Bobbie to go to college, but things have changed. You heard her. You know how good she can sing."

"I've known that since she was five years old. She used to dress up in my old costumes and prance around her room singin' her heart out. What a sight she was. Maybe I should have stopped her then. But Benny's right. Roberta must give it up. I did. It hurt for a while, but I wouldn't trade you children for a million shows. As soon as Benny comes home, we'll all be happy."

Roy put his hand under his mother's arm and gently pulled her to her feet. "I'll take you home now, Mama. It's getting late."

"But Roberta—"

"Roberta'll be along." Roy glared at his sister. "Isn't that right, Roberta?"

Bobbie clasped Sarah in her arms and gave her a kiss. "Yes, Mama. I'll be along shortly."

Sarah clung to Roy as he led her down the dark corridor. As they stepped outside she hesitated. "Have I done what I came here for? Sometimes my mind gets so fuzzy."

"Don't you worry about a thing." Roy urged her on. "Soon you'll be home, and Tallulah will put you to bed. It's late."

Sarah nodded. "If I forgot anything, I'll ask Tallulah. She never forgets."

Bobbie's hands were shaking as she applied fresh makeup to her tear-stained face. Zipping up her costume as she ran to the stage, she pasted a smile on her face just as Chuck introduced her. The welcoming applause helped her get through her first song, and the crowd's enthusiasm helped her through the second. But when she finished her act, she hurried offstage, unable to keep the tears from flowing.

"You really do have family problems," Chuck said as he sauntered into her dressing room. "What was that all about?"

Bobbie looked up at him coldly for his unwelcome familiarity. "What was what all about?"

"Your mother. JoJo told me about her visit."

"My mother's visit is no concern of yours."

"Hey! I'm sorry. You're right. It's none of my business." Chuck stuck a cigarette in his mouth and turned to leave.

"No. Wait."

Chuck stopped and stared at her in silence.

"Mama's been sick."

When Chuck didn't respond, Bobbie continued, "This is the first time she's left the house since Papa died. I wish I could help her. I tried. I thought if she talked about it . . . but she wouldn't say anything. She acted as if nothing had happened, as if Papa had just gone away. I don't think she even knows what year it is anymore."

"Do you?"

Bobbie looked at Chuck in astonishment. "Of course I know what year it is. It's 1921. Do you think I'm crazy too?"

"Is your mother crazy?"

"I don't know. I don't want to talk about it."

Chuck nodded, then picked up the brandy bottle, and half filled two glasses. He sat beside her on a stool and watched as she sipped the drink.

"You got a lot of things you're carrying around."

Bobbie pressed her hand against his face, as though by touching she could discover the nature of the man. Did he really care?

"What things?" she asked softly, as though fearful of treading in uncharted waters.

"Guilt, fear, love. Hate, too."

"No. Not hate. But the others, yes. Especially guilt. I hate the guilt. How do you know what I feel?"

"It's written all over you. The way you walk. The way you talk. The way you look at Roy—and me."

"You?"

Chuck nodded his head. His stare mesmerized her. It was terrifying. He leaned over and kissed her. Only their lips touched.

Too soon, Bobbie thought. We've just met.

Chuck stood up and folded his arms around her. A wonderfully warm feeling swept over her. She felt the hunger of desire and the thrill of being desired. In that brief moment before Chuck pulled away, Bobbie fell in love.

He wants me, she thought. "What happens now?"

"Tomorrow night. After the show. We'll take in an

after-hours jam session. Musicians don't go home till dawn."

Too easy. I'm making it too easy for him. Bobbie nodded. "Tomorrow night."

"Will it be okay with Roy?"

"I don't intend to ask him."

"Your mother?"

"I'll handle Mama."

Chuck stepped away. He opened a gold case and took out a cigarette.

"I don't know if anyone's ever told you, but you have real talent. In a few years you might want to try your luck in Chicago or New York."

"I don't want to wait a few years."

Chuck shrugged, lit his cigarette, and walked out of the room.

For two weeks Chuck and Bobbie made the rounds of the after-hours clubs. Sometimes Chuck sat in on a jam session while Bobbie, along with the wives and girlfriends of the other musicians, sat around a large table cluttered with bottles of beer, whiskey, and soda. Music was clearly a physical craving with the men—women, liquor, and drugs all mattered less to them. They were possessed by some inner drive that only their music could release.

When Chuck made love to her, to Bobbie it seemed more like a duty than a need. Bobbie tried to understand, but this dutiful lovemaking, rather than comforting, left her dazed and depressed. Although their bodies touched, Chuck's thoughts drifted into chasms too deep for her to plumb. The more she pushed, the further he withdrew. One night, unable to bear his silence after lovemaking, Bobbie rolled on her side and touched him.

"I love you, Chuck. You've taught me so much. You've taught me how to love. But sometimes I wonder if it isn't a one-sided deal. Do you love me?"

When he spoke, his voice was that of a stranger. "I'm leaving." He closed his eyes.

Bobbie's heart fluttered. "Leaving! But why?"

"I'm going to Chicago. I'm ready for Chicago. I have to go."

"Do you have a job?"

"No, but I have to go. I have to find out if I'm any good."

"But you are good. You have a huge following right here in St. Louis. Why give it up for nothing? How will you live?"

Chuck didn't answer. Bobbie laid her head on his chest and cried. He didn't touch her or try to comfort her. She had to try to make him understand how much she loved him.

"Take me along. I want to go with you. Please."

"I can't be tied down. A woman would just tie me down."

"No. I'll work. You said I have talent."

"You don't have enough experience. Maybe later."

Chuck's words gave Bobbie a glimmer of hope. "Can I join you in a couple of months?"

"We'll see."

Bobbie watched the sun peep through the partially opened window. The rays crept across the dull gray carpet, then hesitated, touching the side of her face. But it failed to warm her. Chuck had become a stranger to her. He was still staring at the ceiling when she dressed and walked out the door.

CHAPTER XIX

Roy celebrated his birthday in April, 1925, by hosting a grand party at the Savoy. "How many times do you get to be twenty-five?" he asked Willie. In reality, he intended to use the party as an excuse to invite bankers, politicians, and entertainers—to consolidate his influence. He felt that his life, so meticulously planned and organized for five years, was falling apart—not because he was a failure, but because he was a success.

Like an Oriental potentate, Roy surveyed his domain every night from a corner stool at the bar. Dancers and musicians, mayors and aldermen, coquettes and adultresses sauntered by, all wanting to be seen with the fabulously rich, handsome owner of the hottest club in the city. Whites and blacks alike came to swing their feet to the Charleston and watch the floor show where girls with bare bottoms under short, swirling skirts swung to the latest dance craze, the Black Bottom. Roy's gambling operation was flourishing, and although he feigned little interest in Dory's prostitutes, he maintained the house in deference to the aging madame who still kept a watchful eye on the expanding profits.

Roy was afraid of Tony Gianino. He wouldn't admit it to Willie and certainly not to himself, but the Sicilian boss who supplied his clubs with illegal liquor was boasting that he intended to take over the Savoy.

"We'll invite Gianino to my birthday party," Roy had said when Willie told him the rumors. "I'd like to get a feel for the man, see if he's really as mean a bastard as they say."

Willie frowned. "That's like inviting the lion into the den. So far, it's just talk about him wanting to take over the Savoy. If he comes here and likes what he sees . . ."

"I want him to come here and dislike what he sees."

"Come again? He knows you gross thousands every week. The club is famous for its drinks, food, and women. How do you intend to get him off your back?"

Roy's confidence plunged. "I haven't worked that out yet."

Willie headed toward the door. "Let me know when the revelation strikes. In the meantime, I'm interviewing a new dancer. Delta Starr. How do you like that handle? Snazzy, eh?"

"Does she look as good as she sounds?"

"I'll let you know."

Unable to concentrate Roy decided to sit in on Delta

Starr's audition. When he saw the long-legged dancer dressed in a transparent-mesh body stocking complete with strategically placed sequins and feathers, he knew Willie had a new performer.

Two days before Roy's party Willie burst into the office, list in hand.

"Everybody's coming—the police commissioner, three aldermen, Sol Weiss, the biggest real estate broker in town. Slim Hacket, you know him, numbers racket. Mable Smith, bordellos. And Tony Gianino's coming too." Willie didn't know if he should laugh or cry. "Rumor has it he's going to make you an offer."

"Rumor! Rumor! What the hell's all this talk about rumors? Can't you tell me straight?"

Nervously dallying with a sterling silver letter opener, Willie said, "Gianino wants it all. Not just an increase in his liquor bill or upping the ante for protection. That little dago is out to get your businesses. Oh, he'll let you run 'em because he's superstitious about associating with us colored folks, but he wants full ownership. He'll throw you a few crumbs for your trouble."

"But how can I fight him?" Roy's face was lined with worry.

They discussed the possibilities. Force or even the threat of force was absurd. Willie ruled out a compromise; Roy refused to leave town. They puffed on their cigarettes; they poured each other shots of bourbon. An hour later they were drunk but nowhere near a solution until Willie jumped out of his chair with a whooping cheer.

"I got it. It's so simple. Why didn't I think of it before?"

"What? What?" Roy hoped Willie would stop jumping up and down. He was getting a headache.

"I just mentioned that Gianino was superstitious. That's how we're going to get him. Those dagos won't get out of bed without crossing themselves."

"What are we going to do, pray to God that he gets run over by a black cat?"

"Yes, a black cat and two women and a rat's tail."

Roy sneered. "Sounds like voodoo to me."

"Exactly." Willie was grinning from ear to ear. "Everyone thinks we Negroes dabble in voodoo—we are from the Dark Continent, you know. And Catholics have a ritual for exorcising evil spirits, so Gianino must believe in 'em, too."

"Your logic is appalling," Roy said with disgust. "This is the twentieth century, not the thirteenth. And even if he does believe in all that hocus-pocus, what's that to us?"

"We're going to put a curse on him. We'll make him think that if he so much as lays a hand on you, he's dead."

Roy roared with laughter. "I'm supposed to tell Gianino —with a straight face—that I put a curse on him, and he better leave me alone? You're full of shit. You really are."

"No. You don't *tell* him. *Show* him." Excited now, he pranced back and forth in front of Roy's desk, slipping his hands in and out of his pockets. "We'll set up some kind of séance. We'll need two women—one to do all the magic stuff, the other to put the curse on Gianino. We'll need a few voodoo props, maybe a doll dressed like that little dago. I'll snatch a few gray hairs from somebody and tell him they're his. We'll have a fire and—"

"Hold it. You're crazy. I don't believe in voodoo or witchcraft, but I don't want to mess around with it, just in case." He paused thoughtfully. "And even if we wanted to, who would we get? I don't know any witch doctors."

"But you know a priestess."

Roy didn't answer. His face went slack, and he shook his head. When Willie started to argue, he cut him off.

Willie persisted. "Who's to hurt? Sarah would love to help. She hates people like Gianino. She hates anybody who takes advantage of someone's weaknesses. Look what they did to Benny—"

"Gianino didn't kill Papa."

"No, but he's out to get you, and if it means killing you, he'll do it."

At last Roy agreed to talk to Tallulah. But he insisted that Bobbie not be told until it was over.

* * *

Sarah laughed gleefully when she heard the plan; Tallulah drew back, her face dark, like the sky before a storm.

"It be too dangerous. Pretending like you're in cahoots with the devil. It be unholy . . . voodoo unleashes forces best left alone. Calling on Satan to do evil things, that be harming the missus. Don't want that."

"How can it harm?" Sarah asked, pouting. "I want to help. I want to scare those white devils. They killed my Benny. They're not going to get my boy. Won't let'em."

Tallulah finally agreed, if only to placate Sarah. "Well, maybe . . . if it be for a good cause," she said sullenly. "This ain't no make-believe. It be the real thing. When we curse that man, he be cursed."

Roy nodded sympathetically, then told them they had to have their act letter-perfect in two days. Tallulah moaned. Sarah squealed with delight.

Storm clouds moved across the city the night of the party. Roy stood in front of the full-length mirror in his office and wrestled with his black bow tie. He felt the pressure of the next few hours already rising inside, as ominous as thunder. After six attempts at his tie, he threw it on the floor just as Bobbie, stunning in a shimmering black gown, strutted in. Sharing the small mirror with Roy, she adjusted her sequined headband, which was festooned with ostrich plumes.

"Tch, Tch!" she said in a sugary voice. "You're in a lousy mood for your twenty-fifth birthday."

"What the hell do you want?"

"I wanted to wish you a happy birthday, but my timing seems to be off. I'll come back later when your fangs recede."

Roy's face softened, and he leaned down and kissed his sister. "Happy birthday to you, too." Turning back to the mirror, he stared at himself in exasperation. "How do I look? I look like I'm wearing a rented tux two sizes too big. Damn! I told that idiot tailor the sleeves were too long, and that tie is driving me nuts."

Bobbie smiled and stepped in front of her brother.

Picking the tie up off the floor, she drew it around his neck and tied it expertly. "You know," she said calmly, "the major difference between you and me is how we handle a crisis. You panic when there is one. I panic when there isn't one." Bobbie stepped back and looked admiringly at Roy. "You're a handsome devil. I bet you got a dozen girls swooning all over you."

"I don't know a dozen girls, and I wouldn't know what to do with them if I did."

"That's not what the whores say at Dory's place."

Roy glared at her. "I don't want to hear your trashy gossip. And keep out of my life."

"Why, sweets, I wouldn't dream of interfering." Bobbie laughed, then turned and checked her lipstick in the mirror. "But for your own good, I'll pass a little tidbit on. Stay away from Delta. She's absolutely wild about you, but Willie's in love with her, and I don't think he'd appreciate the competition."

Roy's eyes glowed angrily. "And I'll thank you to mind your own business."

Bobbie cringed as Roy slammed the door after him, and a tear rolled down her cheek. Damn! I did it again, she thought. Every time I want to be nice, I end up being a bitch. Bobbie took a compact from her black evening bag. Dabbing her face with powder, she promised herself she wouldn't badger Roy anymore, especially now that she was leaving. She had wanted to tell him tonight so he could find another singer. She was going to Chicago.

After three years, Chuck had finally agreed to let her join him. He didn't have a job, and he didn't have a band, but he promised he'd find work for both of them. I'm gambling a lot on that cold promise, she thought. But I know I'll make it big. Chicago's waiting for me. As soon as Roy and she kissed and made up, she would tell him.

Whites, browns, blacks, chocolates, and creams milled about the foyer, the hall a sea of mauves and lavenders, Chantilly lace, and black lamé. Lacquered blondes sporting brilliant red lips mingled with chocolate-brown beauties

218

with charcoal-black hair. The cloying scent of gardenias clashed with the biting aroma of cigar smoke.

Tony Gianino surveyed the crowd with bulging gray eyes. Squat and solid, he wore a double-breasted pin-striped suit and a hand-rolled fedora that only accented his huge, beak-like nose. Two thick-set men in ill-fitting tuxedos hovered nearby. Roy hesitated a moment. Could this man really be intimidated by an amateur voodoo act? If he called their bluff, Tony wouldn't hesitate to kill all of them. Swallowing his panic, Roy sauntered up to Gianino, his hand extended in greeting.

"I'm Roy Monroe, Mr. Gianino." The aging mobster ignored him. Roy quickly dropped his hand. "I'm happy you could join us. Sid'll seat you immediately. How many in your party?"

One of the bodyguards told Roy they needed a table for ten—near the dance floor and near an exit. Roy helped seat the group himself, holding the chairs for two of the women hovering near Tony. The older one, Roy presumed, was Gianino's wife, Tina. Dressed in a somber, long-sleeved black dress that almost touched her sturdy oxfords, the woman stared straight ahead, oblivious to the activity about her. The younger woman had to be the daugher, Rosanna. Her eyes sparked with excitement. Her skin was alabaster smooth, her well-defined lips were small and pouty. She wore a violet chemise whose only adornment was a row of handmade lace on the high neck and sleeves. Thick black hair, piled high on her head, was secured with two mother-of-pearl combs. Roy was about to introduce himself to the women when one of the bodyguards pulled him aside and whispered, "The boss don't like nobody talking to his women 'less he says it's okay. See to it that we ain't bothered by strangers."

Sid, the muscular maître d', turned to the waiter and ordered French champagne . . ."compliments of the house."

Gianino looked up. The bodyguard grunted, "The boss only drinks Scotch—the real stuff. The women can drink the champagne, but not too much."

Willie had watched these proceedings from the hallway. The presence of Gianino's wife and daughter upset him. He went to Roy's office and poured himself a double Scotch.

"Think I'll join you." Roy lit a cigarette, and relaxed in his father's old leather chair. "I've changed my mind about Gianino. I don't think he'll cause any trouble. He brought his women along."

Willie frowned. "Jeez! Your mood sure changed fast. What'd the man do, slip you a ten?"

"I'm looking at all the angles, and I say Gianino won't try anything with his family here." Roy nodded furtively toward the small storage room where Willie had taken Sarah and Tallulah. "Is everything set up?" he asked nervously. "I want this thing to go off like clockwork. No hitches."

"Quit worrying. Everything's under control." Willie shrugged. "Tallulah's been moaning and praying, but Sarah's excited. They'll be all right." He smiled. "They're something. I swear they're the best actresses in the world or else they really believe in that mumbo jumbo."

"I'm glad they memorized their act. They won't have to stop and think about it."

"I don't think it's an act."

"Oh, come on—"

"Tallulah believes she's a voodoo priestess. She has Sarah convinced she is, too."

"Well, nothing better happen to either one of 'em. I'd never forgive myself, but that wouldn't matter because Bobbie'd kill me." Roy remembered a story from his high school Latin class—something about Caesar crossing the Rubicon. "I'm going to join the Gianino party. There's something mesmerizing about being a part of your own destruction."

Roy approached Gianino's table cautiously. "Everything okay here?"

"Sit down, boy," Tony said with a wave of his hand.

After exchanging pleasantries with Mrs. Gianino and Rosanna, Roy kept his eyes on Tony, trying to ignore the sweet scent of jasmine that drifted from the girl's handkerchief.

"You got lots of important people here." Tony waved his cigar in front of him. "How'd a colored like you make so many connections?"

"My father was Benny Monroe. He owned the Creole Club. He made the connections. I just kept in touch."

Tony nodded, and the ashes from his cigar dropped onto his silk tie. Tina leaned over to brush them away, but Tony raised his hand to stop her. "My wife, Tina . . . she don't like me to smoke, but I tell her there are more dangerous things to worry about, like getting hit by an automobile. Ain't that right, Mr. Monroe?"

Roy nodded as Tony continued without a pause. "That's my daughter, Rosanna. We're celebrating her birthday, too. Eighteenth. Ain't it something how they grow up so fast?"

"Maybe Rosanna would like to help my sister and I blow out the candles on a five-foot cake after the midnight show. It'd be an honor—"

Rosanna was smiling now, and a word formed on her lips. But before she could speak, Tony held up his hand. "No," he said adamantly. "I don't want nobody to get a good look at my family."

Rosanna sat back in her chair; the smile dissolved, but her eyes, still sparkling, remained riveted on Roy's face.

"Anyway," Tony continued, "we won't be staying long. As soon as we eat, you and me can talk business, then we leave."

"Business!" Roy said in surprise. "But I'm hosting a party tonight. I couldn't possibly—"

"Have another drink, boy." Gianino said in a friendlier tone.

Roy motioned to the waiter who brought another round of drinks.

Gianino took the first sip. His heavy lips curled in disgust. "Hey, you mixing this stuff in the basement? I sell you quality booze, and I get rotgut."

Roy quickly tasted his drink. "Tastes okay to me. It's right outta the bottle."

Gianino's face gnarled in anger. "You telling me I don't know my liquor?"

"No, sir. I just said it tasted okay to me."

"Get the bottle. I want to check it myself."

"I assure you—"

"Get the bottle, boy."

Roy hesitated a moment, then stood up. "Whatever you say. I'll be right back."

When Roy returned with a full bottle of Scotch, Gianino looked up and laughed. "Guess you were right, boy. My wife says it's the tobacco. Makes everything taste stale. Finish your drink. You gonna need it." His laughter faded into a deep growl.

Roy turned his attention to Rosanna, who was nervously playing with her champagne glass. "We've had a lot of rain, haven't we?"

"Yes. A lot." Rosanna smiled.

"You in school?"

"This is my last year at Holy Name Academy."

Roy nodded. He fumbled for a cigarette and, lighting it, inhaled deeply.

"You ain't drinking, boy. Don't you like the taste either?" Gianino leaned menacingly across the table.

Roy smiled and took a sip of his Scotch and water. He gagged. The liquid ran down the corner of his mouth. "You're right. This stuff's rotten. What happened? Tasted okay awhile ago."

"Tobacco mouth." Gianino then raised his glass in a toast. "To our business arrangement."

Roy started to pick up his drink when suddenly Rosanna pitched forward in a spasm of coughing. Instinctively Roy slapped her back, then reached for a glass of water. Still coughing, Rosanna grabbed for the glass. As she did, her hand brushed against Roy's drink, knocking it over. Scotch, water, and ice flew into the air and landed on Roy's tuxedo.

Gianino jumped up. Waiters materialized and pressed napkins on Roy's wet pants. Rosanna stared apologetically at the mess she had made. "I'm so sorry. I'm not used to drinking."

Gianino raised his fist, but Tina calmly tugged at his sleeve and nudged him back into his chair. "No need to get excited. No harm done except to Mr. Monroe's suit. Expect he'll be a little damp the rest of the evening."

Roy stood up and casually threw an ice cube on the table. "You're right. No problem. I'll dry off in the kitchen. Shouldn't take long."

"What about our business meeting?" Gianino bellowed. "I ain't got all night."

"My associate, Willie Jackson, is in the office. You can discuss whatever it is you want—"

"I don't discuss nothin' with hirelings."

"Mr. Jackson and I operate as partners. I won't be long." Without waiting for an answer, Roy turned and walked away.

Willie was waiting for them as Tony and his bodyguards entered the office. He had witnessed the accident and had seen Roy head toward the kitchen. Guess I do the talking, he thought, relishing the confrontation.

Tony sat in Roy's chair and stuck a cigar in his mouth. He motioned for one of his men to light it. His eyes glowed with contempt.

"Now that we're alone, we can stop playing games." Tony chewed on the end of his cigar. His teeth were pitted with blackish tar.

"Games?" Willie sat down. "We're not playing games."

"I don't do business with niggers. They do business with me. I been selling you liquor. But my boys handle that. It's routine, you understand. Right now I'm telling you I want this club—the Savoy. I want the gambling house, and I want your nigger whorehouse. How much I gotta pay you for all three?"

"They're not for sale."

Tony's cheeks puffed out like an adder's, and his face turned a deep red. "You didn't hear me, boy. I asked how much."

"They're not for sale."

Tony's eyes closed. "You must have rocks where your balls are, boy. Nobody shuts me out twice." Tony raised his arm, and the two bodyguards stepped toward Willie, walking in unison, their hands in their pockets.

"No sense getting upset," Willie said casually. "If the price is right, Roy could be persuaded to retire or leave town. How much you offering?"

"Twenty thousand for the whole bundle," Tony said in a high-pitched voice that contrasted starkly with his heavy body.

Willie laughed. "Twenty thousand! We clear that in two months." Willie stepped closer to Gianino. "What I'm trying to say is Roy don't own the clubs outright. He'd have to talk to his partner."

Gianino squinted again and puffed heavily on his cigar. "Partner! He said you was his partner."

"He has another one, his mother. Sarah Monroe. She inherited the Creole Club from Benny. Roy ran it for a while. Now they're partners in all the clubs."

"I don't do business with women," Tony said, barely moving his lips.

"Roy didn't know that when he opened the Savoy," Willie said, his voice heavy with sarcasm.

Tony pointed his cigar at Willie. "Well, you're a man, ain't you, boy? You tell his mother you're selling. That's all there is to it."

"We'll all tell her." Willie's voice was calm but his face was taut with apprehension. "She's in the next room. She won't argue if all of us talk to her."

"I ain't doing business with no woman."

"Of course, we wouldn't expect you to, but your presence . . ."

Gianino pulled nervously at his pant leg, coughed, then finally nodded in agreement. "Okay. I'll go with you, but you better not be putting me off or I'll forget about the twenty thousand. I'm doing you a favor. I hope you appreciate it."

"Oh, yes, sir."

Single file, Willie bringing up the rear, the men walked into the room behind Roy's office where Sarah and Tallulah were waiting. Gianino squinted as his eyes adjusted to the dark. Willie quickly closed the door, locked it, and dropped the key in his pocket. Immediately, as though on cue,

Tallulah lit a candle. Tony hesitated a moment, then bellowed like a wounded bull, "What the shit . . ." He pointed to his henchmen. "Open that door. They're playing some kind of trick." He turned and stared hard at Willie. "I'll get you black bastards for this."

Willie smiled and pointed his revolver at him. In a sweeping motion, he included the two bodyguards as well. "Sit down. You said we liked to play games. We want you to join us."

His finger froze on the trigger. "I'll use this thing if I have to," he said forcefully, trying to hide his terror.

Suddenly Tallulah's moans filled the room. Tony gasped when she pointed at him. He shrank back, his eyes filled with horror.

Sarah lit a second candle, the light revealing their grotesque makeup. They were caricatures of voodoo witches— their lined faces creased under thick layers of makeup, their thin lips streaked with purple lipstick. Wearing somber black dresses accented with colorful shawls, they resembled wizened spirits conjured up from the nether world.

Tallulah opened a yellowed, ragged book and began to chant.

> *"Twice the candle's rent by us*
> *Hell's fire can weld it not*
> *Devil men full of avarice and lust*
> *Depart you forever into the dust."*

"What are they doing?" Gianino cried out. "That's a curse. Stop it. Stop. I won't bother you no more. Please—"

"Too late," Willie said. He stood sentinel at the door; the sorcery was clearly having the desired effect. He decided to add his own bit of devilry. "You've entered a coven. There's no turning back."

Moving their hands over a charcoal brazier, Sarah and Tallulah chanted while the burning incense filled the room with a suffocatingly sweet aroma. Tallulah, hypnotized, swayed her large body and sang monotonously, "Cabals, cabats, caldrons . . ." Then, from a flowing sleeve of her shroudlike costume, she drew out a wax image of Gianino. Patches of gray hair were glued on the head of the doll, and a huge, erect penis protruded from its belly.

Gianino screamed and threw his hands over his eyes. "Stop, you dirty bastards. You're the devil. You niggers are the devil."

"If you don't shut up, you'll get a double whammy." Willie glanced at the door. Where the hell was Roy? He was going to miss the whole shooting match.

Tony stared at Tallulah as she stroked the doll dispassionately, then, in one quick stroke, she grabbed a needle and stabbed it in its belly.

Tony screamed.

"Melen, cadze, dasal," Tallulah said, softly at first, then louder and louder. Holding the end of a wire that was wrapped around the doll's neck, Tallulah swung the effigy slowly over the fire. The penis began to melt and drops of wax sizzled as they hit the hot charcoal.

"There be evil men in this room. One named Tony Gianino. Satan claims him when I release him. The fire destroys his manhood. The fires of hell torment him through eternity. Melen, cadze, dasal."

Gianino fell to the floor. The bodyguards didn't know what to do. They too gazed in terror at the melting penis. Gianino was sobbing now, pleading with them to stop.

"Not yet," Willie said. "It's not over yet."

"O Satan, whose demonic power is here implored, take this evil man from us. Keep him in eternal torment 'less he relinquish his malignant plan to destroy us." Sarah spoke in a trance. Her skin was ashen, and her eyes rolled to the back of her head. Willie stared at her, transfixed.

"Usar, soree, tenae. O all ye ministers, I command ye to destroy this evil man if he evermore creates pain against one of us. What say this devil? Will he leave us in peace or shall Satan claim him this night?" Sarah paused, then, taking the doll from Tallulah, she pulled it away from the fire. It dropped from her hand as she fell back against the chair, unconscious.

Tony swore he wouldn't take the clubs. He even agreed to

lower the price of his liquor. He loosened his tie and, taking a handkerchief from his pocket, wiped the saliva driveling from his mouth.

Willie, still brandishing his gun, stepped forward. He agreed to let Tony go, but nodded toward the doll. "If you give us any trouble, all we have to do is drop that thing in the fire. You don't have to be here. We'll send you a note."

Tony nodded, too terrified to speak.

Willie opened the door. Tony and his henchmen hurried into Roy's office just as Roy entered from the opposite side. When he saw Willie, he stepped toward him.

"Is it all over? What happened? Mama! Tallulah!"

"They're all right. Let's get rid of Gianino."

Tony was halfway down the hall when Willie and Roy caught up with him. They followed them into the club and watched as Tony's party got their coats and headed for the door. Rosanna was last, and as she brushed by him, she dropped her wrap. Instinctively, Roy stooped to pick it up. Their eyes met. As she took her coat from him, she thrust a folded napkin into his hand. Roy frowned. "What—" She was gone. He slipped the note into his pocket and hurried back to his office.

A thud, like someone falling, came from the next room. Roy heard the babble of voices, then a scream. "Mama, what's going on?"

The odor of incense stung his nostrils as he entered the room and saw Bobbie kneeling over Sarah's inert body. Tears streamed down Bobbie's cheeks. Her mouth was open in terror. He fell on his knees beside her and tried to comfort her.

"Don't cry, Bobbie. We haven't lost the club. We scared him."

"You fool! You stupid, selfish fool. You murdered Mama. She's had a stroke. You saved your damn club, but Mama's dying."

"Mama!" Roy's eyes shifted to Sarah's body enveloped in the shroudlike costume. "Mama!"

Later, as he sat alone in his office waiting for a call from the doctor, he drew Rosanna's note from his pocket. It was

227

short, almost cryptic, obviously written under great stress. She warned him that his drink, the drink she had knocked over, had contained poison. Her father had tried to kill him.

Roy leaned back in his chair and closed his eyes. Why? he wondered. Why had she told him? He owed her his life. Would she be sorry when she heard what he had done to her father? He hoped not. He hoped she would understand. He hoped she would forgive him.

CHAPTER XX

The city rushed by in a blur as the Illinois Central passenger train slithered through the maze of tracks leading to the heart of the city and Union Station.

So this is Chicago, Bobbie thought, as she pulled a small cloche over her bobbed hair. She strained to look into the night through the rain-smeared window. As soon as the train stopped, Bobbie stood up, tugged at her beige silk dress, and grabbed her purse and hand luggage from the overhead rack.

I don't know why I'm rushing, she thought. No one's here to meet me. Intimidated by the huge station, Bobbie followed a bevy of lively schoolgirls to the exit. A strong wind tousled hats and billowed skirts. A cluster of hands swayed overhead as the girls flagged down taxis. Bobbie, too, hailed a cab, gave the cabbie the address written on the back of Chuck's letter, and twenty minutes later stared bleakly at the dismal facade of her new home. Grabbing her bags, she staggered up three flights of stairs, sidestepping broken toys and empty beer bottles. Bobbie knocked on a grotesque lime green door that was coated with grime. When it opened she was blinded by the light that radiated into the shadowy hallway from a luminous ceiling lamp hanging in the center of a large kitchen.

"Bobbie, sweetie." The young man's light gray eyes bulged under pale eyelashes but his face was friendly. He extended his hand. "Welcome! Come on in. We were worried about you. You're late."

"The train . . ." My God, she thought. Chuck's living with a white person. That would never happen back home. She tried not to stare.

"Oh, never mind. What difference does it make? You're here." The young man grabbed her suitcases and ushered her into the bright kitchen with yellow walls. A massive mural spilled across the living room wall, alive with a dancing elephant and a tall Uncle Sam who pointed to a crimson eagle swooping overhead. Painted underneath the eagle was a wrinkled old woman holding a basket of fruit and dressed in layers of torn, ill-fitting clothes; she sat on a stool and watched the parade from the security of her corner.

"You'll have to get used to us. We're an odd bunch, but we get along." The young man introduced himself. "Everybody calls me Duffy. That's not my real name, but I answer to it." Then, in a loud voice, he yelled a chorus of names.

Doors flew open and three young people ran into the kitchen. They aligned themselves in a row like a string of wooden soldiers, their eyes alert, their smiles broad.

"On the left is Edy Heller, our prima ballerina."

Edy curtsied, stretching a black leotard that barely covered her body and accented her long legs, which were partially hidden under wool lavender leggings.

"You're beautiful," Edy said. "I love beautiful people. What a change from this pack of animals."

"Nels Forbisher," Duffy continued, "America's future poet laureate."

A pale, round-shouldered youth nodded. "I promise to write a poem about black beauty, and I'll dedicate it to you." Nels kissed Bobbie's free hand and waved Duffy on.

"Lastly, Jenny VanDorn—the greatest pianist in the world. Someday. Kissing cousins, maybe?" Duffy laughed at his strained joke about Jenny's dark skin.

"If not cousins, then friends." Jenny planted a kiss on

Bobbie's cheek. She sneered playfully. "I'm really here to show these bumpkins that a colored woman can play something besides 'Old Black Joe.'"

Bobbie wouldn't have been surprised if they had all started singing and tap dancing. Instead, they said their good-byes and disappeared into their rooms, leaving her alone with Duffy, feeling letdown. Duffy, too, had things to do, and the next thing she knew, Bobbie was alone, unpacking her suitcase and sipping a cup of tea. She felt depressed, and missed Chuck. Accustomed to fancier surroundings, Bobbie stared forlornly at the thin wire that spanned a corner of the room. The hangers with Chuck's suits and shirts had slid together toward the center, and her few dresses joined them when she hung them up, their hems touching the floor. She wondered what she'd do when the rest of her clothes arrived. Live out of a trunk, she thought glumly, at least until we can find our own apartment. Bobbie tucked her slips, panties, and stockings in a corner of a chipped bureau drawer. She undressed and, wearing only her new pink satin slip, lay on the double bed and waited for Chuck.

Someone down the hall was playing a concerto by Rachmaninoff. Bobbie listened for a moment, then rolled on her side. It was a record. At least there was a phonograph in the apartment, she thought. Maybe she could borrow it and practice along with Bessie Smith or Ma Rainey, the "mother of the blues." Both black women had recorded on "race records," which were only sold in the Negro community. They were fabulously successful—and often sold half a million records in six months. Bobbie planned to take her place beside these "blues queens"—Bobbie Evans, blues and jazz singer. She was positive people would remember the twenties for its music if for nothing else.

Bobbie took a Camel from a half-filled cigarette pack on the nightstand. Lazily, she blew smoke rings in the darkened room and wondered what Chuck would be like after three years. He didn't love her, but that didn't matter. He would eventually. Did he have another girl? No. Music and money were his passions, not women. Luckily, she thought, she was a combination of all three. Somehow she had to make it. She had to become a star.

It was still dark outside when Bobbie awoke from a restless sleep. She felt something brush against her cheek like the fluttering of a butterfly. Frightened, she bolted upright, only to be engulfed in two arms.

"Chuck!" Bobbie relaxed. Leaning her head on his shoulder, she sighed. "You feel so good." It felt like they had never been apart.

"It's been a long time, babe." Chuck buried his face in her hair. "You're feeling mighty good too."

All too soon, Chuck pulled away. Tapping his finger on her nose, he reminded her that he had been working for nine hours.

Forcing a smile, Bobbie leaned against the iron bedpost and asked him what he'd been doing the last three years.

Chuck pulled the chain on the Tiffany lamp and playfully cuffed Bobbie's chin. "Both of us have lots of catching up to do. What happened to you and Roy and the Savoy? Can't imagine you leaving a gold mine like that."

Knowing a rehash of the family squabble would depress her, Bobbie promised she'd talk about it later. "Please, tell me—what's it like working in Chicago? It must be fabulous." Bobbie stared eagerly at Chuck, waiting for the promise of stardom to engulf her. Chuck threw his dress shirt across the bed and filled a smudged water glass with ersatz Scotch.

"It isn't easy making it in this business." Chuck paced between the bed and the chipped door. Briefly, he summarized his life since leaving St. Louis, bitterly recalling the competition, the poor pay, the streaks of bad luck. He had been lucky to share the rent with four other people. Otherwise, he groaned, he'd be sleeping on a cot at the "Y." Every extra cent he earned was spent on clothes, drinks, and cab rides as he tried to impress club owners, agents, and scouts.

Bobbie wanted to seem sympathetic, but her eyes were riveted on his bulging arms and shoulders, the hairy chest barely visible under a sleeveless undershirt. A slight smile separated Bobbie's lips. The tip of her tongue slid out of her mouth. She positioned it in the center, directing it toward the heart-shaped cleavage of her upper lip. It was a relief to realize she didn't care if Chuck worked or not; in fact, it was better if he didn't. He could spend all of his time with her. He could be her manager, her arranger, her lover. She would be the star.

Chuck talked until the first rays of a cold dawn spilled through a small, sooty transom partially covered with a scrap of plywood. He talked about his roommates, about how they all shared the same poverty and the same dream of making it. After he wound down, Bobbie held out her arms. Chuck stopped pacing, and stared at her blankly.

"I'm not ready. I'm tired and a little drunk."

"I'll wait. Come and lie down. Take off your clothes. You'll feel better after you get some sleep."

Bobbie caressed his body, holding him close to her until she, too, fell into an exhausted sleep.

The sun was warm and a soft breeze blew off Lake Michigan as Bobbie and Chuck ran down the rutted stairs and out into the street. It was three o'clock in the afternoon. They had awakened at one, made love at Bobbie's insistence, and showered together at Chuck's insistence. He claimed it saved water. There was no food in the icebox, so they decided to eat out. A cheap place, Chuck had insisted. Bobbie was starved, but she didn't know how much she could trample on Chuck's ego. She didn't dare offer to pay.

Bobbie's heart sank as they pushed through a swarm of smelly unwashed bodies sitting around dirty wooden tables at Madame Chang's Tearoom.

"How quaint! Is Madame Chang's a meeting place for all the derelicts in the neighborhood?"

Chuck glowered at Bobbie, then shoved a greasy one-page menu into her hand.

Bobbie dropped her menu on the table and studied the waiter for a moment, then giggled when she saw his dangling turquoise earring and matching bracelet. Chuck hurriedly ordered two Hungarian stew specials and two pots of tea. When the waiter disappeared into the back room, Bobbie laughed out loud.

"What was that? God! What a freak. Where do you find 'em?"

"Dammit, Bobbie!" Chuck lit a cigarette and looked at Bobbie in disgust. "You're going to get us kicked out of here. Those guys don't like being laughed at."

"Guys! Is he a guy?"

"Shit! Haven't you seen a homosexual before?"

"Not one wearing green fingernail polish and long earrings." Tears streaked her face as Bobbie roared with laughter.

"Oh, grow up. This is Towertown. Little Bohemia. Hell, everybody's strange around here, including us. We're Negroes, you know. Or have you forgotten?"

"Not likely." Bobbie was suddenly serious.

"Why do you act so ridiculous?" Chuck's brown eyes flashed.

Bobbie dropped her eyes. "I'm sorry. I didn't think. I'm embarrassing you."

Chuck shook his head. "You're twenty-five years old. When are you going to grow up?"

"You don't like me very much, do you?" she said defiantly, at the same time nervously folding and unfolding her napkin.

"Of course I like you. Most of the time you act all right. But I never know."

Bobbie stared hard at Chuck, then slipped her hand over his. "I love you," she said softly. "Really love you."

When Chuck didn't respond, Bobbie wondered if he cared at all how she felt. Maybe he isn't as easy to manipulate as I thought. She leaned closer to Chuck. "If I act stupid sometimes, you have to remember, I haven't had much experience. But I'll try to grow up fast . . . just for you."

Chuck shrugged, his anger gone as quickly as it had come. "Just don't make a fool out of yourself. Right now you're like a squishy peach—kind of spoiled and bruised. In a few months you'll be like a diamond, hard and cold."

"You like your women hard and cold?" Bobbie's penciled eyebrows arched in surprise.

"It's a matter of survival," Chuck said unhesitatingly.

The meal was lackluster, and Bobbie made a mental note never to eat Hungarian stew for breakfast again, but she didn't complain. The tea was hot and strong, and it revived her.

Bobbie had hoped they could go back to the apartment and reminisce, make love, plan for her future. Instead, Chuck wiped his mouth, threw his napkin on the table, and stood up, pulling Bobbie out into the crowded, sunlit street.

Chuck outlined his plans. They would go to the Imperial, a Negro club on the southside, where Bobbie would audition for a singing job. Pay wasn't great, but there would be exposure. Some of the best musicians hung out at the Imperial. Afterwards he promised her a bus ride along the Gold Coast so she'd get a feel for the city, warning her that the slums were only blocks from millionaires' mansions.

The word "audition" rang in Bobbie's ears. Surely he was joking, she thought. I'm not ready for an audition. My songs are stale; I've got to update my style. She tried to argue, but Chuck shrugged off her doubts. It was his last comment, however, that brought angry tears to her eyes. "If you can't get a job in a month, write to Roy and ask if he'll hire both of us back."

Bobbie exploded. "You're using me," she cried in indignation. "You don't give one hoot about me. You want your band, and you want a gig. Well, I won't do it. I'll never go home, and I'll never ask Roy for a favor."

Chuck gripped her arm and held on tightly while he explained his predicament. He hadn't worked steadily since he had left St. Louis and his money was almost gone. Bobbie retorted that she had money. Chuck said proudly that he would only live on what they earned together—"anything else is charity." Bobbie countered his proposal, extending the time limit beyond one month. She offered to buy food if he paid the rent, but Chuck was adamant. He had spent three years trying to build a reputation; he didn't intend to wait any longer. He wanted his own band, and he wanted a permanent gig.

They were silent as the bus pulled up at the curb. Bobbie hurried to a backseat where she stared resentfully out the window. Was that why he had allowed her to come to Chicago—so she would use her influence with Roy to get his job back at the Savoy? Just the thought of being used infuriated her. On the other hand, she realized, she was using Chuck. But that's different—I love him. Still, she wondered how far love would go as she watched the blocks worsen from tacky to downright squalid.

The Imperial was on the bottom floor of a two-story brick building that had seen better days. Yellowing photographs of female singers and black bands were stuck haphazardly behind a dirty plate-glass window. The "co" in the rubber "welcome" mat had worn away.

Inside, a small stage and dance floor filled the back of the room, and a maroon velvet drape hung precariously from a thin piece of wire. They had barely reached the bar when a squat man with beige-colored skin shouted a friendly hello. Moments later, Bobbie was being introduced to Tim, "Tim the Lip," owner and manager of the Imperial.

Bobbie sipped a glass of wine while Tim and Chuck slapped each other on the back, grunting in monosyllables as they appraised her like a prize heifer.

The pungent odor of ribs roasting in tomatoes, spices, and beer distracted Bobbie. She wished they had eaten here.

Tim noticed her furtive glances toward the kitchen and promised her a platter full of ribs. Bobbie finished her drink. Finally, there wasn't any reason not to start the audition. With the torn velvet curtain as a backdrop, Bobbie opened with "Baby, Won't You Please Come Home." She pushed herself to make her voice sound dramatic and sophisticated, something between rural blues and jazz. Tim straddled a chair on the edge of the stage, leaning close when she lowered her voice, tipping back when she raised it, all the while tapping his foot in time with the rhythm.

Maybe I *am* ready for Chicago, Bobby thought, then wondered if it could be that easy.

Tim's roly-poly girth swayed as he ambled across the stage. Impulsively Tim hugged Bobbie, then kissed her, unwilling to let her go. Bobbie was surprised by his adulation. A moment later, Chuck was at her side, wiping the perspiration from his forehead. Tim grabbed his hand and shook it vigorously. It took much chin-scratching, foot-scraping, and throat-clearing before the two men finally reached an agreement: twenty-five dollars a night plus tips for three months. A half hour later, Bobbie and Chuck were running hand in hand down the street.

"I told you you were ready," Chuck said, while Bobbie gushed at having found a job so quickly. She was careful not to compare her coup with Chuck's fruitless efforts of three years.

"Talent," Chuck said, as though reading her mind. "You have it. I don't."

"Nonsense. You're a great drummer. In time—"

"Good, not great," Chuck said, as though acknowledging his limitations for the first time.

"Oh, come on. Don't get down on yourself. You promised to show me Chicago."

Bobbie smiled and squeezed Chuck's hand until he smiled back, grudgingly at first, but as the bus headed south on Michigan Avenue, the Million Dollar Mile, his spirits brightened, and he glibly rattled off the names of the boutiques and specialty stores. When they got off the bus, they walked back the same way they had come, but after a while Bobbie grew bored with the chic shops, the opulent jewelers, the plush clubs. Unless we can buy these things, why should we spend our time looking at them? I feel like I just found out there isn't a Santa Claus. Bobbie glanced at Chuck, who was reveling in the heady atmosphere of wealth. Why would he be satisfied just looking? she wondered.

Bobbie stopped in the middle of the block. It was getting dark. The soft breeze was chilly now and was whipping around her face and ears. She rubbed her hands to warm them. "Let's get a taxi. It won't cost much. I'm cold and tired."

Chuck shook his head. "Hey, babe! I don't have the money."

"I'll pay."

"No."

"But—"

Bobbie was about to flag a taxi and let Chuck get home on his own when the door to a private supper club flew open, and a couple hurried to a limousine waiting at the curb. Bobbie stared at them, enraptured by their elegant good looks, their ostentatious display of wealth. The woman was swathed in black mink, smiling as she waited for the man to open the car door. Bending over, he wrapped her tiny, leather-strapped feet with the billowy froth of her gown as she slid across the smooth leather seat. For a brief moment, the pungent sting of tobacco smoke mingled with the fragrant scent of roses, then the door slammed shut, and they disappeared into the fast-moving traffic.

Chuck noticed Bobbie's wan, almost shocked, expression. He asked if she were ill. She shook her head and walked away, dabbing at the tears that filled her eyes.

"Hey! What gives? If you're that upset, I'll get a taxi."

"God! You're such an oaf."

"Now what?"

"Here we are, surrounded by all this wealth, and you can't even afford a taxi. And what's worse, you're too damn proud to let me pay for it." Bobbie stamped her foot on the sidewalk.

"I'm down on my luck. Give me a chance—".

"You've had three years."

"What do you want?" Chuck lit a cigarette, taking short, angry puffs.

"I want my three years. If I can't make it, then we make other plans."

Chuck turned away. He studied the sparkling display window of The Renaissance Jewelers. Bobbie stepped beside him and pointed to a lavishly designed man's gold and diamond initial ring.

"It's a beauty, isn't it?" She tugged at his arm. "You like nice things. What difference does it make who buys 'em?"

"I don't want to depend on you for my living." He stared at the ring.

"I would depend on you if it were the other way around."

"That's different. The colored woman supports her man, he's a pimp. I don't want to be a pimp."

"Then be my husband."

Chuck spun around. "That's even worse."

Bobbie turned and walked toward the curb. "There's no sense in arguing. If your mind's made up . . ."

Chuck hesitated a moment, then walked past her into the street. He hailed a taxi. As they sped away, Chuck stared out the window, his face taut. "I'll give you one year. But I'll be your manager. I'll work for my salary."

Bobbie smiled. She tried to sound lighthearted. "If we're lucky, I won't need a year."

As they climbed the stairs back to the dingy apartment, Bobbie said, "Can we move out as soon as Tim pays me?"

Chuck nodded in agreement. "I got no ties to these people. We can move as soon as we get the money."

"I'm glad . . . and I promise, I'll work hard. I'll make it. We'll be rich."

"That's important to you, isn't it?"

"Yes, it is." A bitterness crept into Bobbie's voice. She clung to Chuck. "I'm going to show Roy that I can make it too. On my own. I don't need him or his money."

Chuck frowned. "All this is for Roy?"

"No. It's for me. Me and you. But I can't wait to see his face when I make it."

"You'll never go back?"

"Not till I make a name for myself. I want to be a jazz singer. A really great jazz singer," Bobbie said passionately.

Chuck pulled Bobbie closer to him. "Then we'll both work our asses off till you make it."

CHAPTER XXI

Five inches of swirling, drifting snow covered St. Louis, closing schools, clogging thoroughfares. Automobiles, resembling inert polar bears, stood abandoned at the curbs of deserted streets.

Roy glanced up from his desk. His eyes were bleary; his muscles ached. He slammed his ledger closed, startling Willie.

Roy stood up and joined Willie in front of the window. "It's six o'clock in the morning. Don't you think it's time to go home?"

Willie nodded. "I've been trying to talk myself into going out in that icebox for the last hour. Christ! It must be twenty below."

"At least you have a car. It beats waiting for a streetcar like those poor fools." He pointed to the flock of early morning laborers on their way to work. Roy inhaled deeply on his cigarette and shook his head. His reading glasses had left deep marks on his temples. "Where do you think they're headed? A white man's office? A white woman's kitchen?"

"They should've stayed in bed." Turning, Willie walked to the desk and stubbed out his cigarette. "Think I'll get some doughnuts and coffee. Want some?"

Willie grabbed his overcoat and disappeared down the hall. Roy returned to his books, a frown creasing his smooth tan forehead. He flipped through a handful of invoices, then threw them disgustedly back on the desk. He didn't need pieces of paper to tell him what he already knew: losses were up thirty percent from last year. He had begun losing money in 1926, and he had no idea how to turn it around.

"It was bound to happen," Willie said matter-of-factly

when he returned with their breakfast. "All clubs are popular for a while, then they lose their popularity for one reason or another. The public is fickle. It follows trends. Maybe colored nightclubs aren't trendy anymore. The white clubs have done a damn good job of copying our style."

"Hell, you sound like an editorial in the *Wall Street Journal*."

"You asked." Willie propped his feet on Roy's desk and opened the morning paper. Roy bit into a glazed doughnut. Willie seemed immune to financial worries; he hadn't invested all of his money in the Savoy. Maybe I shouldn't have either, Roy thought belatedly, then wondered how difficult it would be to start over again. Willie's shout jolted Roy out of his meditation.

"You scared the hell out of me. What's the matter—did the Dow Jones industrials shoot up again?"

"Industrials, shit." Willie folded the paper in half and handed it to Roy. "There"—he pointed—at the bottom of the page."

Roy's body stiffened when he read that Tony Gianino had returned to the United States—to St. Louis—after spending two years in Naples, Italy. He and his family had come home. Roy crumpled the paper.

"That son of a bitch. What the hell's he doing coming back here? I thought we scared the shit out of him." Roy slumped in the chair behind his desk.

"I wouldn't worry about it." Willie straightened out the newspaper. "I heard rumors that he's coming back to die. Cancer or something like that. I didn't believe it, but I guess it's true." Willie shrugged. "I wonder if he ever got over that night we put the curse on him."

"I don't know about him, but I never did." Roy recalled grimly that his mother hadn't either.

Willie sucked in his cheeks, accentuating his high cheek bones and strong, protruding jaw. Short, gray-speckled sideburns added a hint of maturity to his otherwise youthful face.

"You still blaming yourself for your mother's stroke?"

"It was my fault."

"The doc said she probably would've had one anyway. Something was clogged going to her brain."

"Maybe . . ." Roy drew a series of circles on a pad of paper with his new gold pen. He spoke softly, "Either way, we only bought a few years. Tony's back. I guess he'll try to move his brother, Michele, out of the number one slot. If he does, I've lost my club."

"We can think of a new scam," Willie said enthusiastically.

"Forget it." Roy pressed his fingers against his temples. "I got enough problems."

"Hey, quit worrying, man. It's 1927. The decade's almost over. We survived the Gianinos, the Republicans, and the Ku Klux Klan. What the hell do you want?"

"I want Mama to get well. I want Bobbie to come home. Just to visit. I want this damn prohibition to end, and I don't want to lose the Savoy."

"Shit!" Willie laughed. "You do believe in Santa Claus."

Roy dropped his pen and stared at Willie unblinkingly as though trying to strip him of his cool veneer. He was worried, and he wanted Willie's help.

"Every cent I have is in the Savoy. If I lose it, I lose it all. I can't do anything about Mama or Bobbie or prohibition, but I have to save the club."

"Hey, I can lend you ten grand . . . twenty if you really need it." Willie laid the neatly folded newspaper on Roy's desk.

Roy sighed. "Thanks, but money won't help. Not in the long run. Michele keeps upping the price of liquor. A loan'd just get me through the winter. I need to cut expenses—maybe let some dancers go."

"If you do that, you won't have a floor show. You better not be messing with Delta's number. I won't let you do that to my gal."

"Your gal! Ha! You may have found her, but I hired her."

"You don't own her."

Own her, Roy thought. Yes, I do own her. Willie never

241

found out that Delta and I were lovers, that her bed was still warm from my body when he called and asked if she could come over.

It was fun for a while. Exciting. The danger of getting caught added spice to the affair. But, Roy thought, it's hard to face your friend the day after you slept with his girl. In the end, it got to be too much. When he had tried to break it off, Delta had told him she loved him, not Willie.

Roy shook his head. The whole mess had never been resolved, and he lived in fear that Willie would discover his duplicity some day and realize what a coward he was. Poor Willie. He'll never own Delta, she's mine to keep or give away. Roy would keep her, not because he loved her, but because he needed her. He needed her now more than he had when she had started at the club many years ago. She had been his star dancer. Tall and stately with long legs and a trim, well-proportioned body, she was like an African goddess whom men both worshipped and feared. The attraction was similar to the excitement a man feels when he hunts wild game. The sense of danger coexists with the desire to conquer, to stare into the eyes of a lioness, to be poised on the brink of destruction, then to overpower one's prey and tame it. But once tamed, the thrill of the hunt ceases. The heart slows; the pulse drops. Roy had tamed Delta; she had ceased to be of interest to him. So he used her, and like a faithful pet, she loved him because she needed him in her quiet, domesticated world.

Willie would never own Delta, but he was welcome to her, Roy thought. Willie was welcome to her when he didn't need her anymore.

"I'll keep Delta and Belle." Roy's tone was that of a businessman discussing stock options.

"Delta's the best dancer in the city, but she needs a chorus line to back her up. Two solos a night would kill her. And hell, Belle's just two tits and an ass."

"I didn't say they'd be dancing."

"Then what?"

Roy stood up. He studied his manicured nails for a minute, then slid his hands into his pockets and walked to the window. "Strippers." He kept his back to Willie. "The Savoy is going to have a strip show."

"No! I won't let you."

Roy sneered. "You won't let me! I don't remember asking."

Willie grabbed Roy's shoulder. "You're not going to turn Delta into a stripper. That's final."

"And what if Delta wants to be a stripper?"

"She won't."

"Shit! You may be in love with her, but you can't tell her what to do. She's in love with me. She'll strip if I ask her." Roy's eyes sparked with anger as he stared hard at Willie. "And I will ask."

"Hell! Bobbie was right. You'd sell your own mother if it'd save your fuckin' club." Willie shoved Roy against a chair and stomped across the room. "I wouldn't have used her."

"I'm not going to *use* Delta. I figure she can add a few bumps and grinds to her dance. She's half-naked anyway. What's the difference?"

"The difference is the audience. You know who'll come—drunks and perverts looking for a cheap thrill. Is that what you want the Savoy to become—a two-bit sideshow?—a carny act?"

Roy was quiet for a moment. "I like Delta." He kept his voice under control. "I like her a lot. And I like Belle, too. But I need time to figure out what I'm going to do. If they can buy me that time, I'm going to grab it. All I need is a couple of months."

Willie wasn't mollified. "A couple of months could ruin Delta. She wants to be known as a dancer, not a stripper."

"I've made up my mind." Roy's face was pinched in determination.

"Then I'm leaving. I can't sit around and watch—"

"Don't," Roy pleaded. "If Delta agrees, give me a month. Two, tops. If it doesn't work out, you can leave and take Delta with you."

"Thanks," Willie said contemptuously.

"I mean it. One month."

Willie slammed his hand against the wall. "Damn!" He stared at Roy, his eyes flickering with hate. "I never thought it'd come to this. Not after working for your dad. He wouldn't have asked . . ." Willie shook his head. "Okay, I'll give you a month. But I'm only staying to keep an eye on Delta. Maybe she'll need me to pick up the pieces."

The price of Delta's complicity was dinner, an evening on the town, and a night in Roy's bed. Despite her humiliation, Delta couldn't say no, not if Roy needed her. She was hooked, and her love shone in her eyes. Roy tried to justify his actions by telling himself he was in love, too. He said all the right things, bought her presents, slept with her twice a week. But all the time his mind whirled from the declining receipts and the portents of impending disaster.

Delta wasn't a good stripper. Her body was sleek like a black panther. It had been trained to dance to the growl of saxophones, the rhythmic tinkle of piano keys. Now Delta forced it to gyrate to the thump, thump, thump of a bass fiddle, the shrill whistle of a clarinet, the flatulent grunts of old men. When she stripped her eyes were dull, like those of one being raped.

Willie refused to watch and refused to leave. Roy hid in his office, unable to bear Willie's contempt, Delta's corruption, and the Savoy's death. JoJo was the courier between them. Their messages were curt and infrequent, so when JoJo handed Roy a note late one afternoon he glanced at it indifferently, assuming it was another of Willie's diatribes. Only when he turned it over and read "We have a score to settle," did he open it. Inside it said "I must see you. Please."

Roy shouted for JoJo, who rushed into the office, his face filled with fright.

"Who gave you this?"

"A lady. She hand it to me 'n tell me give it to Mister Monroe. How come you mad, boss?" JoJo stood immobile in the center of the room.

"What lady? What was her name?"

"Don't know, boss."

Roy stepped from behind his desk and grabbed JoJo's arm. "Some woman sends me a threatening note, and you don't know anything! Damn! Is everybody I know an idiot?"

JoJo's hands shook as he tried to pacify Roy. "You can be asking her yourself, boss. She sitting outside."

Roy shoved JoJo aside as he hurried across the room. When he opened the door, he reared back in surprise as a young lady walked into the room. They stared at each other for a moment, then Roy stammered an apology.

"I'm sorry. I didn't mean to yell." He waved her into a chair. "For a minute I thought you might be my sister. This note—it's something she'd write."

"I'm sorry if it frightened you. I shouldn't have sent it." She smiled and sat down, adjusting her dress over her knees. "It's too melodramatic for the occasion, but I was afraid you wouldn't see me."

"It caught my eye." He tried to sound casual.

They smiled at each other. "Look here, if this is some kind of joke, it's okay, but I'd like to know—"

"It's no joke," she said quickly. She pressed the fold of her skirt with her hand several times before she looked up, a smile still on her lips. "I need a job. I thought you—"

Roy raised his hand to stop her. "I'm sorry you went to all this trouble. I'm not hiring. In fact, I don't have a floor show anymore." He shrugged. "And even if I did, I wouldn't hire a white girl. Mixing isn't as open as it was a few years ago."

The young lady twisted the chain of her purse around her finger. She stared at Roy, studying him intently. Roy stared back, acknowledging her extraordinary beauty. When he first opened the Savoy, he wouldn't have hesitated to hire her, but that was a long time ago.

She tilted her head sideways. "You don't remember me, do you?" It was more a statement than a question.

Roy tried to place the face. It didn't seem possible he would forget someone so beautiful.

"I'm Rosanna Gianino. Tony Gianino's daughter."

Roy recoiled visibly. "I don't believe it."

"Oh, please do. I've never been so frightened in my life. I know it was terribly nervy of me to come here, but I need help. You're the only one—"

Roy raised his hand again. "Hold it. There's nothing you and I have to say to each other. I got enough problems without taking you on."

"But I only want a job."

"I'm not hiring."

"You know people who are."

"So does your father. And your uncle. Ask them." Roy took a cigarette out of his case and lit it. When Rosanna asked for one, he hesitated a moment before giving it to her. Their eyes met when he lit it for her. He groaned.

"This is insane. If your old man knew you were here—or does he know? Did he send you?"

Rosanna's eyes flared angrily. "I'm not his errand girl."

"Then why? There must be a dozen people in St. Louis who can help you. Why come here?"

"Remember that night four years ago. My father had someone poison your drink. I knocked your drink over. I might have saved your life."

"I'll never forget that night." Roy shuddered. "And I thank you. That's all you're getting from me though. Just a thank you and an invitation to leave."

Rosanna burst into tears. Roy looked at her, bewildered. "Oh, hell." He handed her his handkerchief.

"This is not a ploy." Rosanna dabbed her eyes. "I'm scared to death, and you're not making it any easier."

"What any easier? You're Tony Gianino's daughter. The man doesn't need an excuse to hate me, and you come waltzing in here like we're long-lost buddies. Your old man'd kill me if he knew you were here. So I want you out. It's nothing personal. Just leave."

"It is personal. You're not the only enemy my father has. Everybody hates him . . . or fears him. But believe me. There's nothing to fear. He's dying."

Roy raised his eyebrows in surprise. "He didn't come back to take over the liquor trade?"

"Never," Rosanna said emphatically. "Uncle Michele would kill him first. They hate each other too."

"He's really dying?"

"Yes. And we're broke. We're living in a three-room flat on Geyer. It's awful."

"Where'd his money go?" Roy asked, surprised at Rosanna's confession.

"Uncle Michele took it when he took over the business two years ago. Daddy never got over the voodoo curse you put on him. He's been depressed ever since, as if he were waiting for an ax to fall. Michele saw his chance. He forced us to leave the country. We went to Italy. To Naples." Rosanna hesitated, her voice quivering for a moment. "Michele sent us enought money for food and rent on an awful little apartment on the bay. Oh, we had a beautiful view, but for two years I smelled like day-old fish. Michele said I had to go to a private girls' school run by the good sisters of something or other, but he never sent a dime for tuition. I had to work in their kitchen. I hated it."

"You hated the kitchen?" Roy found it difficult to be sympathetic.

"Yes, I hated the kitchen! And I hated being poor. Wouldn't you?"

Roy shrugged indifferently, then barely listened as she rambled on about Italy: the insults, the humiliation heaped upon her by her rich, cultured schoolmates. But he perked up when she mentioned the Fascist party and Mussolini, the Communist Workers' Party and revolution.

"You look surprised. Yes, I joined the Communist party, but I did it because all the girls at school, all the nuns who ran the school, and all the priests who ran the nuns were Fascists. I hated all of them."

Roy started to interrupt.

"Please, let me finish." With red eyes and clenched fists, she told him about Giovanni, her Communist lover.

"I was looking for friends and excitement until I met Giovanni, then I became a real radical. But never as radical as Giovanni. He was an anarchist and a Communist. He wanted to destroy everything. He died in his first assassination attempt."

Roy's attention was riveted on Rosanna again. It has to be true, he thought. No one could make up such a tale. Despite his misgivings, he was caught up in her story. It reminded him of Benny's death. The blood-soaked stones, the pain, the screams and laughter, the curses and then nothing. No amount of time could erase the image of his father's murder.

"All I've felt is hate since we left St. Louis. Not love, or happiness, or even real sadness, just hate." Rosanna looked at Roy again, her eyes challenging. "I think you know how to hate, don't you, Mr. Monroe?"

"We all know that." Her tone brought Roy to his feet. He studied Rosanna for a moment. "Why don't you ask your Uncle Michele for help getting a job? He knows everybody in town. Who'd turn him down?"

"Uncle Michele got us out of Italy. The police knew all about my membership in the party. But some big shot called Papa, and Papa called Michele, and he paid lots of money so we could leave the country. Uncle Michele was furious, but blood loyalty was stronger than his anger." Rosanna's eyes were filled with scorn. "Now we live in one of Michele's flats so he can keep an eye on us. Papa's bedridden, and Mama takes care of him. I decided I had to get out of there, away from them. It was like being in prison."

"And you think he's going to let you go?" Roy asked incredulously.

"He has so far. I think he's waiting to see what I'm going to do. I'm sure he wants me to get a job."

"But in an office."

"Or scrubbing floors."

"What will he do if you get a singing job?"

"I don't know. Right now I can't worry about it."

Roy sighed. Opening his address book, he said flatly, "Rudy Weitzman is getting a new show together."

"Oh, Mr. Monroe!" Rosanna's face beamed with pleasure.

Roy raised his left hand to quiet her as he picked up the telephone with his right. In five minutes, Roy had arranged for an audition.

"Ten o'clock. Wednesday morning." Roy replaced the receiver. "The Colony Club."

"Oh, thank you." Rosanna stood up and held out her hand. "Now I owe you. You don't know—"

"Please. We're even. Let's just say you saved my life, and I helped you get an audition." Roy held his office door open for Rosanna, relieved she was finally leaving. He shook his head when she promised to let him know if she got the job.

"It'd be better if you celebrated with your friends. Michele wouldn't like it if he knew you were talking to me, and I can't afford to make him angry. I have to have his liquor."

"I never blamed you for what you did that night. I figured you were only protecting yourself," Rosanna said seriously.

"Thank you. I only wanted to scare him, not hurt him." His expression grew doleful. "My mother had a stroke and never recovered. But that's all in the past. No need to discuss it."

Rosanna nodded in understanding, then disappeared down the hall.

A biting wind was in Rosanna's face as she trudged along the snow-packed sidewalk from the trolley to the Colony Club. It was housed in a seedy-looking building with a dull stone front and a cascade of icy steps. Placards announced the grand opening of an all-new Colony Revue featuring dancers, singers, and a risqué master of ceremonies.

With her patent leather shoes slipping precariously on the ice, Rosanna clutched an iron railing, cautiously propelling herself to the front door. Inside, clusters of young men and women spoke in muted tones while musicians tested their instruments, the shrill wail of the clarinet clashing with a thumping bass fiddle while a pianist pounded out cords. No one looked up as Rosanna approached a balding, middle-aged man whose pudgy, diamond-studded fingers nervously beat the air, pointing first in one direction then another.

Mr. Weitzman studied Rosanna, a dour expression on his

face. After she introduced herself he pointed to the left side of the stage. "Over there. I'll call you when I'm ready."

For the next forty-five minutes, Rosanna sat on a wooden chair, the last in a row of six, and studied the competition: mannequins with frosted hair and lacquered lips that shimmered next to flawless white skin. Rosanna's knee-length dress, an unflattering brown with a worn lace collar, looked somber and dreary next to the soft pastels worn by the other girls. Jut as she began to think that Weitzman had forgotten about them, he walked up to the bandstand and yelled, "We're ready for the singers. Everybody does 'Sweet Lorraine.' You there, in the pink dress. You go first."

One by one the comely pastels sang the sugary tune with some oomph but little talent. After the first few bars, Weitzman wouldn't even listen, hurrying each one through until he finally reached Rosanna. Terrified, she stepped to center stage, hummed a few bars, then began singing, her arms at her side, her voice low. Weitzman shouted at one of the electricians working on the overhead lights. He didn't even glance at Rosanna.

Hoping to salvage her inauspicious beginning, Rosanna tried to add some sparkle to her act. She swayed from side to side, raised her arms, and forced a smile. When she finished, Weitzman thanked all the girls. "Leave your phone numbers with my assistant." He returned to a work table cluttered with musical scores, doodle paper, and coffee cups.

Rosanna picked up her purse and coat and headed for the door. Pausing in the vestibule to wrap a wool scarf around her neck, she noticed that the frosted pastels were whisked away in long, shiny cars, their decoratively shod feet barely touching the snow and ice. As she pushed the door open, someone grabbed her arm.

"Rosanna—wait."

She spun around in surprise. "Mr. Monroe! I never expected . . ."

"I was in the neighborhood." Roy smiled. "I wanted to hear you so I'd know what I sponsored."

Rosanna groaned. "Wasn't it awful? Mr. Weitzman—"

"Come on, let's get a cup of coffee." Roy took her arm.

They sat at a butcher's table in the corner of the club kitchen and sipped steaming hot coffee from chipped white mugs. Despite her naïveté, despite her being the daughter of a mortal enemy, despite her being white, Roy felt that he had known Rosanna all his life. They liked each other. Roy had never felt so comfortable with anyone before, not even his sister—and now that he had found this, he didn't want to lose it.

Rosanna, rehashing the dreadful audition, raged about Weitzman's attitude toward the girls.

"I know you'll get the job. You're a natural for the supper club circuit."

"Translated, that means I look good, I can carry a tune, and I won't interfere with the table conversation. I know I'm not as good as your sister, but how many singers are?"

Roy's face creased in a puzzled frown. "Bobbie? How do you know Bobbie?"

"She sang the night I was at the Savoy. I'll never forget her. Her voice gave me goose bumps. She was fantastic. Does she still sing at your club?" Rosanna chattered on, outlining her plans for an independent future. The first thing was to get the singing job at the Colony, then an apartment, then a roadster—or even a Model T. "I have to have a car if I'm going to work nights."

As if on cue, Roy offered to drive her home in his Cadillac. He was not offended when she asked if he would drop her off at the corner of her block.

A few people braving the wind and bitter cold stared as the Cadillac pulled up alongside the curb. Surprise and curiosity showed on their faces; a fine yellow sedan was a novelty in their insular, working-class neighborhood. There was no outrage when Rosanna stepped out of the car and waved good-bye to the brown-skinned driver. There were many first-generation Sicilians whose skin was darker than Roy's.

The temperature hovered near freezing some weeks later when Roy, bent over his ledgers, realized he was in deep trouble. A month of unseasonably cold weather had cut his already slim margin in half.

If Roy and Willie had been talking, Roy would have agreed that the strip show at the Savoy was a disaster. It had degenerated into an erotic cesspool, attracting the offal of the neighborhood. But they weren't talking, and Roy didn't know how he was going to keep the Savoy open another month. He lit a cigarette and pondered his bleak future. A knock on the door roused him. He looked up and JoJo stepped inside.

More bad news, Roy thought, then sat impassively as the young man explained that Delta refused to come out of her dressing room for the last show.

"Temperamental woman," Roy mumbled. He rushed out of his office and headed to the back of the club. Delta was pinning on her hat when he stormed into her dressing room. Willie stood beside her, holding her coat.

"What the hell you doing? You're supposed to be onstage in fifteen minutes."

"I'm leaving. I'm leaving you and your lousy show."

"And I'm going with her." Willie helped Delta with her coat.

"Stay out of this, Willie. This is between Delta and me."

"Wrong, my man. I'm not going to hang around and watch you destroy everything, including yourself."

"Boys! No need to argue." Delta smirked. We all know the party's over. All we have to do is accept it."

"No." Roy held out his hand pleadingly. "You two mean everything to me."

Delta turned and stared at him. Her eyes were cold, her mouth twisted in repressed anger. "Cut the crap, Roy. Begging isn't your style."

"I'm not above begging. I need you. I need both of you."

"You should have thought of that sooner," Willie said. "We been hanging on, hoping you'd come to your senses, but that little Gianino gal's got you wrapped around her little finger. That's okay if you want to commit suicide. We just don't want to stick around and watch."

"Keep Rosanna out of this," Roy said angrily. "She's got nothing to do with us. I've only known her for a few weeks."

"Oh, but she does, Roy. I was in love with you. I would've done anything you asked, but I'm not playing second fiddle to a wop."

"Delta, what's gotten into you? Has Willie put you up to this?"

Delta sighed audibly. "I told you to cut the crap." She turned and looked at herself in the smoky mirror. She adjusted her hat. "If I stayed here long enough and listened to your pack of lies, I'd end up on that stage again." She shook her head. "You really are something, you know. You could charm your way out of hell, but I'm not buying anymore." Despite her efforts at control, tears cascaded down her cheeks. She didn't bother to wipe them away.

"You can't stop lying, can you? You been two-timing me for weeks—making love to me in the afternoon, then running over to the Colony at night and shacking up with your new girl friend." Delta grabbed her purse and eased her way past Roy, keeping her eyes on the floor. "Well, no more. It's over."

Willie was right behind her. Roy watched, dumbfounded, until they reached the door. "If you walk out of here, you're finished. Don't ever come back. You hear me?"

Willie slammed the door behind him.

Roy ran after them, but they were gone.

Turning his attention from the strip show Belle was valiantly trying to keep alive, a prop man stepped beside him. "What you want me to do, boss? Belle's act'll be over in ten minutes."

Roy looked at the man, but didn't see him. His mind was filled with thoughts of Willie. Willie, who had been like a brother to him. Their ties went back to the Creole Club, where Willie had taught him the tavern business; and later, when he had opened the Savoy, he had depended on Willie, who handled the men who sold them illegal liquor, who knew how to give customers their money's worth during an evening on the town. Maybe I should have closed the Savoy,

Roy thought, instead of making Delta do a strip act. I should have begged them, got down on my knees and begged. Roy bit his lip to hold back the tears. Oh, God, he thought, I've been a real shit-ass fool, but now it's too late.

Roy focused his eyes on the man standing beside him. "Cut the act." He gulped. "Tell everybody to go home. Delta was right. The party's over."

CHAPTER XXII

"Magnificent!" "Jazz Queen!" "Chocolate Honey!" Newspapers, magazines, and the public "discovered" the singer of the decade. In their hedonistic search for new thrills, whites had found forbidden eroticism in the exciting Negro music called jazz. With her sultry beauty and stylish singing, Bobbie Evans shared the limelight with the likes of Bessie Smith and Ethel Waters. She was the darling of the promoters and club owners, who happily paid the five hundred dollars she demanded for a single performance. Exciting, forbidden, extravagant, and rich, Bobbie *was* the twenties. Bobbie knew she was more than a singer; she was a brown-skinned temptress, a rebel. When Bobbie sang about unfaithfulness and free love, she touched the cornerstone of the twenties' new freedom. To the flappers, those gaudy, bubbly, youthful girls who bobbed their hair and smoked cigarettes in public, she not only sang about free love, she epitomized it.

"Well, of course, Negroes don't have the same inhibitions we do." A young girl sporting short blond hair and bright red lips swished gin around an ice cube in the bottom of her glass.

"I heard she has a white lover." Her cherub-faced friend giggled.

"She's Al Capone's mistress," another chortled.

"No. She doesn't like men at all," came the last retort.

Bobbie laughed when she heard the rumors. "If I'm the forbidden fruit, let's make the most of it." She then added to her fame by not denying the lurid accounts ascribed to her. The stories persisted. She was a lesbian; she had a stable of lovers; she was addicted to cocaine. The more sensational the stories, the more Bobbie was worth at the box office.

Over four hundred people ventured out in sub-zero temperatures to hear Bobbie sing on New Year's Eve. Times were still good for the very rich who flocked to the Castle Ballroom to welcome in 1928—a year that promised to be as fruitful as the old year had been. Stocks were soaring and having fun meant spending money.

Bobbie beamed as she took encore after encore; the audience loved her effervescent rendition of "I'm Just Wild About Harry." Jiggling the beads on her white satin dress, she teased the men and shocked the women by slowly rotating her hips and whispering into the microphone. As shouts rose to a crescendo in the smoke-filled club, Bobbie raised the men's lusts to a red-hot frenzy. It was the moment she relished most—having the audience in the palm of her hand. Reluctantly she ran offstage. The cold, dark wings were a miserable letdown after the bright lights and warm applause of her fans. Chuck waited, holding an oversized towel that he wrapped around her shoulders as she scurried to her dressing room, wet with perspiration. Running to keep up, he dabbed at her forehead, while Bobbie, her face grim and unsmiling, upbraided him for the flaws in her performance. She couldn't be heard over the clatter of dishes and the bawling of drunks; the intensity of the lights made her look washed out. "People didn't come to see an albino. They came to see a colored woman."

"They came to hear you sing."

"How could they with some drunk shouting?"

"Hell, I can't guarantee quiet. You're not singing in church. It's New Year's Eve."

"If you can't handle a drunk, maybe I should get another manager."

"Maybe you should." Chuck returned her scowl. It was at times like this, when they fought, that Chuck hated Bobbie. She was a she-wolf determined to devour him if only to prove that she could.

Bobbie walked to the door and called for the wardrobe mistress. At least we don't yell at each other when we have an audience, she thought, then returned to her dressing table where she scooped up a handful of cold cream and smeared it across her face. Chuck retreated to a corner and lit a cigarette, waiting for the next round. But Bobbie lost interest in him as she hurriedly changed into a black crepe gown decorated with feathers and rhinestones. Snapping a diamond bracelet on her left wrist, Bobbie took one last look at her fresh makeup before she turned and walked to the closet where she grabbed two matching black mink coats. She threw one at Chuck.

"We're going to a party," she said curtly. "Mr. and Mrs. Irvin R. Carson requested our presence—"

"He's a fairy."

Bobbie halted in the middle of the room. "I don't care if he's a fairy or a prince. We're going to his party. He has connections."

"What the hell are you talking about?"

"Connections. Meeting the right people, getting better jobs."

Chuck bit his lip trying to restrain his anger. "I'm your manager. I make the connections."

"Some manager! And your connections! You book me into huge halls with horrible acoustics. I want to sing in a nice little club, some place intimate."

Chuck sneered. "Rich and intimate don't buy a hundred thousand records."

"I'm not selling a hundred thousand records, and you know it." Bobbie's eyes were hard.

"You will if you let me make your 'connections.'"

"Damn! I knew you wouldn't understand. Every time I make a suggestion, you say no. Can't you agree with me just once?"

Chuck stepped back. "Okay, babe." He forced a smile.

"You're right. I'm wrong. No argument. You bought me. You have the right to tell me where we go."

"I haven't bought you! You say that whenever you want to make me feel cheap."

Chuck shrugged. "What else would you call it? You bought me a mink coat, a two-carat diamond ring for my pinkie finger. You pay the rent."

"Oh, Christ!"

Chuck took the coats from Bobbie and slipped hers over her shoulders. "Don't worry about it, babe, I'm getting used to it. Just as long as nobody calls me Mr. Bobbie Evans." He draped his coat on his arm and led her to a waiting limousine. "The Carrollton Arms," he told the chauffeur, then sat bowed and tense across from Bobbie in the back seat.

Bobbie nervously picked at a chip in her fingernail polish as they sped north on Lake Shore Drive. Him and his damn ego, she thought. So I pay the bills—why shouldn't I? Money's been pouring in ever since I opened at the Imperial. Why can't he just enjoy it? Bobbie knew the answer to her question even as she thought it. Chuck still dreamed of becoming a great drummer. At least once, sometimes twice a week, he would disappear for a couple of hours to the old neighborhood on the southside. Sitting in with some famous and some not so famous musicians, he improvised for hours. Occasionally he took Bobbie along, and as she listened at the back, she couldn't help comparing "Baby" Dodds's prowess on drums and Chuck's characterless performance.

At thirty-seven, Chuck's technique was set, his skill limited. He couldn't even compete with the youngsters coming on the scene—emerging talents like the new kid, Gene Krupa, who played drums with McKenzie's Chicagoans. Bobbie realized that if they were going to make big money, she would have to do it.

Bobbie reached across the seat to grasp Chuck's hand. He jerked away. She withdrew her hand and stared icily out the window until the limousine pulled up at the canopied walk of a marble-pillared apartment building. A uniformed doorman extended his hand to help Bobbie out of the limousine. Upstairs, the butler ushered them into the foyer of the penthouse on the fifteenth floor. Taking their coats, he announced their names. A sleek, gray-haired man with a gaunt gray face and piercing blue eyes took Bobbie's arm and maneuvered her into the living room, completely ignoring Chuck.

"I'm Irvin Carson. We were expecting you earlier."

Bobbie paused, puzzled. "But your wife, Mrs. Carson, knew I had to perform. I sing—"

Carson's face showed no sign of recognition. "Betsy invites so many interesting people. Come in and meet everyone." Glancing over his shoulder, he said to Chuck, "There are two bars. You might want to try the one in the game room." Without waiting for an answer, Carson whisked Bobbie away through the living room to the music room.

Carson steered her toward a young man, thin and black, with long fingers and a broad smile, who was playing a selection of popular songs on a matching black baby grand piano. Standing up, he introduced himself. "Raoul. It's an honor, Miss Evans."

Bobbie nodded, then took a glass of champagne from a waiter's silver tray. When she pulled a cigarette from her handbag, four lighters materialized as men flocked around her, vying for her attention. Carson disappeared. The pack tightened. Bobbie smelled aftershave lotion and Scotch. Ice tinkled in half-filled glasses. Everyone wanted her to sing, and Bobbie obliged because they wanted it so badly. Watching her perform made it easy for the men to stare at her, at her brown skin and full breasts lush beneath her black sequined gown.

"Wonderful, Miss Evans."

"Marvelous. You must come to my party next month."

White teeth flashed like piano keys on a Steinway. The men, pushing closer, touched her, brushing against her arm, rubbing against her shoulder. Their eyes glistened as they stared at her. She was a Negro—tantalizing and beautiful.

Bobbie saw in their eyes that she was beautiful. Or was it

lust? Chuck would say they were leering. Lust or love—
Bobbie didn't care. If I'm here because I'm colored, I might
as well make the most of it, she thought. She smiled,
accepted another glass of champagne, and sang two more
songs.

When the grandfather clock chimed five o'clock, Chuck
disentangled himself from the clutch of women surrounding
him on the salmon and cream sofa and casually strode into
the music room. It was awash with smoke, the smell of stale
liquor, and a collection of men suspended in alcoholic
hibernation. They hovered around Bobbie, though the
novelty of her presence was wearing off. Chuck wove his
way through the tangle and drew Bobbie aside. Bobbie
chatted amicably until they were out of earshot, then she
exploded, belittling him for dragging her away from her
fans.

"I didn't drag you away. I just want to go home. Hell, it's
five o'clock. I've been up for twenty-four hours."

"So have I."

"Then let's go. I'm tired and bored to death."

"No. I don't care if you're bored."

"What the hell do you care about?"

"My future, that's what. I haven't had time to talk to
Irvin." Bobbie glanced into the music room. Carson had
materialized at the far end of the room. He was deep in
discussion with two other men. Bobbie found it exciting just
looking at him. To her, he represented old money, new
ideas, and absolute freedom to do whatever he wanted.
Irvin was one of the many playboys she met in the clubs
around the city. He happened to be one of the richest.

"Chuck, if you want to go home, go. I don't want to hear
about how late it is." Bobbie rolled her eyes in disgust. "Just
send the limousine back. I can get home by myself."

"I'm not leaving you here with these vultures. They'll
gang rape you the minute I leave."

Bobbie laughed, a cold, derisive chortle. "You've been
hanging around dives too long." She squinted in contempt.
"Men on the fifteenth floor don't gang rape a woman."

"Honey, when a man gets a hard-on, don't matter what

259

floor he's on. He wants some action. Anyway, haven't you seen the way those guys been looking at you? They were almost licking you with their tongues."

"They were not. They were listening to me sing."

"Sing! Bullshit. They want to get you to bed, pure and simple."

"Oh, you're driving me crazy. Just leave. I'd rather be raped than listen to you nag all night."

"Fine with me, babe." Angrily, Chuck turned to leave, then added, "It's a shame, but maybe that's what you need to open your eyes. Just cause you're rich, honey, don't mean you're white. Sometimes I think you forget that."

"And sometimes I think you forget that I'm old enough to stay at a party a whole week if I want, and I don't have to listen to your stupid lectures on whites and colored. Seems like that and money are all you ever talk about."

Chuck didn't answer. Barely stopping long enough to grab his coat and white silk scarf, he stomped out. Bobbie opened her compact, powdered her nose, then returned to the music room. Only a few stragglers remained. Bobbie was only interested in Irvin, but he was still deep in conversation.

Maybe I am being stupid, she thought. I'm exhausted, and I'm tired of singing. God! I hope no one asks me to sing another song. That's all I've done tonight. Not one person talked to me. They looked, they touched, but they didn't talk. Maybe they don't know what to say to a colored woman. How can color make that kind of difference? Bobbie wandered toward the piano, lost in thought. If I can get a gig at the Evergreen Club, I'll rub it in Chuck's face for a month. He couldn't even get a phone call through to the manager. Bobbie's eyes lit up. I bet Irvin can. He's a businessman. Everybody owes him. Wonder if the rumors about him and Al Capone—Bobbie stopped and stared at the man casually plunking out a song at the piano. Who is he? My God, he's gorgeous. He looks like he just stepped out of a fashion magazine. The stranger had broad shoulders and a long square face; his black hair was slicked back, straight and smooth. His olive skin looked as if it would be silky to touch. Bobbie knew that when he smiled he would have beautiful teeth. Where had he come from? She hadn't seen him earlier. Bobbie forced a chirpy hello.

"You look just like a man I saw being whisked away in a limousine on Michigan Avenue. Rich, elegant, detached."

He smiled. He did have beautiful teeth. "And I was with a blonde who was tall and thin and silky."

"Was it really you?" Bobbie laughed.

"Of course. Every time you see a handsome man with a beautiful woman, just yell 'Georgy' and I'll turn around."

Bobbie shrugged and wrinkled her nose. "All men with money look alike to me—just like all Negroes look alike to white folks."

"I'd pick you out of a crowd anytime, Miss Evans."

Bobbie raised her eyebrows in surprise. "You know me?"

"Everybody knows you—in Chicago—around the country."

"Thanks for saying it, but I don't think so." Bobbie found it difficult to chat with such an intense man. Unnerved, Bobbie took a sip of champagne. Her throat constricted, and she coughed violently.

Georgy was at her side in an instant, offering his handkerchief. "Are you all right?"

"Yes. I didn't realize stale champagne tasted so terrible."

"Would you like a fresh glass?"

"Oh, no. I'm going home as soon as I say good-bye to Irvin and Betsy." Bobbie glanced around the apartment. "I haven't seen Betsy for an age."

"She passed out," Georgy said matter-of-factly.

"Oh, you were here earlier?"

"No. It's just that she usually passes out. Between the coke and the booze—"

"Yes, well, I'm sure she'll be all right," Bobbie stammered. "I guess I have stayed too long." Bobbie set her glass on the top of the piano along with other half-empty ones and smoldering ashtrays. She pointed toward Irvin. "Our host is finally alone. I really must say good-bye. I hope I'll see you again, Mr.—"

"Torrio. Georgy to you."

Bobbie nodded, then, not knowing what else to say, smiled pleasantly and walked away. She felt his eyes on her all the way across the room. She shivered. You meet all kinds, she thought, as she approached Irvin Carson.

"Mr. Carson—Irvin—thank you for a lovely New Year's party. Chuck and I really enjoyed—"

"Look, woman, see how it swirls. Doesn't it make you want to jump out in it? Oh, to be enveloped in a vaporish gray shroud."

"What?"

"The fog. Can't you see the fog?" Irvin's thin, gaunt face twitched slightly, and his knuckles turned white as he clenched his fists, pounding on the floor-to-ceiling glass with such force that Bobbie was afraid it would break.

She looked out the window. A gray dawn was breaking in the east, and a choppy, white-capped Lake Michigan swirled turbulently fifteen stories below.

"Mr. Carson, I'm leaving now," Bobbie said, ignoring his outburst. "I wanted to talk to you about a job at the Evergreen Club, but it'll wait." Was he always this crazy, she wondered, or was it just the liquor and the hour?

"Don't go, my dear." Abruptly, Irvin's stern expression faded and a smile spread across his face. "I haven't taken you to bed yet, have I?"

"I beg your pardon."

"To bed. That's why you were invited. Some of the men wanted a little colored gal this evening." He looked down at her, peering over the rim of his glasses.

"You're drunk. Drunk and crazy."

"Not drunk. Just horny." Irvin put his arm around Bobbie's waist and pulled her close to him. He rotated his stomach and hips while he tried to lick her face with his tongue.

"Stop it. Stop it right now! You're the most disgusting—" She tried to push him away, but her feeble efforts only roused Irvin more.

"I love a woman who fights," Irvin whispered as he tried to bite her ear.

"Georgy!"

"Oh, I'm afraid all the gallant men have flown. Only lechers like me are left."

"If you don't let go of me, I'll—"

"You'll what? Scratch my face. How naughty of you. Come on, give Irv a kiss."

Irvin pushed Bobbie against the wall, immobilizing her. His mouth, only inches from hers, reeked of tobacco and whiskey. She gagged when saliva dribbled from his mouth as he tried to kiss her. She spit in his face.

"You are a little bitch." He tightened his grip. "A real bitch."

Bobbie glanced frantically around the now-empty room. Where the hell was Georgy? Bobbie froze when she felt Irvin's hand worm its way into her dress. He pinched her breasts.

"You bastard. If you don't let me go—" She tried to twist away.

"Relax, honey. Enjoy it. Once you have a white man, you won't want a nigger man no more."

"Okay, buster, you asked for it." Choked with anger, staring straight into Irvin's eyes, Bobbie raised her right leg and jabbed it into his groin.

Irvin roared with pain. Clutching himself with both hands, he hobbled away, cursing.

As Bobbie adjusted her gown, Georgy ran up to her, looking distraught. "What's going on?"

"Our host just tried to rape me." Bobbie straightened up and haughtily strode away.

Georgy looked at her, then at Irvin. "You are a real ass," he shouted at Irvin, then ran after Bobbie. He caught her at the door. "I was in the john. I didn't know he was that crazy. He and Betsy are floating all the time. Please, forgive me for leaving. May I drive you home?" he asked solicitously.

"No, thank you. I'm safer by myself." Near tears, throwing her coat over her shoulders, Bobbie stormed out of the apartment, slamming the door in Georgy's face.

The hall was deserted as she hurried to the elevator. Still quivering, she pushed the elevator button, waited half a minute, then pushed again. The elevator refused to budge off the first floor. After two more tries, near panic, she held her finger on the button while she kicked the door. The pungent odor of cigarette smoke wafted toward her. Startled, she turned to face the intruder.

"Chuck!" Bobbie leaned against the elevator door and sighed with relief. "Thank God."

Chuck stepped closer. "Having trouble?" he asked, concerned.

"He tried to rape me." Bobbie tried to control her tears.

"On the fifteenth floor?" Chuck raised his eyebrows in mock surprise.

Bobbie's eyes flew open. "I ought to slap you for that."

"Go ahead if it'll make you feel better." Chuck put his arm around Bobbie and she laid her head on his shoulder. "Buck up, sweetheart. It isn't that bad, is it?"

Bobbie clung to him for consolation. "Not for you. It was awful."

Chuck patted her comfortingly. "I'm sorry. That's why I hung around. I thought something might happen." He paused, then tilted her face upward toward his. "Who was it?"

"Irvin. The bastard. He invited a little 'nigger gal' for him and his playmates. Oh, God! How could I have been so stupid? I thought—"

"Cut it out. What Carson tried has nothing to do with you personally. Tomorrow night he might want Chinese. It's like eating something new every day. Anything to keep from being bored."

Chuck held her until she stopped crying. "How'd you get away?"

Bobbie smiled warily. "I kicked him in the balls."

Chuck roared with laughter. "I bet he yelled like a castrated bull. I knew you could take care of yourself. I don't have to be around twenty-four hours a day to protect you."

Snuggling together, they walked through the lobby where they signaled an indolent doorman to page their chauffeur.

They stepped outside, waiting for their car under the bright green canopy. Bobbie inhaled deeply. The wintry, early morning air revived her. She was happy again.

As they drove away, Bobbie looked out the window at the somber dawn; the sun made no effort to break through the dense clouds. God! I hope I don't get down, she thought. Rain made her miserable, but snow was all right; it reminded her of her childhood, of sledding down icy hills, drinking hot chocolate and falling exhausted into a fluffy feather bed. Memories of her childhood stirred a restlessness inside her, the kind of restlessness she felt when she forgot something and tried to recall what it was she forgot. Mama. Roy. Tallulah. Where were they? What had happened to them? Why didn't she get in touch with them? All she had to do was call them. Yet, she didn't. The hurt was gone, but not the fear, the fear that she would be caught in their web again, that they would try and control her life. Roy could have tried to reach her, she reasoned, but he didn't. Maybe he felt as guilty as she did. She shook her head to erase the painful memories that never quite went away.

Twenty minutes later they stopped in front of a substantial two-story building. The stone front was unadorned except for shuttered French windows and an etched-glass door protected by a black wrought-iron grille. Inside, the hallway was wallpapered in elegant red poppies and white chrysanthemums. In the back of a graceful winding staircase was a small elevator used by the upstairs tenants. Chuck had talked Bobbie into buying the building as an investment so "you'll always have a roof over your head." They had argued about that just as they did about everything else. Bobbie didn't want to settle down. "What if I decide to move to New York or Los Angeles?" she had fumed. In the end, she gave in and was happy she did. She needed the peace and security of a home. It was a refuge, and Bobbie relaxed in the comforting surroundings of beaded lamp shades, overstuffed furniture, and a dark walnut console that housed her new radio.

Wrapped in a flannel robe, Bobbie warmed herself in front of the gas fireplace, a snifter of cognac in one hand, a cigarette in the other. Chuck lolled on the sofa, staring at her with anticipation.

Why can't he want me the way Carson did, Bobbie wondered, knowing that he didn't anticipate making love.

"Let's go to bed." Bobbie threw her cigarette into the fire.

Chuck didn't respond.

"Well?" Bobbie bit the tip of her tongue, then blurted out, "We don't have to make love. I know it's hard for you, especially when you haven't had any sleep." Did I handle that right? she wondered. Why she wanted sex so much she couldn't fathom; it had been months since Chuck had satisfied her in bed.

"I'm not afraid to go to bed with you," Chuck said.

"I didn't say you were."

"You hinted—"

"What do you want to do? Stay up forever?"

"I want to talk."

Bobbie put her glass on the mantel and stalked across the room. "You're really testing me, aren't you? I'm about to fall over from exhaustion, and you want to talk. You can talk to the wall for all I care."

Chuck grabbed her before she reached the bedroom. "I wanted to come home early, if you remember."

"To talk?"

"It's important."

Bobbie's shoulders slumped, she was too tired to argue. She sat down next to Chuck on the sofa, rigid and unaccommodating.

Chuck smiled and spoke in an easy, friendly tone. "I have a surprise. A New Year's present."

Bobbie squealed with delight. "Oh, darling, I'm sorry. I'm such a dunce. What is it?" Laughing, she added, "You shouldn't have."

Chuck pulled away. "No, not that kind of surprise. This is more of a . . . Oh, hell, I don't know how to tell you."

"For God's sake, what is it?" Bobbie turned to face

Chuck. Immediately, she sensed him withdrawing; she leaned away.

"We're going on the road." Chuck blurted it out.

"The road!" Bobbie glared at him, waiting for an explanation.

Chuck straightened up and glared back. "For Christ's sake, don't look at me like I'm an idiot."

"I'm not looking at you like you're an idiot. I have the feeling I'm the idiot. Road! What do you mean, 'road'? Is that like one-night stands and filthy rooms in whorehouses with signs over the doors saying "For Colored Only?"

"It won't be like that."

Bobbie jumped up, ignoring Chuck. "And shittin' in outhouses stuck in the middle of tobacco fields, not to mention the rednecks wanting to lick my black ass?"

"I said it won't be like that." Chuck slammed his fist into the back of the sofa.

"Then tell me, what will it be like?"

"You're getting stale here in Chicago. Where's the competition? It's in New York—in Harlem. But you got to pay your dues if you want to sing at the top spots like Connie's Inn or the Cotton Club. If you make it on the road, if the papers rave about you in Cincinnati, you'll be earning two thousand dollars a night in six months."

"If, if, if. And what if they don't like me in Cincinnati?" Bobbie poured Scotch into a squat monogrammed glass, then topped it with a squirt of seltzer.

"They'll love you, for Christ's sake."

"Oh, shit!"

"It's only for six weeks," Chuck said plaintively. "You're the only blues singer who's never been on the road. Bessie Smith knows every tank town from here to the Florida border. Ethel Waters grew up on the southern vaudeville circuit."

Bobbie gulped her drink then poured another. Was it really better for her career to travel to tank towns, expose herself to racial slurs—but building her following in the bargain? If she stayed in Chicago, she would end up the hometown star—a star that could lose its luster over time. Despite her fears, Bobbie admitted to herself that Chuck might be right.

"Maybe that isn't such a bad idea," she said cautiously. "When would we leave?"

"April," Chuck answered, heartened.

Bobbie smiled. "You knew I wouldn't break my club dates here, didn't you?"

"There's no reason why you should. We'll be on the road from April to the middle of May. We can spend the summer in New York and come back home for the fall and winter seasons."

Bobbie pulled a chair close to the coffee table, and looked unblinkingly into Chuck's eyes. "Okay, tell me all about it."

Bursting with confidence, Chuck told Bobbie his plans, assuring her that he would organize everything: the band, the music, the side acts. All she had to do was sing. "We can even hire a maid," he said proudly, then added out the side of his mouth, "Course she'll have to double as a wardrobe mistress some of the time."

"Have you started auditioning?"

"Just the band."

"The band!" Bobbie was puzzled, then her face lit up. She nodded in understanding.

"We have to have a band. I'm calling it Chuck Jones and His Chicago Aces."

"Are we promoting you or me?"

"Both. I want to find out if I can make it, too."

Bobbie eyed him suspiciously. "Just make sure you don't try to ride the crest on my shirttail."

"I'll make it on my own or not at all." Chuck's eyes were steely with determination.

Bobbie still wasn't convinced. "What about rooms? I won't sleep in a whorehouse, a tent, or a fleabag hotel."

"We're booked in a boarding house in Cairo and hotels in Louisville, Cincinnati and Philadelphia."

"First class?"

Chuck laughed. "Since when do colored go first class?

Even when we got the dough, we can't stay at hotels that are first class." He shrugged. "But they'll be clean."

Bobbie leaned her head on the back of the chair, enjoying the tingling sensation that spread down her spine. I want to go on this tour, she realized. Even Mama went on tour.

CHAPTER XXIII

By April, 1927, Roy and the Savoy were barely afloat. Only sheer determination kept the strip show alive. Belle and three string dancers, performing in pairs, managed two shows a night, but only Belle showed any talent for the act as she gyrated to the throbbing beat of the drums.

Roy quit trying to salvage what little was left of the Savoy and the floor show. Instead, he caught Rosanna's acts at the Colony Club whenever he could. Standing in the wings, the only place Negroes were allowed at the cabaret, Roy listened, enchanted, as Rosanna sang ballads to a graying, middle-aged crowd sipping illegal liquor in elegant, intimate surroundings. Leaning against the baby grand piano, Rosanna toyed with her chiffon scarf as she sang "Sweet Sue," "Margie," and "Carolina in the Morning." Rosanna refused to take her singing seriously. "You know the people like my singing because I don't drown out their conversation. I'm just good background music. Rudy buys me beautiful gowns, and I love my job. I don't have to be great."

Rosanna closed the show with "That Toddlin' Town— Chicago," then ran breathlessly down the hall to her dressing room. She spotted the white florist's box tied with a red ribbon only seconds before Roy entered the room.

"Oh, Roy, you're sweet." She tore the box open. The heavy scent of six gardenias perfumed the air. "They're my favorite. How did you know?"

269

Mama loved gardenias, Roy thought. Sometimes he thought he could still smell them when he walked into her room to talk. It was the only pleasant part of the visit, and eased some of the pain he felt as he looked at the frail shell of a woman who had once been so full of life and vitality. Did Tallulah dust her with scented talc hoping she'd enjoy the smell? Roy looked at Rosanna and smiled. "I like 'em. I figured you would, too."

They bantered back and forth as Roy headed west on Delmar Boulevard toward the Savoy. It's so easy to be happy when I'm with Rosanna, Roy thought.

Rosanna hummed a tune as she fingered the lapel of Roy's evening jacket. "The elegant trappings of an advanced civilization."

"It's my uniform," he said proudly. "All club owners wear tuxes. We even sleep in 'em."

When they entered the Savoy, the hollow tapping of their heels resounded in the club's empty rooms. Roy hurriedly turned on the radio, tuning into station KCVM's night music from Chicago. "Can't stand the quiet." As Roy headed toward the kitchen, he pointed to a table by the dance floor. "You stay put. Everything's ready. I'll be the waiter and serve you."

The champagne cork popped, and Roy filled two long-stemmed glasses. "The real stuff. Right off the boat."

"Must have cost a fortune." Rosanna peered at the French label.

"It's only money." Roy grabbed Rosanna in his arms and swung her around the dance floor.

"I love you, Rosanna," Roy said without thinking. "I don't have the right to love you, but I do." He smiled sadly. "It's okay. It's just for tonight. I won't complicate your life tomorrow."

"Complicate my life!" Rosanna drew back. "Silly! It's too late. You've already complicated my life. I love you more than anything in the world. And I'll love you forever."

Roy stared into her deep brown eyes. His fingers fluttered across her flawless skin bronzed by the candlelight. He lifted her face to his and kissed her lips, softly at first, then harder as his passion grew. In one brief moment of joy, they became one. Moments later, their passion waning, they hugged and kissed and laughed and kissed again. They talked into the morning when they finally fell asleep on the floor, a dusty coverlet pulled over them.

It was past one o'clock the next afternoon before Roy slipped out of their makeshift bed. Pulling on his trousers, he headed for the kitchen and set a pot of coffee on a front burner. I'm in love. Sounds good, Roy thought, but it isn't good. We can never marry, and an affair will never work. We'd be miserable. Roy poured himself a cup of coffee, then, waiting for it to cool, he stared into space. Rosanna startled him as she crept up from behind.

"Guess who." She clasped her hands over his eyes.

"The most beautiful girl in the world." Roy's coffee splashed as he spun around and kissed her.

"Last night I was the most talented, too," Rosanna said teasingly.

"Then the most talented and the most beautiful," Roy corrected.

Rosanna snuggled her face on Roy's chest, held him close for a moment, then looked up at him. "I love you." Her eyes were bright, but with a hint of sadness. "Kiss me and tell me everything's going to be all right."

Roy leaned down and pressed his lips on Rosanna's, holding her chin in his hands. When they separated, he smiled. "The kiss was easy, but I can't guarantee that everything's going to be all right. If it were up to me . . . but I can't control Michele and Tony and the whole stinkin' world."

Rosanna shook her head and moved away. "I can't either." Her voice lost its sparkle. "But we can enjoy what time we have together, can't we? I mean—no one ever has to know."

"How long, my lovely? Can we keep it a secret forever?"

Rosanna thought a moment, a pained expression crossing her face. "Let's not talk about it now."

Roy brooded. "We have to talk about it. You know what Michele'll do if he finds out."

Rosanna nodded. "He'll kill us."

"We can leave town. I'll sell the Savoy. I can still get maybe fifty thou for it. And I have money in stocks. We could manage."

"Where can we run? Michele has contacts all over the country." Rosanna's hair tumbled over her eyes as she poured herself a cup of coffee. She was wearing Roy's maroon smoking jacket, scrounged from the back of his office closet. The silk sash slid open to reveal her soft olive-tone skin, black pubic hair, and long, shapely legs. Roy found it difficult to concentrate.

"We'll both rent an apartment in the same building."

Rosanna started to protest, but Roy held up his hand. "Wait a minute. It'll work. I know a place where colored and white live together. It's in a black neighborhood, but what the hell—"

"Won't Michele ask questions?" Rosanna's frown deepened.

"So what if he does? You got a right to live wherever you want."

"I'm afraid I don't, sweetheart. Uncle Michele doesn't think I have any rights."

"What can he do? He can't put you in prison."

Rosanna stared at Roy, fear glazing her eyes. "He can lock me in a room, he can beat me, he can kill me. That man is not human."

Roy stood up and hurried to Rosanna's side. Wrapping his arms around her, he held her protectively.

"He'll never hurt you. I promise. I'll kill him first."

They grew silent, and clung to each other.

"We'll be careful," Roy said at last, trying to sound confident. "Michele can't watch you all the time, can he?"

They moved into the Arlington Arms in May, 1929, a month after the Savoy closed. Roy had watched the workmen shroud the tables and chairs with white canvas covers, then strip the stage of its props and sound equipment. Roy heard Bobbie's voice wailing the blues, watched Delta kick long, mesh-covered legs high, thrilling the customers with her wicked shimmy. Roy swallowed hard remembering Willie hovering in the wings, alert for trouble, always the congenial jack-of-all-trades.

They were all there, the spirits of his youth. Roy blew his nose, grabbed his hat, and walked out the door. He was twenty-nine years old, and the future looked bleak indeed.

Roy wasn't alone. Even on Main Street the mood of the people was shifting from optimism to wary concern, the hoopla of the early twenties was tempered by economic and social problems that just wouldn't go away.

When the Colony closed temporarily in August, Roy and Rosanna's livelihood was threatened. Rudy hinted that he didn't like keeping the same singer three seasons in a row but rehired Rosanna for September anyway—the times were too chancy to tamper with success.

Freed of her professional obligations, Rosanna told her parents she was taking a vacation. For two weeks Rosanna was the dutiful housewife, cooking, cleaning, sharing Roy's tentative plans for the future. Maybe a new club, he hinted —something less pretentious than the Savoy. He'd hire a combo, one singer, and serve sandwiches, but mostly drinks. In a loud voice, he predicted the end of prohibition. "A noble experiment, but one that's seen its time."

On a stifling Sunday afternoon, Rosanna sat in the sun-filled living room and watched Leadbelly, their black and tan cat, squirm uneasily on the plush gray carpet. Roy dozed beside the animal, the Sunday papers spread around him.

"Let's go for a walk." Tugging at her dress collar, Rosanna stood up and shuffled to the window. "It's ninety degrees in here, and it's only one o'clock."

Roy lazily opened his eyes. "Too dangerous. We better wait till it gets dark."

Rosanna rubbed her stomach. "I don't feel good. My stomach's upset. Maybe some fresh air . . ."

Roy's eyes widened. "You didn't tell me you felt bad. Maybe you should see a doctor. With this heat, it could be food poisoning."

"It's nothing." Rosanna fanned herself in front of the

open window. "We could go down to the riverfront. There are always lots of people there. No one would pay any attention to us."

Roy gave her a sharp look. "Come on, babe. We'd stand out like two Eskimos. Everybody'd notice us."

"We've walked down the street together before and haven't been bothered."

"On a work day when people were in a hurry." Roy scratched Leadbelly's chin and exhaled loudly. "Okay, we'll go, but if it even looks like somebody's going to give us trouble, we're coming right home."

Rosanna was dressed in twenty minutes, and within the hour, they alighted from the streetcar and strolled down the embankment to the Mississippi. When they reached the bottom, Roy and Rosanna walked to the far end of the wharf, away from the crowds of sightseers and fishermen. Rosanna immediately took off her shoes and dangled her feet in the muddy water.

"Oh, this feels wonderful," she said happily.

"How's your stomach?" Roy pulled her gently behind a pylon at the end of the pier to hide them.

"Much better. No aches, no pains. It's great being out of the apartment. I feel so free, just like the Mississippi moving on down to New Orleans."

"There are a lot of snags in rivers."

"Oh, silly. I know that." Rosanna laughed and squeezed Roy's hand. "But looking at all this water moving past us makes our problems seem insignificant, don't you think? We're only here for a little while. The river's been here forever."

"Not quite forever." Roy felt very unphilosophical. "Anyway, what difference does it make?"

Rosanna's mouth turned down in a pout. "You are in a mood today. I know—you're worried about not having a club, you're worried about Uncle Michele finding out about us, you're worried about everything."

Roy shifted to a comfortable position and allowed his legs to dangle down the side of the pier. "You're right. But at least one problem's been settled. I used to worry about making a choice between you and my booze in case Michele found out about us."

"That's wonderful—you would have had to choose between me and a case of hooch. I'm glad I'll never find out what your final choice would have been."

"I'd have chosen you." Roy playfully pecked the side of her cheek.

"That makes me very happy." Rosanna eyed him skeptically.

"Now that that's settled, let's leave." Roy pointed to a cluster of boys a block away. "I don't like the looks of those bums. They got nothing to do but stir up trouble."

Rosanna shielded her eyes with her hand and peered around the pylon. Kegs of beer dotted the area, and boisterous laughter boomed up and down the wharf. Beer and young boys and a hot Sunday afternoon were volatile combinations. It was the type of situation they had assiduously avoided in the past, and now they would have to walk through the milling crowd to reach the street. Swallowing her fear, Rosanna slid off the pier and quickly slipped into her shoes. Without speaking, she walked ahead of Roy, as they'd planned, pretending to be alone, but there was no way they could avoid walking past the youthful rabble.

One of the boys whistled at Rosanna as she hurried past. Soon a chorus of voices rose in a wave of grunts as one boy then another ran in circles around her as she scampered up the hill.

Roy stayed several yards behind. He hoped that they would soon tire and find other pleasures, but they didn't. Instead, they grew bolder, reaching out to pinch Rosanna's hips. She yelled at them to stop, swatting their hands with her purse, but her pleas excited the five boys even more. Suddenly, one of them pulled her close and tried to kiss her. Rosanna slammed her fist in his face. Roused to anger, the boys came at her. Roy didn't hesitate. Racing up from behind, he grabbed Rosanna's arm and they flew down the street, their feet barely touching the sidewalk. The boys were right behind. Roy darted down an alley. My God, this is how Papa died, he thought. In a stinkin' alley. Shit! There's no way that's going to happen to us.

"Rosanna. How fast can you run? We got to outdistance them. I can't fight all five of 'em."

One of the boys turned the corner. Spotting them, he yelled to his friends.

Rosanna stared panic-stricken at Roy. "Uncle Michele—"

"Damn it, Rosanna, forget him. He's not our problem right now."

"No. He has a house just three blocks away. If we can get there . . ."

As the rabble turned the corner, Roy took Rosanna's hand. "Lead the way!"

Zigzagging down empty alleyways, they managed to keep a hundred-yard lead. Out of breath, Rosanna pointed to a red brick house, its backyard accessible through an arched entry at the side. Roy and Rosanna darted through the opening, assuming they'd be safe on Michele's property. Too late they saw that the yard was enclosed, that there was no escape. The boys moved in, their faces menacing and triumphant as they realized their victims were trapped. Roy shielded Rosanna's body, stepping backward toward the fence. Searching the ground for a weapon, he spied a length of wood and snatched it up.

Grabbing his club, the five boys threw Roy to the ground, kicking his face and groin. Beating him with the piece of wood, one pounded Roy's leg until it was a bloody, shapeless mass. Roy freed one arm and fought back, scoring a hit on a nose that crumbled under his fist.

No one heard the click of a revolver over the tumult, but Roy saw two armed men walking across the yard before a blow shut his eyes.

"Hold it right there!" A huge, burly man pointed a shotgun straight at the youths' heads.

The beating stopped.

"Put your hands on the fence."

After the boys had lined up, the man with the shotgun

struck each on the head with the butt of his gun. Blood spurted onto the ground.

"Maybe that'll teach youse guys not to touch a Gianino. Now get out of here, ya scum. I better never see your ugly faces no place or I'll wipe up the street with ya."

One by one the boys shuffled out of the yard. Rosanna, hysterical, fell on the ground beside Roy and tenderly wiped his face with the hem of her dress.

"For God's sake, help him!" She looked up at the men.

They hesitated a moment as though wondering what to do. Finally the man with the revolver stuck his weapon in his pants, dragged Roy inside the house, and dumped him on the kitchen floor. Rosanna started to protest, then saved her energy. Filling a dishpan with warm water, she washed Roy's swollen, blood-caked face. He moaned and tried to push her away.

"It's me, Rosanna. Don't try to move."

Roy clung to her arm and mumbled incoherently.

"I can't hear you." Rosanna leaned down, putting her ear close to his mouth.

"My leg . . . it's broken." Blood-stained tears ran down Roy's cheeks.

Rosanna patted his arm. "I'm going to call an ambulance. I'll be right back." Springing up, Rosanna darted across the kitchen, frantically looking for a phone.

"There has to be a telephone. Please, help me."

The men stared blankly at her, motionless.

"Hell! You're nothing but zombies." She ran to the living room, tripping over chairs and a mahogany coffee table covered with bric-a-brac and dusty artificial flowers. The faint aroma of incense filled the room. Whorehouse, Rosanna thought, spying a telephone at last. She had barely put the receiver to her ear when a hand reached out and took it away.

Rosanna swung around. "Uncle Michele! You frightened me."

Michele Gianino put the telephone back on the stand. Being several inches taller than six feet, he towered over Rosanna. No middle-age paunch protruded from his hard, muscular frame. Rosanna stepped back, hesitated, then squelched her fears and told her uncle what had happened. A twitch in his right eye was Michele's only reaction. When Rosanna finished, he pushed past her and walked to the kitchen. Roy was still moaning, barely conscious.

"Can't you see he's suffering?" Rosanna looked first at Roy then at her uncle. When no one moved, Rosanna fell to the floor and patted Roy's hand. "We have to get him to a hospital."

Michele stepped forward. Raising his hand, he slapped Rosanna across the face, knocking her against the wall. "Keep your hands off that nigger. I know you been sleeping with that bastard, but you're not going to touch him in front of me."

A dull, aching pain ballooned inside Rosanna's head. She felt as though she might faint, but her anger revived her. "That's Roy Monroe. He owned the Savoy. You've known him for years. You have to help him."

Michele's frown deepened. "I don't help no nigger—specially that one. You forget he ruined your father with that voodoo curse? You been disloyal to your family taking up with a nigger. Somebody got to teach you a lesson." Michele grabbed Rosanna by her hair and slapped her again. "I know you been sleeping with this nigger, but I want to hear it from you."

"What difference does it make?" Tears flooded Rosanna's eyes.

"Don't you talk to me like that." Michele's eyes filled with fury. "You're not fit to have the name Gianino."

"I'm more fit than you—"

Michele brought the full force of his fist slamming down on her. A searing pain shot through Rosanna's jaw. She slid across the room and crumpled unconscious in a corner. Michele stared at her with cold, steely eyes, then spat in her face.

Roy watched Michele's violence helplessly, his rage momentarily making him forget his pain. Raising himself on his elbow, he tried to drag himself across the floor. He had barely moved when excruciating pain shot up his leg. A scream rose from deep inside him.

"You want to get up, nigger? You want to help your sweetheart?" A sneer gnarled Michele's already distorted features. "I'll help you, nigger." Michele grabbed Roy's shoulders and pulled him to a standing position. Almost fainting, Roy grabbed onto Michele's shirt and hung on. Laughing at Roy's suffering, Michele jigged around the room, dragging Roy's twisted body along with him. Unable to protect his broken leg, Roy's grip slackened, and as he started to lose consciousness, falling down, he slugged Michele in the face. Enraged, Michele threw Roy onto the floor and kicked him again and again. Finally, when the bloody mass of flesh that had been Roy's body stopped jerking, Michele grabbed the shotgun, aimed it at Roy's head, and pulled the trigger.

Michele stood over Roy's body for several minutes before his anger subsided. Then, kicking it one last time, he returned the shotgun to his bodyguard and growled, "Get rid of 'em. Take Rosanna to the hospital, then dump the nigger in an alley on the other side of town. Make it look like one of his own killed him, not that it matters—nobody gives a damn what happens to niggers."

Rosanna lay in her hospital bed for two weeks, drifting in and out of a coma caused by a combination of drugs and her concussion. After she regained consciousness, she was forced to remain in the hospital another six weeks, her jaw wired shut, a virtual prisoner of Michele's bodyguards who stood sentinel outside her room. Only Rosanna's mother, Tina, was allowed to visit. Stoop-shouldered and shrunken from age and sorrow, the old woman sat by the bedside sobbing softly. Michele had told her all she needed to know: Rosanna had been attacked by drunken hooligans. She would need six months, maybe a year, to heal. Tina nodded and made daily vigils to the Virgin, lighting candles and praying for her daughter at St. Margaret of Scotland church.

By the end of October Rosanna was sent home. Her body

grew stronger but her thoughts tormented her. What had happened to Roy? Why hadn't he contacted her? No sooner had she asked the question than she knew the answer. Michele's bodyguards clung to her like moss. After two frantic weeks of plotting an escape, a thunderstorm gave her the chance to be alone for an hour.

Tina, who usually walked to church on Sunday mornings, asked the bodyguard to drive her because of the heavy rain. Assuming that Rosanna was asleep at six A.M., the man agreed. Before they were half a block from the house, Rosanna was on the phone. When no one answered at Roy's apartment, she called Rudy. Apologizing for the hour, she hastily explained her predicament to her old boss.

Rudy mumbled incoherently, finally woke up, and then spoke quickly, as though anxious to be rid of Rosanna. "Honey, I'm sorry I got to be the one to tell you . . . but Roy's dead."

A throbbing pain exploded inside Rosanna's head. She groaned loudly and Rudy asked if she were all right.

"When?" Rosanna asked, hardly able to speak.

"Couple of months ago. Police said it must've been a robbery. He was beaten up pretty badly." Rudy paused, then added, "Sorry that you had to find out like this. Heard you were in an accident, too. Take care of yourself, kid."

Rudy abruptly hung up.

Rosanna stared at the phone for several minutes, stunned by the news. She didn't cry until she was in her bedroom, then she screamed, pounded on her pillow, and cursed God for deserting her. Moments later she prayed for strength, repeating Roy's name over and over as though the sound of her voice could raise him from the dead.

When she was calmer, she vowed Michele wouldn't destroy her. He'd love to put me in an institution for the rest of my life, she thought. Fit punishment for having an affair with a black man, he'd say. I won't let him do it.

Rosanna sat up and wiped her face. I'll get even someday, she swore. He thinks he's won—he's killed Roy. A cruel smile parted Rosanna's lips. But he won't kill me because I'm blood—and I am going to have Roy's baby.

When the bodyguard returned with Tina, Rosanna was waiting at the kitchen table. Her swollen eyes told them she had been crying, but she was calm. Now she could make plans for her future—hers and her baby's—confident that Michele wouldn't touch the child because it had Gianino blood in its veins.

She was right. Michele growled, but he gave Rosanna a latitude that was as pleasant as it was unexpected. He personally arranged for an adequate supply of milk, fruits, vegetables, and meats for her and scolded Tina when her meals seemed deficient. But he never spoke to Rosanna about her pregnancy after his initial outburst. Rather, he seemed to be waiting, and by April, when the baby was due, Rosanna observed his restraint with suspicion, fearing it like a spring storm.

Expecting Tina to accompany her to the hospital, Rosanna was surprised, angry, and frightened when Michele told her he would take her himself.

I don't want him anywhere near my baby, Rosanna thought, as she packed her bag. Rosanna was in tears as she slid into the backseat of the Chrysler, hunching, tense and terrified, in the corner.

"I'm leaving after the baby's born," Rosanna said.

Michele didn't respond.

"I know you hate me, so it makes sense for me to disappear. I swear, you won't ever hear from me again. I'm going to change my name. It'll be as if I never existed." Rosanna's voice was pleading now, but Michele didn't even turn his head. A contraction, the strongest yet, convulsed Rosanna. Panicking, she threw herself at Michele. Grabbing his lapels, she shook him, while tears of pain and fear rolled down her cheeks.

"Please listen to me. I have a right to my baby, to my own life. You have to let me go. I swear, I won't tell anybody what happened to Roy. I just want to go away."

Michele's iron reserve cracked when Rosanna mentioned Roy's name. In a fury, he slapped her hard across her face, leaving the red mark of his hand upon her cheek.

"Don't you ever touch me again." He squinted with

hatred. "I tell you what to do, you do it. Everybody does what I tell 'em to do. Remember that."

The doctor admonished Rosanna to relax, but she couldn't. It was as if she were trying to keep her baby inside her to protect it from her uncle. Only when the doctor threatened to take the baby by cesarean section did Rosanna allow it to be born. When an olive-skinned boy was finally handed to her, she sobbed tears of relief. Somehow we'll make it, she whispered in her son's ear. We'll run away and hide, even if we have to go to the ends of the earth. Michele will never hurt you, she promised.

For five days Rosanna watched and waited for a sign that Michele was up to something, but the hospital routine never varied. She was allowed to nurse her son, whom she named Roy, Jr., and on the fifth day of her confinement, she was told she could go home. It was close to noon before a nurse came into the room to help her pack. At 12:20 Michele strolled in, a dull, insipid expression on his face. Rosanna looked up, startled.

"Where's Mama? I thought she was supposed to come." As always when Michele was around, Rosanna was overwhelmed by fear. Her throat constricted, and she could hardly talk.

"She was busy," Michele growled. "One of my boys'll drive you home."

Rosanna turned her back to him. "No thanks. I'll take a taxi."

"No taxi. You're going home with my man."

"I'm warning you, Michele—get out of my life! There's nothing I can do about the past except hate you and curse your soul to hell. But stay away from me and my baby." Swallowing hard, Rosanna turned to the nurse. "Please, may I have my son. I'm ready to leave."

The nurse frowned. "I don't understand. He was taken from the nursery an hour ago. The private nurse you hired—"

Rosanna's scream echoed down the hall. She picked up

the water pitcher by the bed and threw it at Michele. He ducked, then threw her on the bed. The nurse ran for an orderly.

Pinning her arms above her head, Michele leaned over Rosanna. "Yes, I took him." His voice was filled with hate. "He's a nigger bastard, but he's got more Gianino in him than Negro. Anna and me never had no kids so I decided to take yours. I told Anna I was adopting a boy. She doesn't know he's yours. She'll never know because if you tell her, I'll fix you for good."

"Kill me! Go ahead and kill me like you did Roy. I don't want to live."

"No." Michele's eyes glistened. "I'm not going to kill you. And you're not going to tell anybody nothing. I got other plans. I already fixed the birth certificate. You and your nigger lover aren't even on it. Anna and me are listed as the boy's parents. We're calling him Johnny. Ain't that something—us getting a baby so late in life. Anna's thrilled. And as for you, I bought a house right across the street from us. That way we can keep an eye on each other. If you're good, you can visit Johnny on Christmas and maybe on his birthday, Cousin Rosanna. Course, if you're bad, then I might have to put you in the crazy house. Wouldn't cost me much to buy a judge."

Rosanna pulled her arm free and lunged for Michele's eyes. Her fingernails ripped across his face, and blood oozed from the wounds. Frantically Michele tried to push her away, but she kept coming at him, scratching, clawing, biting. It took the orderly, the nurse, and Michele to hold her until they could give her a sedative strong enough to knock her out.

"She's been sick in the head on and off all her life," Michele said. "Having the baby tipped her over again. But I'll take care of her, just like I always have. Six months in a home—out in the country. She'll come around." Michele paused, then nodded to himself. "Six months should just about do it." He opened the door and disappeared down the hallway.

The nurse looked at the orderly, then at Rosanna, who was sprawled across the bed unconscious. She shook her head in disbelief. "Isn't he the most wonderful man? Taking care of his niece like that! I wish I had an uncle so concerned about my welfare. And he's rich, too."

The orderly agreed, then they snapped heavy iron bars on the sides of Rosanna's bed.

CHAPTER XXIV

"They pick up the money with their asses," Chuck said, grinning mischievously.

"Their asses?" Bobbie shook her head. "I don't believe it."

"They do. They lift up their skirts and pinch the money off the table. Course, the bills have to be placed just right. Lots of broads get their tips that way."

"It's degrading." Bobbie turned and looked at the Getaway Shufflers, four white chorines, who were practicing a mediocre tap and soft shoe routine. "But I guess they get huge tips," she added indifferently.

"You bet."

"They're not very good, are they?"

Chuck frowned and eyed Bobbie quizzically. "Who?"

"The Getaway Shufflers."

"Who's looking at their feet?"

"I don't want a girlie show." Bobbie mimicked Chuck's frown.

"Don't worry. It won't be."

Bobbie walked past the nucleus of their road show: a pianist, a bassist, and a tenor sax; Cardoza the Great, a white magician, who would stay with them till they reached Philadelphia, and the Getaway Shufflers, who might or might not make it past opening night. It was a motley crew, Bobbie thought, but then, she reminded herself, the public loved the variety they offered.

Bobbie poured stale coffee into a stained mug and stared out the window at the snow covering garbage cans and back-alley litter. Despite the weather, she felt secure and content. If only it could always be like this, she thought. Chuck was happy, maybe for the first time since she had known him. And when he was happy, so was she. Their isolation had ended; their circle of friends had widened. While Bobbie learned new songs and practiced a more sophisticated singing style, Chuck practiced the drums. Bobbie would follow him to the Three Deuces. Even Chuck sounded good when he joined the likes of clarinetist Jimmie Noone and Earl Hines on piano. Returning to the apartment late in the evening, Chuck talked about nothing but his drums, his band, and taking the show on the road.

Slowly the acts began to coalesce. The dancers stayed in a straight line and Cardoza's rabbits stayed in his hat. The band's jazzy blues style was the inspiration for Bobbie's new numbers. All that was left was to hire the maid/wardrobe mistress, a combination that was almost impossible to find.

One more set of interviews, Bobbie thought as she finished her coffee and stood up. Five women were waiting— all hefty, ample-breasted women, all wearing somber dresses and sturdy black shoes, each with folded hands and crossed ankles. The woman sitting on the end . . . a refreshing alertness showed on the woman's warm face. Bobbie smiled, then, rushing to Chuck, exploded with excitement.

"I think I've found her." She grinned broadly.

Chuck kept his eyes on his clipboard. He checked off the names of the dancers.

"Listen to me." Bobbie was bursting with enthusiasm.

"Yeah, yeah. You found her." Chuck thought for a second. "Found who?"

"The maid—the wardrobe mistress."

"Oh, yeah . . ." He shuffled through a pile of papers.

"Will you pay attention?" Bobbie grabbed Chuck's arm.

"I want to hire the woman right now. She's sitting at the end of the row—against the wall. Do you think I should interview her first?"

"Bobbie, I have a million things to do. If you want to talk to her, talk—or just hire her. You know what you want." Chuck found the lost musical score he had been looking for and motioned for Milt Mercer, the piano player, to join him.

Bobbie threw up her arms and hurried back across the room. Extending her hand, she approached the woman and introduced herself.

"Minnie Washington." The woman's voice was friendly but her eyes were crisp and businesslike. "I'm pleased to be here."

"I can tell, Minnie." Bobbie paused a moment, then nodded appreciatively. "You've had show business experience, haven't you?"

Minnie assured her that she had, then recounted her twenty-five years as a bookkeeper, seamstress, and ticket collector in dozens of minstrel shows. "I seen it all, ma'am—everything from a grand performance for President Roosevelt to a lynching on the banks of the Chattahoochee."

"That's some background. I'm looking for a wardrobe mistress and a personal maid. We don't have many costumes to take care of."

"I can be both," Minnie said with a wave of her hand. "Won't be no problem going from one to the other."

"Wonderful!" Bobbie beamed, then drummed her fingers on the back of a chair as she outlined their itinerary. "We'll be on the road for six weeks. First stop, Cairo, then Indianapolis, Cincinnati, Philadelphia and finally Harlem."

"Wooee! Them's some good cities. Had me a few hot times—good and bad—in Cincinnati."

Bobbie laughed, then she turned serious. "You won't mind if we stay in a boarding house in Cairo? We'll be in hotels everyplace else. They'll be clean. No rat traps."

"Ma'am, I done slept in leaky tents set up in the middle of corn fields, shared basements with rats who had their own swimming pool—even slept on blankets we throwed on the

side of the road when we got kicked out of southern towns."
She chortled nervously. "Them signs mean it when they say
that us colored better be gone 'fore sundown. I ain't messin'
with no Jim Crow laws. No, ma'am."

"You won't have to. The minute I see something like that
is the minute I go back to Chicago."

"Knows how you feel, Miss Evans, but I got to warn you,
touring gets in your blood. You puts up with lots of bad stuff
just to get an audience."

"Then you'll take the job?"

"Be proud workin' for you, ma'am."

"When can you start?"

"Right now if you wants. I'm between jobs, if you know
what I mean." Minnie smiled and adjusted her handbag on
her lap.

"That's great. Just great." Bobbie dismissed the other
women while Minnie pulled off her galoshes. Together they
approached Chuck and she introduced Minnie to the
troupe.

"Minnie's a hard worker. She's smart. She absolutely
adores me. Why can't you be more civil to her?" Bobbie's
face was pinched with resentment.

Chuck pushed the choreographic drawing he was working
on aside and looked up, exasperated. "For God's sake,
Bobbie. I don't thank Milt when he plays the piano or Daisy
when she dances. Why should I thank Minnie for a cup of
coffee? It's understood."

"It wouldn't hurt you." Bobbie pouted.

"Okay. What's bothering you? You got five minutes. If I
can't solve your problem by then, you'll have to live with
it."

"Oh, great! The famous, the fantastic Chuck Jones is
going to give me five minutes of his time. What a thrill!"
Bobbie put her hand on her chest and swooned.

"You want it or not?" Chuck stuck his pencil behind his
ear and leaned back in his chair.

"I want you to be nicer to Minnie. She's like family. I'd be
lost without her."

"Fine. You adopt her and let me finish my work. March fifteenth is one week away. If I don't finish this dance routine, I will have to hire a dog act. How'd you like to follow a dancing poodle?"

"And how would you like to be fired!" Bobbie collapsed in tears.

Chuck stood up and put his arm around Bobbie, holding her tight. "What is it, babe? You haven't hit me like this for a long time."

When Bobbie stopped sobbing, she sniffled and talked—about Minnie's sweet personality, her loyalty, her natural ability with figures. "She could easily handle our books. She's already straightened out my personal finances. For the first time in years I know how much I have."

"Minnie's great, but I don't know about you. Are you mad because I've been ignoring you? I've been busy. The show . . ."

Bobbie shook her head. "She's so warm, so full of love—just like Mama."

Chuck sighed. "So that's it."

"What's *it?*"

"Your moodiness. I thought it was the show, but you're really homesick, aren't you? Hell! Why didn't you tell me? You could have taken a week and gone home, but it's too late now."

"I wouldn't go home if you paid me." Bobbie pulled away. "I wouldn't give Roy the satisfaction of knowing I cared if he lived or died."

"To hell with Roy. What about your Mama?"

"What good would it do to see her? She wouldn't even recognize me. The doctor said—"

"Who gives a damn what a doctor says? You'd know her. Isn't that what's important?"

"Yes." Bobbie nodded. "I'd know." She turned around and laid her head on Chuck's shoulder. "But it is too late. We leave in a week. I never realized how much I missed Mama till Minnie came. Have you noticed? She even looks like Mama."

Chuck smiled. "If it makes you happy, I'll thank Minnie when she brings me coffee."

"Don't know if it'll make me happy, but I'd appreciate it."

On March 15, 1928, the troupe left Chicago in a blaze of publicity. Bobbie strutted through Union Station wearing her mink coat, followed by an entourage of reporters, redcaps, and fellow performers. The clickety-clack of her high heels syncopated the staccato conversation she maintained with the pursuing newsmen.

"Cairo, Cincinnati, Philadelphia. Oh, I can't remember all the cities." Bobbie stopped in front of the railroad car that would take them south, but not far enough south to force them to ride in a segregated Jim Crow car.

"Miss Evans, is it true that your next recording for Columbia won't be classified a race record?" A squat, baby-faced reporter stared at her, his pencil pressed hard on a small notepad, his hat jauntily tilted on the back of his head.

"Honey, I don't worry about stuff like that. All I care about is making records so people can hear me sing." Bobbie managed to make her voice sound intimate yet casual. "But I figure if race records are good 'nough for Bessie, they're good 'nough for me." Bobbie's bright red lips split into a broad smile.

The reporter's stare softened into a gaze.

"I hear you're going to Harlem, Miss Evans. Any truth to the rumor you're going to sing with Fletcher Henderson's band?"

"Of course I'm going to Harlem. But I got my own band—Chuck Jones and his Chicago Aces. You know how to spell that, don't you? J, o, n, e, s."

The reporters roared with laughter. Chuck stepped back, feeling blood rush to his face.

The bantering continued for five more minutes. When the conductor yelled, "All aboard," in one last, grand gesture, Bobbie hiked up her skirt, exposed her silk-stockinged leg, arched her back, and broke into a broad smile. The reporters pressed in, angling to snap the most provocative pose. Chuck grabbed Bobbie by her waist and pushed her on board.

"Up to your old tricks again." Chuck was spitting mad.

Bobbie spun around, her smile disappearing. "What are you talking about?"

Everyone in the coach stopped piling their suitcases in the overhead racks, hesitated a moment, then quickly resumed their activities.

Bobbie stomped away. "Not now, Chuck. I'm not in the mood for one of your tantrums."

"You acted like a two-bit whore out there!"

Bobbie froze. The dancers gasped. Bobbie raised her hand over her head to strike Chuck, but he grabbed her arm. Their bodies locked together, their eyes filled with hate.

"Don't you ever say anything like that to me again."

"And don't you forget you're not the whole show. The next time you talk to reporters I'd like you to mention the dancers, Cardoza, and the band. Without us—"

"I did mention the band." Bobbie spat out the words. "And if it wasn't for me, this show wouldn't get any publicity."

Chuck shoved Bobbie and she hit the seat with a loud thud. "Publicity! Hell! That was a show. The next time the press is around, keep your blouse buttoned and your legs together." Chuck turned on his heel and stalked out.

Bobbie collapsed into Minnie's arms, sobbing. "What's the matter with him? Him and his damn ego. Doesn't he know his temper is tearing up all of us? Everyone's nervous and edgy. What did I do to make him so mad this time?"

"Nothin', honey, you ain't done nothin'." Minnie held Bobbie close and gently patted her head.

"Then why—"

"The man's jealous. Anybody can see that."

"Jealous! Of me? Nonsense. I don't play drums, and he doesn't sing." Bobbie's eyes were open now, staring at Minnie in surprise.

"Oh, he ain't concerned about your singin'. You being the

star is what's botherin' him. I imagine the man wants to earn his own million and not be livin' off you, honey."

"Not everybody can make a million—I haven't yet. And anyway, I don't just give him money. He earns it. He's my manager."

Minnie shrugged. "Honey, call it what you will, all I knows is that man unhappy, and he making everybody else unhappy. I ain't sayin' it's your fault."

Bobbie sat up, buttressed by Minnie's support. "I love him, Minnie, but I'm not going to give up everything just so I won't hurt his ego. Still, there must be something I can do."

"There is, honey. And you can start by buttoning your blouse."

"My blouse?" Bobbie looked down and gasped. Her blouse was open to the waist. "How did that happen?"

"I think when you posed for the newsmen."

"Chuck thinks I did it on purpose." Bobbie quickly buttoned up. "Oh, hell, no wonder he's mad. I'll apologize. For the thousandth time, I'll tell him I'm sorry, and everything'll be all right till the next time." As she headed down the aisle, Bobbie wondered bleakly how many next times there would be.

Little Egypt—Cairo, Illinois—was a tough little river town that catered to gandy dancers, stevedores, and the river rats who moved cargo in and out of the heartland of America. The town didn't look like much, but Bobbie was thankful that they had arrived. Relief turned to satisfaction when they checked into the boarding house. Their bedroom was spacious, with solid oak furniture, lace curtains, and a strong antiseptic odor. The Negro woman who owned it assured them that she ran a clean, respectable house. Bobbie had no reason to doubt her.

"Breakfast at eight, lunch at noon, dinner at six," the woman informed them.

Considering their hours, Chuck said they would probably only eat lunch there, but the woman replied that the price was the same. He took it, and after settling everyone in his

room, Chuck and Milt went looking for the Forty Niners'
Club.

Twenty minutes later Chuck and Milt gazed soberly at the
squalid warehouses and honky-tonk taverns dotting the
riverfront. Kicking whiskey bottles out of their path, Chuck
finally stopped in front of a building that had recently been
emblazoned with a sign announcing the Forty-Niners' Club.

"You sure this is it?"

"Shit!" Chuck was stunned. "Bobbie'll never sing in a
dive like this. That son-of-a-bitch agent said it was a supper
club. Some supper club."

"What're we going to do?"

"Go in." Chuck stepped around a derelict car.

Milt shrugged, then followed Chuck inside. Broken chairs
leaned against wooden tables defaced with hundreds of
names. The smell of whiskey and stale smoke permeated the
dark room, and it took a moment for Chuck to locate the
bartender, who was pointing at them menacingly.

"Don't serve niggers. You can get drinks on your own side
of town. At the corner take a right, then go three—"

"We're not here to buy drinks." Chuck stepped closer,
seething from the insult, but managing to keep his composure. "I'm Chuck Jones, and this here's Milt Mercer. I got a
show booked at the Forty-Niners' Club tonight. This the
place?"

The man's face lit up. "Chuck Jones. Sure. Wondered
when you'd be showing up."

Chuck glanced around. A small stage minus a curtain
filled the far corner of the room. Everything looked
cramped and disorderly. "You got dressing rooms?"

"Out back for the colored—combination outhouse and
dressing room. Whites can use the little room right side of
the stage."

"The agent in Chicago said this was a supper club. There
must be some mistake, Mr.—?"

"Smitty. Just call me Smitty."

"Well, Smitty, I don't think my singer'll work here. We
were expecting something better."

Smitty laughed. "Don't let the looks of the place fool you.

The men drop a wad of money in here on weekends. If they like you, you'll earn hundreds a night."

Chuck shook his head. "That might not be enough."

"Here now, you trying to hold me up for more money?" Smitty frowned. "Colored entertainers never complained before. Course we ain't never had niggers from Chicago either."

"Sorry, Smitty, but this nigger from Chicago ain't only complaining—he's not working. My star singer, Bobbie Evans, probably wouldn't even set foot in here, much less sing."

Smitty's mouth became pinched; he grabbed a shot glass and wiped it nervously. "I been advertising your group all week. If you don't work, and my customers get mad and tear up the place, then I'm going to have to take it out on you. Anyway, you got a contract, boy. The sheriff ain't gonna like it if I tell him you skipped town." Smitty shook his head. "You better tell your singing star to slip on down here and do her act. You know what I mean?"

"Yes, I know what he means. He means he has us by our black asses and isn't going to let go," Bobbie said under her breath when she walked into the Forty Niners' Club. "Well, you can tell that no-good, white—"

Chuck drew Bobbie aside. "Shut up. Do you want him to hear you?"

"I don't give a damn if he does or not. I refuse to sing in this dump."

"You can stand it for a couple of nights. For God's sake, you want the sheriff on our tail? Believe me, the jail in this town's got to be worse than this place. And we can leave after the last show."

At the mention of a sheriff, Minnie tugged on Bobbie's sleeve and motioned her aside. "You know what them white boys do to colored when they got'em in jail, don't you?"

Bobbie shook her head no. When Minnie explained, she blanched, put her hand over her mouth, and with tears brimming in her eyes, agreed to sing. "But the first redneck who touches my ass gets his balls kicked."

* * * *

None of the women performers watched as the customers filed in. Only Minnie peered into the room. The men wore pea coats over plaid shirts and bib overalls; the women were arrayed in taffeta and satin, their costumes sprinkled with sequins, feathers, and rhinestones. The redheads looked as if they were straight out of a henna bottle; the blondes had black roots. Their boisterous laughter filled the dance hall.

"Are you telling me we're the only colored in this place?" Bobbie's voice cracked with fear.

"Don't matter, honey. Once they hear you, they be yours—just like always."

Bobbie shuddered, then gulped a shot of gin. In the next instant, a fanfare exploded across the room as the band announced Cardoza the Great and his one and only magic act. Chuck motioned him offstage ten minutes later; the crowd was too rowdy to appreciate his finesse. The Getaway Shufflers fared better. When the scantily clad dancers tapped their way across the stage, the audience went wild, clapping and whistling obscenely.

When the girls took their bows, a shower of one dollar bills floated around them, but the men with the ten-dollar bills slapped them on top of the tables. The bump-and-grind music beat as the young girls tried to pick up the bills with their rear ends, forcing them to straddle, stoop, and sit on the tables. The men guffawed crudely when one of the girls finally succeeded. Tucking the cash between their breasts, the girls taunted the men by pulling the bills in and out and twisting their hips.

What had been planned as a ploy to get bigger tips soon turned into a near riot as the rough men grabbed the girls off the stage, kissing, pinching, nearly mauling them.

Bobbie watched from the corner of the stage, dismayed at the growing violence and Chuck's inability to stop it. When a beer bottle sailed over his head and one of the girls screamed as a man grabbed her, Bobbie walked on stage. Hell, I'll probably get my head bashed, she thought, but I have to do something. Chuck stared at her, unable to comprehend what she was doing. Bobbie didn't explain. Judging by their ages, in their thirties, Bobbie figured that many were veterans; maybe a rousing campfire song would divert their attention so the dancers could escape.

"Play 'There's a Long, Long Trail'" she shouted over the din.

Chuck shook his head; the song wasn't in their repertoire. When Bobbie requested it again, demandingly, Chuck shouted at Milt, who immediately picked out the melody on the piano. The rest of the band filled in, and Bobbie sang two verses of the melancholy air before the familiar strains quieted the rowdy campaigners. Memories of foxholes shared, buddies lost and battles won, overcame them, and they hummed along, one by one turning toward the stage. Bewitched by Bobbie in her red, sequined gown, aroused by her soulful rendition of the popular war song, they demanded others—"Hinky Dinky Parlay Voo," "Over There," "It's a Long Way to Tipperary." Soon the men sat starry-eyed, gazing into their empty beer mugs or off into space.

Smitty, frantically running from one end of the bar to the other, shouted to Chuck, "What the hell you doin'? For Christ's sake! You supposed to be entertaining these slobs, not puttin'em to sleep."

Chuck looked at him, bewildered. "They were ready to tear the place apart—"

"Who the shit cares? They do it every Saturday night. They pay for it. We get it fixed Monday morning."

"That's a hell of a way to run a club."

"Who the shit's askin' you? If that nigger gal can sing somethin' besides those sugar-ass war songs, you better get her to do it before I kick you all out of here."

Smitty stormed away. Chuck took a deep breath. "Did you all hear that?" he shouted at the band. "Let's give the old boy some Chicago sounds."

In ten minutes the crowd was exuberant again, ordering drinks, pinching barmaids. Bobbie sang blues and jazz until her voice started to crack. When she took her bows at last, after three sets, the audience thundered its applause and swamped the stage with bills and coins.

* * *

"I wouldn't have missed it for the world," Bobbie said as the troupe shuffled wearily into her bedroom and collapsed. Chuck, carrying a shoe box under his arm, was the last one inside.

"How the hell were we supposed to know that that ass Smitty let his customers tear up the place?" Chuck asked with irritation.

"I don't care nothing about his ole club," said Mavery, one of the dancers, "but I was sure glad when that bear stopped pinching me. He had me scared."

Bobbie smiled and looked at Chuck. Did he appreciate what she'd done or was he sore because she had usurped his authority?

"We're all thankful you were thinking. It was getting nasty." Chuck kissed Bobbie's forehead, then with a flourish, emptied the shoe box on the bed. "How's that for an evening's take?"

Everyone gasped at the blanket of green and silver money. Evelyn and Mavery jumped in the middle of the bed and tossed the bills over their heads, squealing. "Three cheers for Bobbie!"

"Three cheers for Bobbie!" A chorus of voices rang out.

"I didn't do anything." Bobbie smiled broadly.

A bottle of whiskey appeared. Cups and glasses were quickly filled and quickly emptied as they counted their take.

"Three hundred, four hundred, five hundred." Chuck took the money and scattered it across the bed again. "I like the color." Chuck refilled his glass.

It was after four A.M. when everyone filed out. Slamming the door shut behind them, Bobbie turned to Chuck, a warm glow spreading across her face. "Whoever would've thought." She wrapped her arms around Chuck's waist. "The Forty-Niners' Club—what a dump, but look at all that money."

"Umm, you smell like a million dollars."

"One of these days I'll—we'll be worth a million."

"I'm sure of that." Chuck fell on the cash-covered bed, pulling Bobbie on top of him, rolling back and forth as they kissed playfully. Bobbie laughed and tossed the bills in the air, even stuffing them in Chuck's ears, his pockets, under his arms. They undressed. Bobbie tousled Chuck's hair, relishing the happiness of just being in his arms.

Chuck kissed Bobbie. She responded, content just to respond, afraid to consider his lovemaking an act, but when he rolled on top of her and she wrapped her arms around his neck, their eyes met. There, as always, Bobbie encountered the void, the isolation he felt deep inside.

Why, of all the men in the world, did I fall in love with you? Bobbie thought. There was no answer. The pain of his rejection deadened her; there was no joy, only a dull, empty ache.

Cardoza the Great left the show in Philadelphia to join a circus heading south. When they hit New York, the Getaway Shufflers shuffled off to the theater district, hoping to audition for a Broadway musical. Bobbie and Chuck headed uptown to Harlem along with Minnie and the band.

After renting two cramped efficiency apartments, Bobbie, Chuck, and Minnie moved in immediately. With Chuck urging them to hurry, they threw their clothes in drawers, hung some of them in closets, and shoved the rest, along with their suitcases, under the bed. They rushed to get dressed so they could do the town. At eight o'clock, they headed for the Roseland ballroom, just off Times Square, at Fifty-first and Broadway, where they listened to the big-band jazz of Fletcher Henderson. Later, in Harlem, they hid behind a row of props at the back of Connie's Inn, a Negro cabaret that catered exclusively to white audiences. Bobbie was dumbfounded when the performers recognized her. The biggest thrill, however, was the Cotton Club with its famous "African" dancers who shimmied, tapped, and cakewalked to the beat of exotic African jungle rhythms. After the show Duke Ellington introduced his band to a deafening ovation.

By 3:30, Bobbie and Minnie had had enough of the after-hours clubs. Chuck pleaded for "just one more," so wearily, they followed him into the Rhythm Club. After making a circuit of the room, Chuck returned to the table with a beaming, broad-faced black man in tow. A derby hat was cocked pertly on the man's head.

"Tom Waller—'Fats' Waller," Chuck said with a flourish. "And this here's Minnie Washington." Minnie held out her hand. Waller bowed. When he straightened up, he winked and said, "How ya doin'? Good to see ya! How's your family? How's your husband? How's your cousin? How's your landlord? How's your undertaker? You're looking real prosperous, but you're gettin' uglier every day!"

Minnie looked startled. Waller flirted outrageously with her. No sooner had she warmed to his broad, frisky jests than he withdrew, warning her, "Don't you get sweet on me, sugar. Let's have a gin and talk about it."

Bobbie was holding her sides laughing when he grabbed her and kissed her on her lips. This time Minnie roared at Bobbie.

"And who are you, sweet, sweet brown sugar? Come on and gimme a bite."

"I'm Bobbie Evans. I sing—"

"Do you scat? Do you jiggle? Do you sing the bluesy blues?"

"I sing blues and jazz."

"You wanna star in a Broadway show? Awwww, mercy, dat Broadway's ready for you. Ever heard of the show *Keep Shufflin'?*" You'd be the star if you wanted it, sweet, sweet brown sugar."

Bobbie laughed at this puckish, delightful man.

"Will your offer be good next year?"

"It'll be good forever, my honeysuckle rose, but your man here was talking about jobs. I thought you were in dire distress."

"No." Bobbie was suddenly suspicious. "I have a dozen contract offers back in Chicago." She turned to Chuck. "Why were you telling Tom I need a job?"

"I didn't say who needed one." Chuck's jaw tightened.

"You, *you* need one—here in Harlem! Damn!" Bobbie gulped down her drink, then grabbed her purse and muttered a sullen good-bye.

Tom cringed, apologized, and made a hasty retreat.

Chuck and Bobbie railed at each other all the way home. "We could both start all over again here in Harlem," Chuck said. "A fresh start. We got enough money for six months. Why can't we try it?"

"I got connections in Chicago, connections and contracts. You want me to be sued? And what about my recording sessions? A colored singer can make a fortune on records. I'm not giving that up so you can beat your drums in Harlem."

Chuck sneered. "You're afraid. That's it. I know you're afraid. A Broadway show scares the pants off you."

Bobbie looked out the window and shrugged. "I could do a Broadway show with my eyes closed."

"Prove it."

"I'm not going to prove it 'cause I don't want to do it."

Chuck gave Minnie a hard look, like a man about to strangle a woman. He bit his lip and tried again. "You got six weeks at the Sugar Cane Club. Lot of things can happen in six weeks. You could change your mind—"

"Or you could change yours."

The Sugar Cane Club, a black-and-tan club on 131st Street, featured Bobbie Evans, Jazz Queen, through the month of June, 1928. Bobbie was so popular the management shaved Chuck's drum solos until he was down to two a night, late in the evening when the crowd had returned to their drinks and conversation. Chuck retaliated by staying at the after-hours clubs all night, often not coming home till noon.

Chuck ignored Bobbie, who felt increasingly isolated. He filled in at impromptu jazz sessions, trying to copy the dynamics of Chuck Webb on drums, Duke Ellington on piano, and Don Redman on alto sax. When Bobbie nastily exclaimed that he wasn't fit to shine their shoes, Chuck threw his arrangements across the room and stomped out, shouting that he'd rather be on the chitlin' circuit than put up with her. He didn't return for three days.

Chuck's world centered around Lenox Avenue between

140th and 145th streets. Bobbie sang at the Apollo Theater, the Lenox Club, and the Lincoln Theater, but they went their own ways after each show. By September they had stayed drunk for thirty days; Bobbie's voice was cracking and Chuck often disappeared completely, not even bothering to lead the band anymore.

Minnie pleaded with Bobbie to return to Chicago and her club dates. Bobbie vacillated, afraid that if she left Chuck, he'd never come back to her. "I can't live without him."

"Honey, if you thinks this is love, then you sure likes to punish yourself. That man gonna be the ruination of you. Or the other way round."

"What should I do?"

"Go home. Back to Chicago. Let him decide if he loves you. Ain't no way you ever gonna be sure less you let him make the decision."

Bobbie shook her head. "You make it sound so simple, Minnie. But what if he doesn't come home?"

"You ain't lost nothing you never had."

Maybe it's good we separate for a few months, Bobbie thought as she leaned against Chuck at the Rhythm Club her last night in Harlem. He was attentive, almost affectionate, most of the evening. For the first time in months, he avoided his usual barbs and caustic innuendos, and Bobbie responded in kind. He'd even promised her a surprise later in the evening. She didn't ask him when he would return to Chicago. She didn't ask him how he was going to live. By one o'clock, Bobbie was eager to return to their apartment and make love, knowing that no matter how often they argued and how wrong they seemed for each other, she would miss lying next to him at night and waking up beside him in the morning. He has to want me, too. "Chuck, sweetheart, my train leaves at seven. Let's go. I want to—"

"Hold it, babe. I see your surprise coming." Chuck beamed as he peered across the room.

Following his gaze, Bobbie stared in disbelief at the couple meandering in their direction.

"Duffy! Edy! What in the world are you doing here?"

Duffy and Edy, Chuck's old roommates from Chicago, laughed and kissed Bobbie on her cheek. "Doin' what you are, my love, listening to jazz, smoking reefers, and enjoyin'," Duffy said.

Edy put her arm around Chuck's waist when he stood up to greet them. Bobbie noticed she didn't drop it until Chuck sat down.

"Hear you're leaving us, just when we found one another again." Edy pulled a chair beside Chuck's.

"Oh, just for a little while. I'll probably be back by Thanksgiving unless Chuck returns to Chicago."

"Not much likelihood of that," Edy said. "Not since he and his band are opening at the Starlight Cafe."

"And Edy's going to sing . . ." Duffy rolled his shoulders sensuously.

"Edy!" Bobbie gaped at Chuck. She gripped her stomach as the pain of his duplicity convulsed her. "So that's where you've been going the last month. To Edy's. Working with her. I thought—"

"I got an offer. I didn't want to turn it down just to go back to Chicago and be your pimp. This is my chance to prove—"

"Liar. You set this whole thing up. You knew . . ." Enraged, Bobbie slapped Chuck's face.

"Bobbie, for Christ's sake!" Chuck grabbed Bobbie's arm and looked around, embarrassed by her outburst.

Bobbie pushed him away. "Edy's not even a singer." Hot tears stung her cheeks.

"I can learn, sweetie." Edy grinned.

Bobbie stared at Chuck, overcome with emotion. "I'm tired of messin' with you, Chuck Jones. Just real tired." She took a few more steps, then stopped. "And if you think you've been my pimp, wait till Miss Edy what's her name works on you. You'll find out what a pimp is." Bobbie stormed out of the club, hailed a passing taxi, and felt her life dissolving in shambles.

* * *

It rained the next morning, Monday, September 10, 1928, when Bobbie and Minnie headed for the train station. Minnie didn't dare ask Bobbie what had happened. Ignoring Bobbie's zombie-like stance, she counted their suitcases, then looked anxiously down the track for their train to arrive. Minnie reached out to touch Bobbie, who pulled away as the Penn Central glided into the station. Minnie barked at a redcap to hustle their luggage on board, and without a backward glance, the two women found their seats, closed their eyes, and counted the hours until they arrived in Chicago.

CHAPTER XXV

"It's two o'clock and you still in bed." Minnie pulled the drapes, allowing the cold November light into Bobbie's bedroom. "All that drinkin' and runnin' bound to make you sick. And all because of that man." Minnie shook her head.

Bobbie pulled the satin coverlet over her head and moaned. "I feel terrible, Minnie. What did I eat last night?"

"Eat! That's a good one. Wasn't nothing you ate make you so sick. It be that drinkin' and smokin'. You ruin your voice." Minnie shuffled into the bathroom. Soon the sweet scent of lilacs bubbled from a steaming tub of water. She returned to the bedroom with a glass of water and two aspirins.

"Should just let you suffer." Minnie handed the pills to Bobbie.

"Survival." Bobbie headed into the bathroom. "I'm only interested in survival."

Forty-five minutes later she picked at a soft-boiled egg and absentmindedly chewed on a piece of bacon. "Any mail?"

"That man ain't gonna write. You been waitin' near three months now. He don't answer your letters. He always out when you call that club where he work. When you gonna learn?"

"Please, no lecture this morning." Bobbie dropped her head in her hands. "I can't handle it."

"Can you handle that stack of mail? It's been pilin' up all week. I don't mind handling your money and keeping your books, but you got to decide your club dates." Minnie poured Bobbie another cup of coffee, then threw a thick envelope in front of her. "Look like a contract from the Evergreen Club. You been wanting to sing there long as I known you."

Bobbie opened her eyes. "Oh! Wonder why I'm getting an offer now?"

"Maybe the owner, Georgy somebody, knows you between dates."

"Georgy somebody doesn't own the Evergreen." Bobbie flipped through the sheaf of papers. "Al Capone owns it. Georgy somebody just runs it."

"Maybe, but if you wants to work, you got to sign. Money's the same color no matter who pays it."

"What band's playing there?"

"Bart Hacker and His Dixieland Jazz Band."

"Christ! I can't sing with them. They sound like a New Orleans street band."

"Honey, you can sing with anybody if you wants."

Bobbie glanced up. "But I don't wants."

"How you gonna know less you listen to 'em? They might'n be as bad as you think." Minnie paused. "Maybe you should be thinkin' about movin' to New York. Gotta admit, that's where the action be. Chicago, Kansas City, New Orleans—they all has-beens. Not like you need the money. You is a rich woman. You made some good investments."

"You mean *you* did."

"But you made the money in the first place."

Bobbie shrugged her shoulders. "Money doesn't mean

much without Chuck. Maybe I should've stayed in New York. I'll write him again and ask him if he can find me a club."

Minnie cleared her throat. "My, don't you have a short memory! You write that man every week since you been home, and you ain't heard from him once."

Bobbie's eyes flew open. "Something could've happened to him. He could be sick."

"In a pig's eye."

"You're right," Bobbie said after a moment's thought. "Doesn't matter. I don't need him. I can make it on my own."

"Fine. Then get yourself down to the Evergreen Club and get that singin' job."

Typical, Bobbie thought, as she entered the foyer of the Evergreen Club. She wrinkled up her nose. All clubs look terrible in the daytime—they need people and noise and music to bring them to life.

Gingerly, Bobbie stuck her head through the half-opened door. "Yoo-hoo, anybody here?"

A man looked up from a stack of papers. He motioned for her to come in. "Well, Miss Evans, we meet again."

"Georgy Torrio! I don't believe it." Bobbie stared at him. He still wore his hair slicked back. His white teeth still sparkled against his olive-toned skin. Manicured nails pointed to a chair.

He's the handsomest man I've ever known, she thought. Even better looking than Chuck. Course Chuck had qualities that made him special, she reasoned, noting how easily Georgy moved his large frame.

"I hear it was a success."

Bobbie frowned. "What was a success?"

"Your road show."

"Yes, of course," Bobbie stammered. "I was thinking of something else."

Georgy sat on the edge of his desk and pushed a cigarette into a black and gold holder. "Are you ready to settle down?"

"For a while. I might like to try Harlem again next year."

Georgy nodded slowly. "You got a job here till you decide to leave."

"No audition? No interview?" Bobbie raised her eyebrows in dismay.

"Miss Evans, I've heard you sing at least once a week since you came back to Chicago. You've already auditioned for me."

"Why didn't you come backstage? I wouldn't want to snub such a dedicated fan."

"I didn't hang around. Had to get back here just in case the boss came in."

"And who is the boss?" Bobbie wanted to confirm what she'd heard about Al Capone.

"I'm distantly related to Johnny Torrio. When Johnny resigned, he asked Al if he'd give me a club. I got the Evergreen a few weeks later. Al's a man of his word."

Bobbie racked her brain—Johnny Torrio. Shuddering, she remembered. Johnny Torrio had quit as Chicago's underworld boss in 1925, allowing Capone direct control of the bootleg liquor market and thus of the city's ten thousand speakeasies. Some empire, she thought.

"I'd love to work here. I have the contracts signed and ready." Bobbie pulled them from her handbag.

"Will four hundred a week be satisfactory?" Georgy's eyes were piercing.

"But the contract calls for two hundred."

"I just upped it. Do you mind?"

Bobbie smiled and shelved her self-restraint. "Not at all, Mr. Torrio. Not at all."

The shops along Michigan Avenue glittered with Christmas goodies. Cold white diamonds, creamy pearls, and deep blue sapphires snuggled in plush, satin-lined boxes, their lids ready to be snapped shut and whisked away by contented daddies. Bobbie and Minnie mingled with the crowds and shopped for five days buying gowns, boas, shoes, and jewelry for her debut at the Evergreen Club.

Like a child in a candy store, Bobbie pointed to one glossy

trinket after another. "I'll take that and that and that." She never once glanced at a price. Impulsively, she offered to buy Minnie a mink coat, but Minnie refused gruffly, saying she'd look like a grizzly bear wrapped in all that fur. In the end, she allowed Bobbie to buy her a small diamond ring.

"Isn't this fun?" Bobbie squealed as she threw her purchases across the chaise longue. "Why haven't we done this before?"

"'Cause you let that fool Chuck buy your clothes." Minnie stirred a cup of tea.

"You really didn't like him, did you?"

"He was a weak man, trying to be somethin' he wasn't. Seem silly to me not to know your own strengths and weaknesses."

Bobbie returned to the mirror and held a champagne-colored gown in front of her. "I think I'll wear this my first night."

Minnie nodded. "That'll set 'em in their seats all right. Fact is, that'll knock 'em over."

A bouquet of red roses preceded a tuxedo-clad body into Bobbie's dressing room.

"May I wish you good luck?" Georgy asked, his voice as smooth as the satin on his lapels.

"Never. You're supposed to say 'Break a leg.'" Bobbie laughed. "I'm so nervous. It's like my first night ever."

Georgy stepped closer and pressed the flowers against her body. "I wonder why that is." He brushed the back of his hand against her hair. "You're beautiful. Very very beautiful."

Bobbie stepped back, overwhelmed. "Do you like the gold feather in my hair?" she asked lightly. "If it's too much—"

"You're like a dream." Georgy's eyes probed Bobbie's face.

Bobbie grabbed a powder puff and dabbed her forehead. "You really have to stop these compliments. I might start believing them."

306

"I never say anything I don't mean. Please join me and my guests after the show. We'll celebrate. Champagne to match your dress, caviar to match your eyes."

"I'd love to." Bobbie whisked past Georgy and hurried to the stage.

"Runnin' Wild," a popular song with a fast tempo, opened the set. Flirting with the gray-haired men at the front-row tables, Bobbie broke through the audience's opulent reserve. They laughed, sharing Bobbie's fun. When she finished, they gave her a thunderous ovation.

Georgy was waiting for her in her dressing room. When she saw his face, she was stunned by the admiration in his eyes.

"You were sensational," he said with unaccustomed exuberance.

"Why, thank you, Georgy. It's always nice to know one pleases the boss."

"You please the customers. That's even more important."

"And such nice customers." Bobbie fluffed powder on her nose and wiped the lipstick from the crevices of her mouth. "The Evergreen Club is perfect for me. Small, intimate—and the clientele is so elegant."

"Better than Harlem?" Georgy asked imperiously.

Bobbie's excitement faded, and a chill gripped her as she thought of Chuck living with Edy and Duffy. Jealousy and outrage rose up, almost choking her.

Bobbie pasted a smile on her face. "Let's forget Harlem for tonight, shall we?"

"Whatever you say." Georgy held out his hand. "Come on. I want you to meet some friends."

Georgy hustled her through the club to a booth secluded behind a painted lattice. Casually, he introduced her around the table, including the owner, the infamous Al Capone. Bobbie held out her hand. Capone shook it limply, then retreated to the back of the booth. As Georgy poured Bobbie a glass of champagne, she wondered what all the fuss was about. Capone was a dull, boastful boor surrounded by pepper and honey playmates. Compared to him, Georgy was a man with a difference. She studied the tall, dark man sitting beside her.

Bobbie almost missed Chuck's candid, simple personality; Georgy was intense, almost suffocating. Georgy stared at her. His eyes spoke. With each flicker they said, "I want you."

It was nice to be wanted, Bobbie decided. After years of Chuck's indifference, it was nice to be wanted.

The Evergreen Club was packed every night of the holiday season. Georgy and Bobbie shared quiet, intimate dinners, after the show. With Georgy's flair for the dramatic, exotic flowers were magically transformed into gold rings. Bouquets of roses hid a bracelet or necklace. Petals became diamonds, leaves, emeralds. She protested. He ignored her. As though competing with himself, Georgy tried to surpass each gift with a more grandiose one. In the end, Bobbie gave in and enjoyed the adulation. After her first month at the club, they celebrated her anniversary. A simple dinner, Georgy had promised.

Simple, indeed. The bird of paradise has flown, Bobbie thought, as she glanced at the plain, linen-covered table, its only decoration a colorful centerpiece of chrysanthemums and roses. Georgy sat across from her, partially hidden by the large, heavy flowers. Never one to chat idly, he was even more than usually tight-lipped during dinner. Bobbie was edgy. She peered at him through the stems of the bouquet and compared him with Chuck. More handsome, she thought, certainly richer. Yet, Chuck was more exciting. He was a talker. Sometimes glib, often argumentative, but never dull. Even their fights were better than Georgy's silence. The thought of arguing with Georgy terrified her. She sighed. In two months I'll be finished here, then it's off to New York, to Harlem, to Lenox Avenue. Chuck and I will kiss and make up, and it'll be like old times. I'll return Georgy's baubles before I go. They never meant anything to me anyway.

The waiter cleared away the dishes, then served cappuccino laced with Amaretto. As if on cue, Georgy stood up and lackadaisically plucked a velvet petal from a rose, allowing it to flutter onto the white linen tablecloth in front of Bobbie. She looked up and frowned.

"Don't. You'll kill it." She sipped the hot coffee, trying to hide her anxiety.

Another petal fluttered down, then another. Georgy smiled. "I want to show you the heart of the bud. It's even lovelier than the outside."

Bobbie shoved back her chair and stood up, her face pinched with anger. "I'm leaving, Georgy. Thanks for dinner, but it's getting late."

Georgy grabbed her wrist and gripped it until she winced in pain, then he thrust the rose into her hand. "Here. Open it up. It's a surprise."

Bobbie flinched, but did as she was told. After plucking the outer petals, she saw a gleaming jewel, an oval ruby, surrounded by a halo of diamonds.

"Oh, Georgy!" she gasped, forgetting herself. She stared at the earring glittering in her hand. "It's beautiful."

"Now you know how I feel when I look at you. I've never owned anyone as beautiful as you."

"You don't own me."

Georgy smiled and handed her another rosebud containing the matching earring. Then, in a grand gesture, he broke the centerpiece vase. Inside was a diamond and ruby necklace. It fell on the table. Bobbie was mesmerized.

Georgy finally picked it up and, stepping behind her, draped it around her throat. After securing the clasp, he kissed the nape of her neck.

"I've been wanting to do that since the first time I saw you at Irvin's party. Do you remember?"

"Yes, I remember, Georgy. I also remember the man I was with, the man I still love very much." She raised her hands and unhooked the necklace. Turning, she handed it to him. "I can't take this from you. It wouldn't be fair."

"Wouldn't be fair to whom—me or Chuck Jones?"

Bobbie's face registered surprise. "You know Chuck?"

"I've heard of him."

"As a drummer?"

"No, as your lover—or ex-lover."

Bobbie stepped away. "I'm not going to ask how you found out about Chuck. I don't think I want to know."

Georgy casually lit a cigarette. "I check out all my employees. Company policy."

"With great relish, I'm sure."

"I admit, I was curious about your background—if there were any ex-lovers, ex-husbands."

"You could have asked. I don't have any secrets." Bobbie sat on the back of the sofa and nervously kicked her leg. "I still love Chuck. In fact, as soon as I finish my contract here, I'm going to join him in New York."

Georgy's bland expression returned. "Does he know?"

"Not yet," Bobbie said, flustered, "but I intend to write and let him know."

"Do you think he wants you?"

"Of course he does. We love each other."

Georgy walked over to Bobbie and, staring hard at her, ran his index finger over her mouth, down her chin, her throat, stopping at the curve of her breasts. "He's not for you," Georgy whispered.

"What! I don't know what you're talking about."

"I said, Chuck Jones is not for you. He's a fool. An ass."

"You don't even know him."

"I know *about* him. I know he's living in Harlem with a 'friend,' and you're living here alone."

"By choice, I guarantee you." Bobbie clenched her teeth in anger.

Georgy's suave veneer didn't crack. "Then you don't care who he's living with?—his friend, Duffy Brooks, for instance?"

Bobbie feigned indifference.

"Duffy and Chuck are a twosome, didn't you know?"

"Duffy! You're crazy. Maybe Edy Heller, the little tap dancer who ran all the way to New York to shack up."

"Then you don't know—"

"Know what?"

"Your sweetheart loves men, right now a third-rate thespian. There have been others. He doesn't stay with one too long, not as long as he has with you, but they're not as rich as you."

"You're lying. I don't believe it. He's not that way."

"He was a good lover? He made you happy?" Georgy raised his eyebrows expressing disbelief.

"That's none of your business. Chuck and I—we're going to get married."

Georgy pulled Bobbie to him and kissed her hard on the mouth, his teeth biting into her lips. When he released her, a smile, cold and cynical, distorted his face. "I think you're the one who's lying, or is it wishful thinking?"

Bobbie struggled to free herself. "You enjoy this, don't you, making a fool out of me?"

"I enjoy kissing you."

"You call that a kiss—when you force yourself on me?" Bobbie looked at Georgy in disgust.

Georgy's face pressed close to Bobbie's. "Have you ever had a real man? One who could turn you on five, six times?" Holding her close, Georgy kissed Bobbie's neck, her ears, her lips. Bobbie fought to free herself. Georgy became more aroused. "I should've laid you that night at Irv's. We were taking bets who'd get you." Grabbing Bobbie, he dragged her to the other side of the couch and threw her down. Bobbie tried to push him off, but he was too strong. Without warning, he tore her skirt, reaching for her sex, thrusting into her with brutal strokes. Bobbie screamed as he raped her, but no one came to her rescue. When it was over, Bobbie watched mutely as Georgy stood up, adjusted himself, and zipped up his trousers.

He neither apologized nor gloated. Instead, he stared at her with contempt. Without speaking, Bobbie hurried to the bathroom, washed herself, then returned to the office. Georgy sat behind his desk, brooding over a glass of brandy. Bobbie grabbed her coat and stalked out of the room, slamming the door behind her.

For two weeks Bobbie sat at the bar after the show and

drank, afraid to go home, afraid to face the hollowness of an empty apartment, afraid of the nightmares that stalked her sleep. Except for Minnie, there was no one who really cared.

After a particularly dull Wednesday night when the patrons at the Evergreen had seemed indolent, even bored, Bobbie hurried to the bar. She was suddenly afraid she was losing her talent, her ability to rouse an audience with her voice. Sipping her fourth gin and tonic, Bobbie decided she didn't care. I'm rich, she thought. I don't have to fight anymore. Who cares if Bobbie Evans is famous? I don't. Bobbie finished her drink and signaled the bartender for another. Unexpectedly, Georgy sat on the stool beside her and canceled her order.

"I can always drink at home." She barely looked at him and reached for her handbag.

"Come to my apartment. I'll fix you a drink there."

"And rape me again."

"That was a mistake." There was no remorse in Georgy's voice. He stamped out his cigarette and offered his hand, palm up. "Truce?" He cocked his head to one side. "I'd like to explain, but not here."

Bobbie sighed. Sucker. I am a first-class sucker, but, what the hell. Maybe it's the liquor, or maybe I'm just bored. She took his hand and slid off the barstool. "I've been wondering about your apartment. Does it have walls or bars?"

Bobbie stared out of the tall, narrow windows spanning the east wall of Georgy's twenty-sixth floor apartment in the Regis Towers located just north of the Chicago Loop. Lounging on the custom-made round bed covered with soft calfskin, Georgy watched Bobbie. "I waited too long."

Bobbie turned around. She wished she had a drink, but decided to wait a half hour. One of us has to go slow, she thought. "Too long for what?" Bobbie lit a cigarette to have something in her hand.

"Too long to have you."

Bobbie's laugh filled the room. "Is that what you call it—'having' me?" Bobbie thought a moment then nodded in agreement. "You're right. You 'had' me. You certainly didn't make love." She raised her eyebrow. "Does Georgy Torrio make love or just relieve himself?"

He slid off the bed and approached Bobbie, his eyes riveted on hers. "Yes, Georgy Torrio makes love." Seductively, he led her to the middle of the room.

Accustomed to Chuck's bland, rote lovemaking, Bobbie was mesmerized by Georgy's sensuousness. Excitement, spawned by his raw virility and the gin, inched up Bobbie's spine, and the tingling sensation of arousal erupted wherever he touched her. He slowly undressed her. Her dress, her slip, shoes, stockings. In the soft light from a bed lamp, Bobbie stared at their silhouettes on the wall as Georgy took off his clothes, then circled her, brushing his hand over her breasts, her groin and thighs. Bobbie's eyes gleamed, the light sprinkling them with bits of garnet and amber. She tried to think of Chuck, to put him in Georgy's place, but it was impossible. Chuck never looked at her with so much lust, so much brutal desire.

Georgy knelt down and nestled his head against her stomach. Bobbie felt her blood coursing through her body like the rush of a river, drowning her senses with the agony of her own annihilation. He carried her to bed. Afterwards, they stared blankly at each other. Silently Bobbie rolled over and, as her body cooled, slipped under the coverlet and fell asleep.

When she awoke, Bobbie stretched and glanced at Georgy who lay beside her. Handsome bastard, she thought, but too moody. She felt the moistness between her legs and smiled. But, oh, what a lover! She slipped out of bed and opened the drapes, impressed with his magnificent view of the lake. The cold seeped through the expanse of glass, and Bobbie wrapped her arms around her naked body.

"Come back to bed." Propped up, Georgy looked at her with more than casual interest. "You'll catch cold."

Bobbie nodded then snuggled under the warm covers in Georgy's arms. They made love again, hot and sensual, but again there was no talk of love. Later Georgy slid his arm from under Bobbie's head and, grabbing a silk robe, headed into the bathroom. "Your bath's over there." He pointed to the other side of the room. "We'll eat when you're dressed."

Bobbie hurried and showered. When she returned, Georgy was sitting at a table holding a newspaper in front of his face. Instinctively he stood up and pointed to the chair across from him.

Bobbie toyed with a silver spoon as the valet poured coffee and took her order for breakfast. "Toast, marmalade, and grapefruit."

Bobbie looked appreciatively at the pink roses clustered in a crystal bowl in the center of the table. The same color pink edged the fine bone china, and everything glistened in the light of four tapered candlesticks.

"Do you always have such a fancy table?" Bobbie recalled her hasty breakfasts at home when she and Minnie shared doughnuts out of a paper bag.

Georgy's manicured nails flicked the edge of a rose. "I told you I love beautiful things. I want to be surrounded by them."

"Things or people?"

Georgy smiled. "Both can be bought."

Bobbie smiled back. "I can't."

"Yes, you can. All the little trinkets I gave you—"

"They were gifts—I didn't see a price tag on them."

"You're not a kid, baby. Everything has a price tag on it. You wouldn't be here if you weren't already bought and paid for."

Bobbie's eyes glistened with indignation. "You're a real ass, telling a woman she's a whore."

"I didn't call you a whore." Georgy's expression was impassive. "Just said you were paid for."

"Fine difference."

"It's a compliment. You were expensive."

Bobbie threw her napkin across the table and stood up. "Send me the bill. I'll give you your money back."

Georgy's jaw tightened. He pointed to the chair. "Sit down. We haven't finished talking."

"Maybe *you* haven't . . ." Bobbie stalked across the room.

Georgy was right behind her. Grabbing her arm, he threw her onto the sofa. Bobbie looked at him, frightened by his unexpected violence. A wave of excitement washed over her. She almost cried when she realized that she was as attracted by his fury as she was frightened by it. She smiled. Maybe I've met my match.

Standing over her, threatening and powerful, Georgy stated his terms. "You're going to move in with me. Tell your housekeeper to send your clothes. Tell her you're going to live with the boss."

"I can't walk out. Minnie's not just my housekeeper. She's my friend."

"Then tell your friend she'll be keeping house for herself for a while. I'll send her money. She won't starve."

"I pay Minnie's salary whether I'm there or not. That's not the issue—"

"No. You're the issue, and I want you to live with me."

What had started out as a lark soon turned into a ghoulish nightmare as Bobbie shared Georgy's decadent life—the cocaine, the booze, the demeaning sex. By June, she found herself struggling to survive.

As the summer progressed Bobbie's health deteriorated. Nerves, she told herself, and tried to relax as much as possible when Georgy wasn't around, which wasn't often. He hovered over her, especially after their last fight, when she had told him she was leaving him.

"Nobody leaves Georgy Torrio." He slapped her, sending her sprawling across the room.

Bobbie threw up that day and every day after. She lost weight, her cheeks sunken under hollow eyes. Thank God I'm not singing, she thought, as she curled up in a ball on the edge of the bed and cried. After a week of tears, Georgy finally allowed Bobbie to spend an hour on the beach accompanied by a bodyguard.

Breathing in the fresh air blowing across Lake Michigan and watching the sailboats glide across the choppy waters was like heaven to Bobbie. Waves washed the soles of her feet. She was surrounded by people, yet she felt all alone.

She liked it that way, absorbing the sights, the sounds, and the sensation of freedom for an hour, her thoughts delving no deeper than the joy of being there. Soon, however, she felt the uncomfortable sting of the sun's rays and the bodyguard's eyes upon her. He'll let me know when my time is up. Bobbie buried her head in her hands. God! I'd give anything to talk to Minnie, to hear her voice, but I can't even make a phone call. She must be worried sick about me. Suddenly Bobbie sat up, terrified by the thought that Minnie might be in danger too. Georgy could kill us, and the police wouldn't even find our bodies. Her stomach churned. She gagged as she remembered how just four months before, in February, Bugs Moran's gang was gunned down in a garage while they waited for a shipment of illegal liquor. Newspapers called it the St. Valentine's Day massacre and later acknowledged that Al Capone was the undisputed ruler of Chicago's underworld. When Georgy's man tapped her on her shoulder, Bobbie reluctantly got up and walked docilely to the car.

By the middle of September even the walks didn't ease the terrible headaches and nausea that plagued Bobbie. She would sit for hours in the living room and stare at Georgy, who was usually lying on the couch in a drug-induced sleep. His mouth, which had seemed so sensuous only months before, gaped open. When he awakened and glared at her, Bobbie was terrified anew.

By the first of October, over six weeks after the onslaught of her on-again, off-again illness, Georgy said he was tired of hearing her complain and sent her to his doctor under the watchful eye of the bodyguard. He probably told the man to poison me, Bobbie thought, as she sat in the waiting room and wondered if the receptionist was her enemy too. Once inside the examining room, Bobbie was surprised at the doctor's professionalism as he lectured her about her ruinous habits: the drugs, the liquor, the poor diet. She changed her mind when he wrote a prescription for a drug to make her sleep.

"I'd rather have a vacation in Miami."

The doctor smiled. "No, I want to keep an eye on you.

First three months are crucial. Course I really don't expect you'll have any trouble carrying your baby to term."

Bobbie raised herself on her elbows and shook her head. She felt the jolt of the doctor's words, but the meaning took longer to sink in. She tried to control her voice. "Are you telling me I'm pregnant?"

"You didn't know? You're not spotting, are you?"

"No." Bobbie lay down again.

"Didn't you wonder about your periods?"

"I've only missed two. That's not unusual for me when I'm under stress."

The doctor shook his finger. "No tension. Gotta relax. Walk. Best thing for you."

"When?"

"Whenever you can find time."

Bobbie shook her head. "When is it due?"

"April or May."

"I'll never live that long."

"It seems far away now, but time passes quickly." The doctor was at the door. "The nurse'll give you a list of dos and don'ts. Come back in three weeks—unless you have a problem."

Bobbie laughed out loud when the doctor left. I'm going to have Georgy Torrio's baby. How could this happen to me? After years with Chuck, it has to be Georgy. She couldn't imagine having a child; at first she couldn't imagine being a mother. But later, she asked herself, why not? Why shouldn't I have a baby? Gingerly she touched her stomach, patted it. What difference does it make who the father is? It's *my* baby. Georgy must never see it. He must never know. I'll finally have someone to love who'll never leave me, never hurt me.

Bobbie started when the nurse walked into the room. Her smile was pleasant and intimate, as though she shared Bobbie's secret. She helped Bobbie up, then handed her two pieces of paper black with print.

"Follow the instructions, eat the right foods, get plenty of rest." She sounded like a well-oiled wheel.

Bobbie stuffed the papers into her handbag. "It's so

wonderful. The news, you know." She hesitated. The nurse looked at her blankly.

"My uncle. In the waiting room. I don't want to talk to him right now. I'd rather my husband found out first. Do you understand?"

The nurse thought for a moment, then shrugged. "Yeah, sure."

"My uncle'll know something's going on the minute he sees me." Bobbie made sure the woman understood. "That's why I want to sneak out the back door. I'll grab a taxi to my husband's office and tell him." Bobbie paused. The nurse seemed anxious to leave. "I'd appreciate it if you'd let him sit a half hour. If he catches up with me, he'll spoil everything."

"Yeah, sure." The nurse pulled the sheet off the examining table and pointed to a door. "Go out that door and turn to your right. Steps'll take you outside."

Bobbie smiled and thanked the woman profusely. "Remember," she said conspiratorially, "a half hour."

Bobbie prayed all the way to the apartment that Minnie would be home. When she opened the door, Bobbie fell into her arms and cried, "Thank God!"

Bobbie locked the door behind her. "I don't have time to explain. I have to hide. Georgy—"

"If that man think of hurting you. I call the police." Minnie didn't bat an eye.

"No. Not the police. They can't help. As far as I know, he owns 'em."

"Girl! You shaking like a leaf. What happen to you?"

"He has a bodyguard on me all the time. I got away, but not for long."

"Why you put up with that nonsense?"

"It's a long story, Minnie. Right now I'm scared to death. Where can I hide?" Bobbie's face was filled with panic. She glanced around in desperation.

"In the closet. Under the bed." Minnie's eyes bulged with fear. "I ain't never heard of nothin' like this before. A woman got to hide from a man—"

"Minnie, please. Don't try to understand. Just help."

"Come on. I stick you in the bedroom closet. Wrap some clothes round you."

"They'll look there first. Isn't there someplace they won't think of?"

Minnie thought for a moment then snapped her fingers. "Remember that panel in the bathroom? It come loose awhile back. I checked it. There's a tunnel going outside. The man who owned the place 'fore us was a runner. Brought booze in 'n out that way. It leads to a shed by the alley."

"I remember it, but it's so filthy. Aren't there spiders—"

"Ain't no time to be worrying about that. Come on, we got to see if we can pry it open."

Using two knives, Bobbie and Minnie finally popped the panel off its rusty hinges, while Bobbie told Minnie about her nightmarish life for the last six months. She fell silent when she peered inside the dirt-encrusted passageway. She was about to scotch the idea when the front doorbell rang. Seconds later someone pounded on the door. Minnie shoved her in the dark hole. "I'll get rid of 'em soon's I can. Don't you panic."

Bobbie nodded, but bit her lip as Minnie pushed the panel in place, placed a wastepaper basket in front, then hurried to open the door.

Barely looking at her, Georgy pushed Minnie aside and strutted into the room, his eyes taking in everything at a glance. "Where's the bitch?" He motioned for his two bodyguards to follow him inside.

"Don't know no bitch." Minnie's eyes filled with hate.

Georgy spun around and slapped her hard across the face. "I asked you where she is. I want an answer."

Minnie stepped back, but Georgy grabbed her arm and forced her against the wall.

"She was here a few minutes ago, but she's gone now. She's scared you find her."

Georgy slapped her again. Blood trickled from her nose. She pressed her hand against it and shouted angrily. "All your hittin' ain't gonna change nothin'. She ain't here. Look for yourself."

319

Georgy turned away in disgust, then flicked his fingers. The two men spread out to search.

From her hiding place between the walls, Bobbie heard someone enter the bedroom. Opening the closet door, he pushed the clothes along the rod. Only the back wall of the closet separated them. Afraid he could sense her presence, Bobbie tried to ease herself further down the passage, then realized her dress was caught in the door. Her panic blotted out the sound of the man's footsteps as he walked into the bathroom. Bobbie's hands were clammy as she tugged at her skirt. How much of her blue dress was showing against the whiteness of the panel? She bit her tongue to keep from screaming. The man slammed his hand against the shower curtain, checking the bathtub. Bobbie waited. He would turn now. His eyes would search the walls. She heard his heavy breathing. He didn't move. What did he see? The toilet. The floor. Finally his footsteps echoed against the tiles as he walked out. Bobbie fought the wave of nausea that seeped upward, gagging her.

The voices from the living room were loud and harsh. "She ain't here, boss. What you want us to do?"

Bobbie imagined the look of frustration on Georgy's face. "Cover the front and the back. She's got no place to go but here. She'll be back."

The front door slammed. It was quiet.

Seconds later Bobbie fell sobbing into Minnie's arms. "My dress. I thought he'd see it."

"Hush. It's over. You're safe." Minnie held Bobbie until she stopped crying, then offered her a handkerchief. "Come on, I'll fix us some tea." When Bobby flinched, Minnie patted her soothingly. "There ain't nothin' to worry about. I double-bolted all the doors."

Between sips of tea laced with bourbon, Bobbie told Minnie she was pregnant. Minnie was less than enthusiastic, but agreed that Georgy must not find out.

"I'm going home. That's the only place Georgy won't find me."

"Don't he know you from St. Louis?"

"Yes, but it's too far away for him to worry about. In a few weeks he'll get tired of the chase." Bobbie frowned. "He doesn't want me. He just can't stand it that I left him."

"He's a mean one. You sure he ain't gonna hunt you down?"

"I don't expect Georgy'll be around for long. His business friends aren't at all happy with him. He's crazy. He's made lots of enemies. One of these days when he's walking down the street—"

Minnie shook her head. "Hush, girl. I'm not wantin' to hear such tales."

Bobbie stood up and put her arms around her friend. "I don't want to get you involved, but I have to ask. Can you help me get away?"

Minnie didn't hesitate. "Course I can. What you think friends 're for?"

Bobbie outlined her plan. "I need cash—not much, just enough for a train ticket home and spending money for a month. Since you already have power of attorney, I want you to close out all my bank accounts, sell all my stock, and sell this building. But wait till after the end of the month— just in case Georgy's still snooping around. Then bring yourself, the money, and your clothes to St Louis."

Minnie's eyes widened in surprise. "Girl, you're worth thousands 'nd thousands! You gonna trust me with that kind of money?"

"I trusted you with my life."

"That's different. Ain't no temptation there."

Bobbie smiled. "Well, I'm trusting you again. I want you to dress me up like an old woman and smuggle me out of this house. Can you do that?"

Minnie's face brightened. "Sure 'nough can do that. You tell me how old you wants to be."

"Not too old. I want to turn back into Bobbie Evans on the train. This is just in case Georgy has somebody at the station."

Minnie stood up and headed for the bedroom. "You have to use the passageway to get out. Think you can stand them spiders?"

"Sounds like the underground railroad." Bobbie managed a laugh. As the woman pulled clothes out of a trunk, looking for a costume, Bobbie cautioned her again. "Don't talk to my broker till the end of the month or the first of November. Georgy has spies all over the city."

Minnie nodded, assuring Bobbie she knew just what to do.

CHAPTER XXVI

The city has changed in a hundred ways in five years, but it really hasn't changed at all, Bobbie thought. When the taxi turned off Delmar Boulevard, Bobbie's heart pounded furiously. She rolled down the window and peered through the evening dusk at a row of houses that loomed like dying dinosaurs, relics of an age that was no more—her childhood.

"There it is. That's the house."

"Yes, ma'am." The taxi stopped in front of the two-story home. Dropping Bobbie's suitcase on the sidewalk, the driver counted out change from a ten-dollar bill. Bobbie, paralyzed with fear and anticipation, didn't notice when he pulled away.

It was home, but it looked terrible—the unkempt lawn, the sagging porch, the dirty windows. Suddenly she was furious. Why had Roy let the place get so rundown? It's a disgrace, Bobbie thought. Picking up her suitcase, she climbed the chipped concrete steps to the front porch.

Minutes passed after Bobbie knocked on the glass door before a light went on in the back of the house. Slippers slapped the wood floor, and Bobbie, straining to see through the smeared glass, could make out only a silhouette until the door swung open. An old woman, her black skin cracked with age, poked out her head.

Bobbie threw her hand over her mouth to stifle a scream.

"Tallulah! Oh, my God, Tallulah. You're alive. I hoped, prayed . . ."

"Who be there?" The woman adjusted her glasses and peered hard at Bobbie's face. "I knows that voice, but surely it ain't . . ."

Bobbie pulled the screen door open and grabbed Tallulah, hugging her and crying. "It's me, Bobbie. Roberta. I've come home, Tallulah. I've come home."

"Lord have mercy! Come in, child. Come inside." Tears streamed down the old housekeeper's cheeks. "I been praying all these years, and here you is. The Lord done listen to my prayers."

Tallulah and Bobbie faced each other over the kitchen table. So familiar, yet so different, Bobbie thought. Ever since she could remember, Tallulah's kitchen had been filled with sunlight and the smell of warm bread. What awful thing had happened? Had Roy lost all his money? Were they this poor? Thank God, I've come home.

"Mama? Roy? Are they here? You didn't have to put Mama in a home, did you?" Bobbie was almost afraid to ask.

Tallulah nervously massaged her gnarled, arthritic hands. "Ain't nobody be puttin' my Sarah in a home while I's alive," she said vehemently, then dropped her head, allowing the tears to fall unchecked onto her hands. "But your mama never got no better. She passed a year ago." Tallulah paused, sighed. "Roy, too. They is both gone."

"Not both of them! They couldn't both have passed without my knowing."

"Weren't no way to get hold of you—"

"Don't blame yourself." Bobbie grabbed Tallulah's hand and pressed it to her lips. Her eyes pleaded for forgiveness. "You were all alone, and I . . . Oh, God, all I cared about was myself."

The two women sat at the table, tears streaming down their cheeks. Finally Bobbie asked, "How did they die?"

Tallulah wiped her eyes, then, blowing her nose, told Bobbie what had happened. "Your mama passed first. Weren't no surprise, but it hurt bad. I miss my Sarah. We had our good times. But she with the mister now. Guess she be happy."

Bobbie nodded. "And Roy?"

"He killed. Shot down on the street. Police find him in an alley. Say it was a gang did it, but nobody seen nothing. Police ain't found the murderer."

Bobbie sucked in her breath. Georgy's threats resounded in her ears. Georgy Torrio, Tony Gianino . . . the same scum. Roy didn't get out in time. Now he was dead, and for what? A case of illegal booze. She shook her head in dismay. Poor Roy—he thought he could outwit them. Bobbie felt Tallulah's sorrow, and she reached out her hand. "I'm so sorry you had to carry this alone."

"You home now. That be all the comfort I need."

"I'm staying. I won't leave you alone again." Bobbie forced a smile. I've been on a roller coaster too long, she thought. It's time I faced up to my responsibilities.

They ate a cold supper of cheese, bread, and apples, then, exhausted, Bobbie asked where she could sleep.

"Why, in your old room. I be going up with you 'n find some clean sheets. It bound to be a bit musty after all these years."

Bobbie nodded and stepped gingerly into her past, following the housekeeper down the long, dark hallway, surprised that her memories were as faded as the wallpaper. But as she climbed the steps, she heard in her mind the piano in her mama's room playing ragtime. It reminded her of the ride on the Ferris wheel at the World's Fair and how terrified she was but wouldn't let on. Tears rolled down her cheeks when she saw her papa with his starched collar and straw hat strutting around the Grand Basin as if he were the king of Arabia. Roy's here, too, she thought. She stopped in front of his bedroom door and touched the knob. Maybe if I open it he'll be on the floor playing with his toy soldiers. Will he frown as he always did when I came into his room, or will he smile and ask me to play? Bobbie dropped her hand and walked on. They're gone. I have to remember that or I'll go crazy looking for them. When she reached her own room, she stopped at the door. Her dolls waited in a corner for a little girl to breathe life into them. The blue china tea set waited for a party to commence. Had Tallulah done this?

The old woman lit a kerosene lamp and limped across the room to a closet. "Electric don't work right up here. Don't trust it anyways." She brushed a cobweb off the shelf and stretched to reach the sheets.

Bobbie dropped her suitcase and ran to help. "Here, let me do that."

Tallulah stepped back. "Ain't as fit as I was. Guess I can't be expectin' to run a race at my age."

"At your age you need someone to take care of you. You just get yourself back downstairs and don't worry about a thing. I have money, and my friend Minnie will be bringing it here sometime in November. We're going to be a family again." She paused and felt her stomach. "A real family."

"I hopes so, child. I sure hopes so." Tallulah shuffled out the door and down the stairs. If money buys happiness, Bobbie thought, I've got enough to make us very happy.

"Two cents on the dollar—and that weren't on all of it." Minnie kept her eye locked on the cup of tea in front of her. Bobbie drummed the table with her fingers. She hadn't expected it to be that bad, not even after seeing Minnie's drawn expression when she stepped off the Illinois Central train two hours before. Billions had been lost in the stock market crash just a week ago, but somehow Bobbie thought her money would be secure. She scratched her head, trying not to show her shock. Minnie's suffering enough, she thought, and it isn't her fault. I told her not to sell till after the end of the month. Who in hell would've thought the damn market would collapse?

"How much could you salvage?" A pained expression furrowed Bobbie's brow.

"Two thousand, but only 'cause I start sellin' on the twenty-eighth. Most folks that waited till the twenty-ninth lost everythin'."

"Two thousand seem a lot to me," Tallulah broke in.

Bobbie shook her head. "Tallulah, you've become very optimistic the last few weeks."

The old woman nodded and fervidly slapped the top of the table. "I's ain't alone no more. That mean more 'n a pot a money. Roberta—sorry, child—I means Bobbie, she come home, and she ain't never gonna leave."

Minnie finished her tea. Her face lightened. She grabbed a pencil and started figuring. A few minutes later, she pushed a piece of paper covered with numbers in front of Bobbie. "Tallulah's real smart. She say you come 'home.' Well, if 'home' is free 'n clear, 'n you got two thousand dollars, I figures you, long with us, can make a pretty good living right here."

Bobbie looked quizzical. Minnie explained. "You gots a big place. I thinks we ought to clean it up, paint 'n wallpaper 'n what, then rent out rooms. Jobs are hard to come by for folks like us. This way we'll be independent." She smiled, looked at Tallulah, then at Bobbie, her eyes bright with anticipation. "Well, what y'all think?"

Tallulah nodded vigorously, and Bobbie grabbed Minnie's hand and squeezed it. "I think it's the answer to our problems. Who's going to hire a pregnant colored woman? And who'd take care of Tallulah if you and I had to go out to work? Oh, it's a wonderful idea."

Later, as she helped Minnie with fresh bed linens, Bobbie rambled on. For the first time in months, she dared look forward to the future. "And I was afraid I couldn't take care of Tallulah, and only God knew what I was going to do with a baby. Thank God, you're here, Minnie. You're a genius."

Minnie laughed. "If I were a genius, I wouldn'ta lost you your money. But bad as it seem, you is still lucky you leave Chicago when you do."

Bobbie tensed. "What are you talking about?"

"Georgy. You was right. That man come every day for two weeks, poundin' on the door 'n carryin' on—"

"He didn't hit you anymore—oh, Minnie, he did. And I left you alone—"

"Weren't nothin' I couldn't handle." Minnie stiffened. "I show that man he can't scare everybody. But that ain't what I was wantin' to tell you. Thought you really like to hear what happen to him. Well, two weeks after you leave, he get his. Ain't sayin' it's right, but the way he act, I ain't grievin' over his passin'."

"He's dead?"

"Dead."

"Was he gunned down?"

"Gettin' outta his car in the middle of the afternoon. Course, nobody seen nothing. You knows how that is."

Bobbie sighed. "Thank God, that's over with. Now I can have my baby and not worry that he'll find me. I could never be sure—"

Minnie snorted. "I'm glad he's dead. Now if we is really lucky, that baby be takin' after you."

"I'm going to vote for Mr. Roosevelt." Bobbie folded the *St. Louis Post-Dispatch* and handed the paper to Minnie.

"Guess I is, too," Minnie said, frowning. "I never think I be votin' the devil ticket. Always put my *X* by Mr. Lincoln's party. But there ain't no way I can vote for Mr. Hoover. That man mess up everything."

Bobbie looked up from her sewing. Some days, she congratulated herself for managing everything so beautifully. Running the rooming house, feeding twelve people a day, and taking care of her toddler. But Bobbie could still feel the quicksand beneath her. Her two thousand dollars were dwindling fast. Not that it was her fault. But doctor bills for Tallulah, unpaid rents, and a new roof all took their bite out of her nest egg. The two spinsters and three couples—the average age of the eight was seventy-two—stayed in their rooms most of the time and didn't eat much; but they did have to be fed three times a day, and their rooms had to be heated, not to mention the extra washing. Bobbie felt someone tug at her leg. Dropping the torn pillow case onto her lap, she bent over and whisked the cherub-faced youngster off the floor. Laughing, Bobbie swung her over her head, and the child broke out in a gale of giggles.

Tess—the sun, the moon, and the stars to the three women who doted on her—had just squeaked in on April 30, 1930, and was now two and a half years old. Minnie and Tallulah bickered over whom she resembled.

"She has her mama's mouth, and beautiful hands, and bright, shiny eyes and . . ." Minnie declared. The truth was, nature had divided the parents' features, mixing them just right to make Tess a real beauty. But how am I going to give her the things I had? Bobbie wondered. Piano lessons. I can teach her that. Singing lessons, too, if she wants. I was brought up to believe that God gave us our looks, but what we did with our minds was up to us. More than anything, I want Tess to go to school, to college even. Bobbie leaned back in her chair, remembering her mother's efforts to get her to college, and her grandmother wanting the same thing for her daughter. Just wasn't supposed to be, Bobbie concluded, then wondered how different her life would be now if she had listened.

Tallulah's cry jarred Bobbie out of her reverie. "Lordy! Look at the time. If I's gonna make peach cobbler for supper, you better fetch me some peaches."

Bobbie kissed Tess and pushed her in Minnie's direction. Flipping on the dim light bulb that hung from a dangling wire in the basement, Bobbie stepped cautiously down the rutted steps. Years of accumulated dirt scented the musty cellar and Bobbie sneezed. Spiders scurried for safety into the crevices of the soot-covered walls. Moving along the shelves lined with blue-tinted mason jars, Bobbie counted her accumulated wealth of tomatoes, string beans, asparagus, and corn. On the next aisle were the cherries, peaches, apples, and pears. They're more precious to me than Georgy's ruby necklace, she thought, then rubbed the back of her neck as she recalled the hours they'd spent putting them up the previous summer. Seemed unlikely that Tallulah would be able to do any canning next summer with her legs giving out the way they were. She and Minnie couldn't do it all by themselves, but without the home-canned foods, their grocery bills would soar out of sight. Bobbie grabbed three jars of peaches and headed upstairs. She'd worry about that when the time came.

In his inaugural address on March 4, 1933, Franklin Roosevelt had told the country "the only thing we have to fear is fear itself." Bobbie had been happy to hear that, but she wondered how she was going to pay for another load of coal, another doctor bill, and for having the piano tuned.

"We'll survive," Bobbie said as she and Minnie went over their expenses for the month of February, 1937. "We need more coal again. I swear, heating this house is like heating the great outdoors.

"And we got to keep enough aside for taxes. And Tallulah's medicine and the doctor. If we don't pay the man, he won't tend her no more."

It was too good to last, Bobbie thought. Don't know why I expected Tallulah to keep going forever. Poor thing, could be a hundred years old for all I know. "She's done her share and more. I'll pay the doctor bill if I have to stop eating," Bobbie vowed.

"Don't say nothin' 'bout eatin' to Tallulah," Minnie warned. "She havin' fits worryin' 'bout food. 'Y'all starvin',' she say, and her layin' flat on her back. Truth be, I ain't had no decent greens or corn bread since she took sick."

Bobbie put her finger over her mouth and shushed Minnie. "Bertie'll hear you. She's doing the best she can, but just working part time—"

"I know the woman mean well, but I can cook better'n her."

Bobbie frowned. "Don't think you're going to take on the cooking for twelve people. You'll have enough to do cleaning and keeping the books and taking care of Tess."

"Tess ain't no problem. Anyways, we all take care of her."

Bobbie dropped her eyes and nervously toyed with the salt and pepper shakers, unsure how Minnie would take her pronouncement. I hope she understands and doesn't think I'm running out, but I got to do something. I can't just sit and watch us starve to death.

Minnie eased her chair closer to Bobbie, uneasily aware of her restlessness. "You got troubles I don't know 'bouts?" Her voice was low.

"No, no trouble. Just a change." Bobbie tried to smile, but it wouldn't come. "Changes scare me."

Minnie's eyes were wide, and she clasped her hands together as though for support. "Changes? What kinda changes?"

"I'm going to get a singing job."

"Oh, girl . . ."

"Not in a club. Won't be anything like Chicago. Not that I'd mind the money, but there aren't many places able to afford a singer full time. All the colored clubs just about folded. Musicians got to live on tips, and honey, they're as scarce as hen's teeth." Bobbie paused and flashed Minnie a smile meant to convey confidence. From the frown on Minnie's face, she didn't think she'd succeeded. "Anyway, even if I did land a job in a club, I couldn't afford it. How could I buy a dozen fancy gowns? I can hardly keep myself in house dresses."

"Where you gonna sing 'less at a club?" Minnie eyed her suspiciously.

"Rent parties. They're all over town. Somebody needs to raise money to pay the rent, he hires a singer, a band, brings in some booze, and he's got a rent party."

"I heard of 'em." Minnie shook her head in opposition. "Don't seem like you'd make enough money for the bother."

"Ten bucks a night—plus tips." Bobbie was enthusiastic. "Lizzy Garrett has one every weekend. Said she'd hire me whenever I want to work."

Minnie screwed up her face disapprovingly. "That life never been good for you, 'n music styles done changed since you been in the business."

"My voice hasn't changed, and I can always learn new music."

Throwing up her hands, Minnie finally agreed that an extra twenty or thirty dollars a week would come in handy. Lifting her glasses, Minnie inspected Bobbie, then nodded agreeably. "You still lookin' good, girl—face ain't got a wrinkle on it." She laughed and pointed at Bobbie's midsection. "Your figure still lookin' good, too. Course t'ain't hard keeping skinny round here with all the work 'n so little food." She paused and glanced down at her hips. "How come that don't work for me? I eat the same as you, but it all turn to fat."

Bobbie chortled. "Thanks for the compliment, but at thirty-six, I don't feel so beautiful—or so young. When you go into the business, even if it's singing at rent parties, you gotta gild the lily. Think you can make over some of my old costumes?"

Minnie pushed back her chair and smiled. "Honey, you give me a week, and I have you lookin' like you is openin' on Broadway."

Minnie was as good as her word, even though Bobbie's opening was something less than a first night on the Great White Way. Still, Bobbie was excited as she mixed with the fifty people jammed into Lizzy's apartment while she waited for Eddie Harrison to set up his band. Bobbie caught a glimpse of herself in a mirror. Not bad, she thought, considering it had been eight years since she had dressed up in anything other than her black Sunday dress. Pulling in her stomach, she tugged at the waist of the gold lamé that Minnie had spent hours remodeling into a 1937 fashion. Except for the tightness around the hips, Bobbie thought it looked very chic.

Over the din of voices, Bobbie heard Eddie Harrison call her for the first set. Bobbie pushed through the crowd of people, some smoking tea, some drinking alcohol, which was cheap again, now that prohibition had ended. Bobbie stepped to the front of the band and opened with "Back in Your Own Back Yard." Heads bobbed up and down in time and when she finished, whistles and clapping persisted through the soulful introduction of "The Very Thought of You." Later, when the party mellowed, those who were left sat on the floor, heads touching, as they listened to Bobbie sing the moody love songs "Stormy Weather" and "They Can't Take That Away From Me." Bobbie responded to her audience, as enthralled with them as they were with her. It's good to be back singing, even if it is only a rent party, she thought happily.

Between sets, Bobbie mingled with the guests who ate

fried chicken, chitlins, pigs' feet, and ribs. A plate piled high with food was a dollar, a shot of bourbon twenty-five cents; and while they had their money out, they pressed a few coins, ten, fifty, seventy-five cents into Bobbie's hand. But the money that changed hands in the front of the apartment was nothing compared to what was moving in the kitchen, where a crap game was in full swing. Bobbie loved to watch as the kneeling men threw tens, twenties, or even fifty-dollar bills in a pile and lost it all on one throw of the dice. The sight of so much money was intoxicating; it made the fifteen dollars she earned for a night's work seem paltry. But later, when she handed it to Minnie for the household, it seemed like a fortune.

By June, however, Bobbie wondered how much longer she could sing three nights a week, run the boarding house during the day, and find time for Tess, who at age seven, was growing up to be a sweet, lovable child, but much too withdrawn.

"Bring a friend home from school some afternoon," Bobbie said cajolingly one day. Tess, her eyes riveted on the graham cracker she was dunking into a glass of milk, merely shrugged. "Don't have no friends, Mama, 'n I don't want none. Essie Mae shove me against the fence yesterday just 'cause I ask to play kickball. Everybody laugh 'cept Wyatt."

"See! You do have a friend."

Tess looked up and frowned. "Aw, Mama, Wyatt ain't no friend. He's a boy. I play with him cause I got nobody else." Tess sucked the milk out of the graham cracker, and Bobbie walked into the pantry to get the potatoes for supper, sorry she had brought up the subject.

"Ain't nothin' wrong with Tess," Minnie chided Bobbie later. "Some children likes to be by themselves. It become a problem only ifs you make it one."

Minnie laid a stack of bills in front of Bobbie and then, throwing open her ledger, pointed to the credit column. Bobbie groaned when she saw how little cash they had coming in.

"I knows you workin' yourself to a frazzle already, but

any chance you gettin' more money at them rent parties? We is cash poor."

"I'll see what I can do, Minnie," Bobbie promised, too exhausted to think.

At the next rent party, Bobbie cornered Lizzy and asked her if she could get in on the crap game. Lizzy tossed her henna-dyed hair back and, laughing uproariously, asked Bobbie if she had noticed the bulges in the men's back pockets. She explained that what Bobbie saw was not a friendly neighborhood get together, but professionals playing professionals, and they weren't interested in her cookie jar money. Bobbie looked at the twenty-five dollars clutched in her hand. This isn't any cookie jar money that I saved just to blow on a crap game, she thought. This is our food money for the week. Giving up her dream of turning it over until she had a thousand dollars, Bobbie wadded the bills together, stashed them in her bra, and went back to work.

Somehow Bobbie, Minnie, and Tess, who preferred helping around the house to playing with the children down the street, managed to put in a small garden and in August canned as much as they could. It's not half what we had last year, Bobbie thought, as she lined the tomatoes, corn, beans, and peas on the shelves in the basement. God! I hope it lasts till Christmas. Maybe something'll happen by then. She sighed. With our luck, if something happens, it'll be bad.

The good news was, Tallulah was better. With Tess acting as a crutch, the old woman would get out of bed and hobble across her room. Her spirits improved, too, as Tess gradually devoted all her days to Tallulah.

"I's sure gonna miss you, child, when you goes back to school." Tallulah sat up as Tess fluffed up her pillow after a nap.

"I be missin' you too." Tess sat on the bed and set up the board for their daily game of checkers. Tallulah reached into her bedside drawer and withdrew a nickel. "Money make the competition tougher," Tallulah said, her eyes glittering.

* * *

In September, two of the couples boarding with them paid their back rent. To celebrate this largest influx of cash she had seen in over a year, Bobbie bought a seven-pound pot roast and two bottles of wine. Minnie went to fetch vegetables from the cellar. Humming to herself, she clutched five quart jars close to her body, failing to see the crack in the top step. The wood split and she fell backward, crumbling into a heap on the basement floor. Tomatoes and corn splattered everywhere. In a few hours Minnie was propped up in bed, her leg in a cast, the doctor having admonished her to stay off of it for six weeks. Despite her gallant attempts at coping, Bobbie knew she couldn't keep the house going and sing, too. She had to make money to hire help until Minnie was back on her feet. After a frantic phone call to Bertie, the slatternly part-timer agreed to work a week without wages, but after that, she wanted full pay or she'd quit.

At the next rent party, Bobbie asked Lizzy for extra work, but Lizzy shook her head. "There ain't enough business in St. Louis to have entertainment every night, leastways not singing, if you know what I mean."

"I'm not sure I do know what you mean," Bobbie said, exasperated.

Lizzy exploded in her typical horselaugh. "Ain't you ever wondered where the men disappeared to between sets? First they there, then they ain't."

Bobbie scratched her head. "Never thought about it. Had other things on my mind."

"I got the apartment across the hall, 'n I got girls there, too."

Now Bobbie laughed. "You mean you're running a whorehouse?"

Lizzy pinched up her face in disapproval. "Guess so, if you wants to call it that."

Bobbie apologized. Lizzy shrugged as if to say it didn't matter what it was called—it made money. She asked if Bobbie wanted in on it.

"Fifty bucks a night? That's lots of money, but I don't know . . ."

Lizzy picked at her chipped fingernail polish. "Well, honey, I'm busy. You let me know if you wanna cat for a while. That be the only way I can help you."

Bobbie wanted to question her more. Was it safe? What about disease? How did one handle the weird ones? She turned and walked down the steps. Outside, her high heels clicking as she walked home, she couldn't believe she was actually considering it. I'd be a whore, she thought, then shook her head. No, a prostitute. Sounds better. But who'd know? It'd only be for a couple of months! Nobody'd find out—nobody who matters, anyway. Tess, Tallulah, they'd never hear, and Minnie's bedridden. The women from church can't spread rumors that fast. Fifty dollars—plus the money I make singing. It'd only be for a couple of months.

Two weeks later on a warm night in the middle of October, Bobbie, still wearing her brand-new slip, sat on the edge of the bed while Mr. Jones relieved himself in the adjoining bathroom. Bobbie heard the toilet flush, then water splash from the faucet. Her body was damp from nerves. When her first customer walked into the bedroom with a towel pulled tight around his protruding waist exposing his short legs, she dropped her eyes and swallowed hard, trying to suppress the nausea turning her stomach. He's probably a very nice man, Bobbie thought, as he touched her arm. Very nice. His hand moved across her shoulder and down the front of her slip. When he grabbed her right breast, Bobbie bit her lip, not knowing whether to laugh or cry. It's as if he's fondling a horse, she thought. A damn horse. God! And I was afraid I couldn't handle the passion. He's worse than Chuck when he was dead drunk. She shook her head—it was no time to think about Chuck. I have to concentrate; I have to think of something or I'll laugh in his face. But she didn't laugh. In fact, she didn't have time to prepare herself for Mr. Jones before he raised her slip, knelt on top of her, and finished five minutes after he had started. Five minutes, Five bucks. Easy. Real easy.

Surprisingly, Bobbie discovered that her life changed very little. She was careful about what she talked about at home, but she seldom thought about her "work" during the day. What mattered was to see Tess's eyes light up over a new pair of shoes, and to laugh with Minnie, whose face beamed with pleasure as she tried on her new dress. Tallulah got a warm flannel nightgown, and Bobbie indulged herself with a new coat and a bottle of perfume. Am I trying to hide the stench of being a whore? she wondered. Hell, who cares? I'm paying the bills.

By 1939 most of the country felt the impact of the expanding economy. Government work programs trickled down even to the destitute Negro, and private industry stirred. Manufacturers geared up to produce munitions as Europe tottered on the brink and finally, in September, slid into war. Rent parties lost their popularity as money fed more sophisticated tastes, and nightclubs, supper clubs, and dance halls reopened after ten years of darkness. Clubs were still segregated, but the Billie Holidays, Duke Ellingtons, and Cab Calloways could entertain in the white cabarets as long as they came and went through the service entrance.

Bobbie clung tenaciously to her neighborhood singing job. Almost forty years old, she had abandoned any hope of hitting the big time again. Harlem was a bittersweet memory, Chicago a calliope of reminiscenses. New sounds were being heard; angular, unsettling rhythms provoked old-time jazz enthusiasts to condemn the modern improvisationists who built their reputations in the after-hours clubs: Coleman Hawkins on tenor sax, Dizzy Gillespie on trumpet, Thelonious Monk, piano, and Charlie Christian on guitar. The bebop pioneers failed to capture Bobbie's interest; she continued to sing traditional jazz and blues numbers, and there were still blues purists who appreciated her husky renditions of their old favorites. One of them, Mr. Moody, owned a small club two blocks from Lizzy's apartment.

On a particularly slow Saturday night, Mr. Moody approached Bobbie with a cigar in one hand and a drink in the other. His right eye, twitching nervously as he spoke, seemed to add to the importance of the job he offered Bobbie in his club: sixty-five a week plus tips, nine to one on Wednesday, Friday, and Saturday nights. As though to balance the twitch in his right eye, he winked with his left, and a hint of a smile softened his hard, lined lips. "I been looking for a jazz 'n blues singer like you. You got class, kid, real class, 'n you know how to belt out a song."

Bobbie held her breath and counted to ten before replying. Sixty-five a week! I can double that with tips. And I can stop prostituting. Hallelujah! She looked at Mr. Moody sweetly. "If I take it, I expect I'll get a raise in a few months."

Looking surprised, Mr. Moody thought for a moment, then nodded his assent. "How much depends on how many people you draw."

"Then we got us a deal." Bobbie offered her hand. Mr. Moody, sticking his cigar in his mouth, pumped Bobbie's hand enthusiastically.

Bobbie barely contained herself the rest of the evening as she sang. When she crossed the hallway to undress, she hoped it would be the last time. In two weeks I'll be singing at Moody's Bar. I won't need this money. I'll tell Lizzy tomorrow. Bobbie switched on the phonograph and sang along with Billie Holiday, swaying as she ran a comb through her hair and dabbed powder on her nose.

Her smile suddenly faded when the door opened and her first customer of the evening stepped into the room. She gasped, repulsed by the man who approached her. That he was old—he looked seventy—wasn't as jarring as his dirty clothes and unwashed hair. Tobacco juice stained his grayish-white beard, and his fingernails were brown from decades of hard physical labor. Bobbie didn't hesitate. Flipping her hand in the air, she told him to leave. Ignoring her outburst, the man drew a fifty-dollar bill from his wallet and threw it on the dresser.

Bobbie stared at it, then looked at the man again, a questioning frown etched on her face. Fifty bucks! I could take care of him and call it a night. The temptation was great, but she picked up the bill and handed it back. "Sorry, it's not you. Well, it is and it isn't. You got to clean yourself up. I couldn't begin—"

"Ain't never done nothin' like this before. Don't expect you to believe that, but it's the truth." He sat on the bed and ran his hand through the oily strands of hair lying lankly across his semi-bald head.

Bobbie sighed. "Hey, mister. It doesn't matter. You got fifty bucks that says you can stay as long as you want. All I ask is that you go into the bathroom and wash up a little, especially—well—you know where."

Muttering about being lonely, the man took off his stained overcoat and disappeared into the bathroom. When he returned, he looked a little cleaner and smelled of Ivory soap, but touching Bobbie, his hands were cold and rough against her soft skin. My God, this is going to be the hardest fifty dollars I ever earned, she thought. The man mechanically pressed parts of her body as though anticipating some magical response in his own. When nothing happened after half an hour, Bobbie began to manipulate him. As he lay on his back, his flaccid skin hanging on his bony frame, his lips were pursed in despair. He didn't complain when Bobbie paused to smoke a cigarette, but when she finished, he became agitated and demanded they get on with it. After fondling her for twenty minutes, his breathing finally became labored, his hands more probing. Maneuvering Bobbie onto her back, he squatted on top, lowering his organ into her mouth. Wedged between his legs without a chance to protest, Bobbie submitted, hoping he would soon finish. She counted the seconds as he pumped and brayed. Unexpectedly, he stopped, his whole body becoming rigid as he stared at the sliver of light seeping through the partially opened door.

Bobbie, frustrated at the thought of all her effort ending in failure, bolted upright in the bed and angrily pushed him away. "What the hell's the matter with you? It took me over an hour to get you going, and you quit"—she snapped her fingers—"just like that."

The man pointed to a shadow emerging from the doorway. "You playin' a joke on me? God in heaven, you ain't got'em that young workin' here, do you?"

Bobbie turned to look as the shadow moved closer, then screamed, "Oh, my God!"

"Mama! What you doin'? Oh, Mama!"

The tears streaming down Tess's face didn't obscure the horror in her eyes. Her bottom lip quivered, and she spat at her mother, calling her names that shocked Bobbie.

"Stop that!" Bobbie shook Tess by her shoulders. "Just stop screaming. I can explain."

Tess wouldn't be placated. "You's a whore, Mama. You is nothin' but a whore." Tess pulled away and ran to the door. She paused, looking at her mother, who was kneeling on the floor, naked, while the man hastily pulled on his pants. Before she disappeared she screamed, "I wish you was dead!"

Bobbie was frantic. How did she know I worked here? Why did she come? Unable to think, Bobbie grabbed the telephone and called home. When Minnie answered, she had to ask Bobbie to repeat herself several times before she could be understood. When Bobbie finally told her what had happened, Minnie, too, broke down, and sobbing, explained that Tallulah had just died. Tess had gone looking for her mother so they could comfort each other.

"Tallulah! Oh, my God." Bobbie dropped the receiver on its hook and threw on some clothes.

The first shafts of light were spreading across the eastern sky as Bobbie slipped into her shoes and ran down the stairs. She stopped at the landing when she remembered her purse. I have to have money for a taxi. Tess'll never walk home with me, but I can make her ride with me. She'll have to listen. She'll have to understand. Bobbie hurried back upstairs, grabbed her handbag, then retraced her steps. As she passed a second-story window, she glanced out and saw a little girl with long black hair wearing a red dress disappear down an alley. Bobbie yelled at her to stop, but she was gone. That had to be Tess, Bobbie thought, as she turned on her heel and darted down the steps. Please, God, Bobbie prayed, don't let her do anything foolish. If she hurts herself because of this, I'll die, I'll just die. Racked by guilt, Bobbie didn't see the hole in the worn carpet and her high heel caught in the loose threads. Losing her balance, she fell headfirst down the stairs. When she hit bottom, her neck snapped. She died instantly.

It was several hours before Lizzy found Bobbie's mangled body at the foot of the steps. At about the same time the police found Tess. Wedged between two trash cans in an alley several blocks from Lizzy's apartment, she was crying and mumbling the words "Mama" and "Tallulah" over and over.

Only a handful of people attended the double funeral. The ceremony was brief. The minister hurried through the twenty-third psalm, commented on the stalwart lives of the two women, then, after pressing Minnie's hand and kissing Tess, hurried away in a long black limousine.

Tess kept her eyes riveted on the top of the two gray coffins, her trance broken only by a sniffle or a sob. Minnie had told her to cry, to mourn her loss, but she hadn't since that night when she had found her mother at Lizzy's apartment. She hadn't spoken of it; she hadn't told Minnie what her mother was doing. Minnie found out later but couldn't talk about it. Maybe Tess would forget quicker if they pretended it hadn't happened.

Minnie clutched Tess's hand as they walked away from the grave. "Just us, now. Your mama and Tallulah at rest, lying there next to your granddaddy and grandmaw—'n your Uncle Roy, too. Don't you worry, child, they be lookin' after us from up there." She pointed to the sky. "Don't you know, they is with Jesus now."

Tess pressed her tear-stained face against Minnie's hand. "I kill her, Minnie. I kill my own Mama."

Minnie bent over and kissed Tess's forehead. "Why you talkin' like that? You ain't killed your mama. Jesus took her. It be her time."

Tess shook her head, rejecting Minnie's efforts to comfort

her. "Why didn't Jesus take me? I's the bad one. I wished Mama dead. Jesus shoulda taken me for punishment."

"Hush, girl. I don't wanna hear that kind of talk. Ain't nothing you do kill your mama. You love her. I love her. But she done pass 'n we got to accept that. Ain't no good blaming yourself."

Tess dropped her eyes and walked silently to the waiting car that would take them home.

CHAPTER XXVII

Slipping the black dress over her head, Minnie checked her image in the mirror and thought, it'll do, then, on second thought, realigned her starched white collar and tucked wisps of gray hair into the bun neatly coiled at the back of her neck. There, that's better. She relaxed and sang along to the music drifting in from the living room. Tess was listening to the Hit Parade, her favorite Saturday night entertainment. Minnie knew Tess's ritual by heart: a bowl of popcorn and a Coke, Tess stretched out on the faded maroon sofa flipping through a jazz magazine.

Girl spends too much time by herself—and so moody. Minnie glanced at the clock on the dresser. Got to hurry or I miss the bus. She picked up her white gloves, starched apron, and small black handbag. After checking the mirror one last time, she joined Tess.

"I'm goin' now. Throw the lock after me. Don't want no drunken fool stumblin' in here after I'm gone."

Tess dropped the magazine on the floor. Rolled-up blue slacks and a thin white cotton T-shirt hung loosely on her small-boned frame. Her even features held the promise of transforming her into a statuesque, seductive beauty.

"You look spiffy. New uniform?"

"Yeah, the old man finally bought me a new dress."

Minnie looked down at her heavily starched habit and wrinkled her nose. "It's so black, it makes me look like a lady preacher."

"I think it makes you look like one of them colored maids in the movies, the ones that say yes'm and no'm."

Minnie laughed. "That what I am, and that what I do. I says yes'm and no'm, and them rich white women put a dime in my hand and wait for me to dust 'em off."

"Ugh! How can you stand it?"

"Somebody got to do it, 'n you know we needs the money."

Tess frowned. "You wouldn't have to work two jobs if I wasn't here. You doing it for me. Ain't right."

"Hush. You get me mad 'n I be stewing all night. I'm doing it for us. You 'n me. We're a team. Ain't nothin' gonna change that, specially your crabbing."

Tess hugged Minnie and apologized. "Don't mean to rile you, but I hate to see you work so hard. You're not getting younger."

Minnie patted Tess's cheek. "No need remindin' me of that." Minnie hurried out the door, then waited in the hall until she heard Tess turn the lock.

When she reached the corner, Minnie scowled at the gang of young men milling around. Shiftless niggers, she thought. Ain't gonna do nothin' but cause somebody grief tonight. She hurried on. Ain't gonna be me or Tess. One of these days I'm gonna get us outta here. Filthy slum. Ain't no place to raise a young girl. Glancing down the street, she looked for the Grand Avenue bus. It was nowhere in sight. She sighed. Hate leaving that child alone at night, but what choice I got? Don't make enough at the funeral home. Gots to keep my part-time job at the Paradise. Hate workin' for the man, too. This one's a mean one. Minnie coughed. Seem poor folk gotta put up with a lot.

Nine o'clock on the nose, Minnie thought, as she glanced at the clock over the bar at the Paradise Club. She was relieved to see that the dinner crowd was leaving, making room for the younger set that would drink and dance till one. They tip better, she thought, then pushed open the door to the ladies' lounge, decorated with elaborately scrolled baroque mirrors and dressing tables, a thick Persian-style carpet, and heavy satin drapes. Just the right background for a colored maid, she reflected, as she headed for the toilets where she checked the supply of soap and towels. She shook her head. Lordy! Ain't nobody replace the soap since I left last night, she mumbled, then busily unwrapped three bars and set the rose-scented soap on the sinks. Absorbed in her work, Minnie didn't hear the woman approach her.

"My, my! Ain't you somethin' in that new outfit! I swears, you is fancy enough to be some white woman's personal maid."

Minnie spun around, clutching her heart in fright. "What you doin', Emma, comin' up like that! You wants to scare me to death? And don't be talking to me 'bout bein' somebody's maid. I gets enough orders in a evenin' to last a month a Sundays." Minnie managed a smile for the heavy-set black woman enveloped in white—white uniform, white stockings, and sturdy, white oxford shoes.

Emma laughed as she pushed the toilet doors open and checked each stall. Minnie followed behind, prattling while she walked. "I swear, you act like they is gold-plated thrones the way you carry on. All them women gonna do is sit on 'em and go wee-wee."

"Girl! Ever since Mr. Gianino check up on my work, I be sure everything's spotless. Don't want the man on my tail."

"Stuffy old bastard."

Emma turned and put her finger over her mouth. "Hush, Minnie. You want he should hear you?"

"Heck! That man ain't gonna come in here now. I seen him at the bar when I come through the club. He talkin' to his big-shot friends. He got his boy here again, too. Poor thing. Has to sit around 'n try to act interested while his Papa shootin' off his mouth 'bout all his money."

Emma looked at the last toilet, then joined Minnie in the outer room. "The man got the money. He ain't just talkin'

343

about it. The boy be fourteen now. Guess he be teachin' him the business."

Minnie shrugged. "No concern of mine, just that I had my fill of gangsters in Chicago. Don't like workin' for 'em, but seems like they's all over the place, specially in the nightclub business."

Emma stepped closer to Minnie and peered in her eyes. "What's the matter, honey? You seem down tonight. Got troubles?"

"None a few thousand bucks wouldn't cure."

"Sure it ain't Tess?"

"Tess doing fine. Just be starting her first year of high school. Got all A's. Likes her books."

"Then what's the problem?"

"The girl stays to herself too much."

"Where you living, that be good."

"Oh, I'm thankful she ain't runnin' the streets, but she could invite a girl friend to a show once in a while."

"Honey, I got five of 'em at home, 'n believe me, all they wants is to run. Every time they steps outta the house, it cost me. You just be glad Tess can entertain herself."

"T'ain't normal her sittin' around so much. Don't think she ever got over her mama dyin'."

"That girl smart. She work it out. Them young ones always do. Well, I got to get scootin'. I's in the kitchen tonight, but if one of them fancy ladies gets sick on the cheap liquor they serve 'round here, yell. I clean it up."

Sashaying out the door, Emma almost ran into two women entering the lounge. She turned and winked at Minnie. Just one of their dresses looked as if it cost a month's pay. The gowns were long and slinky—one a vibrant blue, the other an emerald green. The women's throats were ablaze with diamonds. Minnie turned her face into a mask. Like a cigar store Indian, she held two crisp white towels in her hand and waited while the women soiled Emma's spotless toilets. Their light chatter was unbroken as they washed their hands and lifted the towels from Minnie's outstretched arm, their eyes never acknowledging her presence. When they left, they dropped a quarter in the silver bowl on the dressing table. Minnie sighed. It's gonna be a long night, for sure, she thought, then tossed the towels in a closet and draped two more over her arm.

The air was cool, the rainy streets deserted at one thirty in the morning. Minnie stood under the streetlight and opened the envelope holding her tips. Dimes and quarters jingled in her hand, and her trained eye calculated that she didn't have more than ten dollars. Slow night, she thought, then dropped the envelope back in her purse. Ten dollars was ten dollars. She started to walk back to the club for Emma when suddenly she realized someone was standing behind her. She felt someone's breath on her neck. Terrified, she spun around.

"That's the second time tonight," she said, only slightly relieved when she saw Emma at her side. "I swear, I'm gonna put a bell on you."

"What you so jumpy about? You too ugly to be raped." Emma laughed.

"I was countin' my money, little as it be. Last winter I earn twenty-five, thirty dollars on a good Saturday night."

Emma nodded her head and patted Minnie's shoulder. "Don't get yourself in a stew about it. I heard the man talkin' tonight 'n he say Billie Holiday gonna sing at the Paradise next month. Heck! The place be so packed, you 'n me'll be able to retire."

Ten minutes passed before they heard a 1936 Chevrolet sedan, its engine pinging loudly in the still night, turn the corner. Sliding to a stop in front of the two women, the door flew open and a young man, his gold tooth shining in the light of the streetlamp, smiled broadly.

"Sorry I's late, you sweet lookin' things, but I had to drop my gal off 'n one thing lead to another. You know what I mean?"

"Me and Minnie been yessin' all evening. We don't wanna hear 'bout your gal problems." Emma and Minnie piled into the backseat and slammed the door.

"Aw, you ain't late, Junior," Minnie said. "Fact is, we just walked out 'fore you pull up."

"Don't be trying to make me feel better." Junior sped east, then turned onto Grand Avenue and headed south. "I admits to being late."

"Just so's you know I appreciate you taking me home," Minnie said. "Ain't no buses runnin' this time a night, 'n taxis cost a arm 'n a leg."

In front of Minnie's apartment, she tried to press a quarter into his hand.

"Oh, no, you don't. I ain't taking no money for dropping you off. We is friends. T'ain't even outta our way." Junior refused the coin. "Give it to Tess. Maybe she can buy a record down at the Reuse Shop. Tell her it be from a secret admirer."

Minnie dropped the money back in her purse. "I do that, 'n thanks for the ride. See you Wednesday, Emma. Take care."

When Minnie entered the living room, a low buzz of static crackled from the radio, and a tavern sign across the street blinked red and blue across the ceiling. Tess was lying on the sofa still wearing her T-shirt and slacks, her loafers wedged against the coffee table where she had slipped them off.

That girl! I swear. I told her a hundred times not to sleep on that ugly ole sofa. Ruin her back for life. If you wanna sleep, you should go to bed, Minnie had scolded time and again. Serve her right if I let her sleep there all night. Turning down the covers, Minnie changed her mind before she crawled into bed. Padding back into the living room, she mumbled to herself that next time she'd do it for sure.

She bent over Tess and felt a wetness ooze through her toes. Yuck, she thought, then lifted her foot to see what was on the rug. Too gooey for soda pop, she thought, then touched it with her fingertips. It took her a moment to realize it was blood.

"Oh, my God!" Kneeling down, she turned Tess on her back. Tess's arm fell to her side; the movement caused blood to spurt from the slash in her wrist. Minnie fell back, shaking her head in disbelief. Tess! What you do? Dear Jesus, what happen to my Tess?

The red and blue neon light washed across Tess's face, making it glow grotesquely in the shadowy darkness. Minnie stared at her, too shocked to cry, too terrified to move. Finally, after what seemed like an age, Minnie stood up and walked to the telephone as though in a trance. I got to help her, she thought. My baby die if I don't get her to a hospital. Oh, Tess, don't you be dying on me. I don't wanna live if you be dying on me, you hear.

Minnie cowered in a corner of the emergency room at Homer G. Phillips Hospital, staring at the door leading to the treatment room. Tess was someplace beyond the door. Was her body stronger than her will? If so, she might live, the intern had said as she had paused briefly to get vital statistics from Minnie.

"Don't make no sense. Tess seem happy enough. Stayed to herself a lot, but she been that way all her life. Her mama die five years past. Can't believe that botherin' her bad enough to do this. She never talk about it. Figure she forget."

The intern hurried away, and for the next hour, Minnie prayed, making special supplication to Tallulah and Bobbie.

"Mrs. Washington?" The intern approached Minnie.

Minnie raised her eyes in response.

"Your girl's going to make it."

Minnie dropped her head and sobbed.

"She's still very weak. She'll have to stay a few days."

"You sure she's outta danger?"

"As sure as we can be about these things." The woman patted Minnie's shoulder, then pointed to the desk at the end of the hall. "The nurse'll tell you her room number. You can see her for a few minutes."

Tess was at the far end of a row of beds. Leaning over the metal railing, Minnie studied Tess's face. It was peaceful, much as it had been hours before when she was lying on the sofa, but now there was color in her cheeks, and her breathing was calm and regular.

Tess opened her eyes, stared at Minnie for a moment, then closed them again and turned her head. "I'm sorry, Minnie. Can you ever forgive me?"

"Ain't nothin' to forgive, girl. You was cryin' out for help, but I wasn't listenin'. Believe me, I'll be listenin' from now on."

Tears rolled down Tess's cheeks. "I knew you'd blame yourself. It wasn't your fault. It wasn't anybody's fault. Just something inside me said, 'Do it.' Can't explain what I felt 'cept I wanted peace. Didn't want to worry no more 'bout you and Mama and Tallulah. I love you all so much, but I wonder if Mama'd be dead if it wasn't for me. And for sure you wouldn't have to work at the Paradise. I know how you hate that job."

"Honey, you is the icin' on the cake. Without you, I got nobody. I love you. Don't you know that?"

"Course I know. That's what makes it so hard."

"Hard or not, you got to get better. Then you and me got to talk. You hear?"

Minnie's chastising voice elicited a smile from Tess who nodded her head weakly. "I won't try again. I promise."

Tess wore long-sleeved blouses around the apartment to hide the ugly red scars on her wrists. In the two weeks since she had come home from the hospital, she had spurned Minnie's efforts to talk.

"It was a silly thing to do, and I promise I'll call a school friend and go to a show just as soon as the scars heal."

Minnie wasn't convinced. "I knows you tryin', honey, but you still holdin' all your feelin's inside like you don't trust nobody. And I got to get back to the Paradise or I lose my job. But what do I do with you?"

"I'll be all right. Really." Tess plopped herself on the sofa and a pout formed on her mouth. "If you'd stop treating me like a baby . . ."

Minnie knew the look. Tess had shut her out. Arguing wasn't going to change anything.

Two hours later, while she was frying chicken for their supper, Minnie had the answer.

"Minnie, I love you, but you can't ask me to do that. I just won't go to work with you. Not to the Paradise. What would I do? I'd just get in the way." She shook her head vehemently. "Mr. Gianino wouldn't like it either."

"That man only care about money and working us folks to death. I tell him you my niece 'n you needs a job. He understand that. Emma's youngest work in the kitchen, 'n he only fifteen. So I lie a little 'bout your age."

"And what will I do? Wash dishes?"

"Course not, honey. You help me in the ladies' lounge."

"Oh, Minnie. I can't—"

"Ain't so bad once you gets the hang of it."

"Shufflin' 'n scrapin'. That ain't for me."

Tess bit her tongue when she saw Minnie flinch. "I'm sorry. I ain't saying you shuffle. I didn't mean—"

"No need to fret about it. I might bend, but I don't break. Long as I know the difference."

Tess looked at Minnie contritely. "I caused you enough grief. All right, I'll go with you."

Minnie smiled, feeling a little ill at ease for taking advantage of Tess's guilt.

"Ain't you somethin'! Minnie say you pretty, but she don't say how pretty."

Tess turned and looked questioningly at the broad black face grinning at her. "Emma?"

"The one 'n only." Emma hugged Tess, then tilting her head to one side, she spoke intimately in Tess's ear. "Don't you let Minnie work you too hard tonight. You knows we got a special show. Billie Holiday gonna sing. The place be packed in another hour."

"I know," Tess whispered, mimicking Emma's tone of conspiracy.

"What you don't know is I's gonna sneak you backstage so you can see Miss Holiday right up. Maybe even get her autograph."

"Oh, Emma! Can you do that?" Tess's face lit up.

Emma looked at Minnie and winked. "Thinks you can do without your helper for a half hour?"

"Seeing how it's Billie Holiday, I guess I can manage, but right now, hand me a stack of linen towels. The dinner crowd be swarming in here any minute."

"And we'll be ready for 'em." Tess said, her eyes shining for the first time in months.

For the next hour the lounge filled and emptied: between the soup and salad, before the entrée, and after the dessert. Tess was ready for each onslaught, handing out towels, cleaning ashtrays, whisking away soiled linen. Minnie smiled to herself when she saw the diminutive girl stretch to light cigarettes and bend over to retrieve lost purses and popped buttons. And Tess says I step'n fetch, Minnie thought, but wisely kept her mouth shut when she noticed how quickly the silver bowl filled with coins and, on occasion, dollar bills.

Emma returned minutes before the first show. She whisked Tess out of the lounge and, hurriedly stepping over the props, lights, and electrical wires that cluttered the area, stationed Tess close to the stage. Before Tess could thank her, Emma had disappeared.

Gliding onto the stage from the opposite wing, Miss Holiday stepped into the spotlight while Lester Young played the first eight bars of "Body and Soul." A gasp rose from the audience as the yellow orb of light softened her chestnut-brown skin and transformed her gleaming white gown into a mellow cream. Tilting her head back, a delicate brown-tinged gardenia nestled in her thick black hair, Billie began the bluesy torch song. Starting low, at the bottom of the scale, she mimicked Young's growly saxophone, then, moving up, her voice ringing like a bell, she belted out the final line.

By the time Billie finished singing "My First Impression of You," "Mean to Me," and "I Can't Get Started," Tess was intoxicated. "She's better than Mama was," Tess mumbled aloud.

Tess waited until Miss Holiday ran offstage before she turned to leave. Everyone else had disappeared; everyone except a tall, lanky youth, who stood behind her, blocking her path. His face looked familiar, but she dropped her eyes as she slipped past him on her way back to the lounge. He called to her to stop.

Afraid that she had done something wrong, Tess hesitated. He smiled.

"Sorry, didn't mean to scare you. It's just . . . well, I was watching you during the show, and I swear, I've seen you someplace before."

Tess returned his smile. "I think the same thing." She cocked her head to one side. "Where you go to school?"

"A Catholic boys' school."

"Well, I ain't Catholic."

"Maybe here—at the club?"

The mystery unsolved, Tess finally excused herself. "I've got to get back to work."

"Work! You work here?"

"Just for tonight. I help Minnie Washington. She's my auntie, sorta. Anyway, it's a long story, but I got to run. The lounge be packed by now."

Tess couldn't hear his parting remark over the band, which was now playing dance music. The lounge was filled with women, and for an hour Minnie and Tess hustled to supply the guests with clean linen and lighted cigarettes. Less than thirty minutes before the second show, the lounge finally emptied, and Minnie eagerly counted the change in the silver bowl. When she hit fifty dollars, she stopped, dropped the money in a brown envelope, and hugged Tess.

"Couple nights like this 'n we'll be rich." Minnie shook the money beside Tess's ear.

Tess laughed. She listened to herself, enjoying the sound of her happiness, then she laughed louder and clapped her hands when Minnie promised her a new radio. "You earn it, girl. I never seen nobody work hard as you. And we got more comin' after the second show."

Expansively, Minnie gave Tess permission to watch Billie again, cautioning her not to let Mr. Gianino see her. Tess ran off. Within minutes, Tess was caught up in the star's artistry, and she didn't notice the fingers tapping her shoulder. Finally someone tugged at her sleeve. When she spun around, she was face to face with the friendly young man. He motioned for her to follow him. When they stepped inside a musty-smelling storage room, he sighed and closed the door.

"I thought you might not come back." He motioned for her to sit, pointing to a beer case.

Leaning against a broken table, the boy pulled out two Cokes and handed one to Tess. He proposed a toast. "Roses are red, violets are blue, I need a friend, that's why I'm glad I met you."

"What you need a friend for? Seems like you can talk to anybody. Not like me. I get tongue-tied talking to the neighbor's dog."

"You're talking to me."

Tess took a sip of the soda. "Yeah. Guess I am."

"My name's Johnny."

"Glad to meet ya, Johnny." She giggled. "I'm Tess."

"How long you gonna work here?"

"Don't know. Maybe all summer. I'd like to. Bet it'd be fun." Tess dropped her head to one side and eyed Johnny curiously. "What you do here? You ain't a busboy. I can tell by your clothes 'n the way you talk."

Johnny nodded. "No. I'm not a busboy. My papa owns the club. He drags me here whenever he can to teach me the business. Sometimes I get so tired and bored I want to hide. Fact is, that's how I found this place. I come in here to be alone or take a snooze."

Tess's eyes grew large and she whistled softly. "You're Johnny Gianino?"

"Sure. You think that's something special?"

"Yeah, around here it is."

"Naw"—Johnny shook his head for emphasis—"not unless special means getting yelled at more'n anybody else. Papa never stops yelling at me."

"I'm sorry."

Johnny stirred uneasily, looking embarrassed. "Hey"—he jumped up—"you know how to play checkers?"

"Sure."

"Wanna play a game?"

352

"Now?"

"Sure."

Tess thought for a moment, then shrugged her shoulders. "Just one game, then I got to get back to the lounge."

Johnny rummaged through what seemed to be a cache of treasures and triumphantly pulled out a worn board and a bag of red and black checkers. "You do know how to play, don't you?"

Tess nodded, remembering the hours Tallulah and she had spent over the checkerboard.

Tess's hands perspired, and her eye twitched when Johnny advanced across the board, capturing her red checkers as if they were carcasses being carried away by a hungry vulture. Surreptitiously, Tess studied Johnny's expression. My God! He gonna win or else, she thought, then wondered why winning was so awfully important. Even though she told herself it was only a game, Tess felt the pressure mount.

It was too late to salvage the first game. Johnny won the second one, too. Tess straightened up. I'll show him, she told herself, then proceeded to beat him twice. Now Johnny straightened up.

"You're good." Johnny tried to sound convincing, and set up the board again. "Let's play one more. The one who wins'll be the grand champion."

Tess shook her head. "I got to get back. Minnie'll be furious. I stayed too long."

"Please, just one more."

"Okay. One more. I'll get it for being an hour late same as if I was a half hour late." She enjoyed being with Johnny; she just wished they could play for fun instead of this cutthroat competition.

Johnny moved his black piece. Tess's hand had just touched the board when, like a violent burst of wind, the door flew open and Michele Gianino stormed in.

"What the hell you doing in here? I got everybody in the club looking for you." Two beefy-looking bodyguards stepped up behind Michele, anticipating trouble.

Johnny stood up, flushed with embarrassment. "Papa!"

Tess darted out the door, Michele's angry voice trailing after her. She stumbled blindly back to the lounge where she fell into Minnie's arms, crying hysterically.

"Girl! Where you been? We was lookin' all over for you. I thought . . ."

Tess's sobs heightened Minnie's anxiety as she waited for Tess to speak clearly enough to be understood.

"Don't know what's going on. You talking about checkers 'n that man screaming about somebody kidnapping his boy 'n I scared to death you try to hurt yourself again. Lordy! What a night."

"You know what that man said to me? He said I took Johnny in the store room to—to—oh, he was horrible. And I didn't. I swear, I didn't—"

"Course not. The old man knows you didn't, too. That's his way. He blames you, then he blames Johnny for whatever he imagine 'n he don't care one way or another. Dry your eyes. You tell me what happen when we get home. Emma's boy'll come by in a few minutes. You don't have to come back here no more. I'm sorry. I thought . . ." Minnie shook her head. Her face was sad and protectively she put her arm around Tess.

Walking through the club, they kept their heads down, but as they passed the bar, Gianino stepped in front of them. Tess's knuckles were clenched white. She refused to look at the man's face, afraid she would start crying again. From the corner of her eye she saw Johnny standing at the bar, terrified and cringing. Had he been crying, too?

"My boy tells me you was playing checkers."

Unable to speak, Tess nodded.

"And you beat him two games?"

Tess nodded again.

"Don't know how that can be 'less you cheated."

Tess started, and a look of hatred flashed across her eyes. "Don't know how to cheat at checkers. Johnny knows I didn't cheat."

"So you say. I don't believe it," Michele sneered. His eyes, small and grainy like two yellow sand pebbles, darted from Tess to Minnie and back again. He stepped closer; his body smelled of tobacco and whiskey; his breath reeked of olive oil and onions.

Standing tall, Minnie tightened her hold on Tess. "Tess wouldn't do nothing like that. The girl don't cheat."

Michele looked at her contemptuously. "Then you agree to a rematch?"

"A what?"

"A rematch. I want your girl to play Johnny again, only this time out front where we can all watch."

"No, sir." Minnie shook her head vehemently. "I ain't putting Tess through nothing like that."

"Then you admit she ain't up to the competition."

"Don't admit nothing. Just say I ain't gonna put her under the strain."

Michele's face hardened. "In that case, neither one of you come back. I already made a few bets here at the bar. If your girl don't play, I forfeit two hundred bucks, and you forfeit your job."

Minnie gasped. "Ain't right you doing somethin' like that." She pulled Tess alongside her and pushed past Michele. "Guess you just gonna have to get yourself another attendant."

Tess pulled her back. "No, Minnie. Let me do it, please. I'm not afraid. If Johnny can play, I will, too."

Minnie looked past Michele, her gaze falling on the forlorn boy who looked as if the devil himself was about to devour him. Her rancor melted into pity.

"Seems there ain't no end a trouble," she said resignedly.

"Bring the girl back next week. Wednesday. Seven o'clock," Michele ordered. "I'll have everything set up."

Minnie bought Tess a new dress, a new pair of shoes, and manicured her fingernails. "If that man gonna make a spectacle of you, I wants you to look good, just as good as you can. You sure you know all them moves? I want you to beat the stuffings outta that boy. Not that I got anything against Johnny. Just wants you to show the man he can't ride us whenever the urge hit him."

Tess sighed. "Don't you think it'll be worse for Johnny if

he loses than it'll be for me? He's got to live with Mr. Gianino."

"Child, he been living with that man all these years. A checker game one way or another ain't gonna make no difference. You just see to it that you play the best you can."

Tess was calm until she stepped inside the club, then, when she saw Johnny sitting at a card table covered with a checker set, she panicked. He looked like a papier-mâché ghost, his tissue-thin skin drawn across his face like a mask, his eyes flickering with fear. My God! This is worse'n I ever suspect, she thought, as she sidled through the club to the bar, keeping Minnie close beside her. Maybe his papa beat him cause he played checkers with me. Maybe he'll kill him if he loses. Tess stopped beside Johnny and was about to tell Gianino she wouldn't play when the man pointed to a chair and bellowed, "'Bout time you got here. We been waiting half an hour. You and Johnny gonna play five games. First one wins three games'll be the champ."

"I want you to know I don't approve of this whole thing," Minnie said firmly.

"My friends here think it's gonna be real burlesque, but hell, they bet on anything." Gianino pointed to the row of men leaning against the bar, each one wearing a dark suit, white shirt, and two-toned oxfords. They kept their heads bent over their highballs, not even looking up when Gianino spoke.

Just like their women, Tess thought, who come into the lounge and don't even see Minnie or me. Ain't one of 'em ever looked at us. Guess that's why Minnie want me to win so bad, so they look at us. Reluctantly, Tess sat down.

A slight smile softened the hard lines around Johnny's mouth. "I'm sorry, Tess," he said quietly. "He never did anything like this before."

"Let's go!" Gianino ordered. Johnny's hand trembled as he touched the board. He can't be afraid of me, Tess thought, then realized it was his father he feared. Poor Johnny! I hope you win, Tess thought compassionately until she saw Minnie's stern eyes watching her. Please be better than me, she thought, as Johnny moved his piece up one square. I can't let you win. I got to try for Minnie.

Tess moved. Johnny moved. They jockeyed their pieces, but Tess was more aggressive. Elatedly she captured a black piece, only to have her red snatched up by Johnny. The unexpectedness of his move surprised her, and she assumed a more defensive stance. But it was too late. Johnny had the lead and quickly won the first game. And the second. Just like last week, Tess thought. I got to stop him. I can't let him win three in a row. Mr. Gianino'd really think I'm stupid, and Minnie'd be so embarrassed.

Johnny asked for a drink of water. The bartender stepped from behind the bar and placed two Cokes on the table. As she looked up, a thank-you crept out of Tess's mouth. For the first time since she'd sat down, she was aware of the audience they had attracted—Gianino's friends, the cook, the bartender, busboys and waitresses, even Emma, her gold tooth shining when she smiled encouragingly.

Johnny and Tess began the third game like two predators. They hadn't moved four pieces before Tess realized she had the game if she wanted it. Johnny was playing sloppily, moving into her territory without protection. I don't want you to give it to me, she wanted to scream. Fight. Please fight. It don't matter if I lose. Minnie'll understand. Tess looked at Johnny's face trying to decipher the indifference there. If I beat you, I want it to be because you try.

Tess won the third game and the fourth. They were even—two, two. Gianino growled and ordered a break. Puffing heavily on a cigar, the air wheezing from his chest, Gianino motioned for Johnny to join him at the bar. Tess noticed Johnny shiver. Minnie pulled a chair beside Tess, whispering encouragement, but Tess only thought of Johnny and his father.

Muffled threats and innuendos finally led to Gianino's grabbing Johnny by his shoulders and shaking him. Gianino's face was red with fury. "Trouble with you is you're a sucker for that nigger gal who spread her legs for you!"

Johnny lashed out at last. "That's a lie!"

The loud crack of Gianino's hand on Johnny's face stopped all conversation. Johnny reeled, dumbfounded. When he straightened up, he turned his face to the wall.

Tess turned to Minnie, choking back the tears. "I got to forfeit the game. Ain't nothing worth this. Poor Johnny."

"If'n you do, you make that boy feel worse than ever. A man can't stand being pitied. Don't matter if he's young or old."

"But his father'll beat him."

"Better that than lose his pride."

Tess shook her head, unconvinced. She excused herself and ran to the lounge. We got to hurry, she thought, glancing at the clock. The club is opening in half an hour. Oh, dear Jesus, how we gonna act like nothing happen here tonight? Every time I look at the waiters, the waitresses, Emma, Johnny, I'll think about this awful thing. That man is the meanest man alive. Wonder why he got so much hate.

Recovered, Tess returned to the bar, took her seat across from Johnny, smiled, and started the last game.

He's playing again, Tess realized after the first moves. He wants to win. Can't blame him. But I got to try, too.

As Tess made moves, Johnny mirrored them. Looking at him under hooded eyes, Tess tried to imagine his fears, his thoughts, his hopes. She heard the men's heavy breathing, smelled Minnie's dusty rose bath powder, felt the pinch of her new shoes. She listened to her own heart beating furiously, but Johnny seemed beyond caring as he moved a checker, paused, then dropped his hand in his lap and waited for her move.

Excitedly, Tess spied a move that would earn her several of Johnny's pieces. Her hand reached forward, catching him off guard. Jumping first one piece and then a second, she found an opening all the way to his first row where her checker was made a king. Johnny tensed, then responded by capturing one of her pieces. His next move gave him a king and they were even. In pursuing a double ambush, Johnny overlooked a threat on his right. Tess rushed to take advantage and Johnny lost his king, but the game wasn't over. No sooner had she captured two more of his pieces than Johnny retaliated, taking two of hers. Suddenly, all of Tess's pieces seemed threatened. Johnny moved rapidly, not allowing her time to think. Tess lost her king and seemed at his mercy. Panicking, she studied the board, looking for a way out. Several minutes later, she found it. The next five moves rewarded Tess with two more kings, and abruptly it was all over. Johnny dropped his head in defeat. Tess had won.

Gianino bellowed angrily, crediting her victory to pure luck, then stomped away, not even glancing in Johnny's direction. Minnie let out a muffled cry and she and Emma happily hugged Tess.

Regaining his composure, Johnny offered his hand, thanked her for the game, then headed to the back of the club. To the storage room, Tess thought, to lick his wounds. Her mind clouded with remorse over her victory. Should've let him win. How's he gonna face his papa now? Oh Lord, I wish this never would've happened.

At ten o'clock, Tess took advantage of the first lull of the evening and went looking for Johnny. She found him in his favorite haunt, staring blankly at the naked lightbulb.

"You been here all night?" she asked hesitantly, gingerly touching his hand.

"Yep."

"It's so dark and dirty in here. Can't you find someplace else?"

"Nope. I like it here." Johnny's jaw was rigid.

Tess withdrew her hand. "I'm sorry—"

"Don't be. You won fair and square. Anyway, it was just a silly game."

Tess nodded, trying to think of something to say, but the easy camaraderie that had blossomed before had faded. Tess shrugged her shoulders. "I'm sorry," she said again. "It was my fault—"

Johnny was on his feet, pointing his finger at her angrily. "Your fault! Are you crazy? It was Papa's fault. He made fools of both of us, and you're apologizing. I feel like I should apologize, but it wasn't my fault either. Papa's mean and hateful. He treats everybody terrible, even Mama, and

he treats cousin Rosanna like dirt. But this is the worst."
The words choked in Johnny's throat. "I don't understand
him."

Tess reeled under Johnny's outburst. She dropped her
eyes and headed for the door. "I better go. Don't wanna get
you in more trouble. If your papa finds me here—"

"To hell with him. I don't care what he thinks anymore.
Do you?"

"Got to admit I'm scared of your papa. He embarrass
you, but he can really hurt me and Minnie. Maybe fire us.
He seems like a man who don't forget easy."

"He'll carry grudges to his grave," Johnny conceded.
Suddenly, his gloominess evaporated, and he held out his
hand to Tess. "Come on. Climb over the junk. I fixed a spot
right in the middle where we can hide 'n pretend we're in
some deep, dark forest."

Tess shook her head skeptically. "How can we hide from
your papa? If he wants, he'll find us. Lord knows what he'll
make us do next time he gets mad."

Johnny's bottom lip sagged. "You're the only friend I got.
If he scares you off, I'll just sit here by myself till I turn into
a skeleton, then you can hang me on a hook and let my
bones rattle and scare kids on Halloween."

"That'd be awful." Tess half laughed and half cried.

"Then you'll keep me company."

"Don't want you turnin' into a skeleton, but I can't stay
all night. Got to help Minnie, otherwise ain't no reason for
me to be here."

"I'll save a soda for you. Every night you're here. You can
take your break right in the middle of our jungle. You like
Coke or root beer?"

Johnny's brown eyes sparkled for the first time that night
and Tess's heart melted.

Minnie called it puppy love. Tess swore she'd love him
forever. "You're colored," Minnie scolded. "You find some
colored friends at school. Forget the Gianino boy. You're
lookin' at nothing but trouble if you get mixed up with that
family."

Tess ignored Minnie, convinced she was too old to know anything about love. She and Johnny had sworn to die for love if they had to.

Minnie decided to bide her time. There were only seven weekends before Johnny would leave for Mt. Clemens, the Catholic boarding school he attended in central Wisconsin.

"Ain't nothin' like a northern winter to put a chill on a summer romance," Minnie told Emma.

Their last Saturday night together, Johnny met Tess at the club's back door, and they walked silently along Grand Avenue, sidestepping the theater crowd, ignoring bar-hopping soldiers, looking indifferently at the satin dolls, the playgirls, the night people who flooded the avenue. Crossing Lindell Boulevard, they headed toward the College Church. With the majestic steps as their sanctuary, they exchanged gifts—a bracelet for Tess, a small, framed portrait for Johnny, who gently ran his finger across Tess's picture, then stuck it in his shirt pocket.

"Guess we're goin' steady, huh?" Johnny clasped her hand in his.

"I guess so." Tess looked away, trying to hold back the tears she knew would come. It was the first time she had ever wanted time to stand still. I've got no future without Johnny, she thought, then turned her face to his. They kissed.

"Will you write?" Johnny pulled Tess close and leaned his cheek on her head.

"Every day if you want."

"Doesn't have to be every day. What would you say if you wrote that often?"

"Just that I love you," Tess murmured, "and I'm missing you real bad."

"I'll be home for Thanksgiving and Christmas. That doesn't seem so long."

"Doesn't matter if it's a day, a year, a hundred years, I'll wait."

They fell silent again, content in each other's arms. Only when the church bells rang did they stir and reluctantly return to the club.

Gianino yelled at Johnny the minute they stepped inside the door. Tess hurried away before Gianino saw her. The last voice she heard was Johnny's as he made up an excuse as to where he'd been.

CHAPTER *XXVIII*

In September, 1944, Tess began her freshman year at Sumner High School, a solid, dark red brick building with long, meandering hallways faced with metal lockers. Segregated, in the heart of the Negro community, it encouraged typing and bookkeeping, home economics and shop. Meanwhile, at Mt. Clemens, Johnny pursued the classics, history and literature, military scholarship and religion. But through it all, Tess and Johnny maintained their relationship for almost four lonely years of letter writing, clandestine meetings over holidays, and summers shared at the Paradise Club, where Johnny, more and more, took over his father's responsibilities and Tess replaced Minnie completely.

On June 12, 1948, Tess was graduated from Sumner. After the ceremony, Minnie treated her to dinner in a fancy restaurant and presented her with a gold Elgin wristwatch.

"Lord knows what would have happened to me if you hadn't taken me in," Tess said, her eyes glistening with affection.

Minnie pooh-poohed Tess's gratitude. "You was always like my own. Since I was never blessed, you filled my life with so much love, well, I figure I oughts to thank you."

"Thanks to both of us then." Tess held up her ice tea glass, spoofing a toast.

"Best thing is—I sure am pleased you ain't interested in show business."

"Only the money angle, and since old man Gianino

retired, I'm now bookkeeper at the Paradise. Just found out last night."

"Girl! How'd you manage that?" Minnie's face beamed with pride.

"Remember Ted, the bartender? He was handling the receipts, but he didn't know a debit from a credit. I helped him one night. Ever since then I been doing the books, except now I'll be getting paid for it."

"Ain't that somethin'! And me keeping the books at the funeral parlor!" Minnie leaned over the table. "Course you got to remember, that money ain't yours. Can't dip into it whenever you like."

"I wouldn't take a dime of Mr. Gianino's money that I didn't earn. Liable to get myself killed if I did."

Minnie shook her head. "That ain't the only reason that man kill a person."

"If you're talking about Johnny and me, don't worry. We've been very careful. Business as usual. Anyway, since Mr. Gianino's been sick, working at the Paradise has been just that—paradise. It's a different place. He lets Johnny alone, too."

"That man's still keeping his eye on things. His kind never let go till they die."

"He didn't go to Johnny's commencement," Tess said to prove her point. "And he let his wife and Johnny's cousin Rosanna go without him. Johnny said it was the first time he could remember them going anyplace without the old man."

Minnie shook her head. "All the same, you be careful with that family."

Four hundred and fifty miles away Anna and Rosanna watched proudly as Johnny gave the valedictory address to the departing seniors at Mt. Clemens.

Rosanna had bought a new dress and softened her normally severe hairdo, adorning the bun at the back of her head with a silk rose. She looked younger than her forty-one years, especially today as she watched Johnny graduate. She grasped Anna's hand when the monsignor read Johnny's name. The two women, bound to each other irrevocably, responded as one.

"That boy of yours is really something," Rosanna said as they walked toward the podium. "Handsome, smart, considerate."

"And he knows his prayers, too," Anna added. "Father Murphy says Johnny was the best altar boy he ever had."

Rosanna nodded. "I know you wanted him to be a priest, but it just wasn't in him. Can't force something like that."

Anna sighed. "It wasn't so much I wanted him to be a priest, just didn't want him to be like his father. I know what Michele is. I know how he makes his money. Couldn't stand it if Johnny took after him." Nervously, Anna adjusted the black straw hat on her head. The matching black wool suit and sturdy black shoes looked more like a uniform on the squat, aging woman than a fashionable ensemble.

"Johnny'll take over the Paradise, but that's all," Rosanna said with authority. "I ought to know. I handle the accounts for almost all of Michele's businesses. Lou Grazzi's running the numbers, Sonny Williams the dry cleaning—"

Anna held up her hand and shook her head. "Please, not today. I don't want to talk about Michele's business dealings. I want to forget, if only for a little while."

Monsignor David approached Anna, a smile emblazoned on his face. "Ah, my dear Mrs. Gianino. I'm so happy to be able to share this day with you. We've enjoyed having Johnny with us. Everyone will miss him." The priest paused, raised his head, and scanned the faces of the people close by. "And where is Mr. Gianino? I want to thank the good man for his most generous donation. Dedicated Catholics like him keep Mt. Clemens open."

Anna acknowledged the Monsignor's gratitude with a smile, allowing Michele to reap the accolades for her generosity. It was she who had haggled with her miserly husband until he reluctantly agreed to send the money.

An hour later the two women met Johnny at his dormitory, shared his good-byes with his roommates, and were off to the train station to catch the 4:02 home to St. Louis.

Pressed against the plush maroon train seat, Rosanna

remembered the day Johnny was taken from her, her mental breakdown and slow recovery. Her heart, at first filled with hate, then with a cold indifference, finally filled with love for the child she could never claim as her own. But Anna was a good mother, Rosanna thought, and our lives turned out better than I had a right to expect.

Still, Michele can still hurt Johnny, and he would if Johnny crossed him. I just pray that Johnny doesn't do anything that'll rouse him. The man can't live forever, but then, she thought ruefully, the mean ones never seem to die.

Rosanna looked across the aisle at her sleeping son. So much like his father—same small mouth, small nose, curly hair. He has my skin coloring, for better or worse, otherwise Michele couldn't have managed the switch. Michele never really loved Johnny, he was too selfish for that, but he did give him a home, a good education, and a future at the Paradise—one of Michele's few enterprises that wasn't tainted with his illegal activities. As her uncle's head accountant, Rosanna knew whom Michele paid off at city hall, the names of the men in his organization, all the details of his operation. Aware that the FBI would be most cooperative if she ever decided to talk, Rosanna was also aware that she could never betray Michele. Even from a prison cell, the man would find a way to avenge himself and she or Johnny or both would pay the price. Fear of reprisal had kept Rosanna bound to Michele for eighteen years, and it didn't seem as if anything would ever change.

"Can't understand why you want to go to work so soon after graduating," Michele said from the security of a couch that pulsated with telephones, recording machines, and radios. Behind the technological clutter stood a small table holding a respirator, medicines, and tissues, and behind it all stood an oxygen tank. This was Michele's world, as circumscribed as any prison cell.

Johnny jingled his change in his pockets. "I wanna get started. What difference does it make if it's now or next week?"

"No difference, 'cept you seem too eager. You trying to

push me out? I'm sick, but I ain't dead. Just you remember that."

"I'm not trying to push you out, Papa. I got lots to learn."

"Yeah, sure." Michele rested his head on his pillow, the strands of oily hair plastered back. Except for the small, grainy eyes floating in pools of yellowy mucus, everything about him seemed gray—his hair, his skin, his teeth, his fingernails. His body was shriveling, but Michele's mind was still cunning and suspicious. "I'm sending Lou Grazzi to the club for a while to help you."

To help, hell, Johnny thought. You're sending him there to keep an eye on me.

"You got good help at the Paradise. I trained them people myself. Only problem, Ben's doing the books. He don't know shit about books. Hire a bookkeeper. Somebody you can trust. But good, too. Your Aunt Rosanna's got to have the receipts and the cash every day. Two bookkeepers. Double checks. Keep everybody honest."

"Yeah. I'll check around. Maybe Ben knows somebody good with figures."

As Johnny headed toward the door, Michele stuck out his finger menacingly. "You remember I got my boys watching you. Don't step outta line."

"No, Papa. I won't forget."

"My God, I didn't think I'd ever touch you again or kiss you or feel you so close." Tess wrapped her arms around Johnny's neck and squealed with delight. Johnny swung her around the room. Laughing, they fell on top of the soft, calf-leather sofa in Michele's office at the Paradise. It was Johnny's now. They made love on Michele's sofa. Afterward, sipping champagne from a single, long-stemmed crystal goblet, they giggled, imagining what Michele would say if he knew.

"He'd have my scalp nailed to the door," Johnny said.

"And my skin nailed next to it." Tess poured another glass of champagne and lay back on the sofa, trying to balance the glass on her chest.

"When we're married Papa won't be able to do anything about it. We'll just present him with the fait accompli."

"The what?"

"The fait . . . oh, never mind."

Abruptly a look of sadness crossed Tess's face. "Don't talk about getting married. You know it'll never happen."

Johnny took the glass of champagne and finished it in one gulp. "Why can't I talk about us getting married?"

"Because I'm a Negro, and you're white. Because your papa hates Negroes, he hates me, and he'd kill us both if he had any idea we were even seeing each other."

Johnny shrugged. "I'm not going to let him ruin my life anymore. We'll run away. That's what we should do—just run away. He behaves even worse now that he's sick."

Tess sat up. "Michele's only part of our problem, darling. I don't know of one state that allows Negroes and whites to get married."

Johnny stared at Tess in disbelief. "There's got to be one."

"Well, it sure isn't Missouri."

"We don't have to stay in Missouri."

Tess stood up and wrapped her arms around Johnny's waist, leaning her head on his shoulder. "I don't know, Johnny. It's all so hard to figure out. I don't know what's right anymore. All I know is I love you, and if we can be together here at the club, that's good enough for me—for now."

Johnny took Tess's face in his hands and kissed her. "Don't give up so soon."

Tess snuggled closer, pressing her breasts against his chest. Her body ached for him, for his strength and love. She thought he could make evil disappear, the sick well, the infirm walk. Surely he would find a way to handle Michele and the world.

It's like a perpetual honeymoon, Tess thought as she closed the ledger on Johnny's desk, then walked to the washroom where she splashed cool water on her face. Soon they would have the place to themselves before the cleaning crew arrived at dawn. They would spread blankets and pillows on the floor, munch on potato chips and salami, drink champagne and Coke, then fall on each other, making love until light.

"Hello, love." Johnny stripped and fell beside Tess who was lying on the floor, waiting.

"Hi." Tess smiled and rolled on her side. "Did you make lots of money tonight?"

"Yeah, lots. Ever since we changed the floor show. That damn Lou Grazzi finally admitted that my idea was good. Getting some swinging black combos in here makes more sense than hiring big bands or solo blues singers. They had their day. Most of our clientele is ex-GI's. They don't want to be reminded of USO clubs or lonely barracks where they listened to blues records and Glenn Miller. Life's up for them—just like it's up for us. To hell with the past. We're jiving now."

"What does Michele say?"

"You're obsessed with the man. I told you he's letting me run the Paradise. As long as we're making money, he doesn't give a damn if I book a monkey show."

"What about Lou? Doesn't he tell your papa everything that happens? There are spies all over the place."

"Yeah, hanging from the chandeliers, hiding under tables—"

"Make fun of me," Tess said, pouting, "but we're going to be in hot water if anybody tells Michele about us."

"And who'd have the nerve? Lou? He's so scared of Papa, he'd pee in his pants before he'd tell him we're lovers. Everybody else is just happy things are running smoothly."

Tess sighed. "Guess that's what scares me. When things are going too good, I look for trouble. It's usually just around the corner."

"Then don't turn the corner." Johnny kissed her.

Tess watched as Johnny's eyes caressed her, but when he touched her, she tensed. Tess reached up and turned on the radio. Lena Horne was singing "Stormy Weather." It took a long time for sleep to come.

* * *

Tess and Johnny exchanged Christmas presents early, having decided to give each other rings. Tess gasped when Johnny slipped hers on her finger. It was more than a symbol of their love; it was a work of art. Small diamonds were intricately entwined around a large pear-shaped one that sparkled brilliantly. "Forever, Johnny" was inscribed on the gold mounting. Ecstatic, Tess kissed Johnny, swearing to wear it forever.

Minnie tried to look happy when Tess showed her the beautiful ring. "Looks like an engagement ring to me."

Tess smiled. "It is and it isn't. I mean, I guess we're engaged, but I don't need a ring to prove it."

"You sure lookin' for trouble, girl, getting yourself mixed up with that boy. You know his papa."

"Please, Minnie, not today. I know you love me and worry about me, but I made my choice. I love him so much."

Minnie shook her head. "You can pay an awful price for that kind of love. I remember your mama loving a man who wasn't right for her. Just downright no good. Used her, spent her money, then ran off with somebody else. Liked to broke your mama's heart."

"This isn't like that at all. Johnny loves me."

"Yeah, but his papa don't."

"Oh, Minnie, please, try to understand. I can't leave Johnny. He just means too much to me. But I love you, too, and I don't want to make you unhappy."

"There, child, don't get yourself in a stew. You doing what you gots to do. The Lord knows what's right, and if he thinks you and Johnny gonna make it, then I'm happy for you, too."

"I knew you'd understand." Tess tried to smile as tears ran down her cheeks. "You just had to. I couldn't leave thinking you were mad."

Minnie stared at Tess, thunderstruck. "What you mean *leave?* Where you goin'?"

"Johnny and I . . . well, we're going to get married."

"Lordy, girl. You sure straining my emotions today." Minnie frowned. "How you gonna get married? It's against

369

the law in this state for colored and white to live together much less get married."

"Johnny's looking into it. Maybe New York or California. As far away as we can get."

"And you think Mr. Gianino gonna let you be? That man'll haunt you till you dead if you take his son. He ain't gonna sit quietly by while Johnny marry a Negro. He'll do somethin', and I know it'll be terrible."

"That's why we're running away." Tess paused and picked nervously at a hangnail. "No, we're not running away. That sounds like we're kids, and we're not. We're just leaving. We got a right to do that, don't we? Especially, especially since . . ."

"Since what, girl? You ain't . . ."

Tess nodded her head. "Just found out a week ago."

"Oh, Lord!"

Tess jerked up her head and spoke rapidly. "I told Johnny he didn't have to marry me. He was furious. He said of course he didn't *have to*. He wanted to. Now more than ever."

Minnie's body sagged and she slumped in her chair. Slowly she raised a half-filled coffee cup to her lips. "You're right when you say you got to leave. You carryin' that man's grandchild! Ain't no tellin' what he'll do."

"Most men his age would be thrilled to become a grandfather."

"Mr. Gianino ain't most men."

After dessert and coffee Johnny helped his mother and Rosanna clean off the table and carry the dishes to the kitchen. When Anna went into the dining room to scoop up more dishes, Johnny leaned close to Rosanna and whispered in her ear.

"I have to talk to you. Alone. Tonight."

Rosanna frowned, nodded, and, when Anna returned to the kitchen, said, "Johnny offered to help me with my presents. The footstool is too heavy for me to carry."

Anna nodded. "Watch your back. I pulled mine out when I was your age, and it hasn't been right since."

In Rosanna's living room, Johnny sipped a glass of cold beer and stammered, trying to find the right words, "I'm leaving."

Rosanna jerked her head up and pointed to the sofa. "Sit down. I can't talk with you pacing back and forth like a wildcat."

"I'm too jumpy. I feel like I'm committing the crime of the century when all I want to do is leave home."

"That doesn't sound unreasonable to me." Rosanna spoke softly. "Do you want to rent an apartment? Something closer to the club? Certainly Michele will understand that."

Johnny spoke with meticulous care. "I'm getting married, and I'm leaving town. Papa won't approve of my wife to be. I don't want him to know."

Rosanna raised her eyebrows in surprise. "So you're in love. It happens. Don't be ashamed. It's just that you're so young. Can't you wait, at least until you're twenty-one?"

"We have to get married—now."

"I see." Rosanna tapped her fingers on the arm of the sofa. "She's pregnant."

Johnny nodded.

Rosanna stretched out her hand to him, a smile crossing her face. "You don't have to run away. Michele'll storm for a few weeks, but he'll get over it. After all, a grandchild . . ."

With tears rising in his eyes, Johnny grasped Rosanna's hand and whispered, "You still don't understand. Tess is a Negro."

Rosanna reeled under the force of his words. "Oh, Johnny! No! He'll kill you, and her, too. You'll never be able to run far enough—"

"Shit! I'd like to see him try."

"He will."

"Not if he can't find us."

"But where will you go?"

"West. California. We'll use her name."

"And what is her name?"

"Tess. Tess Evans."

Rosanna was on her feet. "Evans? Evans? It can't be the

same . . ." She studied Johnny, her face pinched in pain. "What's her mother's name?" she asked, choking out the words.

"Minnie. Minnie Washington."

Rosanna's shoulders dropped in relief. "Oh, I thought I knew the name Evans. There was a singer—"

Johnny nodded his head. "Yes, Bobbie Evans. She was Tess's real mother, but she died. You knew her?"

"You can't marry her!"

"Oh, not you, too. You're not like Papa. Just because she's a Negro—"

"Oh, God!" Rosanna collapsed on the sofa and sobbed.

Johnny stepped back, flabbergasted. "I'm sorry I got you so upset. I didn't know . . . Tess and I need help, but maybe I can borrow—"

"No!" Rosanna wiped her eyes with the back of her hand. Her bottom lip quivered as she spoke. "I'll help. Whatever you want."

Johnny knelt in front of Rosanna and kissed her hands. "Thanks. Thanks a lot." His face softened, and he looked at her lovingly. "I don't want to get you into trouble with Papa, but we need money. Just till we're settled and I have a job. I'll pay you back."

"That's not necessary. Everything I have is yours."

"I don't want everything. Five hundred'll do."

Rosanna kissed Johnny's cheek. "I'm sorry I shouted. It's just that fate . . . can play gruesome pranks sometimes."

Johnny looked at her questioningly. "You mean Tess and me?"

"Yes." She turned away, unable to look into his eyes and see his father. "If Tess wasn't pregnant, I'd beg you not to get married, but now, well, there's nothing to be done."

"I wouldn't ask you if we weren't desperate."

Rosanna sighed. "I know what it is to be desperate."

"And unhappy. I know you've had a terrible life living next door to us, to Papa. And working for him, too. I don't know why you did it, but I want you to know, I'm glad. It was always easier to talk to you than Mama. I knew no matter what I did, you'd understand."

Rosanna said nothing. He could never know. "Tell me about Tess and about your plans. I want to know everything."

For two hours Johnny reminisced. Rosanna was struck by Johnny and Tess's chance meeting, amazed at the incredible odds of their finding each other. But, most important, she approved of their plans. They would go to San Francisco, use Tess's last name; Johnny could work as a waiter. "If nothing else, I know the restaurant business," he said with assurance. "I figure I'm one of those people who love one person, and that's it. Know what I mean? Just one person means everything."

Rosanna patted his cheek. "Yes, Johnny. I know exactly what you mean."

Michele raged for months after Johnny left. He hired a series of detectives to hunt him down. He personally questioned everyone at the Paradise Club, but the terror he roused in them assured their silence.

Rosanna enjoyed watching Michele thrash impotently, but was frightened by the sorrow in Anna's eyes. Rosanna knew the pain of losing a son.

Eventually Michele's anger ebbed, but he silently vowed he would find a way to even the score.

CHAPTER XXIX

San Francisco was marvelous in July. Accustomed to St. Louis's hot, sultry summers, they relished the invigorating breeze that blew off the bay, making life more bearable for Tess in her ninth month of pregnancy. When Johnny left for work at the Club Colombo, a dinner club like the Paradise, Tess would sit with her back pressed against a hard wooden chair in the kitchen to ease her discomfort and cross-stitch a baby quilt she was sure wouldn't be finished before the baby came.

Still, she felt very lucky. Besides Johnny's waiter's job, which held the promise of advancement, first to maître-d' and then manager, they had found a delightfully airy apartment in an aging Victorian house on Ashbury. Their verbose Mexican American landlady, Carmen Sanchez, quickly became their friend. Carmen doted on Tess during her pregnancy, moved them into her best apartment when it became available, and rummaged through the neighborhood secondhand shops until she found the baby furniture she thought was good enough for her prospective godchild. On the long, lonely evenings when Johnny had to work, Carmen and Tess kept each other company. In many ways, Carmen was Tess's first real woman friend.

Carmen often spoke of her husband, a slight little man who had sold vegetables at a corner stand, then worked his way into a shop and was planning to expand when World War II erupted. With only two months to go before the war ended, he was killed in a kamikaze attack at Okinawa.

"Nothing is worse than sending your man off to war. Life stands still. You don't live 'n you can't die. You just wait." Carmen and Tess sipped their tea in the glare of the overhead light in Tess's bright yellow kitchen.

"I'm sorry, Carmen. Sorry for your suffering. Must've been real bad."

Carmen's broad, round face broke into a grin. "Aw, it was a long time ago. You gets over it even if it does leave a few scars here." She pointed to her heart. "Wasn't like I had family, though. Always wanted a baby." She nodded at Tess's balloon stomach. "Now looks like I'm getting one."

The night Tess went into labor, Johnny was working. It was Carmen who called the doctor, found a cab, got them to the hospital.

Once there, Carmen ran inside and returned a minute later with a wheelchair and an orderly. Forbidden to call Johnny because, Tess said, "We need the money, and there's no sense in his sitting around the hospital waiting," Carmen prayed things would go quickly. Two hours later, sum moned by the doctor, she was told that Tess had delivered a baby girl.

Near tears, Carmen rushed to the telephone. "Tips or not, I think you oughta get over here."

Johnny rushed off without even a good-bye and twenty minutes later was patting Tess's hand and looking at her in wonder. "She's beautiful."

"She looks just like you." Tess seemed bewildered by it all. "And she's perfect—every finger and every toe."

"Naw. She looks like you."

"Well, since we look so much alike, she must take after both of us."

Johnny nodded. He leaned over to kiss Tess, then brushed the back of his hand against her hair. "You look beautiful, too."

Tess squeezed Johnny's hand. "You still want to name her Carmen? You haven't changed your mind?"

"She's a perfect Carmen."

"It'll have to be Baby Carmen."

"Baby Carmen and Mama Carmen. Sounds great—sounds like a family."

"Carmen Evans . . . How about Carmen Roberta Evans?" A melancholy look filled Tess's eyes. "For my Mama."

"For your Mama." Johnny kissed Tess's hand. A half hour later he was back at the Club Colombo, his mood effervescent. He bought a box of Havana cigars from the cigarette girl and absentmindedly offered them to both women and men. Reminded that women didn't normally smoke cigars, he posted an IOU for a box of candy on the kitchen bulletin board, quickly sketching underneath a baby rocking in a cradle, her name, Carmen, printed in bold block letters along the paper's edge.

"Do you realize this is our first Christmas together?" Tess basted the turkey, keeping an eye on the clock and glancing at the baby, who was chewing on the ear of a teddy bear in the middle of her playpen.

Johnny was bent over the kitchen table reading the

want-ads. "If I don't get the maître-d' job at the club next month, I'm quitting." He ran his finger down the job column of the *San Francisco Chronicle*.

"Johnny, you're not even listening to me." Tess stood up, closed the oven door, and gave him a scolding look.

"Yeah, yeah. Our first Christmas. It'll be our last if I don't get more money."

"My God, Johnny, you're not even twenty years old. What do you want?"

"I want the maître-d' job. And what difference does it make how old I am? Alexander the Great conquered Greece by the time he was my age."

"Oh, that was a long time ago. And he wasn't trying to get a job in San Francisco."

"Jeez . . ." Johnny raised his eyebrows in disbelief.

Tess stepped behind him and wrapped her arms around his shoulders. "Please, honey. Don't worry about it now, and don't talk about money in front of Mama Carmen. She worries about us. We'll make it till the first of the year, then I'll get a job."

"No. No job for you. You got enough to do with the baby."

"Johnny, Mama Carmen has offered to watch Carmen. Just for a few hours at night. I already talked to the manager of the supermarket. He says to let him know when I can start. Doesn't pay much, but I'll get a discount on food. That'll help."

Johnny tapped the table with his finger. "Yeah. Maybe. But only till we get a few bucks ahead."

"Sure, honey." Tess kissed the back of his head. "Christmastime is always bad on a budget."

Tess playfully pulled him away from the table and, wrapping her arms around his waist, swayed to the mellow voice of Nat King Cole on the radio.

Johnny took the lead, and they waltzed around the kitchen table.

"I love you, I love you, I love you," Tess shouted over the blare of the music as they spun faster and faster until they finally collapsed into each other's arms on the cold linoleum floor.

"And I love you, too, Tess Evans." Johnny pulled her to him for a long kiss that was both tender and passionate. When he pulled away, his eyes were dreamy and a little sad. "Will you marry me? Please."

His sudden seriousness seemed ominous to Tess. She nuzzled her face into his neck. "We're already married. Leastways as far as I'm concerned."

Johnny refused to be placated. "Not legally. We never said the words."

"Oh, Johnny, I've said them a thousand times in my heart—for better for worse, for richer for poorer, in sickness and in health—"

"It's not right that we can't get married legally. Just because—"

"Just because I'm a Negro, and you're white. I agree, but what can we do? California's as backward as Missouri. No miscegenation."

"You could lie."

Tess frowned, then shook her head. "Say I'm not a Negro, swear to it? No. I couldn't."

"Why not? Who'd know? You're as light as me. We could be Mexicans like Mama Carmen."

"Yeah, and I could fix my hair and maybe pass, but I can't change how I think. I can't forget who I am. It would be like throwing away Mama and Minnie and Tallulah—my whole heritage."

"Do you think they'd mind? Really? Would it hurt you if Carmen passed when she grows up?"

Tess's frown deepened. She shrugged. "By that time I hope she doesn't have to." Tess ran her finger across Johnny's jaw and smiled, her eyes pleading for understanding. "What we got to do is change the laws, not ourselves. I'm not wrong. They are."

Looking sheepish, Johnny hugged Tess tightly. "Makes sense to me, but, in the meantime, I guess we don't get married, huh?"

"For a while we'll just have to pretend."

* * *

Tess's focus on her family world was so myopic she barely listened as the radio announcer described an attack by North Korea against South Korea on June 25, 1950. But Johnny heard every word. "Russian-built T-34 tanks. Southward across the 38th parallel. The capital, Seoul, is in danger of falling."

Johnny nervously outlined the red and black squares of the kitchen tablecloth. He didn't look up when Tess spoke.

"By September we should have enough money saved to make a down payment on a house. Mama Carmen has a friend in real estate keeping her eye open for a good buy. Doesn't hurt to have someone watch out for our interests." She paused and waited and got no response.

"Honey, what's the matter? You look like you've seen a ghost." Fear flashed in Tess's eyes, and she threw her hand over her mouth to stifle a scream. "Michele hasn't found us, has he? My God! I couldn't stand it if we had to move—"

"Tess, for Christ's sake—didn't you hear the news?"

"Well, of course, I heard the news. So what?"

"We've got to stop them."

"Stop who?"

"The North Koreans."

"Stop 'em from what?"

"From conquering South Korea."

"Where the devil is South Korea? And who cares?" Tess stomped across the kitchen and stirred the batter for pancakes. "Sometimes you get so upset over nothing. My goodness! If those people, whoever they are, want to shoot each other, why should you get so excited?"

"Because *those people* represent the communists and the democracies. We'll have to take a stand, especially if the Russians are involved."

"Well, we have the United Nations. They'll take care of it." Tess smiled and dropped two spoonfuls of pancake mix onto a hot iron griddle. Yellow bubbles swelled up, then burst, leaving soft-edged craters around the edges. Flipping them over at just the right moment, Tess was delighted that they had crusted to a light golden brown. She usually burnt them or flipped them too soon.

Johnny slammed his fist on the table. "For Christ's sake, Tess! Sit down and listen to me. We could be heading toward war, and all you care about are those damn pancakes."

Tess flinched. "But why should I care? It doesn't mean anything to me."

Johnny sighed and lit a cigarette. "It does matter to you if we get in a war. There's something I didn't tell you. We needed the money. It seemed like a good idea at the time."

Johnny had Tess's attention now. "What are you talking about?"

"I joined the Marines, the Marine reserves really. If anything breaks out anyplace, I could go—"

"Oh, no!" Tears welled up in Tess's eyes. She clutched his hand tightly.

"Maybe it isn't as bad as I think. And you're right about the UN. They'll probably send the North Koreans a nasty letter, and that'll be all there is to it."

Tess refused to be placated; she had too much at stake. Johnny and Carmen were her life. If she lost one of them, part of her would die. And for what? she wondered. A country called Korea. Where was it? She wasn't sure. Someplace in Asia. It's none of our damn business what they do in Korea.

Johnny held Tess close and spoke soothingly. "Let's not worry about it yet, honey. In a month I bet it'll all blow over."

But it didn't blow over. Tensions mounted the last week of June and President Truman and his Secretary of State, Dean Acheson, took steps that seemed to lead the country inextricably toward war.

On Thursday, June 27, President Truman announced a police action, and at 5:40 P.M. orders went out from Washington committing American combat troops to Korea. The South Koreans were days, maybe only hours, from surrendering. Four divisions of the Eighth Army in Japan were sent to Korea to hold the Pusan perimeter—the southeast corner of the peninsula. If Pusan fell, all of Korea would be in communist hands.

Pusan didn't fall and by August as the war continued, the 1st Marine Division at Camp Pendleton, California, prepared to join the fight. This was Johnny's unit.

Tears won't help, Tess thought as she stood beside the hissing train and said good-bye to Johnny. She forced herself not to cry. "Come back to us." She pressed her mouth close to Johnny's ear. She could barely breathe as Johnny pulled her closer, kissing first her, then Baby Carmen, then her again. She felt his heart beating furiously; she felt his warm, sweet breath on her mouth and the muscles of his arms bulging, pressing, tense, determined not to let go. The conductor yelled.

Johnny released Tess. Unable to say good-bye, he stepped back, turned, and disappeared inside the train. Seconds later Tess watched as the locomotive slowly chugged out of the station. She didn't move for several minutes once it had gone. The tears, held in check for so long, rolled down her cheeks as Tess walked to the street, clinging to Baby Carmen. "Oh, Johnny, please come back to us. We need you so much."

Tess kept abreast of the war through Johnny's letters, which arrived sporadically from Korea. He described the successful Marine landing at Inchon, and mentioned their first quaint target, Cemetery Hill. After the exhilaration of surviving his first battle, the monotonous drudgery of war set in. The march to Seoul, the capital of South Korea, was the turning point. After a particularly bitter battle he wrote:

War is hell. I think General Sherman said that after the battle of Atlanta, but it doesn't matter who said it, it's all hell. Just one more enemy encounter, and it looks like we'll have a rest. If we're lucky, we may get to go to Tokyo. I promise, no geisha girls. I'm saving all my love for you. Anyway, I've seen all the Orientals I ever want to see. Don't worry about me.

I'm attached to the chicken coop platoon. We squawk, we never volunteer, and when we're fighting we stick our heads between our legs and run around in circles. Scares the shit outta everybody. Rumor has it that we got the gooks on the run, and this war'll be over by Christmas. I sure hope so. Believe me, I'll never leave you or Baby Carmen ever again once I get outta here.

Gotta run. Sergeant just reminded us that tea time's over. Kiss my baby and Mama Carmen, and give yourself a big hug. I love you.

Forever,
Johnny

"See! What did I tell ya? Johnny knows how to take care of himself. He'll be home 'fore you know it." Mama Carmen laid Johnny's letter on the table and, forcing a smile, confronted Tess's blank face.

"Every day's so hard. It's like sitting on a time bomb waiting for it to go off. I don't know how much longer I can stand it."

Mama Carmen's smile faded. "You can't let it get to ya. It'll show in your letters, and he'll know how much you're worryin'. He doesn't want that. He doesn't want to be a burden to ya."

Tess snickered. "Burden! Worryin's got me so down, I feel like I been buried alive."

"Then you gotta get unburied. For Johnny's sake."

Tess nodded. "I know. I promise I'll wait three days after I get his last letter before I start panicking. I figure as long as he's writing, he's alive."

"Guess that's better than mooning around here every day." But the sorrow in Mama Carmen's eyes said silently, I been down this road before, and there ain't no turning back.

Waiting for the postman became an agonizing ritual for Tess. When there was no letter, the mailman bolstered her flagging spirits by promising five the next day. One would arrive, smudged with oil, tears, and sweat. Tess kept her promise. For three days, she was happy reading and rereading the hastily scribbled note, but then she returned to her vigil.

After a week without a letter, even the mailman's cheery optimism failed to pacify Tess's gnawing fears. "Gettin' mail from that Marine a yours ain't as reliable as gettin' your gas bill."

Tess nodded, then forced herself not to run to the front door whenever she heard him on the steps. At the end of October, two weeks since her last letter, the doorbell rang. Through the etched glass, Tess caught a glimpse of a uniformed man. She threw open the door, then stopped.

"Oh, I thought you were . . ." She stepped back.

A young man stared grimly at her through the screen door. Taking off his hat, he ran a gloved hand over the top of his neatly clipped hair.

"Mrs. Evans?"

Tess nodded.

"May I come in?"

With shaking hands, Tess unlocked the door. His dress blues are so fine, she thought. Too fine to be worn by a messenger of death. Tess barely heard his words.

"I regret to inform you that your husband was killed in action."

Much too beautiful, she thought, as she pressed her hands over her ears and stared trance-like at his stern, impassive face.

A month later Johnny was buried on a small rise at Jefferson Barracks, a military cemetery for fallen heroes in St. Louis. Its rolling hills were dotted with gleaming, white markers. Tess had called Rosanna, and she, along with Anna and Michele, attended the funeral services. Tess didn't go, remaining in San Francisco and withdrawing from the world, deaf to the pleadings of Mama Carmen and the cries of her neglected baby.

"But you got to eat." Mama Carmen set a tray of food on Tess's bed. "You got to think of Baby Carmen, too. It ain't right, you ignoring her. She needs you as much as you needed him."

Tess stared at the wall. But despite her despondency, the pain slowly eased, not so much from forgetfulness as from sheer determination to survive. Somehow her memories would have to give her the strength to go on. As for the future, there was none. There was only tomorrow and the day after tomorrow.

Six weeks after Johnny's death, Tess crawled out of bed, showered under pelting, hot water, brushed her tangled hair, and slipped into a crisp, clean dress. Mama Carmen was feeding the baby when Tess walked into the kitchen.

"Don't you look nice. And just in time for supper." Mama Carmen blithely ignored the weeks that had passed while Tess had hid from the world.

Tess sat down, smiled, tickled Baby Carmen's neck, and shook her head, the sorrow in her eyes belying her attempt at cheerfulness. "I'll eat later. Right now, I want to talk."

Mama Carmen patted her hand. "That's good. Talking can get you through a lot of misery."

"Mama Carmen, you mean the world to me. If it hadn't been for you, I never would have made it through the last few months," Tess said.

"Hear now, I don't want no thanks. I'm just happy you're feeling better."

"You've been so strong. So loyal. I've been so lucky, having your love."

Mama Carmen patted her hand. "Wasn't hard loving you and Johnny and the baby."

"Then you will try to understand, won't you?"

"Understand!"

Tess hesitated, then blurted out, "I'm going home."

Mama Carmen blanched and tightened her hold on the baby. "But this is your home. As long as you want." Tears flooded her eyes.

"My home is where Johnny is. And he's in St. Louis. I want to visit his grave. Talk to him. I'm so terribly lonely without him."

No amount of arguing about Michele would change Tess's

mind. "He won't find me or Baby Carmen. Anyway, Johnny's dead. What does he care about me or the baby? That part of my life is finished."

Reluctantly, Mama Carmen let go, and within the week she tearfully waved good-bye to Tess and Baby Carmen in the same train station where Tess had said good-bye to Johnny less than a year before. I have to get away, Tess thought, as she blocked out the images, the sounds and the smells of the past. Then, looking tenderly out the window at Mama Carmen, she whispered, "I love you." The train picked up speed, blurred everything—the people, the buildings, the city—heading east, heading home.

Minnie rushed down the steps as the yellow cab pulled up at the curb. She hugged Tess and kissed the squalling baby. "Look at you two! Ain't you somethin'? I been bitin' my fingers for two hours, scared to death you changed your mind."

Too distraught at first to speak, Tess shook the tears from her eyes, then followed Minnie inside. "It's good to be home," Tess said finally.

"Course it is." Minnie untied Carmen's bonnet and set her on the floor. She stared wonderingly at Carmen, then at Tess. "I been praying you come home, but not like this. Not like this."

"You sure we won't be a burden?"

"A burden! Lordy! I barely slept worryin' 'bout you and this baby. Better I worry 'bout you here than you being a thousand miles away."

"I can work. It won't be like when Mama died and you had to take care of me all by yourself."

Minnie nodded. "Life's easier now than it was then. If you wants to work, I got just the job for you. At the funeral parlor. The boss needs a bookkeeper since I quit."

"Quit?"

"Sure 'nough. I'm getting social security, and Mr. Webb got a pension plan, too." Minnie smiled. "We'll do okay. He promised to give you my old job. That way I can take care of the baby while you work."

Tess sighed. "Don't know what I was worrying about. Might've known you'd take care of things."

Gingerly Minnie picked up Carmen and studied the child's features. "Looks just like her grandmaw, don't she? Gonna be a beauty. I see that right now."

Tess studied her daughter. "Sometimes she looks like Johnny, and sometimes she looks like Mama. Thank heavens, she doesn't look like Michele." She paused and looked at Minnie questioningly. "How is the old goat? Still alive, I imagine."

Minnie nodded. "Emma says he's takin' the boy's death pretty hard. She hears he blames you for Johnny getting killed."

Tess bolted out of the chair. "Me! Johnny was killed in the war."

"The old man claims Johnny wouldn't've gone to war if you and him hadn't run away."

"Then he hasn't forgotten."

"That man never forgets."

Tess knelt on the floor in front of Minnie and stared into the woman's eyes. "He hasn't forgotten—he'll never forgive. My God! What are we going to do? Where can we hide?"

Minnie shook her head. "If that man's bent on revenge, there ain't no place to hide."

Two men, their muscles bulging from the strain, carried a wheelchair bearing Michele Gianino to the second floor of his home. Anna and Rosanna followed, neither one doffing her coat or hat until Michele was lying in bed and the oxygen tank was placed alongside.

"I told you the trip was too much for you," Anna scolded as she undid his shoelaces.

"I wanted to see my boy's grave." There were no tears, but Michele's voice quivered as he spoke. His chest heaved.

Anna pulled off his shoes and socks then stopped. "You rest for a while, then I'll take off the rest of your clothes. You gonna have another attack if you don't rest."

"Get out." Michele shoved his wife aside. "I wanna talk to Rosanna alone."

Anna frowned. "Rosanna'll talk to you later. You just—"

"I wanna talk to Rosanna now, woman!" The tissue-thin flesh under Michele's eyes turned blue.

Anna backed away. Glancing at Rosanna, she frowned, puzzled and distraught.

Anna was barely out of the room before Michele barked at Rosanna. "I wanna know where that nigger whore is. You know. You better tell me or—"

"Or what? You gonna kill me?" Rosanna stood at the foot of Michele's bed. "You can kill me, but that's all you can do. No more slow torture. Johnny's dead."

"You and your son had a weakness for niggers, and I don't want no bastard pickaninny claiming my name and my fortune when I die."

"Mark my words, Michele, if you ever try to harm that baby, I'll—I'll—"

"You'll what? Call the police? That's a good one. Little miss nigger lover'll call the cops."

"You've always had the upper hand, Michele, but there are ways to hurt you. I know your weakness, and with Johnny dead, I'm not afraid to play on it—until you let go or die."

"You bitch. You threatening me?"

"You bet."

"You ain't got the guts to do nothing."

"Oh, yes, I do—I'm gonna tell on you."

"The cops? Shit!"

"No, not the cops. I'll tell Anna. I know she's the only person you've ever loved even though you treat her like dirt. I'll tell her I'm Johnny's mother—I'll tell her everything. She'll hate you, Michele. She'll hate you forever."

Michele struggled to sit up. His face was flushed, and the blood pounded in his temples. "You bitch. I should've killed you when I had the chance."

Rosanna backed away. "Tread lightly, Uncle. If you try to hurt Johnny's baby, I'll tell Anna everything."

"You'll put the woman in her grave." Michele dropped his head on the pillow. He coughed until yellowish-white muck spewed from his lungs. Then, exhausted, he closed his eyes and cried out in a weak, breathless voice, "Anna. Anna. Help me."

Rosanna walked to the door. "I'm warning you, let the child alone."

CHAPTER XXX

A chorus of voices sang "Jolly Good Fellow." In the back of the room, two young girls giggled, unable to contain themselves as their boss stood up and blustered around his desk like a chained bull. When one of the workers set a cake, ablaze with thirty candles, on his desk, he shook his finger at the group and resignedly sat down again.

"Well, now, this is a fine how-de-do. Since when do I pay you to give me a party?" The balding Mr. Webb pulled himself up as if to stretch his diminutive five-foot five-inch height to a more impressive stature.

"Didn't none of us think you'd stay late tonight, seeing as how your wife's got a big retirement party planned for you at home." Belinda Berry, Mr. Webb's secretary, pointed to the candles. "Better hurry 'n blow 'em out. Any you miss means you got one less year retirement 'fore you pass on to the next job, if you knows what I mean."

Mr. Webb shook his head. "Can't say if I want to live another thirty years."

"We want you to know we'll miss you." Belinda kissed Mr. Webb's cheek. When she pulled away, tears welled up in his eyes.

"Say now, none of that. We ain't ready for the speeches and farewells. You see, we got another cake. This one's got two candles on it." Belinda nodded to Ruby McLean, the broad-hipped, bejeweled receptionist, who set the cake in front of Tess.

"What's this for?" Tess asked, surprised.

"We're celebrating Mr. Webb's retirement and your second anniversary here at the good ole Webb and Robinson Funeral Home—'If you can't take it with you, leave it with us.'"

"Here, here." Mr. Webb frowned.

Everyone laughed. Tess tried to speak, but the words caught in her throat. All she could manage was "Thank you."

"It's gonna look like the funeral's in here with all these tears," Ruby said.

A young man, his hands shoved deep into his pockets, walked quietly into the back of the room. The women looked at him for a moment, the older ones agreeing he would be a fine catch for some lucky young girl. Clarence Howard was a graduate of Lincoln University in Jefferson City, Missouri. He represented the new breed of Negroes coming of age in the fifties—bright, self-possessed, a man who would survive and prosper in the world of business and commerce.

Mr. Webb approached Clarence with his hand extended in greeting. "You didn't put these women up to this, did you? Isn't it enough I'm leaving, but I got to put up with a punch and cake party?"

"Wasn't my idea," Clarence said, "but if you're really thirsty, I might scrounge around till I find something stronger than punch."

Mr. Webb curled his lips. "I drank some of that stuff sitting in the filing cabinet. Tasted like embalming fluid."

A chorus of "Auld Lang Syne" burst out spontaneously, then Mr. Webb formally introduced Clarence as the new director of the Webb and Robinson Funeral Home.

Tess, who had sat by silently watching her friends and business associates banter and joke, was delighted by her new life in St. Louis. Carmen and Minnie doted on each other, her job as bookkeeper at the funeral parlor was challenging, and for the first time in memory money wasn't a problem. They weren't rich, but occasionally she went to the movies with Ruby, then they would stop for ribs and a beer at King's Bar-B-Que Ribs Parlor after. That was the only amusement she allowed herself. "I'm content," she told Minnie, who scolded her for staying home too much.

"Go out with your friends. Meet a nice young man."

Tess rolled her eyes in dismay. "For the first time in my life I know who I am and what I want. I don't worry about the past, and I don't fear for the future. A man'd just mess up my life. Who needs that?"

She might have added that no man measured up to Johnny, but Tess didn't see any reason to tell Minnie she compared all men to him. Minnie wouldn't understand, she told herself.

A week later when Clarence asked her to work overtime to meet the upcoming income tax deadline, she willingly agreed. Not that I like working all day and half the night, she thought, but everybody has been so good to me. I can't say no. Still, she stared wistfully at Ruby and Belinda as they donned their coats and headed for the door at five o'clock.

"Hey, woman, you're making me feel guilty keeping you here." Clarence had noticed her envious look.

Tess smiled and shook her head. "A deal's a deal. I'll be all right as soon as they leave."

"No, you won't," he said adamantly. "You need a break. Come on, let's grab a bite. I can't work on an empty stomach."

Tess looked up at him in surprise. "You work? But I thought—"

"That you'd be here by yourself? Good God, woman, you'd be here till Christmas. Of course I'm gonna help." He smiled. "But first we eat."

They ate together the first night and every night thereafter until the tax rush was over one month later. During that time Tess learned all about Clarence Howard, and he learned all about her.

Aware that Carmen was an only child, he offered his own life as an example of what not to do in raising her. "I think my parents tried to protect me too much. If I came home with a bloody nose, they acted as if I were dying. But it was how whites treated me that hurt 'em the most. Course they couldn't protect me from them no matter what. Even in a small town where we sure knew our place, there were lots of ways white folks hit at us, such as making us stand aside in the dime store while the clerk waited on the whites first. I remember my mama slapping my hand if I touched anything we weren't going to buy. I got slapped so much, I'm still afraid to move my arms too far from my body."

Tess laughed, but it was a nervous, embarrassed laugh. "I don't ever remember going to the store with Mama or Minnie. We were so poor, we couldn't even afford that. But I know what you mean. Some things you accept, such as sitting in the back of the bus, but others—the nasty remarks, just loud enough to hear—nigger, pickaninny—no, I won't try to protect Carmen from that. Like your folks, I couldn't, even if I tried. Anyway, how we gonna change things if we don't know what we're up against?"

Clarence's face lit up, and he grinned eagerly. "You really mean that?"

"Sure I mean it. Things got to change sometime. Why not now?"

"Then you been following the Brown case?"

"Brown case?"

"Yeah, you know, Linda Brown in Topeka. The N.A.A.C.P. is taking her case to the Supreme Court. The Association's been nipping away at segregation for years, but if we win this one we'll tear America apart. The whole damn social structure based on race'll just crumble up and die. The man's gonna have us sitting next to him in the schools and on buses and in restaurants." Clarence's face was animated as he talked.

"Yeah, and Santa Claus'll come down the chimney." Tess said sarcastically. "That won't ever happen. I'd be happy if we could get better jobs, make more money. As far as the

Brown case, I heard about it, but nothing's gonna change. The boss man's got his world together real tight."

"My God, do you need educating."

"Maybe so. But I don't have time to go to school. I got a family."

"Not school. You gotta join the N.A.A.C.P. We need workers. You'll learn, 'n you'll be helping too."

"But I don't have time. I been working every night for the past month. I gotta stay home with Carmen for a while anyway. Poor kid doesn't even know who I am."

Clarence shook his head. "You're entitled to one night a week. Remember what I told you about raising an only child. Don't lean. If you do, pretty soon you're living her life for her."

Tess eyed him skeptically. "She's only three years old."

They argued for ten minutes. Tess finally agreed to give one night a week to the N.A.A.C.P., and Clarence, as a lure, offered dinner and a free ride "to and from."

Tess hesitated, reluctant to commit herself to spending more time with her boss. A whole new set of emotions were stirring inside; her heart raced a bit when Clarence entered the office. Thoughts of him filled her mind at night before she fell asleep. He's a good friend, she told herself. It's nice to have a man to talk to. He's fun, but serious, too. One of these days he'll be doing some woman good. He says he's never been in love. Hah! Likely story. Even if it's true, he'll be snatched up one of these days. I'll be happy for him. Course, I'll miss him.

Tess laughed when Clarence drove up in a shiny black limousine. It looked big enough to carry a football team, and she told him so, embarrassed by what the neighbors would think.

"I *am* a funeral director," he said jokingly.

"And the whole town's gonna know it."

Good-naturedly their N.A.A.C.P. friends called Tess and Clarence "dicties," high-class Negroes. Their kidding helped lighten the long, often depressing sessions when a handful of people called hundreds of homes and received only a modicum of support in their efforts to raise money and interest in the cause. But no matter how frustrating their evening, by the time they reached Tess's home, they had made plans to try again the next week.

In the months that followed, Tess's uneasiness grew. That man's messing up my mind, she thought. We were just friends, but now I'm not sure what we are. I don't love him—I can't. If I did, I'd lose Johnny, and we got this thing worked out. We talk. He tells me how to handle my life. Not to worry. What would happen to Johnny if I fell in love with Clarence? Would he go away, disappear like fog on a sunny day? I won't fall in love with Clarence. Oh, hell, since when is Clarence in love with you? He can have any girl he wants. Free and clear. But me, I got Carmen. What does he need with another man's child? That's all I got, Carmen, and lots of memories.

By May of 1953, a year later, there was no denying the attraction. Both Clarence and Tess tried to ignore it, but Ruby and Belinda smiled and winked and took bets on when the young couple would come to their senses.

Inadvertently, Tess brought things to a head by telling Clarence she wouldn't go to any more meetings with him because she wanted to spend more time at home. She had rehearsed her speech for a week, but saying the words was hard as she held back her tears. Clarence, sitting across from her at a redwood picnic table at King's Bar-B-Que, seemed unaware of her agony. The May evening was warm and breezy, a night for romance, ideal for a girl's senior prom, her wedding, for falling in love.

Clarence shoved his plate across the table, took Tess's hand in his and asked why.

Tess mumbled that Carmen and Minnie needed her, adding that she hoped they could still be friends.

"Of course we'll be friends," Clarence said, befuddled.

Tess, content to change the subject, wished him well in his bid for the local N.A.A.C.P. presidency, but now the light was dawning. Clarence bit his lip, shaking his head in dismay.

"Oh, Tess, I'm a damn fool. Stupid, dimwitted, you name it. Will you ever forgive me? All along I thought we were friends, fellow workers, buddies. For months I've had this funny feeling inside. But hell, I've never been in love before. How was I supposed to know? If you hadn't . . ." Clarence pulled his chair around the table. Putting his arm around her neck, he drew Tess close to him and nuzzled his face in her hair. "I love you more than anything in the world. You can't stop seeing me. I simply won't stand for it. You're my woman. You have been since our first date. You always will be."

Tess, startled by his sudden outburst, pulled away. "Clarence, don't say things like that. I can't get serious, and I don't want to lose your friendship."

"But you *are* serious. I know you love me. I can see it. I can feel it."

"Then you know I'm afraid. Horribly afraid."

"Of what? Of me? Oh, Tess, I'd never hurt you."

"No, not on purpose, but love means taking a chance on gettin' hurt. I lost three people—Mama, Tallulah, and Johnny. They meant the world to me. What would I do if I lost you? No, it's better not to care." Tess shook her head adamantly. "Anyway, I got Minnie and Carmen to worry about. That's enough."

"I'm not asking you to worry about me. I'm asking you to marry me."

Tess looked at him with sorrowful eyes. "Don't make sense me feeling so bad because you asking me to marry. I should be happy. I care for you, Clarence. But I can't marry you. I'm not over Johnny yet. And I'm telling you, I'm scared."

Clarence kissed Tess hard on the mouth, and she responded in spite of herself. Clarence smiled. "See, you like that, don't you? You got feelings for me. As far as Johnny, you're in love with his memory. He's been dead over two years. You're keeping his memory alive to protect yourself. The poor, pitiful widow, 'cept you're only twenty-three years old. How long you gonna wear sackcloth?"

"Till I'm ready to take it off! And I don't need you to tell me to quit thinking about Johnny."

Clarence reared back. "Okay, okay. Don't get mad. It's just that . . . well, I love you. I love you very much, and I don't want to wait forever. Please, give me a chance. I know I can make you happy."

Tess was silent, then finally said, "Then wait till I'm ready to give you an answer. Don't push me. I don't wanna make the wrong decision."

Clarence vowed to wait and took Tess home. As she watched his car disappear down the street, she cried, partly out of happiness, partly out of guilt. She was being offered a second chance at love and marriage and security. It would be nice. And it would be different from her life with Johnny. She and Clarence wouldn't have to live in fear; they could be married legally. They could grow old together like two brand-new shoes that would wear well over the miles. Yes, she thought. Clarence would wear well. It would be nice to be Mrs. Clarence Howard.

Ruby was Tess's maid of honor at the wedding, which took place on July 1, 1953, at the First Baptist Church. Carmen was the flower girl, and Minnie, enthroned in the place of honor usually reserved for the bride's mother, alternately cried and smiled during the short ceremony. After a punch-and-cake reception, the happy couple opened their presents, then stole away to spend their wedding night at the bungalow they'd bought around the corner from Minnie's flat. They spent their honeymoon papering, painting, and scrubbing, and when they returned to work two weeks later, Tess, exhausted but happy, sat back and appraised her new life. Almost overnight she had acquired a husband, a home, and if her luck held out, another baby. She knew that in a day, an hour, her life could change, some things for the better, some for the worse, but her trepidation was short-lived when she discovered she was pregnant. She couldn't decide if she or Clarence was thrilled the most.

"It's been so long since I've been this happy, I'm afraid to breathe," Tess said, when she dropped Carmen off at Minnie's on her way to work.

"Well, girl, it be time somethin' good happen to you. I never had nothing against Johnny, 'n I mourn the boy's passin', but I's sure relieved you is finished with that Gianino family."

Tess's eyes grew sad. "I loved him, and you never forget your first love. But I was so young." She was silent for a moment, then the chimes on Minnie's living room clock struck eight. "Can't look back." She kissed Carmen and Minnie and headed for the door.

By the time Tess quit work, she was so big she waddled around the office and lumbered up Minnie's steps when she went to fetch Carmen.

"Where's that strappin' man you married?" Minnie asked testily. "You can barely walk, and here you is luggin' this child back and forth."

Tess plopped down on Minnie's easy chair and rested her feet on the stool in front of her. "Don't be grumbling about Clarence. The poor man hardly ever sleeps. If he's not at the funeral parlor, he's at the N.A.A.C.P. office working till midnight or one in the morning."

"What's he doin' that for?"

"Haven't you heard? We're trying to raise money to pay for the desegregation case—Brown versus the Board of Education."

"Oh, yeah. I heard of it. Mr. Marshall trying to get the court to say whites and colored can't be in separate schools no more. Well, honey, don't hold your breath. Them white folks ain't gonna change things. They like it just the way it is."

"But times are changing, Minnie. Clarence says we got a good chance to win." Tess grinned. "Wouldn't that be sumptin' if my kids could go to school with white kids? Might even stop all this hatred between the races."

"Talk like that makes me think you is daft in the head, girl. Even if we win, white folks ain't gonna love us no more'n they do now, and that ain't much."

395

"Maybe, but all the same, it's a step in the right direction, and Clarence is dedicated to it, and he's working like the devil to collect money to pay the lawyers."

Minnie offered to stuff envelopes, but on May 17, three days later, Tess went to the hospital to have her baby, leaving Carmen in Minnie's care.

"I'll call soon as somethin' happens," Clarence shouted over his shoulder as he ran down the stairs to his car.

Two hours later, Clarence reeled under the impact when, almost simultaneously, he heard on the radio that the Warren Court had stated that the "separate but equal" doctrine of segregation had no place in education; and the doctor told him he was the father of a baby boy.

Overcome with emotion, Clarence sat at Tess's bedside. "The same day—I got a son, and the U.S. Supreme Court says blacks and whites are equal, right down the line. What a time to be born!" Clarence gently touched Tess's face. Barely able to focus her eyes, Tess forced a weak smile, then drifted off again.

"How you like the name Stanley? I think we should name the boy after my grandpapa, and his middle name should be Marshall after Thurgood Marshall. He's the lawyer who took the Brown case to the Supreme Court. Is that okay, babe?"

Tess's sonorous breathing was her only response.

Clarence stood up, kissed Tess's cheek and said goodnight. "I'm gonna look in on our boy, honey, then I'm going home. You get a good night's sleep, and I'll be back tomorrow." Halfway out of the room he stopped, turned around, and added, "I love you, Tess."

"It didn't work out the way we thought, did it?" Tess said, talking to Minnie over a cup of tea in her sun-filled kitchen as she waited for Stan and Carmen to come home from school. In 1961, Carmen was twelve years old and Stan was seven, and every year on the anniversary of Brown versus the Board of Education, Tess felt confident that the new year would see her dream of a tolerant, unbigoted society based on justice for all become a reality. Every year her optimism faded. In a fit of despondency, Tess recounted the highlights of the civil rights movement: the confrontation between blacks and whites at Central High School in Little Rock, Arkansas in 1957; the Montgomery bus boycott; Dr. Martin Luther King, Jr.; the Southern Christian Leadership Conference; the Congress of Racial Equality; sit-ins and marches and hatred and violence.

Minnie's face, lined now with age, reflected the sorrow she felt as she listened to Tess. "Never expected that desegregation to go very far, but I never thought there be so much fightin' and hatin'. Scares me when I think what it's doing to Stan and Carmen. It's got to make 'em scared. It makes me scared. I'm afraid to go to the store. Everybody callin' everybody names and shakin' his fists. Sounds like another Civil War."

Tess nodded. "I didn't think it'd take so long. It's been seven years, and nothin' much has changed. Clarence, bless his heart, works at the N.A.A.C.P. office as much now as he ever did. What worries me, though, is his going to CORE meetings. The Congress of Racial Equality is more radical than the N.A.A.C.P. They have sit-ins, stand-ins, and jail-ins. I'm so afraid he'll do something crazy." Tears rimmed Tess's eyes. "If I lost him—"

"Hush, girl. Ain't nothin' gonna happen to that man. He's level-headed. Not like him to go off looking for glory. Clarence, he's a family man, 'n he loves you 'n the children more'n his own life."

"I don't know, Minnie. He sure is caught up in this civil rights movement. He's like a man possessed."

A week later Tess awoke at two in the morning. Drowsily, she moved her hand across the mattress, groping for her husband. When she realized he wasn't there, she bolted upright and snapped on the light. Clarence's name formed on her lips. She peered into the dark shadows of the room. He hadn't been home all night. Panicking, Tess wondered what she should do. Call the police? The hospital? The N.A.A.C.P. office? For a brief moment she envied those women whose husbands had lovers—at least they were safe,

Tess thought grimly. Night after night she suppressed the terror of finding Clarence's body hacked to pieces by a white mob. She was crying hysterically when Clarence finally straggled in, exhausted and depressed.

"Oh, babe. I'm sorry. I should've called." Clarence kissed Tess and slipped into bed. Tess dried her eyes, and when he rolled over to go to sleep, she angrily jabbed him with her finger.

"Is that all you're going to say—'I'm sorry'? It's three o'clock, I've been up for an hour worried sick, and all you can say is, 'I'm sorry.' Well, *I'm* sorry, but I want to know what you've been doing for the last nine hours."

"Oh, babe, can't it wait? I'm beat."

"Clarence—"

"Okay, okay." Numbly Clarence rolled over and, barely coherent, quickly recapped his evening. "I was at the CORE office. We're planning a freedom ride down South."

Tess clutched the edge of the blanket. "Who's *we?*"

"Don't ask tonight. It'll just get you upset."

"Damn it, I'm already upset. Tell me, who is *we?*"

"Me," Clarence retorted. "Me and Sonny and Bob and hell, I don't know all the rest."

"You're not going," Tess said flatly. "You are not going down South and get your head blown off. My grandpaw was killed in a riot. Johnny was shot in a lousy war that nobody even remembers anymore. How many of our men have to die for how many damn causes before it all ends?"

Clarence sat up in bed and, staring at Tess, who was only an outline in the dim light of the room, looked pleadingly at her. "I got to go. I'll be careful, but I got to go."

Something in his voice caused Tess to hesitate. "Clarence, you're forty years old. You've done more than anyone could ask. Letters, meetings, money. Middle-age revolutionaries should be behind desks, not on the streets."

"Tell that to Dr. King."

Tess grew taut. "He's the leader of the movement. That's different."

"No, it isn't. We all got to do our part."

"Well, you can do your part here in St. Louis. What do

you have to go to Alabama for, anyway? Hell, there's enough hatred here to last a lifetime."

"When I get back, I'll take on the problems here. But we decided it was worse down South. We got to break the color codes there or we won't break'em anyplace. Damn it, Tess. You know that." Clarence paused, waiting for Tess's reply.

Finally she sighed and took his hand in hers. "Okay. You got to do it. Why, I don't know. But I'm telling you right now, if you go, I go and so do the children. We'll go as a family."

Now it was Clarence's turn to argue. Dawn was breaking by the time he finally agreed. "But just you and me, not the kids. It's too dangerous."

Tess scoffed, "Well, I never thought I'd hear you say it."

"I never lied. Course there's danger, but I didn't plan on being a hero. All I was gonna do was ride a bus—no speeches, no demonstrations."

"While I sat back here and waited for the sheriff to come to the door and tell me you're hurt or dead." Tess shook her head. "No, thank you. I'll be right there with you. And so will Stan and Carmen. That way I'll know you won't do anything foolish."

Clarence held her tight and nestled his face in her hair. "You shouldn't ask me to put my children in jeopardy. Sounds like blackmail."

"No, not blackmail. I just have the feeling that we'll be safe if we're together.

"You're making this hard on me." Clarence shook his head.

"Look who's talking."

The taxi pulled away from the curb and the Howard family walked gingerly across the sidewalk to the foot of the steps of the Third Baptist Church in Atlanta. The tree-lined street was quiet. Only the muffled shouts of children in a playground nearby broke the ominous stillness.

"You sure this is the right place?" Tess tightened her hold on her children's hands and pulled them closer to her.

Clarence, too, stared uneasily at the church. The long,

horizontal rays of the late afternoon sun softened the red brick, giving the building a drowsy, peaceful facade. "Doesn't look like a place where a bunch of hot-headed revolutionaries would meet," he said.

"I wanna go home." Shifting his weight from one foot to the other, the gangly seven-year-old rubbed his eyes and looked pleadingly at his mother.

Before Tess could answer, Carmen stepped beside her brother and put her arm around his small shoulders. "Don't cry," she consoled. "I'll give you a piece of gum if you don't cry."

Stan's pout lessened, and he allowed himself to be petted by his sister.

While they hesitated outside, the door flew open, and a smiling young man, his hand thrust out in welcome, walked briskly toward them.

"Mr. and Mrs. Howard? I'm Andrew Young. Welcome to Atlanta."

Clarence shook his hand and introduced Tess, Stan, and Carmen. The handsome civil rights leader acknowledged each of them with a handshake, then motioned them inside, saying, "We've been waiting for you." In the church's dimly lit interior, Young introduced them to their compatriots, an animated group of bright-faced men and women, mostly young, brimming with dedication.

"You'll get to know us better when we ride the bus," said Buck, a purple-black Negro with a shiny face and thick, kinky hair.

The group gathered together as Mr. Young instructed them on what to expect on their first freedom ride: "Hate, hate, hate. You're changing their world, so don't expect the white Southerner to thank you for it."

To shouts of "Amen!" and "Ye'sir!" Andrew Young continued: "Stand close together; protect your neighbor; don't resist arrest; answer all taunts with a soft word; don't spout off about your constitutional rights. They know about'em already."

"What if they hit us?"

"Keep down, put your hands over your head, close your elbows in front of your face."

"Can we hit back?"

Young smiled. "You know better'n to ask that. That's a sure way to get yourself killed."

After answering their questions Young commented on their dedication. "I admire your courage. It's folks like you who are gonna change America into something we can all be proud of. Don't have to tell you it's not right blacks can't eat a hot dog at a dime store soda fountain, and it's not fair that we got to ride in the back of the bus. But freedom, like anything worth having, has got to be fought for. And that's what we're doing. We're fighting for what's rightfully ours. Most people think what we're doing is right. But you gonna meet a few who think we're wrong. Whatever you do, be careful, but be proud."

The next morning the freedom riders boarded a large silver and blue bus. Stan and Carmen snuggled together, while Tess and Clarence shared a thermos of hot coffee, then leaned back and tried to sleep as the bus headed southwest to Montgomery. Later the group would sing old spirituals and new fight songs to wile away the hours, but for now everyone was content to speak softly, some voices tense with fear, others charged with dedication. Tess, after her initial fear had dissolved, feeling resigned to the task, told herself that only God could protect them and felt secure that he would.

The trip was uneventful, but tension increased as the bus entered Montgomery. It was dark, and bloodshot eyes peered out of the dirt-smeared windows at the bleak and hostile city. Men and women and a few children milled around in front of the bus station, and when the freedom bus pulled up, they stalked the vehicle like a hunter stalks its prey, lips tight across their teeth, eyes bulging, temples throbbing, their bodies taut and ready to strike. Hatred glistened like beads of perspiration on their faces.

"I don't see any police." Tess took a deep breath, trying to keep her food in her stomach. "Seems like if there's gonna be trouble, the police'd be here."

Clarence patted her hand. "Don't get yourself riled up. They're probably inside protecting the lunch counter."

Buck stood in the aisle at the front of the bus and gave last-minute instructions; their goal was to integrate the all-white section of the terminal—a seemingly simple task, but one in which they could lose their lives.

"We'll form a human chain. Hang onto the next guy's hand. Stay together. Don't go off on your own. That'd make it too easy for 'em."

Snickers, moans, and a few prayers broke the heavy silence on the bus as people stood up, stretched, and grabbed handbags, umbrellas, canes—anything that could be used for protection. Single file, they stepped off the bus. Carmen and Stan were sandwiched between their parents, their eyes glazed with fear. Once out of the bus, everyone lined up and held hands and began to sing "We Shall Overcome." The freedom riders' passivity startled the waiting mob at first, but soon there were angry murmurs and fists contracted and jaws stiffened. The mob moved forward.

Buck stepped out of line to meet them. "We come in peace. We're here to integrate this bus station. Let us pass." His words rang clearly in the warm southern night.

A man in overalls and a straw hat confronted him. They stared at one another, their bodies less than a foot apart.

Clarence nudged Tess and whispered, "It looks ugly. Get the children back on the bus."

Tess nodded. When she stepped back with Stan and Carmen in tow, the line immediately closed in front of them, and they edged furtively along the side of the bus. They hadn't taken five steps before the man in overalls slammed his fist into Buck's face, knocking him to the ground. Then, as if the explosion had unleashed their passions, the mob threw itself against the freedom riders' human chain, raining fists and clubs on their heads. Before she could react, a metal bar whipped across Tess's face. Screaming in pain, she fell to the ground. Clarence shoved the attacker away, Carmen and Stan throwing themselves over her protectively. Shrieks, curses, and moans rent the summer night, and Stan's cries went unheeded as he watched the melee, paralyzed with fear. Clarence tried to pull Tess away from the brawling crowd, but was himself struck with a club. The blow brought him to his knees. A young freedom rider, Yolanda, blood streaming from her mouth, grabbed Carmen and Stan and pulled them, screaming, away from their mother onto the bus, then went back for Tess. Dragging her by her shoulders, Yolanda got Tess inside before collapsing in a seat, holding her swollen jaw and sobbing.

A knee jabbed Clarence in the groin and knocked him to the ground. Sucking air into his lungs, he prayed he wouldn't pass out. A moment's respite allowed him to see Stan and Carmen safe inside the bus. Their tear-stained faces were pressed against a window as they cried out to him to protect himself.

Suddenly the noise diminished, the crowd thinned. Clarence, pulling himself up, sighed with relief. Thank God, it's over, he thought. As he took a deep breath, a sharp pain gripped his chest, prostrating him. Writhing on the bloodied pavement, Clarence saw the booted feet of two men march past him, then smelled the pungent odor of gasoline. Raising his head, he stared, terrified, as the men doused the bus, then laid gasoline-soaked rags on the tires.

"They're gonna burn it! Stop them!" he yelled.

Seeing no one nearby, Clarence grabbed a two-by-four lying next to him and staggered toward the men. Mustering his last ounce of strength, Clarence lifted the piece of wood over his head and brought it down on one of the men's skulls. Blood spurted from the wound, and the man bellowed. Instantly the other man turned and jabbed his fist in Clarence's face. Clarence's body buckled, and he collapsed on the black-topped parking lot.

Carmen watched, screaming and pounding on the window. Soon the place was littered with bodies, and when the police finally stepped in, the mob was already dispersing, content with its night's work.

An hour later, the battered bodies of the freedom riders were lying in a makeshift emergency room of a local Negro hospital. Doctors and nurses fluttered around them, patching, stitching, bandaging. A few were taken upstairs for more intensive care, and Clarence was one of them.

After Tess's wounds were treated, she sat beside Clarence, who had just been wheeled from the operating room. His face was swathed in bandages, only his eyes and mouth visible.

Tess's vigil was broken by a harried nurse, who sporadically appeared to check her patient's blood pressure and breathing. Responding curtly to Tess's questions, the nurse shook her head and told her the doctor would be along shortly.

At five the next morning, a white-coated physician pulled a chair up beside Tess and sat down. He tapped nervously on a chart lying on his lap. "He's going to make it, but we don't know what condition he'll be in when he wakes up. Head injuries are tough. Impossible to predict how much damage has been done."

"But he'll live?" Tess asked in a whisper.

"He'll live."

"Thank God."

The doctor waited until Tess stopped crying. She dabbed her eyes and apologized for taking his time. "I'll be all right. I'm just so relieved. But you said 'his condition'—what does that mean?"

"The blows on the head could have damaged his brain, his eyes, his nerves." The doctor's professional facade never cracked. Only his eyes responded to Tess's sorrow. "But he's a very strong man. There may not be any permanent damage at all."

"I pray you're right." Tess's hand shook as she wiped her face with a tissue.

"And, as for you, I suggest you get some sleep. Otherwise

you'll go into shock, and then you won't be any good to your husband at all."

"Oh, I can't leave him—"

"We'll take good care of him, Mrs. Howard." The doctor was on his feet.

Reluctantly Tess followed him out of the ward. By the time they reached the elevator, Tess had to lean against the wall and close her eyes to keep from fainting.

The doctor studied her with concern. "You sure you're going to make it home?"

Tess nodded. "I'm staying with Mrs. Blanche Gilbert. If there's any news—"

"Just leave your number at the reception desk." He hurried away down the hall.

A month later, Tess, Clarence, and the children were back in St. Louis. Tess's face was still swollen, and she had difficulty talking, but her eyes were bright. She doted on Clarence, who stared blankly at her from the confinement of his wheelchair.

"It's a miracle how well you handled the trip." She tried to force a smile. "Thank God, we're home."

"Amen to that." Minnie looked first at Tess, then at Clarence, all the while trying to hide her dismay at Clarence's broken, mute body.

"It's the first step on a long road, but we're going to make it, aren't we, darling?" Tess pushed Clarence to the middle of the room so he could feel that he was part of the group.

Stan stirred uneasily. "I wanna go outside and play." He kept his eyes on the floor.

Tess stared hard at him. "No. It's too dangerous. You might get hit by a car."

"Aw, Mom—"

"I'll watch him," Carmen interjected. "I won't let him play in the street."

"Let the boy go," Minnie said. "He needs to see his friends. Get back to normal."

"But we have to decide what we're going to do," Tess said.

"Whatever you and Papa decide'll be okay with us," Carmen promised.

Tess sighed. "You be careful and stay in the front yard."

Clarence blinked his eyes as though granting his approval.

For the next hour, Minnie and Tess debated. "How you gonna live?" The bluntness of Minnie's question caught Tess off guard.

"I don't know." She thought a moment. "The funeral home, I suppose. Won't make a lot, but it'll be better'n nothing."

Minnie shook her head. "Don't see how you gonna manage. Who gonna take care of Clarence while you is working?"

"I'll hire a lady from church to come in the mornings. Stan and Carmen can watch him when they get home from school."

"Don't forget about me."

"You?" Tess looked at Minnie's gnarled hands and stooped shoulders, the physical results of the arthritis that was ravaging her. "Dear, sweet Minnie." Tess wrapped her arms around the old woman's shoulders and rocked her gently. "You've done your share. It's time I took care of you."

"Not much chance of that now." Minnie pushed Tess away, refusing to be mollycoddled.

Tess responded sharply. "There's no way I'm going to burden you with Clarence. He's almost too much for me to handle."

"I can fix his lunch, talk to him. Don't need a lot of strength to do that."

Tess patted Minnie's hand, but refused all of her suggestions with a smile. "Minnie! I can't be worrying about Clarence and you too." She thought for a moment. "Anyway, how could you fix Clarence his lunch? We might be living across town."

Minnie giggled to herself as though she had a secret she was about to share. "But you is gonna come live with me."

Tess laughed. "Minnie, you know that's impossible. We'd fall all over one another."

"Ain't the way I see it. Right now you got four in your family. If you live with me, you'll have five. Sure, it'll be crowded, but you ain't going to afford any better."

Tess bit her lip, and tears sprang to her eyes. When does it stop? she wondered. When will Minnie stop taking care of us? The woman's love seemed unfathomable. She nodded and said just above a whisper, "Only till we get on our feet, mind you." She hugged Minnie and tears rolled down her cheeks. "Thank you. Thank you so much, dear, sweet Minnie."

Minnie's smile was a smile of victory. "Don't go thanking me. Ain't doing nothing you wouldn' do under like circumstances. We're family, girl. Families stick together."

Eight years later, on a cold wintry day in 1969, Tess sat at the kitchen table and sipped hot coffee from a mug decorated with Christmas holly. It was a time for meditation. She remembered the day she had come home from work and found Stan and Minnie waiting for her as if they had planned a surprise. Oh, they had been clever, keeping their secret from her all those months, not letting on.

"Sit down, Mama." Stan's face had been spread wide with a grin. He pulled a footstool in front of her chair and lifted her feet onto it. Dear Stan, Tess had thought. He knows how much my feet hurt when I been on'em all day. Before she had time to thank him, Carmen waltzed into the room and handed her a cup of steaming coffee.

"What's going on?" Tess eyed everyone suspiciously. "Who's in trouble this time?"

"Oh, Mama! You always thinking something bad happened." Stan laughed.

"Then what?"

"Drink your coffee, Mama." Carmen winked at Minnie. Too exhausted to argue, Tess leaned back in her chair.

"Close your eyes," Minnie said.

Tess sighed. "Oh, really. Do we have to go through all this? Can't you just tell me—"

"Close your eyes, Mama," Carmen said.

"Okay, but this better be good."

Tess heard feet shuffle, furniture being moved, bodies bumping into one another. Finally it grew quiet.

"Okay, Mama, you can open your eyes," Stan said.

Stan, Carmen, and Minnie stood in a line in front of the alcove leading into the kitchen. After an impromptu fanfare, they separated. Behind them sat Clarence in his wheelchair. He smiled, and raising his arms with the flourish of a conductor, he grasped the wheels of his chair and pushed them, moving forward under his own volition.

"Oh, my God! When? How?" Tess was on her feet, but Stan pulled her back.

"No, Mama. Let him come to you." Stan's deep brown eyes filled with pride and wonder as he stared at his father.

Clarence maneuvered the wheelchair beside Tess. He took her hands and clutched them tightly, the strength in his hands like a steel band cutting her wrists. She cried out in pain.

Clarence released her. He stared at his hands in dismay, as though they belonged to someone else. He turned them over and said, "Almost as good as new."

"Oh, better'n new." Tess reached across the chair and kissed Clarence, who responded with enthusiasm.

How different he looks, Tess thought. Why hadn't I seen it before? His humped, shriveled body had changed. His shoulders were square, his arms bursting with muscles, but even more striking was his face. The worry lines, the drooping mouth and sad eyes were gone. Instead, a newfound joy radiated from him.

"How did you do it?" Tess asked.

Clarence laughed. "That boy of ours wouldn't give me a minute's peace. Made me squeeze that rubber ball till I almost wore it out. Stan'd come home from school and right away, 'Papa, do your exercises.' Down he'd sit 'nd count. Couldn't stop till I did 'em all. 'Come on, Papa,' he'd say. 'Got to show Mama you can do it.'"

They had celebrated that evening. Carmen baked a chocolate cake; Stan bought the ice cream with his grass-cutting money. A month later, Tess and Clarence picked out a van that allowed Clarence to drive to and from the funeral home where he was hired as assistant director. It had been a turning point. Although money was still tight—their medical expenses were still astronomical—Tess felt confident that their lives were improving.

Minnie's declining health, however, had created new problems. Unlike Clarence's infirmities, her arthritis didn't respond to medicine or exercise. The paralysis caused by age and bad health debilitated her, finally confining her to bed. When she died, she barely weighed eighty pounds.

Tess's sorrow was alleviated by the knowledge that her dear Minnie wasn't suffering anymore. She was buried in the family plot beside her beloved Bobbie. Once a week Tess visited their graves. To her, the stone markers represented a record of her life. Every week she laid flowers on the graves of the three women buried there: her mother, Tallulah, and now Minnie. She also included her Uncle Roy when she talked to her family, and she wondered what kind of man he had been, how he had died, what women he had loved. Tess talked to all of them, and when the wind rustled the top of the giant oak shading their graves, Tess heard their replies. They spoke to her, and although the voices could have been silent whispers in her head, they were there all the same.

The visits revived her, renewing her courage, allowing her to face the future with confidence. But when she visited Johnny's grave, in secret, she felt grim foreboding. She sat at the foot and stared at the small, white cross—how long ago it all seemed! Tess had only fleeting memories of the handsome youth who had shared her life, but Carmen was a constant reminder of him. Even now, after twenty years, Michele's ghost tread on Johnny's resting place. Was Michele still alive? she wondered. And Anna and Rosanna? Tess shook her head to block out the memories.

A chill shot through Tess's body as she thought of the Gianinos. She glanced at the clock. It was almost six. My! I'll have to hurry, she thought. She jumped up. After rinsing her coffee cup, she grabbed her coat and hurried out to the car. Can't keep Carmen waiting. Not after promising her I'd stop by for a visit. Poor Carmen! That girl's working too hard. Her voice was on the verge of cracking when she called. Got to make her take a week off. Ain't no sense her singing herself to death.

CHAPTER XXXI

Carmen stuffed a pillow behind her back, leaned against the headboard, and lit a cigarette. The springs squeaked, and the cheap mattress sank under the weight of her body. She was dead tired, her mind consumed by paralyzing terror. For the past sixteen hours her bed had been her refuge; still, she didn't feel safe even with the doors bolted and windows locked.

The previous night as she walked home from the club, a man, a skinny, mole-like creature with frog-green eyes and thin white lips, accosted her. She still felt his claw-like hand tear into her shoulder; she gagged, remembering his other hand clamp over her mouth. Forced against a brick wall, Carmen froze, her eyes silently pleading with her attacker not to hurt her. An instinct, a deep, basic urge to survive, made Carmen slowly lift the hand holding her purse and offer it. Her attacker looked down. When he raised his eyes, a contemptuous sneer distorted his face.

"You ain't got enough money to buy me, broad. What you got in there, ten bucks?" He laughed coarsely. "I want information."

Carmen's eyes fluttered; her limbs went slack. Her body started to slide to the ground as her lungs constricted, cutting off the oxygen to her brain.

The man grabbed her under her arms and slammed her body against the wall. "One scream, 'nd it'll be your last. You understand?"

Carmen nodded. The man's face grew fuzzy and distorted

as she could hardly focus. She fought a wave of nausea that threatened to make her pass out. The man shook her when she didn't respond. She nodded yes. "What's your name, broad?"

My name? she thought blankly. Should I tell him?

The man grabbed her jaw and pinched it harshly. Carmen bleated in pain. Her eyes caught the shiny edge of a knife nestled in the man's pocket.

"Car—Carmen."

"Carmen what?"

"Howard."

His grip tightened. "I been told you're Carmen Evans. Why would my friend lie to me?"

Carmen shook her head. "Don't know. My name's Howard. Carmen Howard."

Oh, God! Mama's maiden name was Evans. Is he looking for her? I musn't let on I know the name.

"Ain't you the singer at the Sunset Cafe?" The man leaned close, his face pitted and greasy. Carmen felt dirty just looking at him.

"Yes."

"Then you gotta be the broad I'm looking for. But the name ain't right." He stared at her with his cold green eyes. He seemed confused. A streak of caution made him release Carmen.

"I'm gonna check you out, broad. If you ain't who you say you are, I'll be back 'nd you 'nd me'll talk again."

Carmen gasped and choked back tears as she watched the man straighten his jacket and walk down the street as casually as a late-night stroller walking his dog. She didn't move till he crept into a white Lincoln Continental, its seats and steering wheel covered with white fur, and drove away.

Sobbing, Carmen ran the two blocks to her apartment. Once inside, she locked and bolted every conceivable point of entry, then sat in a hot bath to try to soak away the man's contamination. The next morning, Carmen called Tess and asked her to come by the apartment that afternoon. Mama might know what the man wanted, Carmen thought. Oh, Lord! Mama has to know.

Carmen lit another cigarette and stared out the window. It had started to snow. Big white flakes blew against the glass where they stuck momentarily, then slid into a puddle of dirty water accumulating on the windowsill. A white-faced clock, five minutes slow, flapped over the door of the ABC Liquor store across the street. The grimy storefront window was crammed with Christmas decorations, imitation pine wreaths, and cardboard mothers and fathers who hurried to some unknown, happy destination with bottles of Seagram's Seven under their arms. A picture of a silver punch bowl filled with golden eggnog and laced with B&B brandy shared the space in a crowded corner. Carmen mused that no one in the neighborhood had ever seen a silver punch bowl, but if he had, it wouldn't be filled with eggnog.

Her own apartment occupied the second floor of an old, brick building on the city's north side. It wasn't much, but it was all she could afford on the salary King Philip paid her. The Masjid Muhammad Church No. 22 occupied the space below her. Still, having her own apartment and a singing job were two dreams that she'd made realities, and she was only twenty years old. Carmen knew the rest would come: the big time, the money, the stardom. Someday she wanted to be known as the best black singer of the decade, and 1970, the beginning of that decade, was just around the corner.

As she looked back, getting her first professional singing job hadn't been too difficult. Six years before, Malcolm Hall had hired her to be the singer for the Blue Devils, the most popular music group at Sumner High. A smile fluttered across Carmen's face as she remembered the fun they had had. Malcolm, the irrepressible teenager, had rocketed the Blue Devils from relative obscurity to the most sought-after band in their league. Sponsors of teen dances scheduled their parties around the Blue Devils' busy calendar.

"We is hot, honey," Malcolm would say, slapping her uplifted hands. "We is hot, and we is good. Ain't nothing gonna stop us. We's goin' all the way to the top."

Looking back, Carmen often wondered how much of their popularity was based on their musical ability and how much on Malcolm's outrageous behavior and colorful costumes. Electric blue satin suits, lace scarves, and purple shoes. He was fun. He made everyone laugh.

When the Blue Devils broke up, Malcolm became Carmen's agent. A musical-pimp, he called himself. He had gotten her the singing job with King Philip, and he promised that, within a year, he'd have her a recording contract. She had never doubted it, at least not till today. Today she was worried because Malcolm hadn't shown up last night. He never allowed her to walk home alone after a show, yet she had waited a half hour, long after everyone else had left, and he never turned up. Danger had crept into her life. The man. Malcolm. The name Evans. What did it all mean? She sighed, then crawled out of bed.

Picking up her jeans from across the back of a chair, Carmen pulled them on, then slipped a plum-colored sweater over her head. Then she stepped into a pair of black high-heeled shoes. She walked to the dresser and studied herself in the mirror. Her jaw still hurt where the man had pinched it, but there were no marks. She dusted powder on her face, then smeared a blue-red lipstick across her mouth. Her hands shook as she plucked her Afro. If only Malcolm had been there; he would have taken care of the man. The doorbell startled Carmen. She checked the peephole before unlocking the door. When she threw it open, she fell into Tess's arms. "Oh, Mama, the most terrible thing happened to me. I'm so scared."

Tess frowned as Carmen recounted her story. To Carmen's "Why?" Tess could only answer, "I don't know. I don't know what the man wanted."

"But how did he know your last name?" Carmen asked, dressing.

Tess faltered as she tried to think of answers that wouldn't give credence to her suspicions. Michele Gianino was foremost in her mind, but if he were alive, he'd be old by now, maybe even senile. Would he have searched all these years to find her and Carmen? Yes, Tess thought. He would. She grabbed Carmen's hand and looked at her daughter with pleading, terror-stricken eyes.

413

"You must be careful. You could be in danger."

Carmen shook her head. "Danger! I don't understand."

"Trust me. I can't tell you everything, but there is a man who . . . who hates us. Maybe enough to kill us. You must take care."

"Oh, Mama. You can't do this to me. You have to tell me what's going on. I'm so frightened I can't move. Please, please tell me."

Tess nodded, sipping her tea slowly. "Yes. I should've told you a long time ago, but I thought it was over. I never dreamt—"

"What, Mama? What?"

Tess talked for over an hour, recalling her days at the Paradise, working and living with Minnie, meeting Johnny, falling in love. It was painful, remembering. She told Carmen about their hideaway, the checkers competition, growing up and running away to San Francisco. By the time Tess reached the end, Johnny's death in Korea, Carmen was sobbing, too.

"He was my Papa?" Her mind was unable to fathom the tragedy of her parents' lives.

"Yes. Johnny Gianino. He loved you very much."

"But why didn't you tell me? I had a right to know who my Papa was."

"You never asked. I thought you didn't care. You were so young. Clarence loved you and you loved him. That was all that was important. Do you understand?"

Carmen shrugged, unable to answer. They grew silent, both lost in their own worlds, worlds filled with love and now terror. Finally Carmen spoke. "You think Michele, my grandfather, wants to hurt us?"

"I think so, yes."

"Oh, Mama! What can we do?"

"I don't know. I'll think of something. In the meantime, please be very careful."

Carmen glanced at the clock over the kitchen sink. "I got to go, Mama. I'm late already."

"Do you have to sing tonight?"

"Of course. But I'll be safe. Nobody'd hurt me in a whole room of people."

Tess had her doubts, but she kept them to herself. She smiled. "I'll drop you off at the Sunset, but don't you walk home by yourself."

"I won't. I promise." Carmen leaned over and kissed Tess, then smiled and patted her mother's cheek. "How sad it must have been for you. Did you love him very much?"

"More than my life," Tess whispered.

"But you loved Clarence, too, didn't you?"

"Yes, and I still do. It's possible, you know, to love two men. Especially when they're as good as Johnny and Clarence."

"You been lucky, Mama."

Tess arched her eyebrows. "Let's hope my luck hasn't run out."

The Sunset Cafe was a carbon copy of the hundreds of plastic and chrome bars that dotted the highways, avenues, and small-town main streets across the country. The usual Saturday night crowd was there: black men, in pastel, double-breasted suits, matching platform shoes, and broad-brimmed hats, snuggled close to sequined, girdled women with faces made up like Kewpie dolls. Loud laughter, the clinking of glasses, the smell of beer, and the wild, sensual beat of Thelonious Monk blaring from the jukebox flooded Carmen's senses. She loved it all: the crowd, the noise, the smells. But it was the people who excited her the most. This was the "Darktown Strutters' Ball." The handshake, the jive talk, the cool shuffle, were all part of their language. Carmen realized that she, like any aspiring black artist, could leave the ghetto for a while, but must eventually return to revive those special sounds.

As Carmen shoved her coat under the bar, King Philip's band stepped onto the stage. Hell, as long as I'm late, might as well make the most of it, Carmen thought, catching the eye of the bartender for a beer.

"Shakin' it a little late, ain't ya, babe?" Nate asked, drawing the beer into a tall pilsner glass.

"Mama came by. Got caught up in that scene. You know how it is."

"How she doin'? It's been over a year since I seen sweet Tess."

"Shufflin', man. Shufflin'."

"You tell her I say hello next time you see her."

Carmen turned and watched the band members take their places onstage. All were there except her: rotund, amiable Bubbles DeCoy, the guitarist and bass player; Matt and Tommy Somers, twins, middle-aged and balding, both masters, Matt on tenor sax and Tommy on bass trombone; Artie Hill on drums, tall and cool; King Philip, the leader, smart, handsome, lean and bearded, who played trumpet and arranged their music; and Larry Page, the youngest, whose deep dimples and wide smile masked the turmoil inside. King Philip described him as a true genius with soul, and he played piano and composed some of the band's most popular music.

Carmen finished her beer and headed for the bandstand. Artie gave her a drum roll as she jumped on-stage.

"Hit it, babe! Do it!" Bubbles cried as he beat his bass.

Carmen launched into "You Make Me Feel Like a Natural Woman." Controlling the direction and passion in her voice, she pulled the listeners into her song. They leaned forward, responding to the melancholy words, excited by her artistry.

She raised her voice in a shout, like the field hollers of black men and women who sang spirituals of generations past. The wail of the gospel song evolved into the blues, and Carmen's magnificent voice tempered it into soul. Her singing shook the house.

When she finished her set the crowd let loose. King Philip took the microphone. "Thank you so much," he repeated several times before the clapping and whistling subsided. The crowd again roared its approval when King Philip invited them to stay for the second set. Wiping the perspiration from his face, King Philip helped Carmen offstage. The band scattered, some to the bar for a drink, others outside to smoke a joint. The jukebox played dance music, and three young men approached Carmen, inviting her to sit with them.

She nodded and pointed to Larry. "Already got a date. Sorry." The men shuffled away, and Carmen and Larry took a table in the corner.

Larry stared at Carmen with affection. "Missed you last night. Didn't even get to say good-bye."

"I waited out back for Malcolm. He never showed."

"How'd you get home?"

"Walked." Carmen bit her thumbnail and turned away.

"Alone?"

Carmen heard the anger in his voice. She cringed. But then, Larry was always angry about something.

"I know it was dumb. I was tired. The club was closed. What could I do?"

"Something happened, didn't it?" Larry asked, his voice rising.

Carmen nodded. "I was mugged—I think."

"You think! What does that mean?"

Carmen's lip quivered. She ran her finger over the back of Larry's hand as she told him what had happened. When she finished, she looked straight at him. His eyes, usually blank and unexpressive, were filled with disbelief.

"He could've killed you."

"He didn't."

"But he could've." Larry held Carmen's hand tightly. "I love you. Don't ever take stupid chances like that again. If anything happened to you—"

"I didn't mean to. I just . . ." Carmen shook her head. "Oh, let's not talk about it anymore. It scares me."

"You should be scared."

"Not just for myself. I'm scared for Malcolm. He's been gone since last night."

"Malcolm can take care of himself."

"He couldn't against that man."

"Malcolm can take care of himself. Nothing's happened. Maybe he had a business deal out of town."

"He would've told me."

"Not if it was a surprise."

Carmen's face lit up as Larry's suggestion took hold. A wave of relief crept over her. "He did say a representative from a recording company was interested in the group."

"Yeah?" Larry cocked his head to one side. "What recording company?"

"CBC Records. The Bear Cat label."

Larry released Carmen's hand. He pulled a cigarette from the pack lying on the table and lit it. Carmen stared at him, feeling him retreating.

"Don't do this to me, Larry."

"Do what?" Larry stared at her blankly.

Carmen returned his stare. He hurt her without meaning to, but her love for him made her vulnerable. "You won't sign a contract if we get one, will you."

Larry smirked. "I'm not interested in selling my soul for some materialistic orgasm."

Carmen's eyes flashed with anger. "What're you talking about?"

"I'm talking about money, my dear. That's all performers want nowadays. Just money."

"Well, of course they want money. What else would they want?"

"Artistic expression. Art for art's sake."

Carmen paused. For months they had had the same argument. Larry accused Carmen of being too concerned with success. Carmen retaliated by accusing Larry of being a drifter, a loner, as though fame and wealth would destroy his natural talent. They had reached a hopeless impasse, but Carmen refused to let the matter die.

"Why can't you have both art and money?"

Larry looked at her with his hollow eyes. "Because money changes people. Money makes them knuckle under. Big recording companies don't care about artists. All they care about are sales."

Carmen threw her hands in the air. "If nobody buys records, what good are they?" -

Larry laughed. He pulled Carmen to him and kissed her lips. Carmen's heart lurched. Their arguments always ended like this, Larry kissing her, condescending to her. This time she pulled back.

"No, Larry. I want an answer."

"An answer?" Larry paused. "Is it music if only the performer hears it?"

"Oh, Larry! Of course it is, but do you play the piano just for yourself? Don't you need an audience?"

King Philip stepped behind Larry and put his hand on his shoulder. "Hope Carmen's question is academic, 'cause we're on." He smiled, then winked at Carmen. "That is, if you two are up to it."

"Hey, man! What do I know?" Larry followed King Philip and Carmen to the bandstand. "I'm just an ole Vietnam vet trying to plow my way through life."

Carmen spun around. "Oh, Larry, stop. You sound so ridiculous. People'll think you're fishing for compliments. Everybody knows you're the best jazz and blues pianist this side of—well, of something."

"Sure, babe. This side of that wall."

"Cool it, man," King said, "we got a show to put on."

At one o'clock King Philip put his arm around Carmen's waist and kissed her, then turned to the audience and bowed. The evening was over. The crowd rose in a standing ovation.

"Thank you, brothers and sisters, for a real cool evening," King Philip said. "You come back real soon. We love ya."

Even as King was throwing kisses to the crowd, the waiters and waitresses moved through the club dumping ashtrays and picking up bottles and glasses. After the show, the band sat around a large, oak table in the back of the room, sipping free drinks and rehashing the evening's performance. Only Bubbles refused to join them, forced, he said angrily, to go out back to smoke a joint. Seconds later, however, he was back, screaming and pointing toward the dark alley.

"Shit! Some dude out there all covered with blood. Shit!

419

What the fuck goin' on? Man killed 'n we just sittin' round gettin' high."

"What the hell you talking about?" Nathan asked angrily.

"Shit, look for yourself. Man out there ain't even breathin'."

The band crowded round the door as Nathan stepped outside, cursed, then dragged a limp, bloodied body back into the bar. "Jesus! Somebody did a job on this dude all right."

In the dim light, no one recognized the injured man until Carmen glanced down, looked at his face, then fell on the floor beside him. "Oh, God, it's Malcolm."

"Easy, babe." Nathan touched her arm.

"Easy, easy. We'll get an ambulance." Larry motioned for Nathan to make the call.

Larry tried to pull Carmen away, but she refused to leave. Instead, she took Malcolm's hand in hers, bent down, and spoke loudly to try to rouse him. "Malcolm! You hear me?" To her surprise, Malcolm squeezed her hand.

His unexpected response roused Nathan, who ran to the bar and poured a shot of brandy. Lifting Malcolm's head, he told him to sip it slowly.

Malcolm let the liquor slide across his tongue and down his throat. He opened his eyes. When he saw Carmen's face, he blinked, and his lip curled up in a tortured smile.

"Oh, honey! You okay?"

"Of course, but you? What happened to you?"

"Some creep beat me last night."

"You been lying outside all this time?" Nathan asked.

Malcolm nodded. "I woke up. Couldn't get up. Crawled to the vent by the furnace." He closed his eyes, weakened by his effort to talk.

Carmen pressed his hand to her face. "Don't talk anymore. You'll be all right. Rest till the ambulance comes."

Malcolm clutched her hand and pulled her down so that her face was inches from his. "No. The man be back. He say he kill you."

"No. It can't be the same man." Fear constricted Carmen's throat.

Tears rolled down Malcolm's cheeks. "Why he wanna kill you?"

"I don't know," Carmen sobbed. "I don't know."

Larry gripped Carmen's shoulders and drew her away. "That's enough." King Philip led her to a table and made her sip his whiskey and soda.

The members of the band stood sentinel over Malcolm's body till the paramedics arrived. Then Malcolm's groans roused Carmen. She ran to the stretcher and held Malcolm's hand till they reached the door.

"I'll come to the hospital. Please, don't be afraid."

"No. Kill you. Run. Hide."

Carmen stood at the door and watched until the ambulance disappeared. When Larry finally drew her back to the table, everyone spoke at once. Questions shattered the uneasy calm that had filled the room, but there were no answers. The men swarmed around Carmen, curiosity mingled with disbelief. Their concern turned into interrogation. Carmen could only shake her head.

Larry sat beside her, hesitant, unsure what to do. Looking at her glazed eyes, her quivering shoulders, he waved everyone away. She was on the verge of hysteria.

"Come on," he said forcefully. "We're going home."

King Philip and Bubbles followed them to the door.

"Need anything, call." King stepped forward and held Carmen in his arms. "We love ya, babe. Don't know what's happenin', but ya got friends here."

Carmen kissed King's cheek, then leaned against Larry for support as they stumbled home.

Carmen's teeth chattered, and she shuddered from fear and cold. Inside her apartment, Larry eased her onto a wooden chair and knelt in front of her. He kissed her hands, her face, her neck. "You're safe now. Everything's going to be okay."

"You don't know that. You saw Malcolm. You saw what that man can do. He's a killer."

"He won't kill you. I promise."

"If he wants to, he will."

"But why would he want to?"

"I don't know. Mama does. I know she does."

Larry paused, then asked cautiously, "What would Tess know? I don't understand."

"When she was young, there was a man who hated her."

"But—"

Carmen's head dropped forward. She sobbed hysterically. "Oh, I don't know. Please—I can't talk about it. Poor Malcolm. He won't die, will he?"

"No one's going to die." Larry pressed his cheek against her head. "If anyone ever tries to hurt you, I'll kill him."

"Hold me. I feel so cold."

Larry lifted Carmen in his arms and carried her to bed. He took off her shoes, her jeans, her plum-colored sweater. Then, after covering her with a wool blanket, he undressed and lay beside her. Her skin was wet and clammy. Gradually her shaking stopped, her sobs diminished, and she fell into a deep sleep.

For an hour, Larry held her, afraid any movement would awaken her. His mind traveled the distance between Carmen and Malcolm and back again. Who was this man with the frog-green eyes? What did he want with Carmen? With Malcolm? There was nothing in their lives to account for this kind of violence. His mind was too clogged with worry, his body too taut with exhaustion, to unravel the possibilities, and he, too, drifted off.

The clock's striking five roused him. Larry opened his eyes. Carmen was lying next to him, her breathing regular, her skin warm against his. A scant odor of perfume and powder hung in the air.

Everything seemed normal: the smells, the sounds, the sights, yet Larry felt uneasy. Tension gripped his heart, his stomach, his bowels. He closed his eyes and lay very still. As the seconds ticked by, his fear mounted, and he realized he was frightened. His heart fluttered; his pulse quickened.

What was it? he thought. Something had awakened him, but what? There was no traffic outside. He listened and waited. In less than a minute he realized someone was in the apartment. He was moving like a phantom through the living room. Larry cocked his head. He heard rubber-soled shoes scrape across the wooden floor, making a soft, thumping sound. In his mind, Larry followed the man as he headed toward the bedroom.

Stealthily, like a jungle fighter, Larry slid out of bed and crept across the floor on his hands and knees. When he reached the doorway, he stood up, pressed his body against the wall, and waited. The intruder hesitated only inches from Larry, who heard the rasping sound in the man's chest and smelled the stale, rancid odor of cigarette smoke and cheap whiskey. When the man stepped into the bedroom, the streetlight silhouetted his craggy profile and small, hipless frame against the papered wall. A revolver, protruding from his uplifted hand, swayed gently as though looking for its target, then, the man's body tensed; his finger coiled around the trigger.

Larry raised his right hand and with the force of a jackhammer brought it down upon the man's neck. Temporarily stunned, his hand still grasping the gun, the man crumbled to the floor.

Beads of perspiration dotted Larry's brow. His temples throbbed. Falling to the floor, he pressed his fingers on the man's neck, sighing when he realized the man wasn't dead. Quickly, he went through his pockets, finding only a set of car keys. No wallet, no identification, nothing.

Larry spun around when he heard Carmen stir restlessly in bed. He pressed his hands on her shoulders, then bent over and kissed her; he kissed her eyelids, her cheeks, her lips, brushing his lips lightly over her face, barely touching, like the fluttering of a leaf. Carmen brushed him away. When she finally opened her eyes, her eyes were full of fear.

"Larry!"

"It's me. Don't be frightened."

"Why did you wake me? I was having a wonderful dream. We were at the club, and this man invited us to have a drink—a talent scout."

"Carmen, listen to me." Larry shook her gently. "The man, the man who stopped you last night . . ."

Carmen peered through the darkness, trying to decipher Larry's expression.

"He's here," Larry continued softly. "In the room."

Carmen's bottom lip quivered. Her hands shook.

Larry grabbed her and held her close. "He's unconscious, but he could wake up anytime. We've got to get out of here."

"How did he get in? Why?"

"He was going to kill you."

Carmen's scream shattered the early morning stillness. Larry's muscles tightened around her. "Get hold of yourself, darling. We don't have time to panic. Get dressed, quickly."

"Where will we go?"

"To King's. We'll be safe for a while. Till we find out what the hell's going on."

Carmen put on the same clothes Larry had taken off her only hours before. Larry dressed hurriedly while he stood beside the man's inert body, watching for a flicker of life. When they were dressed, Larry grabbed Carmen's hand, eased her past the man, and led her out of the room.

"That's him! That's the man!"

"Never mind." The urgency in Larry's voice hurried them on.

When they reached the street, Carmen stopped. "Are you going to leave him there?"

Larry smiled. "He won't steal anything. Got a better idea?"

Carmen didn't answer. She ran to keep up with Larry as they headed up the street, the cold wind whipping around them. Carmen turned up her coat collar and stuck her free hand in her pocket.

"Larry, where are we going? I'm cold. We don't have a car."

"Yes, we do." Larry stopped at the corner. Spotting a Lincoln Continental halfway up the block, he urged Carmen along. "If these keys match that car, we're in business."

Carmen reared back. "But that's the man's—"

"He isn't going to need it for a while."

"Hey, what's happenin'?" King Philip said when he opened the door and stared sleepily at the two of them.

"Trouble," Larry said. The cold crept in with them, and King crossed his arms over his chest.

"What kind of trouble?"

The trio shuffled into the kitchen. King switched on the overhead light, squinting in the harsh glare.

"Give us a minute to thaw out." Larry sat beside Carmen and rubbed her hands until he felt the warmth return to them.

King made a pot of coffee. Occasionally he glanced over his right shoulder at his unexpected guests, curiosity and worry mingling in his mind. As Larry and Carmen sat around the kitchen table, withdrawn and silent, King lit a cigarette and offered it to them. Smoke and the aroma of perking coffee soon filled the room.

"Well?" King said, unable to stand the suspense any longer.

Larry looked at Carmen. "Is it okay? Can we talk about it?"

Carmen tilted her head and finally nodded. "Yes, I want to talk about it. I have to or I'll go crazy. Maybe I'm crazy now. Maybe we're all crazy." Her voice rose as she spoke.

Larry clutched her hands. "The man, the man who attacked Malcolm, broke into Carmen's apartment. He had a gun. If I hadn't been there—"

"Damn!" King said. "What'd you do?"

"Jumped him. Knocked him out. But he won't stay knocked out. He'll—"

"He'll what?" Bubbles asked, leaning against the door frame, his pink silk pajamas peeping through his burgundy satin robe. He walked over to King and stood beside him.

"The dude who got Malcolm came after Carmen. Tried to kill her," King explained.

Bubbles' bottom lip dropped open. "Who's this dude? Why he want to kill Carmen?"

"If we knew that, we could fight back," Larry said, "but, hell, as it is, where do we start?"

"With the cops," King said.

"Cops!" Larry slammed his hand on the table, then stood up and stomped across the kitchen. "What'll the cops do?

425

What *can* they do? A man stops Carmen on the street and asks her name. Howard, she says. He's looking for Carmen Evans. He leaves. Cops aren't going to arrest a guy for asking a woman her name."

"The dude beat Malcolm," Bubbles said, his eyes wide in astonishment.

"We don't know that," Larry said aggressively. All he could see was Carmen being shot or stabbed or run over by a car, and it terrified him.

King poured the coffee. No one spoke. Carmen took a sip and burned her tongue.

"This'll cool it off." Bubbles opened a bottle of brandy and poured some in each cup. Carmen lifted her head and smiled.

"You got to do something." King stroked his beard.

Bubbles paced back and forth across the worn green linoleum. Finally, he stopped and said, "Call the cops. We got to help Carmen. Why the hell we pay taxes if those guys can't protect a citizen?"

Carmen smiled. She held out her hand to Bubbles, who hurried to her side.

"I love you." Carmen wrapped her arms around his bulging girth. "I love all of you, but this thing, whatever it is, has got nothing to do with you or me."

"What're you saying, girl?" Bubbles asked.

Carmen shrugged. "Don't know, but it has something to do with Mama. Mama and my papa. Something that happened a long time ago."

King looked at her in surprise. "You talking about Clarence?"

"Clarence isn't my real father."

King arched his eyebrows.

A glimmer of hope crept across Larry's face. "Call her. Call Tess. Tell her what happened. If there's any way she can stop this . . ."

Carmen was silent, pondering Larry's suggestion. Slowly she shook her head. "I don't want Mama to get hurt. The man asked about Carmen Evans. Evans was Mama's name.

Maybe the man was looking for her. No, I'm afraid. I couldn't bear to think of that man hurting Mama."

"But if she knows anything, anything at all, we can tell the police," Larry said.

Carmen averted her face, afraid to listen to Larry's arguments. Her hand trembled as she picked up her coffee mug. The brandy gave her a shot of hope. She looked up at the faces of the men staring at her, waiting for an answer. How long could she live with this fear? she wondered. The man could find her anywhere. And Malcolm—his beating was somehow tied to this, too.

"Okay," Carmen said finally, her voice trembling, "I'll call Mama. We have to know. We have to stop the man . . . not just for myself—"

Larry smiled and gripped her arm. "Good girl. Good girl."

It was a little after eight that morning when Carmen reached Tess. They talked for over half an hour. Larry, Bubbles, and King caught snatches of conversation, and when she hung up, they held their breaths, waiting for her to speak.

Tears rolled down Carmen's cheeks and she started to laugh. Then she ran across the room and threw her arms around Larry's neck. "Mama says it's going to be all right. She's going to take care of it. It's going to be all right."

Larry whooped and swung Carmen around the room, but when he set her down, he wondered what Tess was going to take care of.

Tess was still staring at the telephone, trying to decide what to do when Clarence wheeled himself into the living room.

"Coffee's still hot if you want some." Clarence glanced at Tess, then picked up the Sunday paper and laid it on his lap. After spying the sports section, he looked up again. Tess was still deep in thought, her hand wrapped around the receiver.

"Something' the matter, darling?"

Tess started. She smiled when she saw Clarence. He had

shaved, and his hair was neatly combed. He reminded her of a little boy getting ready for Sunday school. "No, nothing's the matter." Tess stood up and walked quickly into the kitchen. When she returned, she held a steaming cup of coffee between her hands.

"Gonna be cold again today."

Clarence grunted and continued reading the newspaper.

"Seems too cold to take you out. Might be better if we skipped church today." Tess took a sip of coffee, then turned on the radio. She spun the knob across the stations, then switched it off. "Maybe I'll have to go out later this morning. Got something to attend to."

Clarence folded the paper and laid it on his lap. He held out his hand to Tess and smiled. "Wanna talk about it?"

"Talk about what?"

"Whatever's bothering you."

"Ain't nothing bothering me."

"Woman, I ain't been married to you for all these years without knowing when something's bothering you. Now out with it."

Tess hesitated a moment, then ran to Clarence and fell on her knees beside his wheelchair. "No reason why you shouldn't know. But for a minute, I was afraid, afraid you wouldn't understand."

Clarence arched his eyebrows. "Understand what?"

"I have to see Michele Gianino. I have to save Carmen's life." Tess buried her head in Clarence's lap and sobbed. When she finally stopped, she told him about Malcolm's beating and the attempt on Carmen's life. "It's him. He's crawled out of his hole long enough to get even. After Carmen's dead, I guess he'll crawl back in and die." Tess lifted her head and looked pleadingly at Clarence. "I have to stop him. I'm the only one who can."

Clarence started to protest, fearful for Tess's life, but when he saw the determination, the anger in her eyes, he nodded. "Is there anything I can do?"

Tess patted his hand, then kissed it. "Pray, my darling. Pray."

* * *

Tess's heart was as cold as the weather as she stomped through the snow that had fallen during the night, looking for the address she'd scribbled on a page from one of Stan's notebooks. Rosanna had described her house when Tess had called, but to Tess, the row of plain, brick bungalows all looked depressingly similar. Tess walked with the resoluteness of a sleepwalker, and only when she climbed up the three concrete steps leading to Rosanna's house did she falter.

Tess fell back in stunned silence when Rosanna opened the door. Rosanna's long face, rounded jaw, and rather sad brown eyes brought back Johnny in a blinding flash. Rosanna smiled and invited her in.

"I didn't think I'd ever meet you," Rosanna said in a quiet, tense voice. "I thought it was over."

Tess stared at Rosanna, observing every feature. "He looked like you," she said simply.

The room was silent except for the clock ticking on the mantel. Rosanna waved her hand, motioned for Tess to sit down. "I wanted to call you a thousand times, but I was afraid Michele'd find out. He knows everything. Even bedridden, nothing escapes him."

Tess folded her gloves and shoved them in her purse. "He's going to kill Carmen if we don't stop him. I won't let him kill her."

Rosanna slapped her hands against her thighs and exhaled loudly. "He can't live much longer. He can't breathe without oxygen."

"Will you take me to him?"

A softness crept over Rosanna's face. The tenseness began to thaw. She studied Tess as though trying to recapture a past that had been dead for two decades.

"First tell me about Carmen. Does she look like him?"

"Very much. I see Johnny every time I look at her."

Tears streamed down Rosanna's face. She wiped them away with the back of her hand. "I've waited so long. I wanted to see her, but not like this."

"Carmen's a singer. Soul. Gospel. She's very good. Her grandmother, Bobbie, was a singer."

Rosanna smiled. Her thoughts drifted back to the night she had heard Bobbie sing at the Savoy, the night she had fallen in love with Roy. That was when it all began. She looked at Tess, then her eyes shifted to the window and across the street to Michele's house. And this is where it's going to end, she thought. Then they can all—Roy, Bobbie, Johnny—rest in peace. She walked to the sofa and picked up her coat and scarf.

"We'll stop him. Come along." When they reached the door, Rosanna hesitated, pressed her hand against Tess's arm and said, "Anna doesn't know."

"We'll have to tell her."

"Let me. I love her. I don't want to hurt her anymore than, than—"

"Michele's waiting."

Arm in arm, the two women crossed the street, their black boots crunching in the snow. They rang the bell four times before Anna finally opened the door. Her smile was welcoming yet wary. She led them into the dark living room, blinds and drapes drawn over the windows. A musty smell, a mixture of dust and mold, permeated the air. To Tess, it smelled of age and death.

"Tess Howard," Anna said, responding to Rosanna's introduction. Anna peered through the musty shadows at Tess. "Do I know you?"

"No, Anna," Rosanna said. "You've just met."

Anna nodded. The frown creasing her forehead remained.

"Tess has something to tell you. It's not good news."

"Most news I get isn't."

"It's about Johnny."

Anna cocked her head to one side. "Johnny!" Her eyes watered as she strained to see Tess's face. She dabbed at them with the handkerchief crumpled in her hand.

"Did you know Johnny?"

Tess was startled by the woman's question. How can I tell her that her husband's trying to murder Johnny's daughter? she wondered.

Before she could answer, Rosanna spoke. "Johnny and Tess were living together before he died."

There was silence in the room as the three women stared at one another. Slowly Anna rose and moved beside Tess. "What do you want?"

Rosanna continued, "They had a child, a daughter. She's grown now. Her name's Carmen. Michele knows about Carmen."

"He's trying to kill her," Tess said. The force of her words brought tears to Tess's eyes. She grasped Anna's hand to ease the shock of her statement.

"Michele kept this from me?" Anna's eyes darted about the room as though searching for understanding. "Why? Why did he keep this from me?"

"He's an evil man," Rosanna said. "After Johnny was killed in Korea, he tried to find Tess and Carmen. He would've killed 'em years ago, but he couldn't find them. And now . . ."

Anna shook her head. "Johnny. My beautiful baby. My beautiful son. I don't understand."

"How can anyone understand his hatred?" Rosanna's voice rose as the years of anguish and fear assaulted her. "We have to stop him now before it's too late."

"Michele's old. Dying. Why does he want to hurt Johnny's daughter?" Anna asked.

"I want to talk to him. To beg him to leave us alone," Tess said. "Will you help me?"

Anna's hands quivered. Her breathing was labored. She dabbed at the tears brimming her eyes. Slowly she stood up, straightened her dress, then motioned for Tess and Rosanna to follow her. When they reached the steps, Anna stopped and looked questioningly at Rosanna.

"Did you know?"

Rosanna dropped her eyes. The pain of betrayal was hot on her cheeks. "I knew."

"Why didn't you tell me?"

"I was afraid. I thought it would hurt you too much to know. It was better to forget."

"Oh, Rosanna! I've never forgotten. Johnny's been with me every second, every minute of my life. It would've helped to know he had a daughter."

"I'm sorry, Anna. I was afraid of Michele, too. I've been afraid of him all my life."

Anna thought for a moment, then continued up the stairs. "We were all afraid of him."

As they entered Michele's sickroom, Anna's steps grew firmer, her shoulders straightened a bit, as if on a sacred mission. Standing beside Michele's bed, blue veins pulsed angrily in her neck.

The only part of Michele's frail body that seemed alive were the ever-angry gray-green eyes. Tess hesitated, still intimidated by the violent power those eyes held.

Michele's stare froze on Tess's face as he tried to draw on a lifetime of memories to identify her. When recognition didn't come, he looked at Rosanna and said angrily, "What d' you want? What're you doing here?"

"I've brought an acquaintance to see you. A very old acquaintance. This is Tess. Tess Evans. Johnny's wife."

Michele raised himself on his elbow, and painfully tried to catch his breath. "Get that nigger outta here. She ain't gonna get my money. Her nigger daughter ain't either." Michele jabbed his finger at Tess, then dissolved in a spasm of coughing.

Anna threw her hand over her mouth to stifle a scream. "You knew. You knew about them and didn't tell me."

"She's a nigger. Johnny ran away with a nigger."

"You're going to kill his daughter." Anna gasped as she spoke the words. She leaned toward him, her face alive with passion, as though the mist of age and sorrow had suddenly cleared, and she saw Michele for what he was.

Michele's panting was the only sound in the room as Anna waited for an answer.

"No nigger's gonna get my money."

"Blessed Lord, you do mean to kill her." Anna shook her head. "She's our granddaughter."

Michele laughed. "No, not ours." He raised his finger and pointed it at Rosanna. "Hers."

Anna turned. "What's he saying?"

"I . . . I don't know."

"Liar. You know. Tell . . ." Michele fought for air.

Rosanna turned away, cowering under Michele's wrath.

"What's he saying?" Anna asked again.

"He's going to destroy all of us," Rosanna said, then turned to Michele. "You're evil. Even Anna doesn't mean anything to you, does she? You'd have her know. You'd hurt her now after all these years."

"Know what?" Anna pleaded.

"Johnny's papa was a nigger, a nigger, a nigger."

Anna looked at Michele as one would look at a madman. Rosanna panicked. She screamed at Michele. He didn't seem to hear. Although his face was pinched with pain, his eyes danced as he watched the pandemonium. The excitement was too much, however. Gasping for air, he grabbed the oxygen mask hanging beside his bed. Greedily he sucked in the air. When his breathing stabilized, he spoke with a vehemence bordering on lunacy.

"The nigger lover, Johnny's mama, was Rosanna. Rosanna the bitch. Rosanna the . . ." Michele fell back, unable to continue. Blood trickled from the corner of his mouth. His eyes blazed with hatred as he stared unblinkingly at his niece.

Anna and Tess also stared, hearing, but not believing.

"You're Johnny's mama?" Anna clutched the bed rail for support.

Tess stepped back, reeling under the impact of Michele's confession.

"I'm sorry, Anna." Rosanna gulped back her tears. "You were never to know. He did it. He killed Johnny's father. He took my baby." Rosanna pointed her finger at Michele's withered body.

Tess broke the awful silence in the room. "Roy, my uncle, was Johnny's father? I don't believe it."

"Yes! Yes! I loved him. We loved each other. Michele killed him. Shot him like an animal. Then he took my baby, my Johnny, our Johnny. He threatened me. If I ever told, he'd . . . he'd . . ."

Michele struggled to raise himself. A laugh caught in his throat. "Yeah, I killed the nigger, 'nd I'm gonna kill his daughter. When it's done, I'll pay whatever it costs."

Anna's scream pierced the blackness in the room. She fell on her knees and began to pray. "Our Father, who art in heaven . . ."

Michele's strength was spent. His head lolled and his cheeks were grayish-white. A wheezing sound escaped from his cracked lips. In panic, he reached for the oxygen mask. His claw-like hand pounded the bed and the mask fell to the floor. His hand flapped helplessly; his lips parted. No sound emerged. He lunged forward, then fell back again. His eyes were open when he took his last breath.

An eerie quiet filled the room. Each of the three women, lost in her own sorrow, raised her head, gulped back her sobs, and gazed in awe at Michele's inert body, at the ghastly white paleness of death. Wordlessly they stepped close to the bed. Anna reached out her hand to touch him, then quickly drew back. She continued her prayer: ". . . For thine is the kingdom, and the power, and the glory, now and for ever. Amen."

With tears streaming down her face, Anna pulled the sheet over Michele's body, glanced up at Rosanna and Tess, then turned and walked out of the room.

CHAPTER XXXII

As so often happens in the middle latitudes, an unexpected thaw allows people a respite from the cold, blustery winds of February. Scarfs and gloves are discarded and faces turn upward to catch the rays of the winter sun. "Can't last," old-timers say, then trumpet warnings of cyclones and tornadoes, reluctant to enjoy the mock stirrings of spring.

Carmen, caught in a personal flux, saw the weather as a barometer of her life: winter-spring, freeze-thaw.

Carmen and Larry lay in bed and listened to the melting snow dripping from the eaves onto the sodden windowsill. To Carmen, it had a soothing effect, filling as it did the strained silence separating them. Carmen's mind raced in a dozen different directions for a way to reach Larry. He hadn't spoken since he had announced he was leaving.

As casually as she could, Carmen turned on her side and looked at him. Oh, God, he's so handsome, she thought. His brown skin glistened as though their lovemaking had sprinkled his body with a golden mist. His strong hands tapered off in long, thin fingers, talented fingers. But he had shied away from stardom, hiding his extraordinary gifts by playing in local clubs, refusing to talk to promoters or talent scouts as though fame would ruin him.

Carmen waited for the right words with which to spark his ambition. Then her eyes began to glow; her body tensed with excitement. She wouldn't give up. She would make him see that their love would protect them from the vagaries of the power brokers who would exploit them if they could. She nudged her head against Larry's shoulder and threw her arm over his bare chest.

"You awake?"

"Yeah. How about you?" Larry opened his eyes and stared blankly at the ceiling.

"I'm awake."

"What time is it?"

"Almost seven."

Larry stirred. "Time for you to get ready to go to the club."

"Guess so." Carmen pressed her lips against Larry's neck and covered him with kisses. He laughed and turned on his side to look at her.

"Cut that out. You know I'm ticklish."

Carmen pulled back. "Just wanted to hear you laugh. It's been such a long time."

"Not so long." Larry's hand traced the curves of

435

Carmen's body, her breasts, her hips, her thighs. A chill gripped her, and she snuggled closer.

"What're you going to do tonight?" Carmen tried to keep the bitterness she felt out of her voice.

Larry sighed. "Watch TV. Drink a few beers. I don't know."

Carmen's body grew rigid as anger welled up inside her. She flew out of bed and wrapped herself in a pink, tufted robe. "You're really going to do it, aren't you?" Her stomach contracted, and hopelessness clutched at her heart.

Larry sat up, his face taut. "Darling, how many times do I have to tell you? I don't want to go to Hollywood and become a black superstud musician. I'm a local boy. I don't need fame and a lot of money. I want to play my kind of music, not some tin can stuff, not pushing buttons in a studio. My kind of music is like a cottage industry—small-time."

"We all want that. King, the guys in the band."

Larry sniffed the air. "You don't want it as bad as I do. You're willing to take your chances. I'm not."

"What's wrong with making money?" Carmen's voice quivered with anger.

"Nothing, if that's what you want."

"I want it, but I want you, too. We all want you. We need you. Where will King find another piano player as good as you are?"

Larry's body stiffened. He laughed cynically. "I'm sure Malcolm'll find someone. After all, he got you and the boys the contract with CBC records."

"Yes, and he worked hard for it, too. A month ago he could barely walk, and now—"

"And now he's a big man. I'm happy for Malcolm. I'm happy for King and the guys and you."

"Oh, God!" Carmen turned away in disgust.

"Carmen, don't try to make me do something I don't want to do. I wouldn't ask you not to go."

"Why not? Maybe I wouldn't go to California if you asked. I love you, Larry."

"And I love you, but—"

"But, but, always but." Carmen sat on the side of the bed, tears rolling down her cheeks. She reached over and took Larry's hand. "I'm afraid."

"There's nothing to be afraid of anymore. Your attacker's gone, your granddaddy's dead. That's all behind you."

"I wouldn't be alive if you hadn't been with me."

"I know, babe. I'd never leave you if I thought you were in danger."

"How do we know that's over? How do we really know?"

"Your mama told you—Gianino was a real crazy. It was personal. Now it's over." Larry pulled Carmen close to him. She nestled in his arms. "You're going to make it, babe. It's your time to fly."

"Oh, Larry, I don't know if I can without you."

"Hey, babe, you're going to have to put me on a back burner. Just concentrate on you."

Carmen wiped her face on the edge of the sheet. She looked pleadingly at Larry, her lips trembling when she spoke. "Will you come to the club Saturday night? Nathan's giving us a farewell party. It's our last night before we . . . before we go to California."

"Honey, I can't promise. I may be gone by Saturday."

"Gone?" The word caught in Carmen's throat.

"Yeah. Got an offer to join a combo in Kansas City. They're not as good as King and the guys, but—"

"Larry, you're wasting your life, playing two-bit clubs—"

Larry leaned over and kissed Carmen on her mouth. A sweet, tender kiss, a farewell kiss. Carmen's body grew limp. The feeling of dread she had carried inside her for the past month ceased. She felt nothing but emptiness. It was as though someone very dear to her had died. She stared at Larry, started to speak, then changed her mind. She slid off the bed and walked into the bathroom to shower. When she returned to the bedroom twenty minutes later, Larry was gone.

The Sunset Cafe was festooned with silver and black balloons and striped crepe paper. Nathan rolled a barrel of beer from behind the bar and two waiters hoisted it onto a table set back against a wall. King Philip strutted across the stage, resplendent in his new black tux with its satin lapels. His white silk shirt was frothy with ruffles and his gold cuff links sparkled. He held a Scotch and water in his left hand and tapped out the melody of a song flitting through his mind with his right. As Carmen watched the carnival of musicians and workers ready themselves for the evening's festivities, her face was long and sad.

King sidled up to her perch on the side of the stage and put his hand on her shoulder. "It's going to be all right. Larry's doing what he has to do. We'll do what we have to do. That's the way it is in this business."

"Oh, King. I feel like I'm dead."

"It hurts. Hurts like hell, but you'll pull through." King smiled and sipped his drink.

Carmen snorted. "Easy for you to say."

"No, it isn't easy. Not for any of us. He left a big hole in the band. I can't replace a guy like Larry overnight."

Carmen looked up at King, aware of the anger in his voice for the first time. "We all need Larry." Suddenly, Carmen felt unbearably lonely.

"Otis Jackson's gonna fill in tonight, then I don't know what I'm gonna do."

"We were a team. How could he do this?"

King glanced at his watch. "You better get dressed, babe. First show's in half an hour."

Carmen slid off the stool and walked to a makeshift dressing room beyond the bar. Nathan winked at her. She forced a smile.

The club noise grew louder as Carmen slipped into a sequined gown, put on her makeup, and stuck two rhinestone combs into her hair. She felt a little better. He's selfish, she thought. Selfish and spoiled. If he loved me, he wouldn't leave. What did his love mean if he could walk away and not look back? King's right. I'll get over him. I'll become a singing star. Mama'll be proud, so will Clarence and Stan and Malcolm. They want this for me. I'll show him. I'll—

A knock on the door startled her. Nathan called out, "We're ready when you are."

Carmen opened the door a crack. Nathan's smile defused her anger. Opening night jitters stoked a bubbling excitement inside her, and a vanity born of hard work made her vow to bury her blues onstage.

"Is he here?" Carmen peaked over Nathan's shoulder.

"Is who here?"

"Mr. Kelly, the CBC rep."

"Yeah. He's talking to Malcolm. Why?"

"I was afraid. Thought maybe he wouldn't show."

"What difference would it make? You signed the contract."

"I know, but, well, having the man here who's going to make us into stars . . . it's a real thrill. You know?"

"Sure, honey. I know."

Carmen nodded. "I have to slip on my shoes and take a few deep breaths. I'll stay in here till it's time."

"King's getting nervous."

"Aren't we all?"

King was going over the songs with Otis when Tess entered the cafe with Stan at her side. Clarence maneuvered his wheelchair to the center of the room. They waited as Nathan rushed forward to meet them.

"Sweet Tess." Nathan kissed her cheek, then turned to Stan and Clarence and offered his hand. "Some night, eh?"

"Wouldn't have missed it for the world," Clarence said.

Nathan led the group to a large table in front of the bandstand. "Front row center." He seated Tess, then cleared a space for Clarence's wheelchair.

"Guess you're gonna miss that girl of yours when she goes to California," Nathan said.

Tess smiled. "Not for long. We're going to join her in a few months. As soon as she can find a house."

"Hey, you're gonna love L.A." Nathan's eyes twinkled. "But you better watch Stan. All them cute young things'll turn his head."

"And I'll turn it right back again."

"Tess's midwestern values might collapse a little once we get on the other side of the Rockies," Clarence teased. "That woman needs to lighten up."

"Nothing's wrong with remembering who we are," Tess countered, frowning.

"Tonight all you got to do is sit back and enjoy." Nathan glanced over his shoulder. "I'll send a waiter over to get your order."

Before he left, Tess grabbed his hand and pulled him close. "We're expecting a friend. She'll be alone. Will you seat her— Oh, never mind. There she is."

Nathan looked up. A woman stood inside the door, clutching a small black handbag. Nervous tension distorted her features. Only her eyes, sparkling with anticipation, betrayed her excitement. Nathan hurried to her side, then escorted her to the table.

Tess rose to kiss her. "This is a dear friend, Rosanna Gianino. I'm so happy you came."

"I'm so happy you asked. I think I've waited for this night all my life."

The two women twittered and chatted until finally Clarence cleared his throat and said, "I don't think we've met."

Tess blushed like a schoolgirl, then introduced Rosanna to Clarence and Stan.

Clarence held out his hand. "You'll forgive me if I don't stand up." He smiled.

Rosanna returned the smile. "Only if you'll forgive me for staring. I can't help thinking how lucky Tess is to have had two such handsome men in her life."

Clarence acknowledged her compliment. "And she was lucky to have you, too. It must have been awful that day . . . three women confronting Michele Gianino. How can we ever thank you for saving Carmen's life?"

Rosanna dropped her eyes. Her bottom lip quivered, and she fell silent. Michele's ghost hovered over them still.

Stan, however, immune to the sorrow that had plagued Rosanna's life, leaned forward and smiled broadly at the two women. "I think it was neat what you did. That old goat should've gotten his a long time ago."

Rosanna sucked in her breath, held it, then exhaled, expelling her anguish and fear. She looked at Stan, her face soft and radiant. "Yes," she said with a note of finality in her voice, "it was about time someone got the old goat."

Artie Hill rolled a fanfare on his drums, and King Philip stepped forward to introduce the first set.

"A medley of old favorites." King tapped his right foot and raised his hand and the band broke into a popular forties song, "That Old Black Magic."

Tess and Rosanna swayed to its familiar rhythm, and at the end, Rosanna sang the words under her breath while memories fluttered like butterflies across the chasm of a lifetime.

Rosanna clapped wildly when the band finished. She leaned over and pressed Tess's arm. "I wish Anna had come. She would've enjoyed this so much, but her eyes bother her, the smoke and everything."

"Tell her she's welcome to visit us anytime."

"Yes, but I don't think she will. She's lost in the past. She loved him, you know. I begged her to move in with me, but she won't leave her home. Just as well. In the end all we have are our memories. Maybe that's all we ever have, really."

A chorus of whistles and shouts accompanied Carmen's introduction. King rambled on for several minutes, eulogizing her talent, her beauty, her pending stardom. Then, as though to heighten the tension, King waved his arm and directed the spotlight to the right of the stage where Malcolm sat.

A short, skinny young man, his Afro like a huge, frizzy halo, stood up and raised a fist over his head in a victory salute. His left arm was still in a sling, and he wore a patch over his eye, the last vestiges of the beating he'd suffered over a month before, but his face beamed; his grin stretched from ear to ear, and a gold tooth glittered like a rare jewel against his coal-black skin.

"I owe it all to my babe, Carmen Howard," Malcolm said, then added, "Course, next to Carmen, I owe everything to this man." Impishly, he bent down and hugged Mr. Kelly from CBC records.

441

The spotlight moved on, stopping when it picked up the red glitter of Carmen's dress. Like a firecracker about to explode, Carmen lifted her hands over her head and snapped her fingers. Her face was one broad smile. Artie beat a drum roll and Carmen strutted across the room to the tumult of shouts and cheers. When she reached the foot of the stage, she turned and bowed, then turning again, lifted her foot to climb the bandstand. Halfway up she stopped, the hem of her skirt caught on a splintered piece of wood. Embarrassed, she tugged several times and was about to bend over to unhook it when a man stepped out of the darkness and pulled it free. Blinded by the spotlight, Carmen thanked him, then moved up another step. She stopped, turned, and then said quietly so that only he could hear, "Larry. You came back. Oh, my God. You came back." She bit her lip to keep the tears from ruining her makeup, then she laughed. "Why?"

Larry smiled, took her arm, and helped her to the stage. "I've always been a sucker for a pretty face." He pursed his lips into a kiss and winked at her.

"You mind, Otis?" Larry asked, at the piano.

"Be my guest." Otis slid off the seat and off the stage.

Carmen stood just to the left of the band. King raised his hand, and, as if a painting had magically come to life, the band began to play an introduction.

"This is for Mama." Carmen threw a kiss to Tess, then began her song—"Satin Dolls."